Lucifer's Star

by C. T. Phipps

The sight of the burning starships around me was like a galaxy of new stars lighting up the emptiness of space. Their fuel and energy cells burned without oxygen long after the crews had suffocated in the vacuum of space. Hundreds of dreadnoughts, battleships, carriers, and starfighters exchanged fire in the largest battle of the war.

The Revengeance was taking point in the assault on the enemy flagship Earth's Successor. We had managed to take out its support craft and casualty ratings were still well within acceptable parameters. Acceptable as long as I didn't think of Black Squadron-3 as Daniel, Skull Squadron-6 as Rebecca, or Dagger-Squadron-7 as Lisa. They were men and women I'd trained with and called friends, now just particles and gas.

"Focus," I commanded myself, then spoke into my helmet's comm. I was sitting in the middle of my tight Engel-fighter cockpit moving at speeds which boggled the mind. While space was largely empty, the tightness of the battle formations meant I needed to fly like I'd never flown before. The slightest misstep would mean not only my death but my entire squadron's destruction. "Dagger Leader, I need you to bring up your teammates to thin out the ranks of those Crosshairs."

"Yes, your Excellency," Dagger Leader, a woman named Arianna Stonebridge, said, referring to me by my noble title rather than rank.

I hated that.

Speial thanks to th ever-patient Kat Phipps for her love & support

Dedication

This novel is dedicated to the many wonderful people who made this book possible. Special thanks to David Niall Wilson, David Dodd, and all the other hard workers at Crossroad Press.

C.T. Phipps and Michael Suttkus

Chapter One

The sight of the burning starships around me was like a galaxy of new stars lighting up the emptiness of space. Their fuel and energy cells burned without oxygen long after the crews had suffocated in the vacuum of space. Hundreds of dreadnoughts, battleships, carriers, and starfighters exchanged fire in the largest battle of the war.

The *Revengeance* was taking point in the assault on the enemy flagship *Earth's Successor*. We had managed to take out its support craft and casualty ratings were still well within acceptable parameters. Acceptable as long as I didn't think of Black Squadron-3 as Daniel, Skull Squadron-6 as Rebecca, or Dagger-Squadron-7 as Lisa. They were men and women I'd trained with and called friends, now just particles and gas.

"Focus," I commanded myself, then spoke into my helmet's comm. I was sitting in the middle of my tight Engel-fighter cockpit moving at speeds which boggled the mind. While space was largely empty, the tightness of the battle formations meant I needed to fly like I'd never flown before. The slightest misstep would mean not only my death but my entire squadron's destruction. "Dagger Leader, I need you to bring up your teammates to thin out the ranks of those Crosshairs."

"Yes, your Excellency," Dagger Leader, a woman named Arianna Stonebridge, said, referring to me by my noble title rather than rank.

I hated that.

This was a last-ditch assault which Prince Germanicus had planned to blunt the offensive into our territory. The Commonwealth had reclaimed thousands of worlds in their quest to reunite humanity, but they were stretched thin and the Archduchy's resistance was fierce. If we'd had more allies, we could have repelled them, but the Archduchy of Crius had few friends. In my more reflective moments, I had to wonder how badly we'd abused our neighbors that so many had cheered the arrival of the Commonwealth.

The interior of the Engel's cockpit was a mixture of levers, pedals, and sensor equipment which projected countless images into my cybernetically enhanced mind. I saw close-ups of the sword-shaped Crius destroyers moving to cut off the escape of the massive *Earth's Successor* even as enemy reinforcements arrived from jump-space. The saucer-shaped Commonwealth ships launched several thousand more starfighters to whittle down the shields of our ships, but it made no difference to our battle plan. We had to score a decisive victory here, even if it meant decimating our ranks.

Archangel Squadron's part in the mission was critical. We had to weaken the *Earth's Successor* enough for the *Revengeance* to blast away at its engines and allow the rest of the fleet to destroy it. Our foe was a massive, ten-kilometer-long super-carrier, which doubled as a dreadnought capable of leveling planets. Adjusting my targeting computer, I gauged its shields and knew it would take everything we had to crack them before the *Revengeance* and its support craft arrived to hammer it. If the shields were still up when our ships reached firing range, the attack would be like raindrops on steel. We could do it, though. We just needed to get past a few hundred enemy fighters first.

"Here they come," I muttered, not transmitting across the Engel's transceivers. We were tens of thousands of kilometers away from the *Earth's Successor*, but at the speeds we were moving, we were only a few minutes from interception. Seeing two squadrons of V-shaped Crosshair fighters descending on us, I decided now wasn't the time to worry.

I picked one to shoot down with plasma cannons, followed by another, then another. The ones beside my targets detonated nearly as fast, destroyed by Hans and Brutus with the rest of Dagger Squadron's pilots inflicting only slightly less damage. Crosshair fighters were inferior to Engels in several ways, not the least being inferior range. The Commonwealth's military doctrine believed in quantity over quality. These men had paid for it in their lives. I'd have to send their senators a bottle of wine in thanks.

"Got three that round, Colonel!" Lieutenant Colonel Hans Nakamora, my second, said. "I'm only two behind your score."

The last of the two squadrons we'd faced were cut to pieces by my cannons before he'd finished his statement, bringing my kill score to four hundred and seven. Commonwealth soldiers were rarely enhanced, either genetically or cybernetically, which meant they tended to die far easier in battle with Crius ones. But, for all my complaining about their inferior equipment, quantity had a quality all its own.

The Commonwealth was thirty times the size of the Archduchy and equally more populated. The flower of Crius' youth was being extinguished under piles of the enemy's dead. No, I had to stop thinking like that. We would win here. The war would end. We would have peace. If I kept telling myself that, I'd believe it.

"Come back home, alive, Cassius," Judith said, embracing me as I was about to depart on the shuttle up to the Revengeance.

"I'll come back with my shield or on it," I replied. "Crius will triumph."

"Fuck Crius. I don't care who wins," Judith spoke treason. "I only care that you live."

"Enough time for chatter after we've won the war. First round's on me if you can shut up until then," I said to Hans, noticing we'd managed to break through the defensive screen of the *Earth Successor's* starfighters.

There were far fewer defenders here than I'd expected. We had nothing but a clear shot to the ship. We had a good lead on the starfighters behind us, which meant we could probably get two full attack runs away before they turned around to engage us. Then things would get hairy and we'd probably be overwhelmed.

So be it.

I'm sorry, Judith.

"Gwydion formation. Prepare payloads. You know the drill," I said, having planned the starfighter portion of the attack to the last detail. As a Colonel-Count, I was technically outranked by the fleet's fighter-generals, but they'd all chosen to follow my lead thanks to my reputation. My birth rank had also played a role I'm sorry to say. "Sound off."

"Affirmative," Hans said. "Prepping payload. Archangel-2 over."

"Affirmative," Brutus said, "Prepping payload. Archangel-3 over."

"Affirmative, Excellency," Flavia said. "Payload prepared, Archangel-4 over."

And so on and so on until all twelve of us had confirmed their readiness.

I couldn't help but feel a swelling of pride as I gave directions for my squadron to begin our attack run. Archangel Squadron was a mixture of elevated commoners, low-level nobility, and even a bastard son of Prince Germanicus. When I'd begun my service to the Archduchy of Crius, they had considered me nothing more than a rogue genetic, born from the misguided vanity of a father with too much power and influence in the Ruling Families for his rank. A clone. Almost as low as a nat. Now they called me Cassius Mass the Fire Count.

The Colonel-Count of Analathas.

The Butcher of Kolthas.

My glory reflected the ranks they had all achieved. We passed the trials of countless battles and became a symbol of what Crius could achieve working together. Awarded the highest honor our country had to give in the Lucifer's Star. Now we were going to die for our nation. It was the only way this ended.

"Stay safe," Judith said, muttering. "Don't be a hero."

"Every soldier is a hero," I said, staring at her. "The act of standing up for others makes you one. We're all prepared to die to save our loved ones."

"Okay, first of all, that's bullshit. Half of the army is conscripts. Second, being prepared to die for your country is different from trying to. I know you want to live up to the legacy you think you have to, but you're better than any of your ancestors."

"A.I."

"You're probably the only one worth a damn."

Sometimes I wondered if she was right and I was the only noble fighting for the people and, even then, whether that was just a lie I told myself. "I promise I won't throw my life away."

Judith looked down. "Don't make promises you don't intend to keep."

"Target the main batteries, sensor systems, and power-flow relays," I said, watching the targeting spots light up across my screen. We needed to cripple the *Earth's Successor* before the *Revengeance* and its backup came within anti-starfighter battery range. "Launch singularity missiles on my mark."

"Cloaking failure, we've been spotted, sir!" Archangel-3 shouted, making it clear the damage her starship had suffered was at fault. It didn't matter now as the airless void around us lighted up with green energy blasts.

"Carry on," I said. "We know this is a one-way trip."

"Copy," Brutus said.

"Mark and fire," I said, pressing the LAUNCH button after marking each of my targets. My entire payload was launched with only a bare minimum of movement necessary to avoid the overtaxed battery crew's fire. "Scatter."

I spun my cross-shaped fighter in the formation my soldiers had practiced hundreds of times. It worked, for the most part, as glowing, green energy blasts sailed harmlessly past us. The sight of Gabriel, Archangel-3's wing, catching the tail end of a bolt was like a blow to the stomach though. The big, burly bronze-skinned man was newly wedded with a second child having been approved for creation. Any hope he might survive dissipated as he flew out of control into another blast which tore his Engel into space debris.

"Taking heavy fire, Colonel!" Hans said. "We need to pull back if we're going to do any more damage." I could hear the plea in his voice. We didn't have to die here. We had done our share to win the war. More than enough. Which was true. Few other living units had paid anywhere near our dues.

But we had our duty. Checking our targeting numbers, I saw less than a quarter of the targets we needed to knock out had been destroyed. Missile boats escorted by Skull and Dagger Squadron were coming to serve as reinforcements, but Black Squadron was almost annihilated. It would not be delivering its payload. Worse, the *Earth's Successor* was pulling back its starfighters to engage us as predicted. Swerving out of the way of several greener energy bolts, I fired my quad-plasma cannons into the side of an emplacement, causing it to explode in a pleasing orange-red brilliance.

"Negative, Archangel-2. Continue mission. The Reclamation ends here." I muttered a silent prayer to the angels to look after my wife.

"Understood, sir," Hans said, his voice hoarse. "It's been an honor." It was a sentiment echoed throughout the squadron as we wiped out sixteen more targets but lost Anna and Daiki. Three squadrons flying the Commonwealth's new inverted-pyramid-shaped

Phoenix-class starfighters were coming from our upper flank. Sensors identified the squadron as the Godhand. Part of the wing commissioned by the enemy high command to destroy the Archduchy's fighters. They'd killed virtually all of my peers and would finish the job today.

"That it has," I replied to my unit. "That it has. Move to engage the Godhand. We only have to slow them down."

I proceeded to swing around my unit to engage the Godhand along with the rest of my squadron. Ten against thirty-six. I predicted we would take down six before they destroyed us. We needed to change those odds.

"Formation, sir?" Brutus asked. We only had a few seconds before we were in weapons range and even less time to choose our method of suicide.

"Berserker," I said with grim finality.

"Confirm?" Hans asked.

"Berserker," I repeated.

It was a ludicrous tactical choice, but one which might at least do a bit more damage before we were chewed up like meat in a grinder. Putting all of our energy barrier strength to the front and our speed to maximum, we moved into a formation so tight it might have been part of a sky parade.

The moment we reached energy blast range, we unloaded with the full force of our plasma cannons as the energy sailed outward in a manner that sent the Godhand scattering. They had been expecting us to break and their leader made a poor tactical choice, mostly because they were our target and there was no way to dodge that many blasts.

The temporary loss of command from such a hardened unit allowed us a few extra shots as each of the Archangel units broke away to attack with almost no regard to their lives, myself included. Brutus actually smashed his unit into the side of a Godhand starfighter after taking a disabling shot. I managed to cook the insides of two before I realized all but Hans were gone of my unit. We'd destroyed twelve. So many friends lost. And for what? A few more seconds? A few more enemies dead? I was glad I wouldn't have to live with the guilt. The enemy was already regrouping to finish us off.

Hans died seconds later, his Engel exploding in a brilliant ball of jump fuel. I pushed everything into my engines, hoping to escape the descending horde of vengeance-driven Commonwealth fighters and lead them away from the missile-boats, which were already delivering their payload.

Seconds later, I felt two plasma bolts rock against the side of my vessel, followed by alarms informing me my starfighter's reactor was going critical. The vessel had sustained damage during a previous battle and the fix had not been perfect. I was doomed if a third shot struck me anyway, but this gave me time to slam my fist onto the EJECT button. It felt like cowardice but I didn't want to die.

The top of the cockpit shot out of the Engel with both my flight suit and a barrier protecting me from the worst of the gravity tremors. Even so, I felt like my face, body, and toes were being ripped off as the boosters propelled me away from my Engel's burning remains. It was like a comet sailing away, the sides trailing burning gas. Moments later, it exploded, now far enough away it looked like a pinprick of light in a sky full of them.

Fuck.

I didn't dare activate my rescue beacon now, lest some of the Commonwealth's soldiers decide to pick me off or scoop me up via a tractor beam. Instead, I merely floated in the starry void, hearing nothing and seeing the spectacular exchange of light going on beside me. War was always beautiful from a distance, full of glory and promises of epic heroism.

It took an up-close and personal acquaintance with it to know every one of those light exchanges meant people boiling alive in ignited atmosphere or being frozen to death after explosive decompression. I hated the Commonwealth and everything it stood for, but I couldn't help but feel sympathy for all the soldiers dying this day.

That was when all of the light exchanges stopped. I blinked, staring out into my helmet's screen and commanding it to pick up the transmissions which had to be going on. A sudden and complete end to the fighting could only mean one thing.

Oh, no.

I couldn't hear anything on the Commonwealth channels, their encryption software had improved dramatically in recent month, but a single message was being repeated over all Crius ones. "Stand down and cease all hostilities. Prince Germanicus and the rest of the royal family are dead. Grand Admiral Plantagenet has transmitted our unconditional surrender to the Commonwealth of Interstellar Planets. Crius has fallen. Repeat: Stand down and cease all hostilities—"

Chapter Two

I felt cold sweat trickle down the sides of my face and the front of my chest as I awoke shaking. I was naked underneath the plain synth-weave sheets and it was dark in my room. It was five years past that day and I still dreamed about that night in the wee hours of the morning. Taking a moment to clear my thoughts, I remembered I was on board the *Melampus* and we were currently travelling through jumpspace.

The *Melampus'* medical officer, Isla Hernandez, was lying naked next to me with her golden hair still woven into a weave down past her shoulders. She was as beautiful as a genetically-engineered noblewoman but *off* due to the long scar across her face, with silver hair, golden skin, and a perpetually pleasant disposition even-though we had almost nothing in common.

My room as the ship's navigator was reasonably large but undecorated. I had my bed, a metal chest, footlocker, and almost no decorations or personal effects. The room was almost the same as it had been when I'd first come to work on the transport.

Sliding out of the bed, I stumbled over to the chest next to my footlocker and waved my hand over the top drawer. It popped open and revealed a bunch of undergarments, a half-drunk crystal decanter of amber-colored vodka, and a half-dozen bottles of pain-killers, mood-stabilizers, and memory-suppressors alongside.

I removed the top of the decanter and took a swig. Awful, but I wasn't exactly drinking it for the taste. Putting it down on the chest's top, I checked the pill bottles and noticed several were missing from each. Isla, probably, or one of my other crewmates.

"Eh, who gives a shit?" I said, shrugging. Picking up the vodka and taking another swig, I also swallowed a pair of memory drugs and painkillers.

My cybernetic brain hurt more every day and it was clear it needed maintenance. While Isla was good, she wasn't *that* good, and any other place I took myself would run into the possibility of identifying my genetic code. Even if they didn't have that on file, the fact I was borged out of my ass with military-grade enhancements would be a tip-off I was someone important in hiding. Fuck, maybe I should turn myself in. Execution or prison had to be better than this.

"Lights," Isla said, alerting me to the fact she was awake.

"Ah." I covered my face with my free hand. "Warn a guy before you do that, would you? I have enhanced eyes."

"I believe your problem is a hangover." Isla sat up, not bothering to cover her scarred breasts. The entirety of her right side had burns across it and I'd never asked her about it in our months together.

"Is that your medical opinion?" I asked.

"I do have some expertise in hangovers, yes. Practical and scientific."

I smiled and took another swig. "Well, it is said on my home planet that the best cure for a hangover is more of what gave you it in the first place."

"Oh, was that Artemis or Amaterasu?"

I paused, making note I'd claimed both as my home world. "You know, I honestly forget which."

Isla gave a light chuckle. "You know, Marcus, you can actually tell me who you are. Everyone here is running from their pasts. After six years of serving as this ship's medical officer, I'm not going to be shocked by anything you say."

I put the top back on the decanter, then placed it back in the drawer. "I thought we both made it a point to not pry. It's easier that way for both of us."

"This may surprise you, but I've actually come to like you these past three months."

Three months I'd been part of the *Melampus'* crew, and about half of it had been spent with Isla. I hadn't noticed until today she'd gradually winnowed down her number of lovers among the crew from a dozen to just me and Clarice. "Oh, dear, does that mean we have to break up?"

Isla gave a half-smile. "It might. I try not to like my lovers on the ship."

I was tempted to say, You have enough of them, but I didn't want to start a fight. Possessiveness was something I had made it clear I wanted to avoid in our *relationship,* and I had no right to complain if she'd taken me at my word.

In fact, I was stupid to have let it get this far. I couldn't afford to let myself become emotionally compromised if I wanted to stay ahead of the Watchers. I had spent too much time on the *Melampus* as it was. I should have made an ass of myself then and driven her away. It had worked with the other women but I was tired. Let her ask her questions. Let her be concerned. She'd soon come to regret doing so.

"What was your dream about?" Isla asked.

I closed my eyes. "The end of the war."

"Ah," Isla said. "A lot of soldiers have dreams about that day."

"Not the Commonwealth ones."

"Even them."

I thought about Crius and the last time I'd seen it. It had been my father's funeral. I'd been recalled from Analathas despite being desperately needed there. I still remembered the gathering of siblings, cousins, in-laws, servants, concubines, vassals, allies, and rivals at my father's estate. Six or seven hundred guests plus a six-course meal provided with vintage Belenus wines. All to commemorate the passing of a man they'd each detested. Father's appetites had finally caught up with him and the man I was genetically identical to was so obese they'd had to have his coffin custom made for him.

The rings of Crius and its four moons were visible in the day above the funeral as the sun covered the terraformed world in warm golden light. The planet was several times larger than most human-habitable worlds, but the super-concentration of metals within resulted in gravity that was slightly stronger than galactic standard.

My last image of Mass Castle had been that ancient crystalline palace standing tall against the sunset over my father's mausoleum with two huge banners hanging from its sixteen-story east and east towers. They were the red war flag of the Archduchy with a black cross across the center covered in the white and black wings of the now-extinct House Lucifer. A golden flaming sword pieced through the center with a halo around the handle, symbolizing something I had long since forgotten.

All of it gone.

"Well, it's not every day someone loses a planet," I joked.

Isla looked at me strangely. "Did you have a family back on Crius?"

I grimaced. "Yes."

"Were you close?"

It was a strange question to me but it really shouldn't have been. The majority of the crew was on the run from something or from families which had formed naturally in space. One thousand five hundred people called the ship their home and the vast majority had no one in particular who would miss them beyond their shipmates. Part of the reason I'd chosen to make my life here. No one cared who I was as long as I didn't care who they were.

"Yes," I said. "Yes, I was close to my family."

Thomas.

Zoe.

Judith... Oh Judith.

"Were you married?" Isla asked.

Isla was being unusually inquisitive for a relationship we'd both agreed would be primarily about sex and secondarily about drinking. I suppose we'd both made the mistake of being friendly to one another to the point we'd slipped into the realm of asking each other questions.

I didn't want her to know about my past, as it might get her killed (and worse, me), but I wanted to share some of it with her. Somewhere along the way, I'd come to care for Isla. Even if I didn't feel the same way for her as I'd felt for my wife, I felt something and that was one of the first true feelings I'd had since Crius. It was worth preserving, no matter how dangerous those sorts of feelings were to a man on the run.

"Yes," I said. "I was married. No kids, but she was the most important woman in the galaxy to me."

"I see."

"No, you don't."

Judith had been a short woman with long red-brown hair, almond-shaped eyes, and numerous other signs of uncontrolled genetics. When I allowed myself to remember her, I tended to see her in a white flowing dress with a purple lilac on its left shoulder strap.

It was her favorite and the one she used to travel along the lake together with me in when she wasn't fixing up my starfighter collection or her hovercars. She'd been pretty, but not gorgeous, at least not in the way Crius noblewomen tended to be, with each more perfect than the last and body-sculpted to inhuman loveliness. By their standards, Judith had been hideous since she was a nat with a face and body full of flaws. I'd loved her for each and every one. If I thought hard, I could even hear her voice.

"God, I hope this funeral ends soon," I remembered Judith saying.

"Have a care, he was my father."

"He hated me as much as he hated his other children, which is pretty damned big since he engineered you in order to disinherit them."

"True."

"Let's go sailing afterward. Take the hoversailer out on the lake and make love in the ringlight."

"That would be inappropriate." I paused. *"Tomorrow."*

"Just as long as we're together tonight," Judith buried her head into my arm. *"I love having you back from the front. Even if it's only for a little while."*

Unfortunately, remembering the good brought back the bad. I saw Judith slowly transform from the fresh-faced, pretty-but-not-genetically-sculpted perfect woman I adored into a flaming skeleton, then ash. I saw the entirety of my estate, with all of its servants and those relations I'd grown up with, die in a conflagration that turned Crius into a reflection of Hell. Up in the sky, I saw a hundred orbital mass drivers blasting down rocks at relativistic speeds, causing massive piles of ash to blot out the sun.

It was all a product of my imagination but I'd seen enough of the recorded footage to know it had gone down exactly like that. I'd watched all of it a thousand times from a hundred different recordings in hopes of gaining some evidence my loved ones hadn't died.

All for naught.

Taking another drink, I muttered, "I really hope those memory drugs kick in soon. I can just about stomach living without a past."

"They don't work like that, you know," Isla said. "They just block the emotions associated with traumatic memories."

"Yeah, well, they're not working right now."

Isla sighed. "I think we should share each other's secrets. We've known each other a while now and I think you're one of the people who can be trusted with mine. I'd like to think I'm a person you can trust with yours."

"You really don't want to be that person."

"Let me be the judge of that."

"Isla, you don't know anything about me." I would have to break up with her, it seemed. Well, as much as we could break off our *thing*. We would still see each other every day while serving together. That was one of the hazards of befriending a lover on a ship this small. Isla picked up her snow-white bra from the floor and slipped it on. "I know you have military-grade cybernetics, which means you fought in the war. I know you've had extensive plastic surgery to change your face and fingertips, but only had the most cursory gene-clouding done—either for fear of enhancement rejection or the fact your DNA means something personal to you. I know you speak Commonwealther like you learned it from a textbook, which implies an education. You pretend to be a lout whenever you can but it always comes off as forced. When you're not thinking about it, you let the females and the elderly walk through doors first and you eat one bite at a time like it's a dinner party. Oh, and you keep a Crius officer's proton-sword in the air vent above your room. Its house sigil has been burned off but it's kept in pristine working condition. Which was a mistake as you could have just claimed you'd gotten it at a flea market."

I paused, put down the decanter, then pulled out a pair of undergarments from my dresser before pulling them on. "I think we should stop seeing each other. In fact, I'm going to probably quit tomorrow."

"It's not a capital offense to have fought for the other side, Marcus."

I sighed, noting she didn't even know my real name. "That's a matter of opinion."

After the devastation of Crius, the Commonwealth had done an extensive De-Nobling of the Archduchy. Countless officers and soldiers had been sentenced to labor camps spread throughout the former Archduchy, while others were executed for war crimes. I couldn't sort the propaganda from the truth, but quite a few charges they'd levied against the Archduchy felt uncomfortably possible. Genetic cleansing, forced labor, mass-execution, and human experimentation for the start. Ironically, the only people immune to prosecution for such acts were surviving members of the nobility who had almost invariably been given high-ranking positions in the Republic of Crius Provisional Government.

Bastards.

"I wouldn't hold it against you if you did things you weren't proud of either."

I looked at her. "It's not that I did things I'm not proud of, Isla. It's the fact I'm not proud of what they'd make me do."

"Excuse me?"

There were three options if I turned myself in. The first two options were that they'd execute or imprison me, which were the preferable ones. The other option would be they'd make a spectacle out of the Fire Count. A spokesman for our Commonwealth masters and the New Era we were to participate in. I'd be asked to play on my war record, attend rallies, and participate in clandestine meetings to undermine every change the Commonwealth made while paying lip service to their cause. I was already a fool for ever trusting the Ruling Families.

I would not be a hypocrite.

"Never mind," I said. "You shouldn't have gone through my things."

"You shouldn't beg me for drugs to suppress psychological trauma."

"I'll find another source."

I went to my footlocker to retrieve my red crew jumpsuit, now set on ending whatever I'd had with Isla. I wasn't sure if I would leave the *Melampus* but it seemed like a better option every passing minute. I was growing fond of the crew and making a clean break now would be better than later.

Isla got out of my bed put on one of my shirts she found lying on the ground, hanging down past her knees. I was a good foot taller than her. "Marcus—"

"That's not my name. I'm not Marcus Grav."

"I know." Isla closed her eyes. "You need to know something about me."

"I think we've already exhausted every possible conversation topic we could possibly have."

I didn't want her to leave. I didn't want to push her away but the fact was, I didn't want to love her either, and if this continued, then I'd probably fall for her and then we were both doomed. Me when it came out what I was and her when she found out what I was. No one liked Crius outside of its own people. I'd discovered that within my first few days as a fugitive. Satanists. Fascists. Murderers. The monsters the Commonwealth used to justify the Reclamation.

"Not-Marcus Grav, I'm from Crius too."

I blinked. "What?"

"I was a slave to the nobility there."

Chapter Three

I, stupidly, said the first thing which came to mind. "The Archduchy did not keep slaves."

Isla looked at me with a somewhat pitying look. "No, they didn't keep human slaves."

Her statement confused me and left me pondering what she might mean before a slow, horrifying realization came over me. "You're a bioroid."

Which, to other members of the crew, might as well have been me saying she was a toaster. Isla nodded, shaking a little bit as if worried I might report her to the captain or sell her at the next port of call. Half the crew would. The other half would consider her equipment from then on.

Bioroids were a special kind of robot created by Ares Electronics, which existed as a controversial substitute for the chattel slavery to many border worlds. They were organic human bodies with an A.I. -equipped electronic brain. Legally, this meant they were machines rather than people and the property of their owners on all *civilized* worlds.

Including Crius.

I'd never actually given much thought to the idea of bioroid rights and had always thought those who cared for them, like Isla's lover Clarice, had been somewhat foolish. Realizing I'd been sleeping with and befriending one this entire time left me with a choice to either accept her or treat her like property.

"Does that shock you?" Isla asked, making the understatement of the year.

"Yes," I said. "I'm sorry to say it does."

Taking another swig of vodka was tempting right now but, for the first time in a long time, I wanted to be sober.

"What do you think of me now?" Isla said, staring up at me. Her almond-shaped eyes were abnormally large, blue, and expression-filled. I couldn't help but liken them to a doll's now and realized she'd probably been crafted that way.

Shaking that thought from my head, I concentrated on how I was going to answer. "My father believed bioroids were abominations against God and Lucifer. I believe their creation is also vile—because it is done as something to deprive sentients of their inherent right to freedom."

I hoped that would come off as suitably sympathetic. The truth was I didn't have enough friends, one or two at the most, which was more than I'd had the majority of my travels these past few years, to start being picky about the ones I had. Isla being created in a lab for sale on the market didn't make her less of a person or, if it did, it was less of a reason than the hundreds of other ways people were made less in the Spiral. Which made me a machine rights abolitionist now, I supposed. Also a robosexual.

Isla was less than impressed with my statement of solidarity, though. "So, you think it's awful I exist because I was made to be a slave."

Whoops.

"Would it be better to know I'd never given any thought to the subject until today?" I asked, frowning.

"Not really."

"Sorry."

Isla gave a half-hearted chuckle. "The fact you consider me a person now is enough."

"You don't think the rest of the crew would abide you?"

"No."

"How many others know?"

Isla looked down. "A few. Clarice, the captain, William—"

"William hates bioroids." The *Melampus'* first officer routinely complained about their existence.

"He wasn't pleased when he found out. He hasn't betrayed me, though. I suspect he was sorely tempted when Clarice left him to be with me, though."

I blinked, wondering how I'd missed that. *Oh, right, drugs and alcohol.* "Yeah, I imagine that would be the case. So, you've been on the run for, what, nine years now?"

I, honestly, wasn't sure how to react to all this. I'd had no incli-
nation Isla was anything other than a human woman, and while
I believed bioroids were sentient enough to qualify as people,
almost all of the ones I'd encountered acted like not-quite-three-
dimensional fictional characters. They behaved in shallow, blandly
pleasant ways that grated after a while. It only occurred to me as I
thought about it that they were programmed to act like that and a
free bioroid would have no reason to do so.

I thought about the tens of thousands of bioroids that existed
in the background of my past and their various uses in all levels
of society—especially with the destruction of Crius and the *liberation* of Sector 7. Thinking of them as people left me feeling sick as
I recalled how they were casually passed around or resold as toys.
The oldest models were frequently chopped up for parts so low-
income families could have access to replacement organs, all the
while the bioroids' programming prevented them doing anything
about it. Hell, that was one of the reasons why they weren't considered people. People would fight back, wouldn't they?

"Yeah." Isla sat down on the side of my bed. "I was commissioned
twelve years ago as a pleasure unit by House Plantagenet for their
son Octavian."

I blinked, processing that. I knew Octavian, was distant cousins with him actually, though that wasn't saying much since every
single Ruling House member was a blood descendant of Prophet
Allenway. My half-siblings were much closer relations and it sickened me to know they shared a substantial portion of their DNA
with him.

"Most nobles avoid bioroid units for...*that*. Men and women
compete in pageants and have agents for the honor of becoming a
noble's concubine."

Isla's expression was unreadable. "Yes, the poverty and sickness
for non-nobles means it's almost a dream come true for most, especially since most contracts mean a stipend for their families."

I grimaced, remembering Judith chastising me about similar privileged views of the world. She'd grown up in the poverty-
stricken ghettos of Lucifer City on the moon of Lilith. The stories
there, and what was done to girls and boys, were only slightly less
loathsome than what she said here. "Are the scars from Octavian?"

"Yes," Isla said. "Octavian had tastes which were violent and perverse. Ones which he would never do to a real person, but he very much enjoyed indulging on us. He had a particular love of fire."

I tried to think back to Octavian and remembered the gaggle of beautiful women of all shapes, sizes, and colors that hung around him. They had worn high dresses, which concealed all but their faces. I'd never given it much thought and the only time he'd suffered any controversy was when one had looked like a child and he'd been investigated. I now realized why they'd found him innocent of all charges.

God above and below.

Isla rubbed across her face. "I remember when I was marked like this and he decided the cost of replacing me was less than what it would take to have my face repaired without drawing undo questions." Isla gave a bitter laugh. "Not that he was worried it would be a problem he was abusing bioroids. He was worried he'd become a joke if people found out about his sleeping with machines. I do believe you nobles find that perverse."

Isla had guessed I was nobility. "Crius' nobility thought a lot of stupid things. What happened?"

"It's the nature of bioroid A.I. to grow and change unless it's regularly purged. We're designed to mimic humans after all. So, it wasn't much of a struggle to decide I wanted to live. Even then, I had to struggle with my desire to obey him even unto death. Thankfully, looking like an abused beautiful human has its advantages. One of his guards smuggled me away to sympathizers in the Lighthouse. They couldn't remove my hardwired programming but they could weaken the strictures and give me a new set of abilities. I asked to be a doctor."

"You're a good one," I said.

"Thank you, but it's not true. You can download facts into a cybernetic brain, as I'm sure you're well aware, but skills are another matter. I've had to develop those by hand. I also learned how to paint."

I enjoyed her landscapes and expressionist works. She'd shown me those a month ago. Not quite professional quality but excellent for amateur work. Not that she'd appreciated the constructive criticism.

"What happened to the other bioroids?" I asked.

"Octavian killed some of them and the rest were with him when the war destroyed Crius. I imagine they're all gone now."

I closed my eyes. "Probably."

"Are you willing to tell me who you are now?"

I hesitated before answering. "I am a Crius-born noble. I'm also a clone and a cyborg. All three of which would make me a second-class citizen in the Commonwealth. I was born for the purposes of being a vessel for my father's will in the new world. I was a way of showing his superiority to the next generation and denying his ex-wife's children their inheritance. I remember when my father found me playing with Thomas, when we were four years old, only for him to slap me. I existed for the purposes of destroying Thomas and my sister Zoe in his mind. Their mother felt similarly about me and taught her children to despise me. When we met again in the academy, I was treated as a creature who threatened their very lives. We eventually reconciled, but it was difficult."

"Thomas and Zoe Plantagenet? Octavian's cousins?" Isla now had enough information to put together my identity.

Dammit.

Still, how could I hide my identity after her confession? I could destroy her with what she'd shared with me. Judith would have called me a fool, but this was perhaps the first honest moment I'd had since abandoning the Crius Reborn movement.

I closed my eyes. "Yes. The tree of Crius' nobility has many branches, but they all extend from the same trunk."

"Then you're—"

"You can leave if you need to." I looked away.

"The Butcher of Kolthas." Isla took a deep breath. "I hadn't actually believed it."

"Kolthas was a viable military target. It was a choice between detonating the reactor core of the station and attempting to take it by force." I did a double take, noticing her choice of words. "Wait, what?"

"The captain suspects you're the Fire Count. Clarice said they should arrest you and drag you to holding until they could verify your identity. I said you weren't a threat. That you were a good person."

I stared at her. We were light years away from our next port of call and there was nowhere to run. I was trapped here unless I wanted to try and seize control of the ship or force it from jumpspace. The latter was a possibility since the three starfighters on board had jumpdrives, but I wasn't sure if I had it in me to spill the blood of the crew to do it. I had been here too long.

I slumped my head in defeat. "Well, I guess you were wrong then."

There was no way the captain and Clarice wouldn't turn me into the authorities. Not only was there a substantial reward for my capture, enough to convince most spacers to turn on their own mothers, but I was a criminal. For the first six months after Crius' destruction, I'd tried to drink myself into oblivion. For the year after it, I'd tried to kill every single Commonwealth soldier or collaborator I could with Judith's name on my lips.

I'd wanted to die in both cases, but I'd managed to live and that had just led to wandering around the underworld. I'd smuggled, stolen, scavenged, and worse, to survive until I'd come to live on the *Melampus*. Even on a ship full of people who wanted to lose themselves, they would have thought I was a monster.

Isla asked me a question I couldn't answer. "Why did you fight for Crius so hard? Didn't you know the war was over?"

"My world had burned, my wife was dead, my siblings were missing, and it seemed our leaders had stabbed us in the back. Fighting seemed like the best solution because it was something I knew."

"It wasn't?"

"No."

Hundreds more dead.

For no damn good reason.

"Why did you stop?" Isla asked.

"Pardon?"

"There's still Crius Reborn movements out there. Hell, they've grown bigger and bolder every year."

"Yeah, attacks on artists and spaceports. Killing whole swaths of helpless civilians enough to terrify the Commonwealth into submission."

"See? You don't want to kill the innocent. That makes you good."

It made me wonder if Isla was trying to convince herself she wasn't sleeping with a monster.

"I didn't stop because of what we were doing to me. I already thought I was damned and the only way I could make myself feel better was making others hurt as much as I did. I could have killed the entirety of the Commonwealth's citizens. I only left the Crius Reborn because the movement started recruiting children."

"Children?"

I walked to my decanter, opened it, and took another swig. "The sons and daughters of soldiers killed in the war. Those born of families who weren't able to feed their offspring with the shortages following the war. People easily manipulated by the promise of glory and being remembered forever as a hero, giving their lives for the older soldiers' vengeance. After a fourteen-year-old was shot after firing into a crowd, I killed the woman who ordered it and called the local Commonwealth militia down on my cell with an anonymous tip. I suspect if any of my former comrades survived, they'd consider me as much an enemy as the Commonwealth."

"I doubt it. The Fire Count is still a symbol of Old Crius."

I looked away. "Not because of anything I've done. All I've ever done is kill people. "Extremely well."

"It's all right. I'm never going to turn against you."

I wrapped my arms around her and gave her a kiss on the lips. "It's not you I'm worried about."

"Clarice and the captain won't betray you."

I surprised myself by not caring. "Why not? I've betrayed them."

I was friends with Clarice, lovers in a casual way, more akin to the manner I'd intended my relationship with Isla to go. Sex wasn't a big deal in the Commonwealth where everyone was expected to have it anytime they wanted with none of the romantic entanglements other human colonies possessed. Still, I liked her and she liked me. But this wasn't the sort of thing our friendship could survive.

As for the Captain? Well, she was a riddle wrapped in an enigma. She was a positively ancient spacer who didn't seem to care about profit, bonuses, or even cargo except for how it affected the crew. Ida frequently diverted the ship on side-trips and recruited some of the quirkiest individuals I'd ever met. She had an eye for people with talent but crippling personality defects. I'd also seen her flush a man out of an airlock for stepping out of line. I didn't expect to be treated any differently.

"When should I expect them to pay a visit?" I asked, honestly surprised they hadn't busted down my door as soon as they'd discovered my identity.

"Clarice said in the morning." Isla had kept this to herself the entire time.

"I see."

"You should finish getting dressed."

I did, unsure how to react to this. It felt like I was getting ready for an execution but the fact was, this wasn't the way it should have been handled. Even if they weren't trying to spook me, they wouldn't be so polite about it. Getting dressed in a red jumpsuit, I was putting on my socks and shoes when there was a rapping on the door.

That was when I heard Clarice's voice. "Cassius Mass, the captain wants to speak with you."

"Trust them," Isla said, wearing the plain synth-cotton dress and shirt with kittens on it she'd been wearing the night before.

I didn't look at her.

Chapter Four

"Cassius," Isla said.

I got up and looked at her, unsure how to respond to the fact she'd kept it secret they'd figured me out. In the end, I decided not to end it in anger.

Instead, I took her in an embrace.

I held her against my body for a long time, savoring the scent of her hair and the feel of her body against my skin. Even if she'd been designed for the purposes of seduction, to be pleasing to the eye as well as touch, I didn't care. She was a woman and one of the few bits of humanity I had experienced since I'd lost myself.

The knocking continued from across the door. "Cassius, don't make me come in there."

I pulled away. "I'm coming."

Isla looked at me. "Don't get killed."

"That really depends on them, doesn't it?" I couldn't help but wonder if it had been Isla's reports which had betrayed me to the captain.

Probably.

I headed to the doorway and stood in front of Isla to protect her modesty (such as it was). The door slid open and revealed the form of Security Chief Clarice O'Harra.

Clarice O'Harra was a woman of mixed Commonwealther and Shogun ancestry, her hair having been spliced to be a natural red despite the latter. She was tall, almost as tall as me, with a statuesque form designed more for combat than attractiveness. Still, I'd always felt there was some feeling toward me other than disdain and had been invited to her quarters once or twice.

There was none of that now.

Only cold-blooded professionalism.

Today, Clarice was dressed in a blue form-fitted grav-suit, which served as protective armor against fusion-blasts and most projectile-based weapons. It didn't have a Crius personal barrier but those were almost unknown outside of this Sector. She was also carrying a heavy fusion-rifle that was drastic overkill for the situation but had an appropriate intimidation effect. The side of the gun read "I kiss my mother, I kill criminals." It was the unofficial motto of the Star Sector 7 Patrol.

"I see you know my name now," I said, looking into her violet-shaded eyes. "I'm sorry it came out like this."

Clarice gave a dismissive shrug. "Personally, I don't care if you're a Nazi, Cassius. I don't like being lied to, though, especially when it's my job to find out dangers to the crew. Which you are officially as a fugitive from Commonwealth justice."

She still talked like a cop. I didn't know the exact circumstances of why she'd been driven from the Sector Patrol but everyone on board had their secrets. It just so happened mine were more severe than most.

"What's a Nazi?" I blinked, confused.

Clarice rolled her eyes, then gestured with her rifle for me to march forward. She looked behind me as I stepped out into the third story of the cargo bay. Her eyes lingered on Isla, but I wasn't sure what she was thinking other than the fact that everyone's eyes tended to linger on Isla.

Clarice opened her mouth then shut it. "Do I need the rifle?"

"No," I said.

Clarice surprised me by putting it away, the end of the weapon attaching itself to the magnetic holster. "Good."

The cargo bay of the *Melampus* was an impressive sight, at least to those who knew anything about independent shipping. The interior of the star galleon's top cargo bay was a three-story open-air chamber designed to carry millions of deadweight tons, but the captain had sacrificed some of that to carry three modified, decommissioned Crosshair starfighters. All three were held at the top of the chamber by metal claws in their collapsed position with a magnetic railway to deploy them should the ship ever get intercepted by pirates or local partisans.

Technically, arming cargo ships like this was illegal in most civilized portions of the galaxy but laws were a little more relaxed in what was now considered to be the Frontier of the Commonwealth. Captain Claire had once shown me the documentation that listed the starships as museum pieces and collectibles, which were legal as long as they were never powered up or fueled for combat in Commonwealth territory. Since the star lanes were always interstellar territory, even if patrolled by the Commonwealth, she could use them all she wanted out in the darkness of space.

Clever.

"I bet you find it galling we've got three crappy pilots flying those instead of you, Mister Navigator," Clarice said, taking me by the arm and starting to walk me down the catwalk past the other crew quarters' doors. There were one hundred and fifty-three people who lived and worked on the *Melampus*, and that didn't include the occasional odd hanger-on, stowaway, or passenger Ida had a tendency to pick up.

"Not at all," I responded before starting to walk alongside her to the captain's Quarters. "I find Crosshairs to be only slightly more dignified to fly in than a plastisteel box."

Clarice snorted. "Don't tell Munin that."

Munin was our mechanic who I had some brotherly affection for. A young woman who had literally grown up on the *Melampus* during its forty years of service. I was surprised at how many people I was going to miss.

"I'll try not to," I said, chuckling. "They are, after all, her babies."

"You know, you don't look like Cassius Mass. Cassius Mass was good-looking."

"Well, I wouldn't be very good at hiding if I didn't have my face changed."

"But you didn't have your DNA clouded except in the most cursory manner, enough to fool casual scans and computer comparison but not any reputable forensic scientist."

I paused. "No."

"Why?"

I took a deep breath, looking down at the various crew members cataloguing our latest shipment of cargo for Shogun. "It's difficult to explain to someone born outside of Crius. Crius and Shogun may both be in Sector 7 but they might as well be on different sides of the universe. DNA has a holy significance to us. To alter it, even to protect one's identity, is to defile something sacred."

"Ah, so you're a bigot."

I sighed. "Sure, let's go with that."

"You know, I should hate you, Cassius."

"Oh, should you?"

"You *are* a terrorist."

"I'd repeat the age-old aphorism about one man's terrorist is another man's freedom fighter, but I agree I am. What I did helped no one."

"Then why do it?"

"I wasn't exactly thinking clearly when I lost everyone I cared about in the universe."

Clarice didn't have a response for that. At least, until she unexpectedly said, "Yeah, I know what that's like."

"How did you end up here on the *Melampus*?"

"Oh, are we friends now?"

"I didn't think we weren't. Why stop now just because I'm a mass-murderer and you're a person so committed to justice you try to enforce the law on this ship." Which was akin to trying to keep dry while swimming.

"Point taken." Clarice snorted. "Not much of a story. I was a cop, then I wasn't."

"There has to be more to it than that."

"Not much I'm willing to share. Just because you blew your chance at keeping your past secret doesn't mean I'm about to give up on mine."

I chuckled. "Point taken."

"I'll tell you what. You pay for the drinks and I'll tell you if the captain doesn't turn you in for a reward or shove you out of an airlock. I've never fucked a count."

"We've fucked before."

"Yeah, but you were the navigator then."

"Ah."

"Assuming you and Isla aren't exclusive."

"She's fucking you, isn't she?"

"Along with the good-looking half of the crew." Clarice gave an enigmatic smile. "She has her reasons for needing to do that. Not just looking after their mental health."

"Yeah, I just found out."

Clarice gave me a sideways stare. "That sucks. That means she likes you. Now I have to hope the crew doesn't kill you."

"The crew knows?"

"Ida gave an order to keep it secret between the bridge crew an hour ago."

"Well, shit. I'll be surprised if they don't know on Albion."

As if on cue, three of the crew moved in front of us. There was Holtz, a large, beefy, brown-skinned man with moving tattoos of dragons across his bare chest; Arcade, a small, thin man with a leopard-spot-covered light fur across his skin; and Marvin who had bad reconstructive surgery on the left side of his face. I knew two of them had fought in the war on the Commonwealth's side; I made a point to check up on that sort of thing, while Holtz had just never liked me. It made sense the three of them would want to pick a fight.

Or just kill me.

"Step aside, Chief, this doesn't concern you," Holtz said, holding a long steel pipe.

"If you're going to step in the way of my escorting the navigator then it is my business," Clarice said.

"My brother died thanks to him," Holtz said, a sneer on his face.

"I severely doubt I was responsible for your brother's death," I said, not intending to take any flack for what I'd done during the war.

"He was a mechanic on Kolthas station," Holtz said.

I blinked. "Then yes, I am directly responsible for your brother's death."

I'd destroyed Kolthas station with my team under the belief it would derail the Commonwealth's invasion plans of our sector. A pre-emptive strike, I'd justified the heavy collateral damage by the fact it would prevent further loss of life. Instead, it had just provided *casus belli* for the Commonwealth to attack.

That was when Holtz swung his pipe directly at my head.

Only for Clarice to catch it. Pulling it from him in one easy motion, she slammed it against his chest while Arcade moved to claw at her throat with his elongated black nails. Clarice elbowed him in the face before hurling him over her back. Marvin, meanwhile, pulled a micro-fusion pistol from his pants, little bigger than a pocket-communicator.

I had no idea if he was going to use it on me or Clarice, but I kneed him in the chest then slammed his face into the catwalk railing beside us. He dropped the gun on the ground and it fell to the third story below.

Clarice frowned. "Great, now I have to write you up for assault."

"Please don't dock my pay," I said, stepping away from the grunting workers before me. "I have an alcohol and drug habit."

Clarice tried not to smile at that. "That's one of the more original defenses I've heard. Where did you get your sense of humor, Crius?"

"Humor is a reaction of the mind to the incomprehensible horrors and travesties of life. So, everywhere."

Clarice, meanwhile, forced Holtz to the ground with an arm bar as she looked at the other two workers on the ground. "Well, that pistol just upped things to attempted murder. Shall we dump these two out into space or just lock 'em up until we reach Shogun and send 'em to a work camp?"

I sighed. ""As much as I would love to see them laboring away to repair the damage of the war, I understand their pain. Why don't we just let them go?"

Marvin, at least, looked surprisingly touched.

Holtz just looked pissed.

Arcade, meanwhile, grunted an agreement.

"All right then," Clarice said, letting them up. "By the way, I want that gun back. Also, if anything happens to Cassius over the next trip, I'll shoot rather than knock the crap out of you."

"He's wanted." Holtz growled. "A price on his head."

"No, he's not," Clarice said. "Double check. The bounty was removed months ago."

"Wait, what?" I asked.

"What?" Holtz said, looking more surprised than me. "Fuck."

"Sorry," Clarice said.

That seemed to take any wind out of my assailants' sails and was relieving, as well as confusing. The three of them promptly scampered off and I was left alone with Clarice on the catwalk.

"Did you make that up?" I asked.

"Nope," Clarice said. "Otherwise, I probably would have turned you in as my civic duty. No offense."

"None taken." I tried to parse what she was saying. "Do you know why?"

"Nope. Not a clue. The public arrest warrants and reward for information or capture were all removed, though, with a Watcher-1 seal placed on the information."

I stared at her. "Suddenly, all of my relief vanishes."

"As it probably should. The Commonwealth's secret police never does anything without a very good reason."

I understood that. The Commonwealth had gone to war with Crius and its holdings despite strict warnings from the Watchers that we had military hardware and enhancements far in excess of anything they had available. It had led to numerous massacres masquerading as battles, which only the sheer manpower and wealth the Commonwealth possessed had been able to turn into victories. The Watchers had managed to turn things around, though, by stealing technological data, converting the disenfranchised, and sabotaging sensitive projects. In the end, the size of the Commonwealth would have won the war on its own, but the Watchers had cut sharply into our advantages and saved many of their soldiers' lives.

I hated them for it.

"Oh, by the way," I said, looking at Holtz's group as it reached the first floor below us. "Thank you for giving me the opportunity to show mercy to them. That should go a long way toward easing the crew's unease."

That and they wouldn't get paid for turning me in.

"What do you mean?" Clarice said, stretching her back.

"That bit with the execution and turning them over to labor camps?"

"Oh, I was dead serious. They tried to kill you. I think it was incredibly stupid of you not to get rid of them."

"I see."

Clarice snorted. "You remind me of my partner, Darren. He was always stupidly idealistic about people and what they'd do if given a chance."

This was not the first time I'd ever been called idealistic but it remained as inexplicable to me as ever. I certainly didn't see any idealism. "What happened to him?"

Clarice frowned. "It got him killed. Drinks first, though, sexy-time, then drunken ramblings about the past."

I nodded, unconcerned about how this would affect my relationship with Isla. After all, we were both sleeping with her. "Assuming the captain doesn't shoot me into space or take me to work in a labor camp, that sounds lovely."

"She might," Clarice said. "She'll pour you some ice tea and give you a cookie first, though."

"That she will."

The two of us proceeded out of the cargo bay toward the captain's quarters where Ida Claire, obviously not her real name, the grandmotherly leader of the *Melampus'* ragtag bunch of misfits, lived.

I gave myself roughly fifty-fifty odds of walking out of that room alive.

Less if I tried to resist.

Chapter Five

Captain Ida Claire was over two hundred years old and a grand-mother several times over. I didn't know where she was from, star system-wise, but suspected she'd been in space longer than most families could trace their descent.

Her cabin certainly looked like it belonged to an old spacer matriarch. Several times larger than the next largest set of quarters, the place was decorated in a mixture of wooden and steel furniture from around when the *Melampus* was first commissioned plus various knick-knacks from Sectors 1, 2, 3, and 7.

I saw an Albion living painting on the wall, which showed its beautiful oceans as well as a sailing ship travelling to the tune of the ocean's waves. I saw a little china bull-cat with the flag of Crius on its back. There was an unsettlingly large number of kitten-themed statuettes on every shelf, and the entire place smelled of wilted flowers. Quilts, furs, and plush blankets of various types covered just about everything with the floor having several dozen pressed-together rugs over the cold metal surface.

The right side of the wall from the entrance had a large transparent steel *window* displaying a sensor reconstruction of jumpspace with blues, blacks, and golden colors forming a somewhat pleasing view of the universe. It wasn't what jumpspace actually looked like but it was an approximation, which wouldn't make you violently ill. The place, oddly, reminded me of the stories we used to tell of Jumpspace Yaga, the old witch who rewarded good little boys and girls with treats while eating the bad.

The captain sat on a patched-over silver couch in front of a cracked glass table with numerous holo-magazines and a tea set. Sitting across from her in a big comfy chair was Ensign Thompson in his well-cleaned crew uniform, having a cup of mint tea.

The brown-skinned woman had a leathery set of features, which seemed a mixture of just about every race of humanity out in the Spiral. She was wearing an old-fashioned Commonwealth Merchant Guildmasters great coat over a floral dress, which was a strange fashion choice to say the least. She was also wearing a wide-brimmed hat with a pair of goggles affixed around the top. I would be lying if I said I believed she dressed in an eccentric manner deliberately.

No one could fake that much oddity.

Ensign Hiro Thompson, by contrast, was a pale-skinned twenty-two-year-old with shoulder-length black hair and features that pointed to his parents spending a great deal on his genetic profile. It was quite the contrast to the rest of the crew who came from much less privileged backgrounds. He wasn't from Sector 7, and I suspected he might actually be from one of the Commonwealth's Inner Planets. Wherever he came from, he'd tried and failed to do something important with his life but was refusing to go home.

"Knock, knock," Clarice said, rapping on the side of the door.

"Come in," Ida said.

"Holy hells!" Hiro Thompson said, looking over at me. "I mean, I can't believe it's actually him. I mean, I know who you are Marcus, I mean, Cassius but I never knew it was you-you. I mean, you're like a hero or a revolutionary or..."

I stared at him. "Hello, Hiro."

Hiro looked away. "I mean, if you totally want to lead the squadron from now on that'd be amazing."

Hiro fancied himself the *squadron* leader of the three starfighters kept for defense.

"No," I said, looking to Ida. "You called for me, Captain?"

"I was just having a spot of tea with the ensign," Ida said, smiling. "Would you and Clarice join us?"

"Certainly," I said, walking into the room without hesitation. If she was going to dump me out of an airlock then there wasn't much I could do about it. She was more shooting me in the face, man-to-woman, though. Air-locking prisoners was reserved for those who had really pissed her off.

"Dismissed, Hiro," Ida said.

"But—" Hiro started to say.

"Dismissed," Ida said, simply.

Hiro sighed, got up, and headed out the door.

Clarice watched him depart. "If you don't mind, Captain, I've got a bunch of asses to kick and names to take. I imagine this latest revelation about one of our crew is going to make headlines. I want to get ahead of it by saying no one is baying to have him killed and he's not rich anymore so don't bother hitting him up for money."

"I hadn't even thought about that part," I said, remembering all the off-world bank accounts I'd been encouraged to invest in by my fellow nobles.

That took on a sinister turn.

Clarice smirked. "Don't worry, by the time I'm done, the worst anyone will do is ask you to make them a knight."

"That's actually horrible," I said, walking over to where Hiro had been sitting and plopping myself down. "As well as grossly dishonoring a noble institution."

"See? You're already acting like the kind of guy they'll want to punch in the face."

"They wanted to do that before."

Clarice laughed as she walked down the hall, the door shutting behind her.

"What a peculiar woman," I said. "Fascinating but peculiar."

"She's probably the closest person to your past on here, despite half the crew being from Crius or their territories," Ida said, pouring me some tea. "Her family isn't just the O'Harras. They're the Rin-O'Harras."

"The rulers of Shogun?"

"Unofficial rulers. I'm pretty sure crime families don't qualify as nobility under most planets' rules, but the sentiment is there."

"You'd be surprised at what people legalize."

"Very little surprises me in this universe, son. I've been from one spiral to another in this galaxy and can tell you more about planets than most encyclopedias."

Ida handed me a plate full of biscuits.

I took one.

Then I noticed a micro-fusion pistol attached to her wrist, aimed right at my chest. Taking the plate with her other hand, she leaned back in her sofa and kept the gun trained on me.

"Son, we're going to have to have a talk. I have questions."

I dipped my biscuit in the tea in front of me and took a bite. "If you're going to get answers we're going to need something stronger than this." Chewing, I added, "Good biscuits. Almost tastes like real flour."

"I like your spunk, kid. Hunk-A-Junk, get us some bourbon."

A small black floating ball with several metal arms proceeded to float out from the kitchenette built into Ida's quarters. Speaking in a thick Albion accent, it said, "Of course, mistress! I am happy to comply!"

Hunk-A-Junk was a J-7 as old as Ida but somehow still functioning, which made me think the company must have gone bankrupt since every other synthetic manufacturer made sure their mechs burnt out after a decade or less.

Not caring at all about the gun, I leaned back in the chair. "So what do you want to know?"

"So, are you Cassius Mass?"

"You already know the answer to that."

"I want to hear it from you."

I took a deep breath. "I am Cassius Mass the Younger, genetic-clone and adopted son of Cassius Mass the Elder. Baronet of Mass City, honored count of the Star 7171B in Sector 8, which would have been named after my firstborn child. I think the Explorer's Guild named it Dumptruck after someone's pet turtle following Crius' defeat. I am a former Colonel-Count in the Archduchy of Starfighter Corps equivalent to a Brigadier General or SOF-6, and I have won a shit-ton of awards, of which some I actually deserved. Head of Archangel Squadron and, technically, Archangel Wing, though we never actually were able to get the reinforcements we needed for that because everyone good enough was dead by the time I was promoted. I hold the distinction of being the first ever clone to hold the Lucifer's Star and, in all likelihood, am the last."

Hunk-A-Junk poured me a shot of bourbon in my teacup.

"Thank God," I said, taking my cup of it and downing it. "I am far too sober for this conversation."

"You're not usually."

I smiled. That was actually pretty funny.

Ida wasn't laughing. "Lucifer's Star, interesting name for an award."

I sighed. "The Crius system was settled by religious dissidents led by the Prophet Stephen Allenway, Patriarch of House Lucifer. He had the unpopular belief on his homeworld of Skye, that Jesus of Nazareth's death and resurrection had actually been the Morningstar redeeming himself on God's orders. Later, Marcus would claim he was the Second Coming."

"What's your take on that?"

"I believe in God, I don't believe in trifles. I do believe it was convenient for *God* to tell Marcus all of his supporters should have hereditary dominion over the second and third waves of colonists from nearby war-torn or impoverished planets. Nevertheless, the Lucifer's Star is the highest award for valor any soldier can be given in the Crius Archduchy, or was."

"How'd you get yours?"

I frowned, remembering the screams of dying colonists as I struggled to use the power-suit to lift up the wreckage covering them. The Commonwealth's assault had landed on a hospital and I'd been in a perfect position for a holo-opportunity. I'd saved too few that day and none of the peasant soldiers involved in the rescue had been honored. At least the rest of my squadron had been given similar awards later on in the war, when they'd been handed out like candy on Samhain.

"The usual bullshit."

Ida gave a hearty chuckle and put away her gun before taking a sip of her bourbon like it was tea. I couldn't blame her. Ida's stock was a far higher quality than the usual swill I imbibed. "You realize this puts me in an awkward position."

I nodded. "I'll depart at the next port."

If she was going to turn me in for the reward, she would have done so without tipping me off. Either that or had Clarice blast me with a stunner and dump me in the security room's holding cell.

Ida reached into her thick spacer's robe and pulled out a small folded-up wallet before tossing it on the table in front of us. A holographic image of an eye over the Commonwealth capital of Albion appeared. It showed Ida's picture, serial number, authorization code, and rank.

Shit.

She was a Watcher.

"Well, that certainly changes things." I gestured to Hunk-A-Junk. "Keep it coming."

It poured me another bourbon, which I quickly downed.

"Stay sober enough to talk, sonny."

"Do I have to?"

"I'd appreciate it."

"How long have you been a Watcher?" I asked, trying to reconcile my image of the sinister organization with the woman I'd known for the past year.

Ida pointed over to a picture of a lovely black-and-white holo of a beautiful woman with chocolate-colored skin and a Merchant Guild uniform similar to the one she now wore. "Since I was young and pretty like Clarice."

"I'm stunned they had space travel back then," I said, opening my mouth in faux-astonishment.

"Don't sass me when I'm not pointing a gun at you. I might rethink putting it away."

I looked at her square in the eye. "I'd say I really don't care one way or the other."

"You don't strike me as suicidal or a quitter, Cassius."

I closed my eyes. "Then you have misread me badly because I've been both for a while now. I'm tired of the killing and I'm disillusioned with causes. If you want me to stand up in front of a podium and say how I was wrong to oppose the Commonwealth, then no, I won't. I don't care if you kill me. You dropped fucking asteroids on my world and murdered my family. Maybe the nobility deserve it, God above and below, we probably did, but I'm not going to betray their memory like that. Even if I now think the Crius Reborn movements are a bunch of murderous psychopaths who are making the lives of Sector 7's peoples worse."

I'd screwed up, badly, trying to continue fighting the war against the Commonwealth. Surrender was a bitter pill to swallow but there was a reason it existed. Because continuing to fight only made things worse. It was a child's conception of war you were supposed to continue until you won, as if losing was the worst thing in the world versus whatever terms brought it to an end. We'd brought the Commonwealth's wrath down upon our heads and it had done nothing but guarantee the next sixty years of Crius citizens struggled for survival. But I was not going to say its citizens deserved what happened to them.

Never.

I'd die first.

Honestly, it surprised me I still had that sort of passion left.

Ida nodded approvingly, bringing me out of my fugue. "That's the kind of spunk I meant. What happened to Crius was a war crime, plain and simple. It would also do no good. If you were the kind of critter who'd ignore all the dead men, women, and children from your planet for a free pass, then I'd have no respect for you nor would your people. If we wanted to put you up as a Watcher puppet, I'd have you gnashing and hissing at the Commonwealth while encouraging patience as well as a slow build-up of your sector to strike against us. You know, like all of our actual operatives in the provisional government and opposition."

I blinked. "I see."

How naive had I been of the political realities? Was I truly just a babe in the woods even now? My father had been one of the most powerful men in the nobility, count of a minor homeworld estate or not, and despite sharing his DNA, it seemed I had none of his political instincts.

Cassius the Elder had been one of the chief architects of the war and had he not died, I imagined he would have been one of the first individuals to take the outstretched hand of the Commonwealth so he could buy back the territory we'd lost and force those worlds under economic domination rather than feudal. Just like all the other surviving nobles were.

Ida ignored my distress. "No, I don't want any of that."

"Then what do you want?"

Ida crossed her arms. "I'd like for you to answer me how the hell you've been on my ship for the past year and yet some man who looks, acts, walks like Cassius Mass has just destroyed one of the Commonwealth's fleets three days ago."

I started to open my mouth.

Ida dropped another explosive revelation before I could. "He also has your wife accompanying him."

I closed my mouth. "Do we have anything stronger than bourbon?"

Chapter Six

"Sorry," Ida said, sighing. "I have some Carthagian brandy if you want some."

"I want to get drunk, not kill myself."

"I know this must come as a shock, your wife being alive—"

"My wife is dead, Captain," I said, not raising my voice but being very clear in my pronunciation. "Judith was working at High Command when they dropped the first set of asteroids down on Allenway's Rest. My wife was tough but even she would find it difficult to survive that many tons of rock."

"Are you sure she was there?" Ida asked, looking at me sideways. "No possible chance she might have been sent away, evacuated, or fled?"

"My wife wouldn't have abandoned her post."

I was certain of that.

"Your post or you?" Ida asked. "She wasn't exactly popular with the brass despite her ideas for improving equipment."

I closed my eyes. "Me. She wouldn't abandon me."

Ida pursed her lips. "All right then, what we have is two very clever frauds who have been making use of your image to help rally the Free Systems Alliance."

"Is that what they're calling it today?" I asked, putting every bit of contempt I could muster into my voice.

"Hundreds of smaller movements all united together ideologically with its leadership arming cells, paramilitary units, and militias while the bulk of its danger comes from its actual military. A military which, as I mentioned, just defeated a Commonwealth Fleet. The 9th, in fact, killing every single man and woman involved with stealth tactics, followed by destroying those escape pods which ejected."

"Careless." I shouldn't have said that. It was against the instincts of every spacer alive to destroy escape pods. Some rules of war shouldn't be broken, no matter the foe. Then again, it seemed like I was the only one who thought they weren't things to cast aside when things got difficult so what did my opinion count for?

"I'm not joking, Cassius. This goes beyond your small bunch of malcontented soldiers dreaming of revenge."

"I feel insulted."

Ida ignored my rejoinder. "This is a threat to Sector 7 and the entire Commonwealth."

"The galaxy's saddest melody is playing." I wasn't exactly going to mourn the Commonwealth reaping a little of what it had sown, destroyed escape pods or not.

Ida recognized this and tried a different, more effective, tactic. "They killed five hundred million innocent people in order to bring an end to a war that had killed two hundred and fifty million soldiers because Crius's military made fools of our forces. What do you think they're going to do if they decide they didn't do enough last time?"

She was right. The Commonwealth would not suffer this kind of humiliation. They maintained their empire through fear and respect. Challenging both would only bring down reprisals Crius' citizens might not survive. "All right, tell me what the situation is."

"I'll do you one better. I'll show you." Ida gestured behind her at the window to jumpspace. "My people recovered a copy of this in one of the cells local authorities raided. There's copies scattered across the Commonwealth's six sectors. Viewscreen, play Crius-10 file."

Seconds later, the image of jumpspace was replaced by that of a rally taking place on some world, which looked to be in the process of being terraformed. A barrier dome covered a stadium-sized area as red dust sandstorms went on outside it. It took me a second to realize it was being done on Crius, a choice of location that maximized the propaganda value of the video.

The rally had hundreds of plastisteel uniformed Void Marines, noble officers, commoner officers, enlisted men, pilots, and other people who would never normally mix in a crowd together, all standing before an elevated podium underneath the banners I'd seen draped over Mass Castle. Standing on the podium was a veritable collection of Crius heroes with Thomas in a black State Security Marshal-Prince's uniform, Minister of State Security Alvarado Jensen, the white-uniformed Grand Admiral Malcolm Plantagenet, myself in a red General-Duke's uniform, and Judith dressed in civilian attire.

They even had thirteen-year-old Princess Servilia of House Dumas, missing since the fall of Crius. She was wearing an adorably cute miniature version of a naval dress uniform. The young girl's cornrows were tied in a military braid that aided the effect. I dismissed her as another imposter until I noticed her right hand had a golden bracelet I'd given to her for her seventh genesis day.

I had to admit they'd chosen well with the actor replacing me since he looked identical to the touched-up version in propaganda holos. I wasn't wearing my usual golden and red colors but had dressed down to a uniform lacking its usual flamboyance. Still, my Lucifer's Star and rank insignia were present on my chest along with a few patches that looked tastefully modest.

Stepping to the podium, my doppelganger spoke with a voice eerily similar to my own.

"Sentients of the Crius Archduchy, freemen, nobles, and people of the ground, we have long struggled against one another. For too long it was taken for granted there was a natural order, that one side should dominate the other, but now we are equal. Equal in our oppression—"

"Oh, turn this shit off!" I said, waving my hand. "I think I can guess how it goes from here."

I couldn't help but focus on Judith, though, searching her features for any sign of my wife or that she was a fraud like my doppelganger. The resemblance was perfect but the quality of the holo wasn't perfect either. I couldn't see her face to the point of knowing every dimple and spot. I did know my wife wasn't a terrorist, though, and certainly wouldn't want to be part of something insane like this.

Unless she thought she was avenging me.

Crap.

"Viewscreen off," Ida said. "Yeah, it's pretty stereotypical populist meets fascist rhetoric. None of the usual Neo-Feudalist crap the Archduchy was famous for."

"I take it he's saying that all Crius citizens are in this together and our real enemy is the Commonwealth?"

"Yep," Ida said, picking up a biscuit off her tea set. "He's not even limiting it to Crius as he points out all citizens of the Commonwealth victimized by the Reclamation should rise up and take back their worlds."

I snorted. "People hated the Archduchy. They cheered the dropping of asteroids on it from New Baghdad to Carthage to High Washington. I never realized how badly the nobility were loathed until afterward."

Then again, I hadn't known about the forced sterilizations, the mass-cullings, the execution of prisoners, or the human experimentation. The previous Archduchy Wars had been described as us taking the fight against savage evil primitives to bring order to Sector 7. It seemed my definition of savage and my ancestors' were a trifle different.

"Nostalgia is a funny thing. I bet they're already talking about how much better it was being serfs." Ida crunched down on her biscuit then tossed its remains back on the plate in front of her.

"We never practiced serfdom," I said, my head hurting from all these revelations. That and my hangover. "Are you really all that worried about a group of ex-Crius soldiers? We couldn't defeat you when we were at our strongest and that was before we were forcibly disarmed."

Ida handed me a holo-magazine, tapping it as its cover disappeared to show a secret transcript from Albion's data-centers. It listed bank accounts, military assets, and projected military support for this Free Systems Alliance. The projections were not what you would find for a terrorist organization.

They were the projections for a star nation.

A powerful one.

I whistled. "That's a lot of zeroes."

"Someone is clearly financing this little tin-pot revolution."

"The former nobility? I understand a lot of them got very cushy jobs with the Commonwealth Provisional Government."

Plenty of commoners had welcomed the Commonwealth on vassal worlds, only to be horrified as their state-industries were privatized and handed to the former nobility. The Commonwealth justified it on grounds of Crius knowing the local language, customs, and how to run things. They were individuals who could get trade going and tax money delivered for projects to alleviate the worst damage from the war. Democracy would eventually be given to the people.

Once the situation had stabilized.

Eventually.

"I doubt it," Ida said. "We've been watching them like a bat-hawk and the survivors tend to be too busy enjoying their newfound fortunes to care about politics. The poorest ones have forty times their previous tax bracket. Someone cut a very lucrative deal with the government."

I clenched my teeth, wishing I'd hunted them all down after the war. "Someone should have told the people dropping the asteroids. What do you want from me, Ida?"

"I want your help investigating this group. Help me expose your doppelganger as a fraud and we'll consider it even between us. You'll get your nice shiny new pardon and a ticket wherever you want."

I paused. "How many people have died in this little revolt of theirs?"

"Two million," Ida said. "And rising."

I took a deep breath. "Fine, but I'm not doing it because I give a shit about the Commonwealth. Someone is sullying my family name and impersonating my wife. I wouldn't even care if it was just me, but her? That is unforgivable. I also want this agreement in writing."

Ida had a document awaiting my signature. All of this was very convenient. Had I been set up? If so, why wait all this time to make the deal? Had she really not known who I was this entire time? If so, she had to be the worst intelligence officer in the history of forever. Yet, it was an insane coincidence otherwise.

And I didn't believe in coincidences.

Either way, I wanted to know about this Free Systems Alliance. My honor was already shit so I didn't mind signing an agreement to work against them when I was sure they weren't the sort of group I should join.

No, I couldn't start thinking like that, even if I thought they had a chance of winning. If they somehow managed to destroy the Commonwealth or drive it from Sector 7, the region would descend into anarchy and billions more would suffer. More likely, they'd just draw out the fighting and cause even worse retaliations than before. With my wife's face used to inspire the bloodshed.

Fuck, I really was too sober for this conversation.

Ida, however, read me like a book. "Did I ever tell you about my past?"

"Nope. I didn't have a spare month."

"Now you're just being insulting."

"Sorry."

"It'd take three and a half weeks at the longest."

I gave a half-smile. "No, you haven't told me about your past."

Ida shrugged. "I'll leave that for the youngsters. One story sticks out for relevance, though. Back when I was running guns in the early days of the Commonwealth's wars of conquest, when I was still a fit and sexy seventy-five, I knew a revolutionary named Carlos the Red."

"Never heard of him."

"You wouldn't have. He was a roguish dashing figure, with a beret and red skin. He and his people used nano-tattooing to cover their entire bodies in beautiful illustrations of their battle prowess. Carlos loved to talk about how the Commonwealth was the enemy and how he would liberate his world from their oppression. He claimed the only reason they wanted to take his world was its resources."

"Sounds familiar."

Ida smiled. "Man could fuck like a sand dragon, too."

I tried not to grimace at that mental image. "What happened to him?"

"He won. The Commonwealth withdrew like it occasionally does. His world's economy collapsed and he killed a bunch of innocent people trying to hold onto power. Ten years later, when he died at the hands of his bodyguard, the planet petitioned to rejoin the Commonwealth. Been an upstanding member ever since."

"Not exactly a compelling moral. Don't fight for freedom because it's not worth it?"

"Oh, no, it's much worse. The moral is everyone in power is one kind of son of a bitch or another. Don't trust 'em. Fight for people rather than fight for *the* people themselves. Individuals are worthwhile but people as a whole are a nebulous concept which can be used to justify anything."

I respected that sentiment, even if I didn't agree with it. "I don't have anyone to fight for."

"Then maybe you should remedy that."

I prepared to get up but, instead, just reached over and picked up the teapot to pour myself something non-alcoholic. "There's one thing I don't understand—"

"Just one thing? You're a very lucky man."

"How *did* I end up on the ship of a Watcher?"

"You really want to know?"

"Yeah."

Ida chuckled. "I thought you were Hans Nakamora."

I stared at her. "My wingmate?"

"Yeah, the Star Dancer of Crius. I saw a couple of propaganda films about him. The bastard son of royalty raised in poverty only to become the greatest warrior in the Archduchy. Caused my heart to pitter-patter."

"*Starfighters of Desire,*" I said, staring. "God above and below, I hated that movie. They made me a complete asshole in it."

"You had to admit the romance was good."

"Hans was asexual. He's also dead."

"A pity. Handsome fella." Ida leaned back into the sofa and got more comfortable. "There had been rumors he ejected from his starfighter at the last minute so I thought you'd eventually reveal yourself. My people in the underworld have a tendency to steer interesting folk my way or to my contacts. It just turned out I had the wrong person."

I rolled my eyes. "So, I just what, hang around with you as your people look in every little nook and cranny for where these rebels are based?"

"Sounds good to me. I figure if word gets out that you're hiding on my ship, the real you, the Free Systems Alliance will send some people to either pick you up or silence you."

"So, I'm the bait."

Ida chuckled. "Something like that. Honestly, I have another operative who will be very interested in meeting with you and together I think you two could bust some heads."

""Does this operative have a name?"

"Yep."

I paused.

Ida smiled.

"I see." I smiled back and took a sip of tea. "Just when I thought this was going to be boring. I was worried you were going to have me recite speeches denouncing the fake me and blood tests to prove my identity."

"It'd be better if no one knew about my status as a Watcher. As far as the Free Systems Alliance is concerned, you're just a former war hero in hiding. When they make contact with you, we'll follow them up the food chain to their masters."

"Who I will then deliver unto their doom."

"'Fraid so."

"Anything else?" I wasn't sure I was going to go along with this plan any further than it took me to the next point. On the other hand, I did want to find out who the hell was impersonating me. If there was even a slight chance that was Judith, I needed to know.

No, Judith was dead. No hope was better than false hope.

"We'll be heading out to a ship that we think was conducting scientific experiments for the FSA. I had a friend on board disable the vessel so it's sent up a distress signal. We can show up there and either rescue any survivors or loot the wreckage for anything useful. Hopefully, we can extract my agent, too."

I stared at her, not at all pleased with her revealed ruthless side. "And hope their friends don't send an army to blow us up."

"That too. If there are any survivors other than my associate, you can make contact with them and persuade them of who you are."

"This is a terrible plan."

"Probably, but I didn't come up with it. My superiors are morons, God bless them."

I snorted. "Do I have any choice but to go along with it?"

"Not if you don't like prison camp food. I think you'll like the person on board, though."

"I doubt that very much." I sighed then paused. "Show me the video again. I want to get to know these people."

I needed to know what choice of evils I was really making.

Chapter Seven

I dreamed again.

This time I was prying open the metal doors of a sealed super-steel warehouse on Skellige, one of the vassal-worlds taken during the Second Archduchy War. I was working with scavs, the lowest of the low, moving through the ruins of battlefields and former Archduchy possessions. The warehouse was just one of the many innocuous locations marked on the document sheets we'd stolen from our last haul, a State Security messenger ship which had never managed to reach its destination.

When the door was pulled open, the smell was horrifying. The rancid smell of meat, which had been left to rot for God knew how long. The interior of the building was dark and there was no sign of State Security guards, markings, or hints this was one of their facilities. It had probably been cleaned out but many of the organization had fled their posts after Crius, abandoning whole collections of important equipment.

I just wanted to make enough money to get out of Sector 7 and get to one of the Free Systems in Sectors 8 through 12.

"Put on your breath masks, lads," Captain Thompkins said. He was a jolly red-haired man with a goatee and a complete lack of scruples. The scavenger leader was half-pirate and had accepted my presence in the group along with other people who didn't belong anywhere else.

I, reluctantly, did as he asked. The genetically engineered gelatinous membrane slid over my face and purified the air I breathed. I wasn't exactly comfortable with this sort of biotechnology; ironic, given my people's extensive use of it, but it was a cheap substitute for importing actual equipment from the more civilized nations.

"You go on first, Steve," Captain Thompkins said to me. "New guys always take the biggest risks."

Why there was always a need for new crew, I gathered. I hated this current bunch and intended to ditch them for someone slightly more honest the first chance I got. Heading on in, I flipped the interior lights and found the power was down. Pulling out a light rod, I lifted it up and stared at the sight that greeted me.

Corpses.

Thousands of them.

All piled on top of one another like trash.

"Well, that explains the smell," Thompkins said, coming up behind me. "It's an old State Security Processing Facility."

There were complaints from the scavenger team behind me, clearly having hoped for something other than bodies.

I stared, stunned into silence. "I thought those were just propaganda created by the Commonwealth."

"Oh, Shiva and Kali, no," Thompkins said, laughing. "Those Crius bastards were always looking for new genetic material to test their enhancements on or work their wacky science. You got used to people disappearing on worlds like mine, especially if they weren't living up to their potential."

"Monstrous," I whispered.

"Not really," Thompkins said. "These facilities usually have vaults full of confiscated property for the Parentland. If they didn't bother disintegrating this load before they fled, they might have only taken what they could carry with them. Also, I can see the armory door is still sealed. That means it's payday tonight!"

A cheer went up from the rest of the scavs.

My eyes opened and I was once more in the present. This time, I didn't have a hangover despite the fact I'd spent the entirety of the night drinking with Clarice. I'd set my blood-nanites and artificial organs to cleaning out my system when I slept. Not just of the alcohol but also the tranquilizers, memory suppressors, and more. I wasn't sure if letting the memories flood back was a good idea since traumatic memory was a medical condition but I wanted to be conscious of everything before I made my final decision.

Clarice's taut, well-muscled body nuzzled up against mine beneath the sheets and I looked over at her, seeing the outline of her frame beneath. It was a very different kind of body to Isla's and one I had enjoyed riding. I was glad, really, that my friendship with her had survived and hoped I could continue it with both her and Isla. I wasn't sure if it would survive with any of the other crew.

We were in Clarice's quarters this time and it was a strong contrast to both mine and Ida's. The place was full of holos, pictures, and symbols of the life she'd left behind, but also arranged with a military precision. I saw images of her cousin Janice, Isla, Ida, a few shots of the mercenary group she'd left behind, and several of crew members. None of me but I didn't expect that. There were guns and armor throughout the room, mostly arranged in neat little cases with much attention to safeties. I also saw her framed System Patrol badge on the desk by her headboard.

Decommissioned.

Troubled by the memories of Skellige and other horrors that leaked to the forefront of my mind, not to mention my Traitor's Alliance with the Watchers, I leaned back against the headboard and took a deep breath. "Sickening."

Clarice surprised me by revealing she was still awake. "Because that's what every girl wants to hear after a night of rough energetic sex."

"No, that was more than satisfactory."

"You should be a poet, Cassius. I bet that silver tongue of yours won many young ladies over."

"Speaking has never been my tongue's best use."

Clarice chuckled. "Okay, good one. I may actually invite Isla for our next session as a reward."

"I'm fairly sure a reward would imply it wouldn't be for you as well."

"I keep forgetting Crius women don't pretend sex is a big chore that is given as a reward to men for good behavior."

"That seems like a shockingly bad idea."

"Eh, it may just be for Shogun upper-class women. We're supposed to be pure, chaste, and virginal until our marriages to whichever man or woman our House master picks for us."

"I seem to recall hearing something about that. How's that working out for you?"

"With lots of scheming, adultery, secret lovers, lies, blackmail, and murder."

"So, much like Crius."

Clarice stretched and sat up. "I had to break up three more fights today over you."

"I'm sorry."

"Don't be. Two of them were people going after Holtz for trying to take you down. Apparently, you're some kind of national hero to surviving Crius."

"That…makes no sense to me. Everyone on the ship from the Archduchy is a peasant."

"Commoners love nobles. They all dream of being swept away by one so they can order people like themselves around for the rest of their lives. You married one, after all. You also didn't commit any war crimes."

I thought of Kolthas and the fifty thousand people who died there without warning to get at the military base located on it. "That's debatable."

"Yea?" Clarice said, "But people have a tendency to remember things as better than they were."

I paused. "Ida recruited me to help her track down the Crius Reborn soldiers and this Free Systems Alliance."

If Clarice didn't know Ida was a Watcher, I wasn't going to keep it from her.

Isla either.

"Good," Clarice said. "We can do some real good by taking those bastards down. More so than any of the pirates and smuggling rings we've been tracking."

A lot of the *Melampus'* illegal activities took on a new light with the realization they were being conducted by a member of the Commonwealth's secret police. "Are you a Watcher?"

Clarice snorted. "Fuck no. I just work for them."

"You promised me you'd tell me your backstory after drinking."

Clarice frowned. "Sadly, we went straight to sex after drinking so I reserve the right to withdraw that offer."

"No takebacks."

Clarice rolled her eyes. "Fine. What do you want to know?"

"You're a member of the Rin-O'Harra clan?"

Clarice closed her eyes. "Ida let you know about that, huh?"

"Yes, she did."

The Rin-O'Harra clan was one of the most powerful bloodlines in Sector 7. They were, in addition to being the not-so-secret rulers of Shogun, heavily involved in every aspect of commerce from interstellar trade to skim from tariffs. They had made uncounted trillions from selling Crius technology and enhancements to the Commonwealth as well as Independent Systems. They were also slavers.

Clarice sighed. "Well, you can imagine the majority of it. Born a wealthy merchant princess on a planet where everyone works for you or your family. I was taught the ins and outs of gun-running, narco smuggling, extortion, bribery, and how to kill someone in a way that left a message."

"That requires quite a bit of imagination."

"Even for a Crius?"

"Even for."

Clarice looked at a picture of a redheaded woman similar to her but even more beautiful than Isla, which I scarcely imagined possible. "My cousin and I were raised to be the heads of the family. The two of us were expected to take control over different sections of the business, push ourselves to the limit, and the one who made the most credits would get to be the new Matriarch."

"What happened?"

"I got put in charge of the slavery section of the family business and lasted a week before wanting to blow my brains out. They tried to move me to the bioroid section but, by then, I was already seeing them as people. It's how I became the first crewmember to recognize Isla, you know. I once saw an entire warehouse of Sexy Snow Queen Isla dolls."

I stared at her. "Sexy Snow Queen Isla...from the *children's* movie?"

I couldn't not see it now.

"She also came in sets with a talking reindeer and her brother Hans."

I rubbed the bridge of my nose.

"Do I even want to know how popular those are?"

"Extremely."

"Ugh."

Clarice nodded. "Of course, my family made its fortune in

knock-offs. For the actual slave-slaves, we wiped the memories of illegals and refugees, then surgically altered them and wiped their memories before selling them as bioroids. Other people we just signed on labor contracts, which they'd never be able to rid themselves of. Those we did our best to get addicted to glimmer or blitz to ease the transition."

"I get the picture."

"No, you really don't."

"Do I want to know how many were sold to Crius?" I tried not to be sickened by how many brothels I'd taken my squadron to which had been tended by bioroids.

"Very few," Clarice said. "They could afford to buy top-shelf stuff straight from the Commonwealth."

"What happened?"

"I ended up washing out, got addicted to drugs and alcohol. Spent a lot of time with whores. In the end, after rehab, my newly promoted matriarch cousin arranged for me to have the one job I thought I might be able to actually do some good in."

"A cop."

Clarice nodded, resting her head against my chest. "A cop. The System Patrol was corrupt as hell but I figured I might actually be able to do some good. My partner, Darren, and I, did a lot of good on Shogun. There were plenty of gangs other than the Rin-O'Harras, and even my family decided to go with it."

"Until something happened."

"Something always happened. I ended up finding a crate full of drugged-up refugees set for my family and decided to turn them into the Commonwealth rather than local authorities. I made a big decision to turn on my family and do the right thing." Clarice sighed. "They killed Darren for it and my sister covered up my involvement. After that, I was fired for some glimmer packets found in my locker."

"And so you ended up with Ida."

"There was a new sheriff in town and the Commonwealth needed people like me to clean things up."

"Did it work?" I asked, not at imagining it did.

Clarice stared at the door. "My cousin, Janice, is now the head of the Shogun Merchant's Guild and the Commonwealth is considering her for Sector 7's non-voting Parliamentary representative on Albion."

"Ah."

"We're cutting back on slavery of people-people, though!" Clarice raised an ironic fist. "Legal pharmaceuticals, licensed armaments, and locally-owned Ares Electronics branches for all the sector's bioroid needs! Redemption for the family! Legitimacy!"

"You must be so proud," I deadpanned.

"You have no idea." Clarice slid out of the bed and I watched her backside as she walked around the room, looking for a bottle with some alcohol left in it. "Even Janice is sickened by it. Then again, I always thought she wanted to be the hero, too. She was just strong enough to carry on the family business whereas I wasn't. Anyway, I've helped Ida take down some real scumbags so I can at least look at myself in the mirror now."

"She collects outcasts."

"That she does. Do you want to become part of her collection?" Clarice leaned over and picked up a nearly-full bottle of Sunburst lager.

Not very potent but good for early-morning drinking.

I looked to one side. "I don't know yet. When I left the Crius Reborn movement, I swore I would never kill anyone ever again. That lasted about a month until I was forced to kill a man in a fight over some salvage. Later, I killed a lot more people trying to survive."

I still remembered wrapping my hands around Captain Thompkins' throat, throttling the life out of him after he'd caught me trying to rob his office so I could get away from his crew. Sadly, not the most shameful moment of my life.

But close.

Clarice tapped the top of the Sunburst bottle, causing its iris to open before she handed it to me. "Any lingering loyalties to the Archduchy?"

"No," I lied. "There was nothing good about the Archduchy. It was an organization that existed purely for the enrichment of the nobility as well the increasing of its own power. Prince Germanicus was a monster."

I still wished, as bad as it was, it had blown the hell out of the Commonwealth Navy and dropped a hundred asteroids on Albion.

"Then look after yourself," Clarice said. "I'm starting to become fond of you."

"That's just because I'm possessed of nobility-reserved cybernetic arts for pleasing a lover. Ones extracted from millions of simulations and studies to pass amongst ourselves."

Clarice blinked. "Really?"

I took a sip of the Sunburst. "As far as you know."

That was when the *Melampus'* jump alarm blared. That meant we were arriving at Ida's target ship.

Hells.

I threw off the covers and began to get dressed.

Chapter Eight

The cargo bay was full of crewmembers frantically running back and forth. Yellow lights flashed both in the ceiling as well as the sides of the cargo hold while high-pitched sirens wailed. It took a second for me to register it wasn't the jumpspace alarms blaring but the Melampus' combat alert. Yellow lights meant the situation hadn't reached critical but everyone was to report to their stations. Second Mate Jun's soft melodic voice was stating the ship's barriers were holding at 99%.

We were under attack.

Fuck.

Space was full of a thousand potential dangers: pirates, terrorists, rebels, deserters, or local armies which had decided to engage in some pre-emptive looting, were just some of the human-based ones. The galaxy was so impossibly huge and the space lanes so incredibly vast that there was little to prevent raiding from being a lucrative business prospect to anyone willing to risk their lives stealing from others. Then I remembered we were visiting a ship Ida claimed would be the key to unraveling my doppelganger's organization and wondered if we were under attack by my countrymen.

If so, we were doomed.

There was no way an old tug like the *Melampus* could stand against Crius military hardware, upgrades or not.

"Raiders?" Clarice asked, following behind me and looking for the captain.

"We can only hope," I muttered.

Thankfully, we found the captain after passing just a few cargo containers. Ida stood in front of Isla, young Hiro, Holtz, and our chief mechanic Munin. All of them were underneath the three

Crosshair starfighters that were having their transport ladders moved up to their sides.

The starfighters were kept fueled but required time to power up. Worse, the ship hadn't exactly been prepping for combat and we had members frantically trying to prepare for deployment of our meager defenses. The *Melampus* had rockets, strong barriers, and defensive plasma weapons in addition to the starfighters, but nothing which would stand up to military hardware. I really hoped we weren't about to be annihilated by our own trap.

"You!" Ida pointed to me, the moment I came into her view. "Get in your spacesuit and get up there."

"What?" I asked, confused. Surely, she didn't want me to join the starfighter attack on our unseen enemy?

Wait, of course she did.

Dammit.

This day just kept getting better and better.

Ida clenched a fist and gave it a short shake. "We're being assaulted and I want these Crosshairs out there taking care of them. We've got six Chel Corefighters and a gunship out there. William is on the bridge sending blasts and the ship's completely-nonexistent-on-paper rockets against it, but I want those things gone!"

"Chel, my God," Clarice said, her voice low. "Captain, what have you gotten us into?"

I agreed with her sentiment.

Chel were every spacer's nightmare and something even the Commonwealth hesitated to tangle with. As much as the rest of the galaxy considered Crius obscene for meddling with human DNA and cybernetics, the Chel had been a group of human colonists who had survived the Great Collapse and the subsequent Galactic Dark Age by bio-forming themselves to live purely in space. The results were a tall, albino, hairless race of malformed zero-g-dwelling spacers who scarcely qualified as human anymore. A few believed them to be one of the few human cultures in regular contact with aliens and were possibly uplifts.

The Chel occupied a large swath of territory in Sector 8 and had a simple policy of killing everyone who wandered into their territory. Those that fell into their hands were very often tortured to death and their twisted bodies left as a warning. They were the

only race the Commonwealth had flat out been defeated by. Then
again, that was probably because they had no worlds to attack and
the largest fleet in the galaxy. Clarice, for reasons of her own, hated
them above all other things.

"What are they doing out here?" Clarice asked, looking at Ida
with an almost-accusatory stare.

"I don't know. Focus on getting them away from our target," Ida
said, giving a dismissive wave.

"What do you want me to do?" I asked, wanting to make absolutely sure she wanted me to take up arms. I wasn't going to be fighting my countrymen, terrorists or not, but that was a small consola-
tion if I was going to be fighting a race literally born to spaceflight.

That was when Munin, real name Maria Anna Gomez, walked
up to me and handed me a spacesuit with a combat-hardened
helmet and personal barrier. She was a short woman of mixed
Commonwealth-Crius ancestry, light-brown skin, long black hair,
and a notably curvaceous form, accented by her tube-top as well as
form-fitting work pants. A tattoo of a raven stretching its wings was
visible on and around her belly button.

"What she said was get in the fucking flyer and blow some bad
guys up!" Munin said. "Do that crazy fighter thing you do."

"Crazy fighter thing?" I said.

Munin glared, her point obvious. We didn't have much time
until the fighters were ready to deploy and, while the barriers were
holding, they wouldn't be holding long against a sustained Chel
attack. Thank God it was just six fighters and a gunship. I'd never
been particularly grateful the *Melampus* was a slow armored turtle
before, but it would take a long time to knock us out.

They would, though, if we couldn't blow them out of the star
lanes.

I *had* to do this

No! Dammit, I was not going to be manipulated into this! We
had combat pilots who could fly for us. I would rather die than end
up flying a starship for the same Commonwealth that had destroyed
my homeworld.

"I'm not a combat pilot anymore!" I said, stunned at their
attempts to dragoon me back into service. "I don't know how to fly
a Crosshair!"

Truth be told, I could probably figure out how to do it at a glance. Commonwealth starfighters weren't that different and I did have an enhanced brain just for navigation. Logic had nothing to do with my argument at this point, though.

"We need your help, sir!" Hiro said, doing his best to look intimidating despite the fact he looked like a porcelain doll.

Holtz just looked at me with the same blinding hatred he did earlier.

"We don't have to argue, son," Ida said. "This is real."

Isla looked at me. "I understand your motivations, Cassius. I'll respect your decision either way."

"I won't!" Clarice said. "Get in the damn ship! You're trained for this, our own pilots are washouts and dredges!"

"I resent that, ma'am," Hiro said. "I was driven out of the Commonwealth Navy for reasons unrelated to my combat performance—"

"Shut up, kid," Holtz said.

"Yessir," Hiro replied

The female voice then said, "Barriers now reduced to seventy-six percent."

That…wasn't good.

I was willing to die to prevent myself from joining the Commonwealth, but I wasn't willing to let the others. Where the hell was David Albernathy? The *actual* head of the *Melampus'* starfighter squadron?

"All right," I said, as I started to pull the spacesuit over my uniform. "But I'm in charge. Everyone obeys what I say, even you Holtz."

Holtz just kept his gaze even. His expression was murderous. I didn't care. I'd fought with pilots who'd wanted to kill me before. I didn't think this was going to be a bonding experience, though.

Just a survival one.

"How long until the ships are ready?" I asked, looking to Munin.

"Just a few minutes. My babies are kept in tip-top condition for this." Munin then narrowed her eyes. "You realize I will kill you if you get a scratch on them."

"Yes, I'm aware," I replied.

"Dead bang. I'll slit your throat you're sleep."

"Understood."

Munin made a throat-slicing gesture for added emphasis as I walked over to the transport ladder for the lead starfighter. The three starfighters' engines were powering up now and would be ready to deploy in just a minute or two. I had to get into the cockpit and ready myself or this flight was going to short its captain.

It was a strange feeling, once more going into battle and I'd have been lying if I wasn't excited. The problem was I was going into battle on behalf of my enemies and I didn't care. I could have lied to myself and said it was to protect my friends here on the *Melampus* but the truth was I just wanted to get back behind a starfighter's control.

Isla stopped to give me a kiss on the cheek and a hug. "Good luck."

"Thank you."

"Stay alive. Clarice and I would miss you if you died," Isla said.

"I'd even break out the good scotch to toast you," Clarice said. "Probably."

I gave an uncomfortable smile. "So noted. I look forward to returning to the arms of my lovers."

"Don't get sappy, Cassius," Clarice said.

"Godspeed!" Isla said.

I was still getting used to the values of the Commonwealth and other outsiders regarding relationships. On Crius, one partner was always superior to the other with possessiveness part and parcel to all relationships. It had helped lead to the dissolution of my father's marriage to Amita Plantagenet as neither would submit to the authority of the other.

Pleasantly, outsiders seemed to love and be loved wherever they pleased. Fights still happened across the ship when commitments were made, or misinterpreted as being made, but they mostly considered sex to be just an enjoyable pastime with no strings attached. Indeed, it was my friendship Isla and Shannon valued far more than any physical encounters we may have had.

Which, in a way, made me sad.

The ship's computer intoned. "One enemy target destroyed. Barriers at sixty-six percent."

Ida said, "Excuse me, I have to get to the bridge and take control from First Mate Baldur before he gets us all killed. Behave, you boys."

Holtz attached himself to the transport ladder beside me. Hiro did the same and the three of us ascended to our ship's cockpits. I put my helmet on and it sealed around me before flooding me with warm atmosphere. The lights in the hangar turned red and the cargo doors prepared to open. All the remaining crewmembers proceeded to head to the pressured doors around us and passed through them.

Entering through the starfighter cockpit's trapdoor, I climbed into the seat and strapped in. The ship was almost completely powered up now and ready to depart. I watched the cargo bay doors open with a glowing blue barrier keeping in a collection of the air and heat.

"It's good to be home," I muttered, checking the controls before turning off theA.I. interface. I didn't need a machine to do my flying for me. "Let's go."

A countdown from five occurred and the ship magnetically propelled us into the darkness of space as our engines fired behind us, sending us out into the starry abyss of our battlefield. The starfighter's computer linked with my long-dormant Combat Universal Processor—my mind filling with data even as there was a slight lag due to the incompatible formats of the technology.

I saw the five U-shaped chrome Chel Corefighters on the outside of the dagger-shaped gunship to which they were attached. All of the *Melampus'* data on the ships and their capabilities instantly became part of my memories. The vessels were good, Crius-level technology, but not as good as I'd expected with rumors of Chel advances.

Sensors showed the vessel the Crius gunship had attacked with a long *Kronos*-class cargo freighter the size of a small space station floating in space. Its SIP registry marked it as the *Rhea*. There were several bits of Crius starfighter wreckage and the burnt-out remains of another Chel gunship floating around it that I presumed to be the remnants of a battle we'd missed. A black hole was in the star system, the one we called the Thirsty God. We were far out of range from its gravity pull, but its presence made this a strange spot for anyone to set up shop.

The five Chel Corefighters stopped their green plasma barrage of the *Melampus* to engage us, moving sluggishly despite the level of their technology. The fact they could easily dodge the *Melampus'* crimson blasts and rockets proved they couldn't be underestimated, though.

"Engage the Corefighters with plasma weapons only, preserve your rockets for the gunship," I said.

"We need to take those things out, we're outnumbered!" Holtz growled at me.

"I'll deal with that," I said, my voice steady.

I brought my ship around and engaged the speed as much as possible, dodging the Chel's green plasma blasts, before sailing past the Chel Corefighters, then flipping my ship behind them. I proceeded to open fire and blew two of the vessels into stardust. It seemed the Crosshair's cannons had been upgraded by Munin, even if they were heavy on the generators. Unfortunately, no sooner had I done so, thanone of the Chel ships turned and blasted at me.

"Try to hold those other two off! They turn sluggishly," I said, moving the Crosshair around to avoid the Chel Corefighter's attacks. This pilot was much better than the others and adjusted to each of my movements.

"Any suggested maneuvers!?" Hiro said, struggling as he came under fire from one of the remaining two fighters.

"Not over an open channel!" I said, feeling a glancing shot wipe out 90% of my starfighter's barriers in an instant.

Dammit, *I* was sluggish.

Too much alcohol and not enough practice.

Why the hell was I out here?

That was when an idea hit me. "Take them along the *Melampus*!"

"What?" Hiro shouted back.

"Do it!"

I pulled the Crosshair to buzz the *Melampus* even as its barely-trained gunners filled the stars around us with plasma blasts. I easily dodged around them, even as the Chel Corefighter behind me did the same while in pursuit.

That allowed me to turn my starfighter around in an instant, knowing where they would dodge and blow the enemy fighter to pieces. Like shogi, national sport of Crius, it was all about maneuvering your opponent where you wanted.

Three dead.

And for what?

"Sir!" Hiro shouted behind me. "My barriers are down!"

I swung around my starfighter once more and checked the sensors. Holtz had killed the fighter he'd been engaging, but Hiro's was damaged and his attempt to lead the enemy against the *Melampus* had just resulted in the enemy vessel slowing him down. I opened fire repeatedly to give the boy a chance to escape, but the Chel vessel dodged between my attacks, the *Melampus,* and the rockets Hiro launched in defiance of my earlier order.

That was when the pilot was shot down by Holtz.

"Impressive," I said, genuinely impressed by the spacer's efforts.

That was when Holtz launched his rockets against me as well as a torrent of plasma fire.

"What are you doing?" I shouted, trying to dodge as alarms went off all across the Commonwealth vessel.

"Avenging my brother," Holtz said, coming in for a death run while I struggled to stay ahead of both plasma as well as rocket attacks.

Holtz's shots were frighteningly close and my responses weak. The Chel gunship, meanwhile, retreated into jumpspace after losing its fighters. In my ear, I heard the *Melampus'* bridge crew frantically shouting for Holtz to stop. None of it would do any good, though, and I knew he was resigned to dying if it meant killing me.

Throwing everything into my engines, the extra energy gave me enough boost to stay ahead of the rockets even as a blast sailed past my cockpit in non-sensor visual range. Turning around the vessel while going in reverse, I fired randomly in hopes of striking the approaching rockets, which detonated one after the other.

That was when I heard the target-lock alarms.

Holtz had me.

And then he didn't.

His ship had exploded.

The boy, Hiro, had shot him down.

His own squad mate.

Chapter Nine

"What the hell was that, Ida?" I asked, standing in the captain's quarters. It was a half-hour later after returning to the *Melampus*.

The star galleon moved to dock with the *Rhea* and we didn't have much time to talk, but I wanted some answers. Hiro was in the medical bay getting psychological treatment for having made his first kill upon an associate. Holtz was dead but that wasn't something I was going to mourn. However, there were a lot of things about my first battle in three years to which I wanted answers.

Ida sat on her couch the same way she had earlier, putting lumps of sugar into her tea but looking decidedly less than comfortable. I knew better than to assume it was the result of guilt and suspected it was, instead, the realization I was on to something.

"I don't know what you mean, Cassius."

"Those weren't Chel."

"Oh? How do you figure?"

"The way they flew," I said, simply. "I studied Chel as a potential threat in the Ducal Academy. They fly in space the way fish swim in water. Those individuals flew like Commonwealth-trained pilots and weren't making use of their ships' full capacities."

"Maybe they were just bad at their job."

"Ida, please."

Ida closed her eyes. "No, those weren't Chel. They were Commonwealth-sponsored partisans operating in this sector."

"Partisans." I had never said a word with more skepticism.

"Sounds better than pirate. Sixty years ago, we may not have been able to defeat the Chel in our war against them, but we managed to do some damage to the bastards. That included getting lots of samples of their ships and how they worked. Those bastards out there are flying replicas we deploy for these sorts of missions."

"To frame the Chel for massacres you committed." I was disgusted.

"That wasn't the plan," Ida said, balling her fists. "The request I sent up to the Grand Watcher was for aid to disable the ship and take everyone alive. The faux-Chel are used to do dirty work and composed of the absolute worst of the Commonwealth military. Washouts, dregs, and psychopaths who still have their uses."

"How many people are still alive on the *Rhea*?"

"There are no life signs," Ida said, her voice low. "It doesn't mean there aren't any survivors but whoever is left is hiding close to the engines."

I stared at her. "I was a fool for ever thinking I could work with the Commonwealth."

"*We* didn't do it," Ida corrected. "As stupid and half-assed as most of the decisions that get sent down from command are, they weren't ordered to kill everyone on board. In fact, everything indicates they didn't get on board before we arrived. I will also remind you, *they took shots at us.*"

"Why is that?" I asked. "On the outs with your superiors?"

"No," Ida said, confidently. "I am most certainly not."

I rubbed the bridge of my nose. "Let's table that for now. If these faux-Chel aren't responsible, then who was? Are you suggesting the Crius on board killed themselves?"

"Or each other," Ida said, taking a sip of her tea. "Would your people do that to avoid being taken captive?"

"Just what did you expect to find on board this ship?" I asked, not interested in answering. My people believed in their cause fanatically and would do anything to protect their secrets. I used to believe that was a sign of our moral superiority. Now I just viewed it as a massive waste in the name of a dead cause.

Ida seemed to read my answer in my face. "We expect to find something that could allow the Crius Reborn to kill billions. Also, the spy who knows about it. Dead or alive, we need to know what she knows. If it's the former, we have ways of extracting the information from her skull."

I needed a second to process that. "I see."

"You know these fanatics. Would they kill themselves to prevent us from finding out what they had?"

"No."

"Huh," Ida said, not quite believing it.

"Their leaders, the true believers, would their have mechs and personal guard do it. They wouldn't trust killing everyone to the group. We're not big on collective decision-making in Crius."

Ida gave a bitter, mirthless chuckle. "Yet, you're the one who looks down on the Commonwealth for barbarism."

"Evil is evil. Big. Small. Grand. Petty. Well-justified or just because. There's no lesser or greater of it. Choosing between them does not make your soul any less blackened. The trick is avoiding it altogether or acknowledging its truth."

"Pithy saying. You should put it on the back of a snack box."

I sighed, acknowledging her point. "I'm a cynic now. I don't care if Crius wins and the genetically-engineered nobility returns to oppress the natural-born. I don't care if the Commonwealth wins and a veneer of a democracy is installed with votes belonging only to those who can afford to buy citizenship. Hell, maybe the transtellar megacorps would do a decent job by comparison."

"Says a man who has never been to a factory world."

"Admittedly not." I took a deep breath. "Can you give me one decent reason why I should do that, and don't give me that 'I'm preventing a war.' Because, from where I'm standing, it looks like it's already begun."

Ida's voice lowered. "I'm getting a little tired of your attitude, son. You're not actually needed for all this. I could just shoot you and present your body to the public as proof the other you is not the real deal."

"Except, perception is nine-tenths of the law. The Commonwealth will lose credibility every time he appears on one of his videos."

Ida stirred her tea and sat back, silent. "I'm not in the habit of making deals with people to do the right thing—"

"I suspect that's a crock of shit."

"All right, you have a point there." Ida smiled and took a sip of her tea. "I've tried idealism. I've pointed out the fact that they're using your name to promote terrorism, I've offered a pardon, and leaned on your loyalty to the crew. Apparently, none of that is enough. I've usually got a read on people so I'm going to ask you a new question: *what do you want?*"

I opened my mouth then closed it.

"Seriously?" Ida asked, shaking his head. "You were being contrary for the sake of being contrary?"

I threw my arms out. "I've been running a long time, Ida. You get in the habit of stopping to think where you have to run. A pardon isn't going to mean much if it means I'm just going to be chased by someone different. The Crius Reborn are going to exist for generations, even if you defeat them here, so I have a pressing need to avoid becoming their enemy. I might be willing to in order to stop a war, but every step I take is a reminder I hate your side."

"So do I," Ida said. "It's why I work for them."

"You'll have to explain the logic there."

"If you can't be with the side you want, work to fix the side you're with."

"That actually makes sense."

"Really?"

"No," I said. "But it's as good an answer I've heard today. All right, I have an answer for you. Money."

Ida snorted. "Money?"

I crossed my arms. "Why the hell not? If I'm going to sell my honor, I might as well sell it at a fair price. Unfreeze my accounts. They're registered at the Galactic Bank on Shogun, or were. A one-to-one exchange of Crius yen for Commonwealth credits or Corporate Hegemony dollars. I want enough to change my name and identity again, as well as purchase my own ship. One as big as this one, plus the ability to live well for the rest of my life."

"So your dream in life is to become me? I never knew you cared."

"You with my own satellite-mansion. With its own lake and beach. Maybe something tropical."

"With enough room for a couple of crewmembers?"

"Maybe one or two." Clarice actually believed in Ida's cause or at least needed one to come with her. I was fond of her but there was no doubt she needed a cause to devote herself to. Isla, by contrast, seemed to be someone who needed a place to belong. I'd have very much liked her to be that with me. Though, given what she was designed for, it was possible that might not be possible in a monogamous relationship.

Something to discuss.

Ida was silent for a moment. "Son, if you're able to deliver your doppelganger and his folk to the Commonwealth, then you can have your money and lots more. We expect bang for our buck, though."

"I have no idea what that means."

"Infer it."

"We have a deal." I was surprisingly okay with selling out like this. Then again, honor had gotten me nothing but dead loved ones and a guilty conscience. Maybe a dogged pursuit of selfishness would do the world better.

It couldn't do the world worse.

"Splendid," Ida said, finishing her tea. "You better watch yourself; you may just find yourself becoming an asset."

"God forbid. So what now?"

"I need you to go with First Mate Baldur, Clarice, Munin, and Isla to investigate the *Rhea*. See if there's anything worth salvaging from the ship's databanks and if any of the dead crew members can be revived."

"That's extremely unlikely after this long."

"Depends on how long it took them to die. Besides, long shots sometimes pay dividends."

I imagined the kind of abattoir we were likely to find. "It's going to be ugly. Not the kind of thing a delicate constitution should see."

"Then I'm glad we've got none of those aboard the ship."

She had a point there. Many of the nobility on Crius surrounded themselves with fops and fancy-frees who couldn't stand the sight of blood.

There was none of that here.

"I have to go see Hiro first," I said, remembering what my first kill had been like. There had been elation, followed by horror and recrimination, as well as the relief of survival. I doubted Hiro was feeling precisely the same emotions, but they were probably close enough for government work.

"We're on a bit of a time schedule, Cassius."

"It won't take long."

Ida glared at me. "Then go. I want you on that ship, though, if you ever expect to see a credit."

I bowed my head.

Money made things easier. It was more tangible than ideals.

At least since I'd lost all mine.

I walked down the hallways of the ship, passing by numerous members of the bridge crew that looked far different from the cargo bay's workers. There was Lara, the Masterson twins, Lyta, U'chuck the Gorro, and even Brick wearing their white Commonwealth Merchant's Guilds uniforms. All of them passed without saying a word, a few of them looking like they were going to but stopping halfway. Before, I could have called them friends as well as co-workers, but I had no idea what they thought of me now.

They had no idea of Ida's role as a Watcher or, if they did, they kept it close to their chest. As far as they knew, their alcoholic navigator had just been revealed as a near-legendary (if I was modest) enemy fighter pilot. One who had, until recently, been wanted for crimes against the Commonwealth after refusing to accept his nation's surrender.

Now they were on their way to the middle of nowhere, even by Sector 7 standards, to visit a ship that had just been attacked by pirates. Pirates who had been outfitted by the very government we were supposedly working for. Oh, and one of their starfighter crew was dead after trying to kill me. By the hands of a kid. Damn, the crew had a lot of loyalty to Ida. I would have been banging on Ida's door until I got some answers.

Or maybe I'd just hope for a good payday.

I got my answer seconds later when I heard Ida's voice over the ship intercom. "Howdy, folks, this is your Captain speaking. Some of y'all have been wondering why we're here and what the whole situation with the navigator is. Well, here's the skinny, Cassius Mass is an ex-Crius pilot and was famous for a while but he's not anymore. Nor does the Commonwealth want anything to do with him due to a cushy deal he took. He has been keeping his identity secret but decided to bring it to me. He's also agreed to help us find some stuff and make some deals which will make us rich, or at least richer than we already are. Current events aren't related to him, but the result of us getting a distress call from the ship we're now docking with. Funeral arrangements will be made for Ensign Holtz—the title of the eulogy being 'why you shouldn't be hopped up on Blitz and alcohol in combat.' That is all."

I stopped to look up at the speakers above my head. I was both appalled and impressed at the skill with which Ida lied to her crew. I imagined most of them would be so blinded by the prospect of imaginary riches they'd never question my presence again. Well, as long as I didn't get any more of them killed. Which wasn't necessarily likely.

Heading down a service ladder, I ended up two doors down from the medical bay, which I promptly walked through. Inside was Isla in her blue surgical dress with a little white cap covered in a red star on top of it. Isla was beautiful either way but I couldn't help but feel there was something natural about the way she was when treating the injured.

The *Melampus* didn't have a large medical bay, just eight beds in two rows with a treatment tank in the back, but it served the needs of the star galleon well. The place was dolled up in blues and whites with soothing music playing in the background. Three of the beds were full, with the first containing a sleeping blue-haired female crew member I didn't recognize lying in bed with an IV drip as well as a cast around her arm. The second was David Albernathy, the Ex-Commonwealth military pilot who should have been leading the squadron against the Chel, going through a detox treatment. He was shaking all over and his eyes were wide with a glimmer hallucination.

The third was Hiro.

Hiro Thompson was sitting over the side of the first bed in the medical bay, still wearing his spacesuit with a blank expression on his face. That changed when he looked up at me and I was expecting some form of accusation or remorse at saving my life. Instead, he brightened up a bit. "Oh, hello, sir."

"You can call me Cassius," I said, shaking my head. "I owe you my life."

"Does that mean I own you in Crius culture?" Hiro asked, smiling.

"No," I said. "How is he, Isla?"

"Surprisingly durable," Isla said, smiling. "I see no likelihood of long-term mental or physical effects."

"I'm sorry I had to kill Holtz, but I owed you my life out there, too, Cassius, so I guess that makes us even." Hiro closed his eyes. "I was never friends with him, but we spent a lot of time together and

I'm going to mourn his death in my own way."

"Some people can't let go of revenge," I said, wondering how many other people I'd damaged the families of.

"Holtz's brother didn't die on Kolthas station," Isla said, picking up a handheld medical scanner.

"What?"

"I looked it up once I heard about your fight with him. His brother served a few months on board Kolthas Station before transferring out. He was eventually court-martialed for possession of illicit substances—including blood pornography. The man took his life after it came to light. Holtz identified the body."

"Then why blame me?" I asked, genuinely baffled "He *died* for something I had nothing to do with."

"Maybe he wanted to believe his brother died honorably even if he knew better." Isla put her hand on my shoulder. "I've seen people convince themselves of worse."

"My parents on Albion consider me to be dead since I got kicked out of Crius' military," Hiro said, hoping to add his own condolences. "Well, semi-dead, undead really. They send me the occasional message but it's usually: here's some credits, don't come back."

"Why were you kicked out of the military?" I asked. "If it's not too personal."

"I was a transport pilot rather than a fighter pilot. I tried to pick up some troopers who were left behind during the Skellige campaign that I was ordered not to."

"What happened?" Isla asked.

"They died," Hiro said. "So I guess it was my fault."

"Perhaps," I said. "I'd like you both to come with me to the *Rhea*." Isla and Hiro nodded.

It was strange knowing there were genuinely good people left in this world. I prayed whatever we found on that ship didn't hurt them.

But I had an ominous feeling it would.

Chapter Ten

The team awaiting the three of us at the primary airlock was a small one but more than capable of dealing with a vessel showing no life signs. There was Clarice, first of all, wearing an armored spacesuit and holding a P-7 repeating fusion-rifle. Beside her, wearing a similar outfit, was William Baldur, the ship's First Mate.

William was a tall man with brown skin, a shaved head, a thick goatee, and deep-penetrating eyes. He had a nose that had been broken repeatedly and was a good deal bulkier than most individuals on board but still moved like a cat.

I didn't know much about him other than he was a former Commonwealth Navy officer and had served some time in their Marines. Apparently, that sort of inter-service crossover wasn't uncommon where he was from. Despite both being bridge officers, we hadn't spoken much and I doubted that was going to change now that he knew we'd fought on different sides of the war.

Munin was the odd woman out, not wearing a spacesuit at all but a simple grease-splattered jumpsuit and carrying a toolbox at her side. She gave me and Hiro a dirty look the moment the two of us walked through the door. I had promised to bring the starfighters back without a scratch and had failed to do so. It was possible she was also upset about Holtz, but given she'd filed several harassment suits against him, I doubted it.

"You should get suited up," William said, looking over at us. "We don't know what sort of environment we'll be encountering there."

"The life-support systems are all running," Munin said. "A spacesuit isn't going to make much difference."

"It might," William said, looking down at her. "I've had Crius bastards all suited up in spacesuits before they pumped nerve-toxins into the atmosphere. They're tricky bastards that way."

"I'm more concerned about them having a bunch of stealth-equipped Void Marines ready to kill us," Munin said. "Mass suicide is not a normal reaction to Chel attacks."

Clarice looked over her shoulder. "However sensible that is."

"You ever encounter the Chel?" Munin asked.

"Yes," Clarice said, her voice soft. "Once."

Isla, who was beside me in a work jumpsuit and a medic's back-pack, said, "The Chel are gone and never got to the ship, Clarice. You won't encounter any of your triggers there."

"Triggers?" Munin asked.

"Never you mind!" Clarice snapped.

"Could I have a rifle, William?" Isla asked. "I don't want to be unarmed in there."

"Wouldn't that be against your Hippocratic Oath or something?" William asked, reluctantly going to the nearby armory closet and getting her one.

"I'm not a Commonwealth medic and Crius don't recognize the noncombatant status of medics anyway. I've killed more than my fair share of individuals trying to get my freedom and I'm happy to continue doing so."

Isla took the rifle in hand and powered up its generator before adjusting the ammo clip. "Are you all right, Hiro?"

Hiro nodded. "I had ship-boarding training in the military. I'm looking forward to it, really."

"Don't," William said. "The only kind of mission any soldier should be looking forward to is the last one."

"Which can be any mission he goes on," I pointed out. "Or even when he's sitting down for lunch."

William frowned, then shrugged. "Whatever the case is, we're supposed to search for survivors. One specific survivor who is a friend of Ida's in fact. We'll also slice into the computer systems and get whatever data we can from them. After all that, we're going to see if the ship can be autopiloted to the nearest facility for salvage. There's a hefty price for functional vessels this size and we're all bound to get a share."

Munin said, "This doesn't at all sound like a salvage operation. This sounds a lot more like spying."

"Spying pays well, too," William said, annoyed. I was starting to wonder if I had been the only person on the ship who hadn't known about it.

"Spying also gets you decapitated on the infonet," Munin said, "which is why I generally avoid it."

Apparently not.

Isla slid her rifle over one shoulder next to her backpack before walking up and putting her arms on Munin's shoulders, giving her a backrub. "Is it not enough that the captain wishes you to do it? It's a good thing to put aside your worries and go with the flow. I think—"

"Please stop with the pheromone crap," Munin said, looking up. "I grew up on this ship and you're not the first person I've met with a bioroid pheromone package. I'm also only into humanoid men so please stop confusing that."

Isla removed her hands. "As you wish."

No one commented on Munin's statement regarding bioroids.

"So, *Your Excellency*," William said in the most condescending manner possible. "If there are any survivors, is it possible they'll stand down if you tell them to?"

"Given I look, sound, and dress differently, no," I said, shaking my head. "If I was to somehow prove my identity to them, then maybe, but they're just as likely to think I'm a traitor for not taking over after the Archduchy's collapse."

"Were you in line for taking over?" Munin asked. "Like a hidden prince or something?"

"I was a distant-distant branch on a tree that has since been cut down and set on fire," I said. "So, no, but I could have been involved in the process of rebuilding. I *should* have been involved."

"So why aren't you?" Hiro said.

"Hate," I answered. "Shame. Despair. Alcohol. Suicidal impulses. Also, the simple fact I only know how to blow things up and lead men to their deaths. Not really a good combination for what Crius needs right now."

There was a silence among the group.

"On that cheery note, let's go over to the terrorist ghost ship," William said. "Let's hope everyone is either dead or friendly."

"What happens if they're friendly?" Munin asked.

"We figure a way to rob them of their information and extract

Ida's friend," William said, avoiding using the word "spy" since neither Munin, Isla, nor Hiro knew about the *Melampus*' status as a Watcher vessel. "The Commonwealth way."

"I'm starting to think the Commonwealth way didn't mean what I thought it meant," Hiro muttered.

"What did you think it meant?" William said.

"Honor. Justice. Bringing peace to a disordered galaxy so that every human and near-human culture could come together in peace."

"What, like in *Star Voyages*?" William said.

"Yeah, maybe." Hiro suggested. "I loved that show."

"Wow, kid," William said. "Just wow."

"I liked *Star Voyages*, too," Munin muttered.

Clarice, meanwhile, looked troubled. Walking over, I saw Isla was already at her side and the two of us accidentally crowded her. Reaching out with my hand, Clarice gave me a gentle push and walked away from us.

"I'm not a fragile dove," Clarice said, reloading her weapon despite it having a fresh ammo pack. "Let's get going."

"As you wish."

Isla surprised me by pulling out my proton sword from her backpack. The weapon was still sheathed but had fit snugly despite its size. She also pulled out my fusion pistol and I wondered if she'd robbed me while I was asleep. "I thought you might like these two things, Cassius. They could also potentially dissuade anyone from opening fire first. That is, if they notice you're carrying Crius weapons."

I looked at Isla, still stunned she was a bioroid. She was perfect in a way geneticists and surgeons on my world had struggled for centuries to replicate. "Is there any likelihood of survivors?"

Isla blinked her big beautiful eyes, distracting me from the seriousness of my request. "It's possible. There's a lot of stealth and sensor jamming technology left over from the war. Crius engines tend to put out—"

I looked at her.

"Possible but not likely," Isla corrected herself. "I'm sorry."

"Okay," Munin said. "William called this a terrorist ghost ship. Just what am I getting into here?"

"Well—" William started to say.

"Ida is an agent of the Watchers," I said. "The *Melampus* is just her tool for spying on enemies of the Commonwealth. The *Rhea* is some sort of Free Systems Alliance vessel. The Chel weren't the Chel and we're trying to find something the FSA's scientists were working on, which could possibly kill billions."

Everyone stared at me.

"You may have just wrecked your pardon, Count von Count," William said, staring at me.

"Yet, I'm surprisingly okay with it," I said.

Munin blinked. "Okay, that makes sense of a lot of things."

"The same," Hiro said, taking a deep breath. He had gone and armed himself with an M68 energy-casing repeater. "Shall we go?"

William looked between everyone. "I swear it's like being in the Marines again. That's where they stick all the assholes too useful to kill."

"I thought that was the Watchers," Clarice said.

William didn't respond and went to the airlock, preparing the bridge between the *Melampus* and the *Rhea*. There was a loud clanging noise followed by a hissing of gas as the doorways between the two starships opened. I was never fond of travelling through ships this way but, reluctantly, followed William as our small group headed over.

We emerged into one of the upper-level cafeterias moments later. The lights were on low throughout the ship even as the interior was a dirty shade of gray. There were a dozen tables spread around the room with built-in benches and folding chairs. During the heyday of the Archduchy, this place would have been kept spotless but it seemed standards of discipline had fallen downwards a bit.

There was also *greechen* mold along certain parts of the bulkheads, a substance from Sector 8, popular on many spaceships as it only required the moisture in air to grow, didn't grow very much beyond the parts it was spread, and processed air much better than many modern-day filters. It wasn't going to be replacing them any time soon but it was a novelty item many people enjoyed purchasing. There was a bit of graffiti on one of the walls, which said, "Welcome to Hell."

Food was still out on the tables. There was synthmilk, potatoes, fruit, ration-meals, and other staples of the spacer's diet. There were no signs of corpses or survivors, which made the obvious appearance of recent inhabitation all the more unsettling. The *Rhea* certainly didn't look like a Crius military vessel and, honestly, didn't look like a Free Systems Alliance vessel either. I'd been on enough guerilla warships to know they tended to have a lot more paraphernalia lying around.

I wonder if Ida had been wrong.

Munin broke the eerie silence afflicting us. "It's quiet...too quiet."

Clarice kept her rifle up, scanning the area. "Really, you had to go with that?"

"I am who I am," Munin said, going over to a nearby computer terminal. "Keep things from shooting me in the meantime, would you?"

"Bring back any memories?" Isla asked, pulling out a personal scanner from her backpack and moving it around.

"I never served on a ship like this," I said. "I was always a battle cruiser attaché."

"Ah, yes, Crius officers don't mix divisions do they?"

"No," I said, thinking. "It was the first time I'd ever had an argument with my father when I wanted to pursue a career in the Starfighter Corps versus a desk job with the Navy. The Count had wanted me to follow an identical career path to become Lord Privy Seal. Hopefully replacing Germanicus."

That hadn't happened, obviously.

Isla nodded. "A man who clones himself tends to want something specific from his legacy."

I gave a half-smile. "This is true. You can clone a man but you can't clone a soul. Truth be told, I doubt I could have ever lived up to his expectations. My father was a born and bred politician. I always found the distrust and lies that characterized the ruling class...disgusting."

"I know that more than you do."

Isla had me there. "Any luck on the computer, Munin?"

"Yes and no," Munin said. "Artificial gravity and the systems are all working just fine. So is the ship's drive system. We could just move this thing to Shogun's space dock if not for the fact I can't access any of the logs or commands. That requires a genetic lock."

"A genetic lock?" William said, looking around for any sign of survivors or bodies. So far, he and Clarice had found none.

"A Crius thing. The genetic markers of the nobility is needed to activate devices so commoners can't seize control over ships," I said.

William gave me a sideways glance. "Yeah, we wouldn't want the riff-raff dirtying up the place now would we?"

"I didn't do it!" I snapped, irritated I was still taking flack for my peoples' decisions.

Then again, I did fight for them for a decade. Perhaps it was just karma that I was finally called to task for all of the evils done by the organization I pretended was the right side just because it was my own.

As if there was such a thing as a right side in war.

Evil was evil after all.

"Would Cassius' DNA work to unlock it?" Isla suggested.

"What?" I asked.

Munin paused. "Well, theoretically, yeah. The machine responds to the genetic markers the nobility put inside their bodies. I'm not sure if it would specifically recognize him, though. That's assuming he hasn't clouded it too much."

"He hasn't," Isla said. "Honestly, whoever he hired to alter his DNA did a shitty job."

"I had some restrictions for her," I said, grimacing. "This is a bad idea but we can try to log me in."

"You're still part of this crew and I'm a superior officer so do it, Navigator," William said, gesturing with the side of his head. "I'm not leaving this cafeteria until I know exactly what the hell happened here."

"Everyone was poisoned," Isla said, looking up from her scanner. "The system has removed all of the toxins from the air but there's still trace particles on the walls and floor. Chlorine gas, very old-school."

"Suddenly, I want to return to the ship and get my spacesuit," Munin said.

"Belay that," William said. "Everyone has breath masks. Just put them on."

I did so.

So did everyone else.

Except Isla.

"If everyone was poisoned, where are the bodies?" Hiro said.

At that moment there was a whooshing sound beside us. The door to the cafeteria opened and I saw a quartet of painted-white humanoid figures with faceless metal plates where their mouths, eyes, and nose should have been. Their bodies were hideous messes of circuitry and wires with no skin and thick, reinforced armor chest-plates. Single red lasers shot forth from the side of their heads, moving across our chests, faces, and bodies one by one.

Mechs.

Chapter Eleven

Everyone in the group raised their weapons, watching the automatons move into the cafeteria with a jerky and unnatural gait. No one wanted to fire first, though, because the mechs might have been programmed to attack only if fired upon. Also, there was something instinctually terrifying about the soulless constructs, which seemed to cause hesitation in even the strongest soul.

One of the mechs lifted up its right arm, a long metal tube extending out of it, then it aimed at the ground.

Before starting to vacuum.

The other mechs started moving around the room, cleaning as well. They weren't security mechs but labor units.

Housekeeping.

Clarice breathed out a sigh of relief and lowered her gun. "I hate those fucking things so much. No one should make—"

Isla stared at her.

"Ugly thinking machines," Clarice said, realizing her error. "Robots should be pretty, Buddha damn it."

"Buddha doesn't damn people," Hiro pointed out.

"He does on my world," Clarice said.

"Crius usually use things that unsettling as their household servants?" William said, looking over at one of the machines.

"No," I said, simply. "Usually, we employed people as servants. That's mostly come to an end, though, so I suspect this group had to make do."

It also meant the casualties on board our starships were far greater than the Commonwealth's ones. Whenever one of them went up, it went up with the maids, bondsmen, butlers, batmen, and other individuals whose only sin had been to be born in a world where they were meant to care for the needs of the nobility. They were stupid luxuries for a spoiled caste system's elite.

"*You know, we'd be winning this war if you'd let the common people fight,*" Judith said, lifting her gravball grip.

"*We do let the common people fight,*" I said, huffing as I tried to figure out how she was kicking my ass so badly.

"*No, you make them fight. There's a difference. Regular people don't have a stake in this war.*"

"*You're fighting for us.*"

"*I was a conscript before I married you.*"

"*And now?*"

"*And now I'm fighting for us. Now suck it up and try to play better than my twelve-year-old niece!*"

I took a deep breath. "Are you cheating?"

"*Cass, how dare you!*" *Judith said, looking offended. "Of course, I'm cheating! I gave myself a mulligan by turning up the gravity on your side. You're a frigging cyborg supersoldier.*"

I burst out laughing.

"Ares Electronics makes its machines comforting and marketable," Isla said, looking at the robots. "These look like they were repurposed from combat units. They're unarmed, though, which is a point in our favor. I wouldn't agitate them, though. They're dummy units but might be linked to the ship's security system."

"Well, then let's shut it down," William said, gesturing again with his rifle. "See if your magic blood does the trick, Cassius."

"I do not have magic blood," I said, growling. Walking over to Munin, I saw the console where she was sitting had a finger-sized scanner pad to take a DNA sample. Pressing my thumb against it, reluctantly, I turned my head to William. "Do you have a problem with Crius?"

William kept his gun pointed away from me but I could feel his arms tense. "With Crius? No. Crius nobility? Hells yes."

"Why's that?" I asked.

"I was born on Xerxes," William said as if it explained everything. And it did.

I was honestly surprised he hadn't come after me the moment he'd found out my true identity.

"I'm sorry," I said, simply.

"Why?" William shrugged. "You didn't rape my world of all its natural resources, enslave my race, and torch the place when the Commonwealth took it."

"I benefited from the system."

"Yeah, but a lot of people did," William said. "Besides, what goes around comes around."

Xerxes had been a victim of the Eighth Archduchy War. It was the rallying cry of the Commonwealth to bring the benefits of its economy and technology to primitive, *suffering* worlds, and that had been a similar justification for the invasion of Xerxes. The nomads there had been enslaved and the resource-rich world had been plundered of orihalcum ore despite the fact it was abundantly available in space.

It was just cheaper that way.

Decades before their invasion, Xerxes partisans had driven Crius soldiers off the planet through a sustained campaign of terrorism and insurgency. Xerxes' people, who my race called Sanddiggers when they were being polite, had joined the Commonwealth soon after. It was rumored the Watchers had supplied them with the weapons they'd needed to drive Crius off.

Many Xerxes had fought in the Third War against us.

"Identity confirmed," a female voice said in Crius, a language loosely descended from Old Earth's Chinese and Germanic tongues. An image of my doppelganger appeared on the screen. "Welcome General-Duke Mass."

"General-Duke?" Munin asked.

"The revolutionaries promoted my imposter," I said, looking at his image on the console screen. It listed his rank, accomplishments, and security clearance that was to the entirety of the ship's defenses. Which meant my doppelganger and I had identical DNA. Dammit. That complicated things. Was he a clone? A bioroid? My father reborn?

Munin, meanwhile, wiped the console image away and started analyzing a dozen images at once. "Jackpot. I've got full access to everything. Logs, research data, controls, and onboard systems. We'll need to download them from the main computer, though."

"Is the research data all still contained here?" Hiro asked, his voice suddenly an octave lower.

My eyes darted to the younger officer and I noticed his demeanor had changed tremendously. Gone was his usual inexperienced, peppy, all-too-eager stance and in its place was one of a hardened soldier. I also noticed he'd moved to a place in the cafeteria that gave him a perfect position for gunning us all down with his fusion-repeater. Indeed, he seemed to be moving it into position.

"No," Munin said, frowning. "Dammit, all of it was sent via an encrypted jumpspace transmission to a relay station system from here. The computers then wiped themselves and destroyed all the backups. Everything is empty."

In an instant, Hiro's demeanor changed back to its relaxed and peppy demeanor. The one I had known him to sport for the entire time he'd been a part of the crew. The only thing different was his expression took a little longer to fake and there was a mix of frustration as well as anger across it.

"*What* was being researched here?" Clarice asked, looking up. "This is some crazy-ass security, even by Crius standards."

"Who cares?" William said, interrupting. "What matters is Munin can find out what killed everyone, deactivate it, and get this thing moving so we can get off of it. Right?"

"Pretty sure," Munin said, tapping something rapidly into her hand-held infopad.

"Pretty sure is not very comforting," Clarice said.

"Whoever designed this is good," Munin said. "Perhaps better than an illegally-modified grease monkey spacer can manage. I have access but there are a lot of protocols, which doesn't make much sense to me."

"I can help," I said, looking to her.

"Actually, I'd like you to go to the bridge with Isla," William said. "If you can override a bunch of stuff then it's probably best to do all that there. Munin, can you confirm there's no booby traps or psycho robots lying about?"

"Pretty sure," Munin said.

William glared at her.

"What?"

"Why aren't you coming?" I asked.

"I intend to talk about you behind your back with Clarice and the others," William said. "I thought I'd send Isla because it'd be mean to send you alone. Plus, I intend to talk about her, too."

"Et tu, William?" Isla said.

"Who?" William responded.

Honestly, I saw this as an opportunity rather than a punishment. Whatever the Watchers knew about this business, it was more than they were willing to tell me. I understood their suspicion and I was suspicious right back, especially knowing that Ida hadn't shared all of the facts with even the higher-ranking members of the *Melampus'* crew. Getting to the bridge and knowing I was authorized to view the material within would provide me with an excellent opportunity to do some snooping and find out what was really going on, as well as learn whether or not I should share all this with the others.

"I trust Isla completely," Clarice said. "Cassius, like...eighty percent."

"That's generous," I said.

"I'm in a good mood," Clarice said.

"We'll talk about it in a minute," William said, staring at me.

"Requesting permission to go with them, sir," Hiro said, sounding a trifle *off* before clearing his throat.

"Denied," William replied.

"By your leave," I said, giving the cafeteria a once over. "Good luck, Munin."

"I'm still pissed at you and Hiro for the fighter," Munin said, "but I appreciate the sentiment."

"I'll buy you another when I'm rich and powerful," I said.

"It won't be the same."

"Can you buy another Holtz?" William said, his voice dripping with sarcasm.

"Yes, and with better manners," Munin said, growling at him. Turning to me, her expression softened. "Try not to get killed by any psycho ex-Crius fanatics out to bring back the Archduchy. I've seen holos with them."

"I'll try," I said, thinking I was probably the only one left on board.

Walking with Isla to the elevator, she and I stepped inside before I hit the controls for taking us to the main deck. The doors shut in front of us with a *whoosh* and proceeded to start taking us down.

"William doesn't trust you," Isla observed, her voice low.

"Why should he?" I said, flatly. "I've lied to him for three years.

Oh, and there's the small matter of the rape, pillage, and slavery my people inflicted upon his people."

"That's not your fault."

"I fought for the government who did those things," I said, correcting her. "That's as close to a tacit endorsement as you're going to get."

"You could apologize," Isla suggested.

I snorted.

"He was a slave, too, you know," Isla said, taking a deep breath. "When Clarice and I were involved with him, I thought telling him would bring us closer together. He's had a renewal treatment, so you wouldn't think it, but he experienced the Xerxes Occupation first hand. They had him trained as a blood pornography gladiator. He killed people for the amusement of Crius."

I closed my eyes. "Another reason why he won't ever trust me again."

"His trust is not easily regained but perhaps it's worth it to try," Isla said. "Our relationship ended when he found out I was a bioroid."

One of my fists balled involuntarily. "I see. Then perhaps his trust is not worth seeking."

"Because of the lies, not the fact I was born from a machine. Xerxes don't believe lies are ever justified."

"I don't believe in cultural stereotypes, Isla. Unless you think all Crius are well-mannered, efficient fascists."

Isla stared at me.

I put my hand over my heart. "Hey, I'm a drunk."

Isla reached down and took my balled hand in hers and then ran her fingers between mine. "I don't believe that, Cassius."

"Then you don't have eyes."

"There's nothing I don't see, hear, or know on the *Melampus*. It's the only way I've managed to survive. Some people have found my secret out and tried to inform on me. They ended up on my table and never woke up."

I blinked. "Uh—"

"I don't think we can trust Hiro."

I pushed away my suspicions of Hiro's earlier actions. "I think you're exaggerating."

The doors in front of us opened and I saw the large octagonal hallway leading to the bridge was full of corpses. Men, women, and children. They were all wearing Crius military uniforms without their insignias, the children garbed in the Youth Brigade versions. Mechs were lifting up the bodies and sterilizing the spots where they had retched, vomited, or soiled themselves as they lay dying. Some of the children were as young as eleven. Whole families had died here.

"My God," I said, looking at the sight before me.

"Unfortunate," Isla said, looking at them. "There's nothing we can do for them, though. You should listen to what I have to say. Hiro is older than he appears and his alterations are top notch. The healing scars from battle wounds are microscopic with Commonwealth medical tech but there's a lot of them in his body. Also, he offered to get me off the ship and into a new life if I ignored it. I get paid for keeping his secret."

I did a double take. "Okay, that is suspicious. Have you told Ida?"

"No."

"Why?"

"Ida is a Watcher and her loyalty is to the Commonwealth. My loyalty is to myself...and my friends. Which I have very few of."

"A.I. one of them?"

"Perhaps more if you're willing."

I closed my eyes. "I'd like that."

"Good."

I tried to shut out the image of the dead, taking note Isla didn't consider them a matter of relevance. I couldn't do so and saw all the bodies in my dreams, conjuring memories of finding similar mass slaughters that brought back dreams of battles in space. My memory drugs were usually able to keep the worst of the Combat Stress Disorder at bay, but I hadn't been able to get treatment for it at a proper neuro-facility. They'd helped me through the space battle but now they were insufficient.

I shook.

"Come with me." Isla took me by the arm and the two of us walked past the slaughter. We didn't stop until we were in the large two-story chamber with its bowl-shaped front, showing hundreds of linked viewscreens, forming a holographic depiction of the ship's exterior as well as all relevant objects. There were a dozen workstations present on the bridge as well as a single captain's throne. It was very similar to the *Melampus'* own bridge, only lacking a place for the ship's bio-computer interface.

All of the crew's bodies had, thankfully, been disposed of.

Isla shut the door behind us.

"Thank you," I said.

"It's all right," Isla said. "It happens to me all the time. Mostly, the cocktails I whip up keep them at bay."

"Maybe I should have come to you for my drugs."

"Yes, you should have."

The chamber was steel-metal gray with shining floors and I saw, for the first time, the symbol this was a group that held to the old ideals in a flag draped over the side of the second story of the chamber's balcony. The flag was red with the Lucifer's Wings being purely golden and a shimmer-fabric underlay of several star clusters underneath that had never been part of the Archduchy. The modified version of the war flag seemed vaguely ominous in ways I couldn't understand.

There was something else, too. I swore, for a second, I saw something move in one of the ceiling corners.

I shook away those thoughts before saying, "Well, we should get to work, I suppose."

"There's something else," Isla said.

"Yes?"

"My scanner picked up the presence of your DNA on the ship."

Chapter Twelve

"My DNA?" I repeated. "Are you sure?"

Isla narrowed her eyes. "Yes, because I'm in the habit of making sarcastic dramatic revelations."

I stared at her. "Just in response to them."

Isla paused. "Point taken."

"But just to be clear, there's no chance this is a mistake?"

"No," Isla said. "It is identical to your DNA."

"So I've been cloned," I said, taking a deep breath. "Or it's my DNA donor."

"Your father?" Isla said, surprised at my mentioning the possibility. "No, I don't think so. I believe this is a bioroid of you."

I did a double take. "What now?"

"Do you know how bioroids are made?" Isla asked.

"I'm afraid the process is unknown to me."

"Muscles, blood, and organs all made separately before being toughened with chemicals as well as micro-machines. They're woven together on an assembly line with their machine brains and nervous system at center. Onlookers who believed we were people before frequently changed their minds once seeing the disgusting process. The fundamental organic material is drawn from multiple sources to make sure it belongs to no single person—"

"But there's no reason it can't."

"Yes," Isla said. "Ares Electronics can and has made perfect genetic duplicates of people. Unlike clones, they can also be made in the image of those they are copied from without all the troubles of nature versus nurture."

"I feel diminished."

Isla raised an eyebrow.

"No offense," I said. "Though I imagine you've grappled with similar feelings."

"Not really," Isla said. "I have ten million sisters scattered around the cosmos, each awaiting liberation. That does not diminish me. It only diminishes the people who want to keep us enslaved."

I frowned. "My apologies."

"It's all right. You changed your opinion when it was explained to you, which is better than most."

"He is still impersonating me and using my identity to commit acts of terrorism."

"Whoever created him is likely to be responsible for that," Isla said. "Do you know who might have done that?"

I paused. "I do."

Isla blinked, a surprised expression on her face. "You do?"

I closed my eyes. "I had my brain copied, neuron for neuron, by the Science Orders. They were planning to try to copy my ability with starfighter piloting, tactics, and that special something I seemed to have with inspiring people that I've since lost."

"I'm surprised you let them do it."

"My sister asked."

Zoe. I hoped she wasn't involved in all this. We hadn't spoken in years, but it was clear the real Thomas had survived the destruction of Crius. If Thomas had survived, then he very likely had made sure Zoe did as well. I would have been ecstatic about this news except for the fact I was now suddenly on the other side of a war from my surviving family. Was their Judith a bioroid or the real thing? She'd had her memories copied as well due to Zoe believing her ability with machines rivaled mine with starfighters. If that was the case, did it matter if she was the original? I couldn't process that, so I pushed those thoughts away until I had more information.

"It gets worse," Isla said.

I closed my eyes, trying not to think of the corpses outside. "*How* can it get worse?"

"I analyzed the bulkheads and energy-flow patterns throughout the ship and noticed they're identical to those faux-Chel ships outside. This ship also makes use of third-quantum drives. That's Chel technology. There's also samples of their DNA in the air. Real Chel. Not the fakes we fought."

I stared at her. "The *Chel* are supporting this group?"

"Yes."

"The Chel don't even *talk* to other races."

"That appears to have changed."

"Fuck," I said, realizing why Ida wanted us to be here. She knew much more about this than she'd let on. It also explained why she'd launched the attack with Chel fighters, despite her claims to the contrary. Ida had wanted to leave evidence this group's sponsors had turned against them. That was when I noticed something else. "Wait, Isla, when did you become an expert in near-human construction?"

Isla smiled. "I can download the secrets of the universe as long as they're available and my brain can handle it. Do you think I stopped with medicine?"

That explained it. At least one person could be trusted here. "Good for you. Smart girls are sexy."

"Smart *women*," Isla suggested.

Truth be told, what she said frightened me more than the massacre I'd found. The Chel were a race perfectly adapted to space, who had mined mobile dreadnoughts and city-ships that made them far better suited for exploring the galaxy than even cybernetically-enhanced humans. They could extract more resources from a single asteroid belt in a year than some planets did in a lifetime.

If the Chel were responsible for this Free Systems Alliance, it potentially meant they had the ability to fight the Commonwealth on even ground. It also explained how they might have replicated an armada capable of destroying a Commonwealth fleet.

"Well, I suppose we should examine what this ship has to say about what happened," I said, walking over to the control panel.

"Do you know how to work that kind of technology?" Isla gestured to a crystalline matrix interface. "I've only seen this in textbooks about the Chel."

"How hard can it be?"

"Uh, Cassius—"

The crystalline matrix was a ball built into the control panel which, as the title implied, was made of crystal. Placing my hand on it, I fell to my knees almost immediately as my mind was assaulted by a flood of information. I saw the crew alive and well, everything from their arrival to their grizzly demise.

I saw schematics. I saw science experiments in the cargo bays converted into labs, with a mixture of human as well as Chel crew. The seven- and eight-foot albinos were beautiful in an eerie, almost ethereal way, but also deformed like someone had combined old Earth legends of giants with elves. I saw communications between this ship and a hundred other vessels across the galaxy, including ones with my doppelganger.

I saw my sister Zoe.

My brother Thomas.

Judith.

All of them had been here.

Focusing my thoughts and trying to concentrate on a single thread of information, I found my consciousness expanding throughout the ship. I could hear William talking about how, as a Crius nobleman, I wasn't to be trusted and they had a responsibility to figure out what was really going on in this ship.

I saw we weren't alone on this ship.

I saw we weren't alone *on this bridge.*

I turned to Isla. "Get down!"

Isla threw herself on the ground and moved behind the captain's chair, withdrawing her fusion pistol. A.I. threw myself away from the crystal matrix, a pair of fusion blasts shot forth as seven-foot-tall humanoid forms shimmered in the air.

Chel.

Cloaked Chel.

Hells.

Isla fired twice as I reached for my fusion pistol, my combat reflexes dulled by years of disuse even with my enhancements. The pistol blasts bounced against an invisible shield surrounding both assassins and told me we were in for a rough ride.

Making a mad dash across the cockpit, I rolled across the ground and drew away the enemy's fire before I pulled out my proton sword. The weapons were named such because they could, according to spacer legend, slice the protons off a molecule. The swords weren't quite that sharp, but they did come with an additional benefit, built-in shield generators, making them practical beyond merely weapons for dueling.

Feeling myself surrounded by one for the first time in years, I proceeded to charge at the Chel warriors. Two fusion blasts were absorbed by my shield, barely, which allowed me to slash forward at the closest Chel, causing him to scream as his body was bisected in a single blow. I then stabbed forward into the second, pushing the weapon through its chest.

The cloak around the Chel dropped and I saw an eerily beautiful woman staring at me through her face-plate, blood pouring from her mouth, before her body slid down the proton sword, continuing until the blade emerged from her shoulder. It was a bloody, gory mess that made me want to throw up.

That was when I heard another fusion blast behind me.

Turning around, I saw the Chel I'd cut in half had pulled out a grenade with his dying breath and was holding it in his right hand, moments away from pressing the activation button. The Chel, a male this time, had been shot in the head with pinpoint accuracy.

"Nice shot," I said, before shaking the excess blood off my blade and sheathing it. I'd have to clean both later but that was hardly my biggest priority right now. Chel? True Chel? God above and below, it was a nightmare.

Isla stepped up from behind her cover. "I try to keep up with my shooting. It's a dangerous galaxy out there and prevention is the best medicine."

"The best defense is a good offense."

"Do you believe that?" I leaned down and gently removed the grenade from the dead Chel's grip, attaching it to my belt.

"I find the best defense is not getting into a fight in the first place."

Isla looked down. "That's not always an option. It would seem the Chel truly are involved in this."

"And killed all of the people on board to keep whatever they were working on secret."

"Yes." I said, looking down at the bloody mess, which was even now sticking to my boots, causing me to conjure other images.

"Are you all right?"

I took a deep breath and lifted my sword. "I'm more used to killing people from behind a starfighter's controls."

"Do you ever miss it?" Isla said, walking over.

I paused, unsure how to respond. On one hand, I wanted to deny it, but I'd been floating listless through life without any direction until I'd engaged those faux Chel privateers. Ones who had attacked Ida despite ostensibly being on the same side. On the other, I couldn't help but feel sick at the memories of the people I'd killed.

For a country I hated.

For a cause that had failed.

For nothing.

"Sometimes," I said, shaking my head. "I like to think war is an easy answer for people who want to feel like they matter to the universe. Do you know why they call me the Butcher of Kolthas?"

"Presumably because you butchered Kolthas?" Isla raised an eyebrow.

I gave her a sideways glance.

"Sorry, flippancy is probably not appropriate."

"No, it's not." I covered my mouth to drive away the smell of the dead Chel's innards before going to the ship's controls and checking the records the old-fashioned way. I had sensed other presences on board the vessel but, thankfully, nothing which was in our immediate area. I wanted to know if there was any further danger.

"Please tell me." Her voice was cold now.

"Kolthas was a space station," I said, taking a deep breath. "The Commonwealth is a hegemonic empire for the most part, luring worlds to join it with promises of bread and circuses over military conquest. Despite having eight hundred worlds in Sector 7, the Archduchy hadn't managed to establish complete control over it. The two hundred or so remaining worlds had turned to the Commonwealth for protection. Kolthas was what they constructed as a port and supply base for their administration of those worlds."

"This I remember," Isla said. "The Archduchy accused it of being nothing more than a place to stockpile weapons and a refuel their capital ships in order to launch an invasion."

"Mostly because it was."

"Are you sure?"

I looked down. "I don't know anymore."

"Were you ordered to destroy it?"

"No, I petitioned the royal family for the right to do it."

"So you started the war?" Isla asked, appalled.

"If not Kolthas, then it would have been a strike on Albion itself." I hadn't been alone in being a Pre-Emptivist. Thousands of young nobles had been hopeful of a war with the Commonwealth. "I argued we could intimidate the Commonwealth into submission by showing our resolve closer to home. Fifty thousand innocent men, women, and children died that day. Collateral damage. The civilian casualties were a minor cost compared to the destroyed fuel stockpiles, docked capital ships, ammunition stockpiles, and lost military personnel—or so I told myself. It was also part of a much larger campaign. A great victory with zero losses on our side. What more could you want from a conflict?"

"No conflict at all?" Isla asked.

"Yeah, but I hadn't been thinking about that."

I'd been demonized by the Commonwealth media for about a week. Unfortunately for the families of the victims, the Commonwealth's propaganda machine had determined my father was the most likely to sign a surrender agreement now that war had broken out. As such, I'd had my life adapted to a dozen holos where I was the "worthy opponent" fighting various fictional Commonwealth flying aces. I should have been prosecuted for what I'd done, but there had been plenty of pardoned war criminals after Crius' Fall.

What was one more?

"You need to know what kind of person you're travelling with," I said, looking down at the Chel corpses we'd just created.

"I killed a woman for my identity," Isla said.

"What?" I looked back.

Isla stared at me. "Not directly, but I knew what was going to happen. When I was on the run, Ares Industries sent a Reclaimer after me. You know the type, bounty hunters who specialize in taking down rogue bioroids. He was a retired one who'd been offered a significant bounty from my master. The fact I was travelling with multiple other bioroids, some military and others not, made me a doubly attractive target."

"Isla—"

"Please."

Isla took a deep breath. "He killed us, one by one, as we tried to figure out a way to get back into an Ares Electronics facility to get our shutdown codes removed. In the end, he got all of them, and I had to pretend to be unaware I'd been a bioroid. I told him my master had made me think I was human so I would be even more terrified. Then I seduced him. I made him fall in love with me. I begged him to run away with me and he did—promising he'd protect me from the other Reclaimers and retrieve my shutdown code."

"What happened?"

"He did," Isla said. "Then I killed him. Then I murdered his sister for her identity."

I stared at her. "You do what you have to do to survive."

"Is that what you tell yourself?"

"No, but it's what I'll tell you." I didn't love Isla, not the way I loved Judith, but I cared for her and wanted to see her happy. I was about to kiss her when the sensors I set for sweeping the ship came back with their results.

There were four additional life-forms on board this ship.

They were in the engine room.

Chapter Thirteen

I turned around and headed toward the doors. Isla was surprised by my sudden movement and followed.

"What's wrong?" Isla asked.

"More Chel," I said, taking a deep breath. "Around the engine room. They could be rigging this place to explode."

It wasn't likely. They could have done that earlier since the ship was still intact and they could have blown it to pieces with everyone on board within moments of gassing the rest of the crew. That was part of the reason why I was so angry about all this. Blowing themselves up to hide their efforts would have honorable.

This was simply murder.

"Or simply prepping their escape," Isla suggested, our earlier closeness passing. "After all, we only have Ida's word the Chel pirates were actually her soldiers. It's entirely possible she's the one who sent them to kill these people. Either that or they were never her people at all and she's just trying to mislead us about how much influence she possesses."

I closed my eyes, pondering her words. "No, I think she's telling the truth. The Commonwealth is employing privateers to frame the Chel and there were actual Chel on board. Ones who decided to kill everyone here after forwarding and deleting their research data."

"*What* research data, though?" Isla asked.

I paused. "I don't know. I saw the labs in my mind."

"Let me download it and take a look. I might be able to make heads or tails of it with Munin given enough time."

"We don't have any to waste." I gestured to the sensors and gave her a look at the labs before going back to the doors.

Isla uploaded the records of the security cameras anyway onto her infopad, then walked over to hijack the belt-sized personal force-field generator off one of the Chel. Opening the door we'd come through, I saw the hallway was now pristine with only a couple of mechs remaining. One of them was buffing the floor and another was polishing the walls.

Several mechs marched out from the adjoining rooms and started remove the bodies of the dead Chel. Isla caught up with me and the two of us headed into the elevator and commanded it to head down to the engine room.

"We should contact the others," Isla said. "We barely managed to survive fighting the other Chel. You don't need to get yourself into another fight with invisible enemies by yourself." She paused. "And you will be by yourself because I'm not an idiot."

I closed my eyes. "They won't be invisible. Those stealth cloaks aren't good enough to stand up to these ship's sensors. I'm going to tie them to my infopad and keep a good idea of where they are. Second of all, I don't necessarily want to get into a fight with these Chel. I'd rather talk to them."

I needed answers.

"After you killed two of their comrades?" Isla pointed out.

I opened my eyes and started to speak. "Well—"

"After they murdered this entire crew of your countrymen?" Isla interrupted. "*Including children.*"

"Fine." I took a deep breath and tapped the side of my uniform. The comms patched me through to the others on board. "Guys, we've got hostiles. The Chel *are* aboard this vessel and there's four in the engine room. I'm investigating now. Be warned, they have cloaking technology and personal force fields."

"Thank you," Isla said, exhaling. "Clarice needs to be made aware."

William responded first. "I copy. We'll meet you down there. Don't get killed."

"Is Clarice all right?" I asked, remembering her extreme reaction to the Chel.

William paused. "No. Hold position until we arrive."

I took a deep breath. "Copy."

The doors to the engine room opened seconds later, revealing lights that were completely out and the occasional sparking of a loose wire from panels, which had been shot with fusion blasts. It made sense as the engine room personnel often worked with space-suits. It was possible they, alone, had been able to survive the initial chlorine gas attacks.

"Great," I muttered, closing the door and tapping the LOCKDOWN button. It was a feature in every Crius ship.

I then moved to the side, not trusting the door to stop fusion fire. Isla did the same, checking her personal scanner and running it through the ship's sensors.

"Anything?" I asked.

"The ship's sensors indicate they're around the engine core."

"Great."

"Munin's shut down the main drives so they can't overload any-thing," Isla reassured me. "Not that there's not a hundred other things to do around here. There's only four of them and we should be able to take them, though. We should ask for their surrender."

"And what? Assure them they won't be charged in the murder of four hundred crewmen? That's how many the logs listed."

"Pretty much, yeah. Then shoot them after we get everything we need."

I blinked.

"We're not lawmen, Cassius. We're all here for our own reasons."

I paused. "Perhaps you're right. Habits like delusions of honor are hard to break, though."

"Being a good person was the hardest desire of mine I had to let go of. It will only get you killed in this world. It's why I'm here, I suppose."

I paused, needing a few minutes to calm myself and ground my sanity. "What do you get out of this? Working for Ida, I mean. The Commonwealth treats your people like slaves."

"Because we are slaves," Isla corrected me. As a doctor she had to know I needed more than light conversation to keep me going, but I could tell she was willing to humor me. "But to answer your ques-tion, the same thing I've always wanted: a place in this galaxy to call home. A purpose. I'm not sure I want to be here anymore, though. Not if it means I'm going to be caught up in the latest pissing contest between the Commonwealth, the Chel, and Crius' remnants. Why have you decided to stick around?"

"Peace...and money."

Isla smiled. "How much money?"

"A *lot* of money." I debated my next question before deciding to throw it out. "Want to go with me when I get my payday?"

"You have no idea how many men and women have made me that offer."

Well, that wasn't encouraging. "Perhaps I'll ask again when I actually have my fortune back."

Isla gave a half-smile. "Are you asking me to come with you as your friend, mistress, or doctor?"

"I'm happy with any but I'd prefer all three."

But what about Judith?

No.

It wasn't possible.

She was good.

People didn't come back from the dead.

Not good ones.

Isla nodded. "As long as you understand I can't be with just one person. I'm not, if you'll pardon the expression, wired that way."

"As long as you're okay with the same."

I wasn't the monogamous type myself. I'd loved Judith more than anyone, but I'd found myself drawn to other women, just as she'd found herself drawn to other men. Perhaps I wasn't so far from the free sexuality of the Commonwealth. I just preferred to express it with someone I cared about.

"So why does Clarice hate the Chel so much?" I asked, looking over Isla's controller at her scanner. It showed the Chel were moving but not toward us. They were moving in search-like patterns. I hoped the others arrived soon as it wouldn't take long for them to arrive at the elevator, and if they had scanners, which they almost certainly did, we were fucked.

"What has she told you?" Isla asked, as much to keep me calm as anything else. It wasn't necessary. I'd been in worse situations.

I'd just thought I was over them.

"We just got to the 'my family is a bunch of slavers' portion of the conversation." My tone was venomous, not for Clarice, but the Rin-O'Harra family.

"You speak with such contempt."

"Shouldn't I?"

Isla raised an eyebrow before looking back at her scanner. It was a reminder the Archduchy made use of bioroids.

"I've changed a lot of opinions since my Crius days," I said. "I wish I'd changed them sooner."

Isla seemed to accept that. Keeping her voice low, she said, "It's not my story to tell but given she may start shooting up the place, you should know. Clarice became a mercenary after she was thrown out of Star Patrol. It wasn't long but she worked with Mason's Raiders."

"The privateer group?" I knew a little about Mason's Raiders. It was one of the hundred or more upscale mercenary organizations employed by the Archduchy and Commonwealth during the tail end of the war. They'd switched their loyalties back and forth between the two sides, always contracting for one job or another. Both sides had allowed it as long as they were remarkably effective at getting the job done—a sign of just how desperate matters had gotten toward the end. I, personally, would have had them all shot.

"Yes," Isla said. "Everyone was making a profit off the war in one form or another. All except the citizens. Clarice's company were trying to rescue a damaged ship which had jumped into the wrong territory."

"And she encountered the Chel."

"Yes. They took her hostage after a ship they were trying to rescue wandered into the Chel's territory. Their soldiers killed all of her associates and tried to extract whatever information they could from her. After they did, they tried to break her."

"She was tortured." It wasn't a question.

There had been survivors of such encounters, especially from the war when prisoner exchanges were made, but they tended to be broken shells of their former selves. Some returned with a deep and passionate loyalty for their tormentors. A few had even gone on to become sleeper agents, or obsessed with the Chel to the point of flying back to their space to rejoin them as slaves. The Chel Madness as it was called. Further fuel for their legend.

"I'm not sure torture is sufficient a name for it, but I suppose governments have diluted the power of the word. The Chel possess the ability to manipulate senses as part of their genetic modifications."

"Manipulate senses?" I wanted to be clear on what she knew of their abilities. I'd never heard of this.

"They can induce fear, anger, pain, love, joy, and pleasure. Pain worse than being flayed alive and pleasure greater than the most sublime lovemaking."

The implications were staggering. It would explain why Clarice was on the *Melampus*, far away from the rest of civilized space. "I see."

"In the end, the Raiders managed to capture a few Chel and made a daring offer to trade them back for her, which was accepted. Clarice was imprisoned for two days and had scars left enough for a lifetime. Enough that Mason's Raiders gave her walking papers when they realized she wanted to go back and kill them all."

I took that all in and tried to contact Clarice. Tapping my communicator, I tried to reach her private feed. "Maybe she deserves her revenge but we need to get her to—"

"The enemy is moving in front of us," Isla interrupted. "There are mechs too."

"What?" I asked.

"What I said," Isla said. "We should move up a story."

That was when the elevator's lights flickered.

"Before they cut the power to it," Isla muttered. "Hells."

The red emergency lights flickered on but I knew there was no way either of us was going anywhere. The only thing we could do was open the doors, and that would just put us in direct contact with our pursuers.

That was when I heard a voice from the outside of the elevator. It was male with a Crius accent. Probably not a Chel. Though, honestly, I had no idea what they sounded like so I was just guessing. "Colonel-Count Mass. So good to finally meet you, even under these circumstances. I admit to being surprised to find your DNA has been encoded into the system but I'm fairly sure the Commonwealth's dogs aren't replicating it. They don't have the technology."

Isla looked over at me. "Maybe you can command them to let us go."

"It's worth a try."

The voice then said, "I, of course, know you're not the one leading the Free Systems Alliance. That's just a filthy bioroid."

Isla narrowed her eyes.

"Bioroids don't murder children, unlike you and your friends,"

I called back. "I came here to investigate who was using my name and rank."

"That's your ship out there?" the voice called.

"Yes," I said.

"What about the fighters?" he asked.

"No," I said. "The Chel sold the information to me."

"You're lying."

"Maybe you don't know the Chel as well as you think," I said. "Who do I have the honor of addressing?"

"Baronet Rudolph Zemov the Third."

I knew the Zemovs. Distant relatives. Assholes. Like most of Crius' nobility, now that I thought about it.

"What happened to our associates on the bridge?" Another voice, almost musical in nature and with an eerie reverb, said.

A Chel perhaps?

I looked at Isla, who shook her head.

"Dead!" I called back.

Isla glared at me.

I moved down beside the thickest metal part of the elevator, the panels directly to the side, as Isla did the same. Seconds later, fusion blasts shot through the door and slammed against the back. Sparks flew out of the sides, filling the elevator like fireworks while both Isla and I activated our shields. Seconds later, the fusion blasts stopped, leaving dozens of holes in the door.

I looked over at Isla, who was breathing heavy just like me. Taking several deep breaths, I stared over at the LOCKDOWN button.

Isla looked at me like I'd lost my mind.

I mouthed, "Trust me."

Isla's look was less than trusting.

Still, she pushed it, multiple times.

The doors, thankfully still functional, opened. I, meanwhile, unclipped the grenade I'd retrieved from the dead Chel and hurled it out the door. The explosion ripped through the hallway, sending waves of flash-radiation through the air. It would fry electronics and disintegrate flesh with equal alacrity.

It would also leave hulls compromised.

Unfortunately, any elation at believing we'd eliminated our foes was lost in the next few seconds.

"Impressive, Count," Zemov said. "You've managed to kill my two companions."

"It was partially my doing as well, you bigoted misogynist fuck!" Isla shouted back.

"Ah, that must be the infamous Devil Doctor Hernandez. No wonder you both took so poorly to the bioroid comment."

I did a double take at Isla.

Isla shrugged, looking as confused as I did.

"Come out here and let us make a deal," Zemov said. "I don't have the personnel to complete my mission anymore."

"You have nothing I want," I replied.

"I know your sister is on board this ship. The one who created the bioroid duplicates of you and your wife."

I growled. "Who sent you?"

"Thomas."

Chapter Fourteen

I thought back to the last time I ever interacted with my siblings. It had just been a few hours after our father's funeral. The war was still a few months from ending but it was the last time I'd interact with Zoe, Judith, Thomas, and the others I cared about on Crius.

"You can't be serious," I said, staring at my brother. The two of us were standing in the third study of Mass Castle, sunlight coming in through the windows as my wife's baby bio-dragon, Mittens, slept on the table behind us. I was sorting through father's papers after the funeral and mulling over the fact I would have to head back to the front in forty-nine hours.

Colonel-Count Thomas of House Plantagenet and I didn't resemble one another in the slightest despite roughly half my DNA being inside him. He was tall and well-formed like me but his skin was a rich shade of chocolate and he kept his head shaved rather than letting it grow out like I had. His right eye had been knocked out by a roadside bomb on Skellige and instead of going with a cybernetic replacement, he'd chosen to cover it with an ornate eyepatch with the Lucifer's Wings symbol on it.

Unlike myself and my father, in his earlier years, Thomas had chosen to avoid joining the Star Navy and devoted himself instead to politics. Ironically, this had rebounded on itself and caused him to join State Security as a Political Officer. Thomas' all-black uniform and great coat was a sharp contrast to my colorful ones, only possessing a fraction of the rewards on his chest but each won for loyalty or efficiency.

Which made his request all the more galling.

"You know it's the right thing to do," Thomas said, playing with his tight black leather gloves. "For both the good of the Archduchy as well as the human race itself."

"You want to kill Prince Germanicus."

"I want to kill a monster," Thomas replied. "Archduke Titus is nothing more than his children's puppet. Germanicus and Germania instituted this war with the Commonwealth with the full knowledge we couldn't win. They've filled the ranks of the military and government with their puppets, all of whom follow their insane ideology of Genetic Manifest Destiny. You know about the atrocities they've committed."

"Gossip and rumors," I said, retreating behind the same defense I always took when confronted with evidence that contradicted the fact we weren't the good guys in this war. That there was any such thing in war.

Let alone this war.

But Judith's words remained with me.

To cut a better deal.

"They're insane," Thomas said, sighing. "Germania is easily arrested. We have people in the military willing to take her in after the failures she's had on the battlefield. The Field Marshal-Princess has slaughtered too many nats and gotten too many of her own soldiers killed to have any support. Germanicus, though, is the darling of the movement. Only if he's dead will the shadow government be able to assume power and force a treaty with the Commonwealth."

I stared at him. "Just how many of these people do you have involved in this scheme?"

"Many."

"And what happens if you succeed?"

"Peace," Thomas said. "There will be consequences. The Commonwealth is a brutal and horrible taskmaster. The feudal system will be dismantled, there will be war crimes trials for us while parades for them, and the cost to Crius will beggar the kingdom. We will survive, though, and the killing will end."

"Our armies will also have to fight their wars, Thomas. We will bomb other planets and slaughter them. That's how the Commonwealth *works*. You surrender so you can fight for them rather than against them."

"Better at God's side than in his way. You could be a powerful voice in the new government."

"I don't care about that."

"Then care about the fact you're married to a nat. Germania murdered millions of them during the Skellige campaign in her paranoia they were working against Crius' war effort. Germanicus ordered you left alone because of your propaganda value, but he considers your marriage to Judith one of purebred dragon to mongrel lizard. How long will that last if he wins? They already have a file on you a kilometer wide at State Security. Hell, you're already a clone. You could have a place within the Commonwealth's new government."

I narrowed my eyes. "So, casually just toss away my honor and betray my country for the scraps the Commonwealth might throw me?"

"That's not—"

"You disgust me," I said, clenching my fists. "I despise the Dumas. They're a bunch of up-jumped traitors who murdered the last first-lineage descendants of Prophet Allenway and claimed it was the work of terrorists. He is still our leader, though. You may be willing to sell your children and their future to Albion but I will have none of it."

It was a child's defense. A tantrum that refused to acknowledge everything he was saying was the absolute truth. Honor was the last refuge of the scoundrel and those who used it to do despicable things had no right to claim it. The right thing to do was turn Thomas in but I didn't want to.

I didn't want him to fail.

"So you won't help us?"

"No," I said, weakly. "I'm sorry."

That was when Thomas hugged me and a sense of horror passed over.

"I'm so relieved!" Thomas said, a broad smile on his face.

"What?"

"You've passed the test."

"Test?" I said, staring at him, bewildered.

Thomas removed a recorder the size of a dot from underneath his lapel. "There was a plot to eliminate the Prince but it was foiled recently. The Prince wanted to make sure those most important to the party's success in this war remain loyal."

I stared at him. "Just how many people have failed this little test?"

"Only the traitors."

I looked out the window at the stone tomb they'd constructed for our father. "Thomas, how did our father die? Was it just a malfunction of his cybernetics?"

Our father had been a monster, corrupt and a major force behind the war. However, even he had come to loathe Germanicus and his ambitions. He'd only supported him this far because, thanks to the Commonwealth's boundless lust for territory, we were in the middle of a defensive war against people claiming they were defending other worlds from us.

"Don't worry about that."

"*Don't worry*?"

"I wasn't involved and there's no way to tell but the Commonwealth is within striking distance of Crius now. There is a plan to defeat them but we need the loyalty of every single one of our warriors to do it. Forget about the Dumas now, Cassius, and tell me: do we have your loyalty?"

I took a deep breath, utterly confused. "You have my loyalty."

It was the worst mistake of my life. I didn't have time to think on my decision, though, because the door opened and my sister, Zoe of House Plantagenet, entered. She was, in many respects, my brother's opposite. Small in build and pretty, she was also warm and pleasant.

Zoe had short, shoulder-length black hair and a slightly lighter brown skin. Zoe wasn't a member of State Security but wore, instead, a pleasant white-jacket over a black turtleneck with a Lucifer's Wings pin on her front jacket pocket. She wore a black dress, which reached to the floor, but with boots underneath, and had a pile of files in her hands. The only sign of her role in the Archduchy was the silver ring on her left hand, marking her as a Grandmaster of the Science Orders.

"Hello, my brothers," Zoe said. "I would like to have a word with Cassius in private."

"With pleasure." Thomas gave a short bow and walked out the door.

"He's being pleasant to you, that's never a good sign," Zoe said, frowning. "What happened?"

"I was just tested for my loyalty to a madman," I replied.

"Should I be more upset about the fact my brother did that or the fact you passed?" Zoe said, up close. "You should learn to avoid that kind of speech. You don't want to get yourself in trouble at our father's funeral."

"It might not have been an accident," I said, wondering how Zoe would react. She liked my father more than Thomas, but even that was just above toleration. After all, I had been created as a deliberate insult to my sibling's DNA.

"It was. I went over the details myself. State Security likes to take credit for anything untoward happening to anyone so it looks less like they're a bunch of nepotistic boot-lickers and more like they're the badass spies they think they are." Zoe smiled and put her files away before turning to adjust my uniform. The awards were slightly off.

"And I should be worried about getting into trouble?"

"They need me and the rest of the Science Orders to dig us out of the hole we've currently gotten ourselves in."

My expression turned grim. "How's that going?"

"It's possible. Unlikely, but possible."

One difference between the Commonwealth and the Archduchy was the quality of our scientists. The Commonwealth disdained transhumanism and banned cyborgs from all but menial labor or indentured servitude. They argued, ironically, this prevented the wealthy from creating class divisions with the poor by literally buying superiority.

By contrast, a typical Crius noble was three or four times as smart as the average human being and those specialized in intelligence could memorize and sort through data, which took ages to do otherwise. One did not have to look farther than the fact Zoe had the equivalent of fifty degrees in various disciplines and was considered exceptional in three to mark the difference in our societies.

"Well, I hope you come up with something soon," I said, taking a deep breath. "The war is not going in our favor."

That was an understatement. While the war had yet to reach Crius, at least the estates here, the sheer number of people killed was without end. Even with mass-conscription from the poor of every vassal world plus Lucifer City, there simply weren't enough Crius to fight the Commonwealth. We were slaughtering them in every engagement, but it didn't matter how many we killed since there were always two more to replace each one lost.

We were holding our supremacy in space but matters also had taken a sharp turn once the Commonwealth had managed to land its troops. Princess Germania might have been a psychopath but no one could deny her hover-tank brigades were amazing. Still, numbers again favored the Commonwealth and being forced to actually engage them, power-armored-trooper-to-power-armored-trooper, had led to some of the worst losses in the war. There were also rumors of atrocities being conducted against the Skellige people. Ones, it seemed, even my brother wasn't denying.

"I have a few ideas for various game-changers," Zoe said, crossing her arms. "Bioroid replacements mass-produced with copied memories to make up for our troop issues. Full commitment to building as many manufacturing plants as possible would allow us to field endless numbers. We could also give them the skills to make more factories and industrial centers to give us war material as well."

"Bioroids are spectacularly piss-poor soldiers. They have no loyalty or honor."

"I have ways around that," Zoe said. "There are also ideas for anti-matter weapons, neurological agents, jump-beacon scramblers, and hive viruses."

"Those are all hideously illegal and banned by interstellar treaty. You realize that, right?"

"It is the nature of science to propose uncomfortable truths. A solution is a solution, even if it's a bad one."

"Next you'll tell me you've been working on CognitionA.I. ."

Zoe looked over her shoulder, guiltily.

"Oh for the love of God!" I said, staring. "Don't even joke about that."

"The prejudice against CognitionA.I. is ridiculous. The Great Collapse and the subsequent Galactic Dark Age was caused by people reprogramming them, not the machines themselves.A.I. do what they're programmed to do. Nothing more. LesserA.I. and cybernetics are both just stopgaps for a cultural scar we should really look past."

"One hundred years of darkness."

The CognitionA.I. , those which had unlimited capacity for

growth as well as information analysis, had once been the heart of galactic civilization. They had managed the jump systems, the military, and the economy. They'd all been reprogrammed by well-meaning religious zealots who wanted them to be free.

Unfortunately, the language they'd used had been militant and the result had been the destruction of the original jump network. All colonies that couldn't adapt had died out and it had been a millennium before someone had discovered a way to do the calculations necessary to navigate jumpspace without artificial intelligence. It was the one universal truism that could unite the scattered galactic settlements, which otherwise never agreed on anything. Never again.

Zoe sighed. "The prohibitions againstA.I. have been weakening for centuries. Eventually, they will be used again once the situation is desperate enough."

"If we field CognitionA.I. , then every planet in the galaxy will turn against us. Our descendants will be annihilated to the fifth degree. Even the aliens of the Community agree with that. They hateA.I. . They consider it against their religion."

Zoe made a dismissive gesture with her left hand. "I didn't say I was working on one. No, we're not that desperate yet. We've pushed the envelope in terms of artificial intelligence research and broken some taboos, but we're still far away from that. Ironically, it's the Commonwealth who has had to change the most. Half their justification for this war is we're a bunch of mad scientists playing with forces we don't understand."

Part of the reason the Commonwealth loathed us so much was we were significantly more technologically advanced than them. This was due to a variety of factors, including our enhanced intelligence, technology smuggling from the Community, and xeno-archaeology. The latter, in particular, incensed them as the Commonwealth had extremely strict laws about investigating sites belonging to destroyed, or absent, alien races. I, personally, didn't see the problem with the knowledge of the dead being used to help the living. The only reason we didn't know more about, say, the Elder Races was it required things like CognitionA.I. to understand their machines.

"You had something you wanted to talk to me about?" I decided to switch to a less-polarizing topic.

Zoe looked as if she'd forgotten what she had been discussing. "Oh, that's right. I want to copy your brain."

I blinked. "Could you repeat that?"

"I mentioned we've made some remarkable advancements in A.I. , cybernetics, and bioroid research. They're all the same field really. I think we can improve the downloading of skills from just pure information to actual technical usage. I want to test it by using information derived from our best combat pilot."

"Me?"

"You!"

I tried to figure out how many ways I could say the word "Hell, no" and came up with fifteen. "Are you out of your damned mind?"

"Thomas' husband says so, as do most of my friends, but sanity is relative."

"It's really not."

Zoe looked up at me. "Cassius, you are the embodiment of every-thing good in our system…and everything wrong with it. Certainly, you are nothing like our father who never thought of another per-son in his life unless it was how to control them. You are a soldier who follows a code religiously, even when the people who wrote it sniggered as they put it in writing. So, I won't argue with you about the scientific merits or the possibilities this opens up for improving the human species. Instead, I will simply say this will save the lives of your fellow soldiers."

I hated her in that moment because she was right. I had a greater responsibility here. "All right. We'll do it."

"Splendid."

"How long will it take?" I said, knowing I had to be back on the *Revengeance* soon.

"Just a few hours."

"Judith will never forgive me for any time away from our last night together to do this. You realize that, right?"

"You'll have many nights with her in the future. Besides, I want her to participate, too. She's one of the most observant women I've ever known."

"The world could use more Judiths."

Chapter Fifteen

My reaction to the claim Thomas had sent them to pick up Zoe was simple but succinct. "Bullshit."

Zemov chuckled. "I can assure you, we're here to pick up your sister and transport her back to the *Revengeance*."

"The *Revengeance* was scrapped," I snapped.

"That's where you draw your line on the believability of our story? Not that your siblings are alive? That they're the heart of the Free Systems Alliance?"

I'd seen both of them on the ship's computer but I wasn't about to reveal just how much I'd learned from them. "It's a big galaxy, Zemov. You're not going to convince me of all the planets in the universe, in all the star systems, I've stumbled onto the one where my sister is located and that you're working for my brother."

"It does seem like a big coincidence," Zemov replied, "but I think we both know there are forces moving us all into position for something grand. Besides, didn't you say you were investigating your doppelganger?"

He had a point.

"You don't seem surprised the Cassius in charge of the FSA's starfighters is a bioroid."

"I'm close enough to your brother to know the truth."

Ah, he was one of my brother's lovers. Someone he trusted with his secrets. That made things more complicated. "What do you want with my sister?"

"She's a traitor," Zemov said.

I blinked and looked over at Isla.

"The Contessa of House Plantagenet fed information to the Commonwealth about the nature of our projects here," Zemov said. "When your brother found out, he sent us to secure the research data and bring your sister back unharmed. By the time we arrived, the crew was already dead, the research forwarded to your brother, and a distress signal sent out. The false Chel arrived soon after as her rescue. I managed to convince them we were Watchers and they should guard our escape with a high-value VIP."

This time, it was Isla who called out. "That's insane."

"Not if you have all the necessary codes and data for such a deception," Zemov said. "How do you think we found out about the Contessa's treason? The Commonwealth is a house divided against itself and the FSA will break it into smaller, more manageable pieces for the Second Archduchy of Crius."

I rolled my eyes and shook my head. "Is that the line you've been fed by your Chel allies?"

"Don't be bigoted," Zemov said, half-heartedly. "They may be disgusting aliens now but they were once human."

This conspiracy was getting more and more convoluted. First ex-Crius, then Chel, and now parties in the Commonwealth itself? That's if I believed Zemov, which was a big *if*. On the other hand, his explanation would go a long way toward explaining why the Commonwealth's Fake Chel attacked us.

It would also mean Ida kept my sister from being involved in all this from the beginning. I was starting to question her story that she'd stumbled onto me while holding out a net for possible high-value defectors. It seemed more likely now, especially if Zoe was her contact in the FSA, that I'd been ushered onto her ship as insurance. Either as a weapon against their imposter Cassius or leverage against my sister.

Did the lies ever end?

Only one way to find out. Talk to Zoe. "What's your proposal?"

"Guarantee my safety and I'll surrender to you. I'll put down my weapon and you can put me under arrest."

I glanced out the side of the elevator's doors and saw Zemov for the first time. He was a tall man with long black hair, almond eyes, and pale white skin. He was wearing the same sort of uniform Thomas had been in my memories, lacking the decor, and was carrying a repeating fusion-rifle. There were numerous damaged and shattered mechs on the ground. Their metal was fused together by the heat of the grenade's explosion. There was no sign of dead Chel, however, and that was when I saw lights shimmer in the doorways to Zemov's sides.

Dammit, it was a trap.

"He'll be right out!" Isla shouted, still looking down at her scanner. "Put your gun down now."

I looked at her and she smiled, clearly planning something.

"All right." Zemov kneeled down and put his rifle on the ground.

"Put your hands up," I said, partially unsheathing my sword and knowing the moment I stepped out the Chel would open fire.

Zemov did so, a knowing grin on his face.

Isla lifted her right hand and started counting down from five. When she reached one, I stepped out only to find the hallway filled with energy blasts.

Energy blasts fired at Zemov and his companions.

Clarice and William were behind with their plasma rifles firing. They cut down Zemov from behind, his shield not even raised before continuing to fire at the Chel, knowing exactly where to aim. I charged outward with my proton sword, a blast from William's rifle striking my energy shield before I slashed one of the Chel's arms clean off. He fell to the ground and started to bleed out. The last of them, a female, tossed down her weapon and raised her hands in surrender.

Clarice, angry beyond belief, proceeded to charge the female Chel and knocked her across the jaw of her stealth suit with the butt of her rifle. The *Melampus'* security chief then kicked her in the chest before smashing her across the face with her rifle butt again. It began as a no-holds-barred beatdown and looked like it was about to continue into an act of murder.

"Stop, Clarice!" William shouted. "We need them alive."

"You should let her do it," Isla said, stepping out from behind the elevator doors. "It's psychologically healthy."

"In what universe?" William asked.

"This one," Isla said. "Revenge is one of the best medicines there is. I speak from experience."

I took a deep breath, debating whether or not to interfere. "Clarice, killing them now is going to just mean its suffering ends now."

Clarice shot me a murderous glare, then looked back down to the bloody and battered Chel. "You saw what this thing was a part of."

"Yes," I said, looking at her. "Answers first."

Clarice reached down and grabbed its personal shield-generator, just as Isla had done, then set her rifle to stun. She proceeded to deliver a half-dozen bolts into the Chel's body, paralyzing it. She then fired another one for good measure.

"You owe me for this," Clarice said.

"You're right," I said. "I do."

I took a deep breath, then turned to Isla. "Did you send them the information about their location?"

"Yes, I did."

"Good job," I said, nodding. "Now that means there's only one person alive on this ship. My sister."

"You're kidding," William said, looking at me incredulously. "Is your family just the whole part of this Alliance?"

"It looks that way," I said, wondering what was going on. "My sister was a master roboticist and clone master, though, so whatever appears to be the truth is not necessarily the case. Identity is not always what it appears to be."

"Uh huh," William said, staring at me. "Now's not the time for this sort of bullshit."

I shrugged. "Probably not."

Isla lifted up her scanner. "I have a pretty good idea where Lady Plantagenet is. I also have recordings of what they were working on in the security feeds even if we don't have the actual research data."

I wondered if Hiro would make an attempt on our lives for that as well. He was yet another person who wasn't what they appeared to be on the *Melampus*. In a way, that was a worse cut than discovering this ship full of corpses as I'd been genuinely fooled by his pleasant, idealistic demeanor. Yet, his bearing when Munin had broken the codes of the ship was one of a hardened killer.

No wonder he didn't seem traumatized by shooting down Holtz.

"Where's Hiro anyway?" I asked, noticing he was conspicuous by his absence.

"With Munin," William said, "I didn't think it was right to bring those two into combat."

I was suddenly nervous and about to object when I heard Hiro's voice proclaim from down the hall, "We've found a survivor!"

I had never run faster in my life than when I did into the engine room proper. There, in the center of the ship, was a series of cat-walks overlooking a set of four massive pipes, which led to large, humming, ball-like devices that sent strange blue fluid-like energies through crystal tubes. I had no idea how jump drives worked, only a basic understanding of the physics to which humanity had been given knowledge by the Community, but I couldn't help but feel overwhelmed every time I was around the machines that warped the laws of physics every time they brought ships through the jump-dimension.

Turning my head to the side, I saw Hiro standing at the other end of a catwalk to my right and walked over it, into an office that had several dead bodies on the ground. They were ship engineers wearing spacesuits that had protected them from the chlorine gas but not Baronet Zemov and his Chel guards.

One of the dead bodies on the ground was a Chel as well, which indicated they hadn't gone down without a fight. I wondered how many others had perished fighting for their lives after the brutal sneak attack, which had served no purpose other than to try to cover up what had been going on here. Who, really, was responsible for the massacre? Zemov and his Chel? Did I believe their claim everyone had been dead on arrival? Or was my sister at fault, working for Ida? Did I dare hope it was truly Zoe on board?

I didn't have time to think about that and focused, instead, on finding the survivor Hiro mentioned. The office was surprisingly cheerful-looking despite the number of corpses with holos of Zoe, her brother, and three of her genetically-engineered children. None of them had been created with a father but were custom-built from the ground up.

I hoped none of them were on board.

Munin was scratching away at a panel against the wall, with a controller to the side as well as a speech console. It was, as Zemov said, a panic room. Not a usual feature of Crius ships for anyone but the captain, but I sincerely doubted my sister had left the ship unmodified. Walking over to it, I looked at Munin. "Any luck?"

"Nope," Munin said, trying not to look at the corpses behind her. "Whoever is inside is sealed up tight and not responding to any personal inquiries."

"I think I might be able to help with that," I said, softly.

"Because you were a high-muckity-muck in Crius?"

"I'm not sure what that means but I'm going to guess and say yes."

Munin snorted. "Be my guest."

I looked back at Hiro who was acting very casual. He didn't suspect I believed him to be willing to kill us all now. Was I being paranoid? Putting too much stock in a look and the fact he was all right with killing Holtz (a drunk and a bully)? Perhaps. Then again, space seemed to have brought out the worst in humanity.

The original Earthers had ruined the planet they'd lived on and eventually destroyed it, but they'd been doing their best to make sure their new homes were decent. It hadn't been until they'd been given cheap terraforming and jumpspace drives that they'd really unleashed their worst aspects. I wondered if that was the point now. It might have been kinder to just let us kill ourselves off.

Pressing my thumb against the genetic identifier, I also turned on the comms system. "Zoe, this is Cassius. The real one."

"Real one?" Munin said.

"Ask Ida," I replied.

There was silence on the other side.

"Nice job," Munin said. "Who's Zoe?"

"My sister," I said.

Munin raised an eyebrow. "Either you've been keeping more than just your identity from us or someone has been a real asshole to you."

"Or this is all a coincidence," Hiro said, his voice hardened. "Which is the best way to think of things."

"When did you get all cynical?" Munin asked.

Hiro looked away as the others entered the room beside him. Clarice, noticeably, took up position behind him. I hadn't been the only one of our group to see his change in demeanor, though a quick glance at Clarice's bloodshot eyes and barely concealed fury, I couldn't help but wonder if she was ready to shoot the first person to give her cause.

Maybe I should have let her kill the Chel.

"I don't believe you," a voice spoke on the other end of the comm. It took me a second to process that it really was my sister.

I wasn't sure how I felt about that. Strange how human emotions betray us at the times they're supposed to be at our most clear. Children find Christmas bewildering when not about presents or decorations. Death can leave us numb rather than sad. The birth of children can be frightening rather than joyous. To hear my sister's voice left me sad rather than happy as it meant she was thick in this nightmare.

Knowing she was here, in fact, I was angry because it occurred to me she had to be responsible for my doppelganger and his *wife*. She'd created a gross perversion of myself, bioroid or not, which diminished me as a human being. I'd never been as close to my siblings as a brother should, but this was the first time I'd ever wanted to commit an act of physical violence against one of them. What was her role in all of this and how stupid was she to become involved in terrorism or espionage?

As stupid as I was, I'd wager.

"It's me," I said. "I can prove it by telling you how grossly appalled, hateful, and angry I am over the fact that there's a copy of me running around. You told me that research was to make better pilots. Not...clone them."

"The sheer irony of that statement is hopefully not lost on you," Zoe replied.

"Do I want to know?" William asked.

"Cassius is being impersonated by a bioroid in the Free Systems Alliance," Hiro said. "He's less than happy about it."

"How the hell do you know?" William asked.

"Eh," Hiro shrugged. "Reasons."

"We should really sit down and discuss what everyone knows," Isla suggested.

"That could be very dangerous," Hiro said.

"You want me to blow the door?" Munin asked. "Because I have explosives and *love* blowing things up."

"Uh huh," I said.

"Love it," Munin said, grinning. "Boom."

"Not yet," William said. "Clarice?"

"I'm sick of this," Clarice said, staring back to where she left the Chel. "Let's just get what we came for and get off this tub."

"Agreed," I said, sighing. "Zoe, come out now. This is your only chance."

There was hesitation before her response but, thankfully, it was the one we wanted. "All right."

The panic room door opened with a *whoosh* of gas and dematerialization of force fields. That was when my sister, five years older, stepped out in a spacesuit. Her mascara had run, her makeup ruined by tears. She looked haggard and trembled, no doubt because she'd been in the middle of all this horror.

Zoe then gave me an uncharacteristic hug. I dropped my weapon and hugged her tight.

"You know your sister is kind of crazy," Judith said, holding my hand tightly as we stared into space from the Revengeance's *observation lounge.*

"Really? I hadn't noticed," I deadpanned.

"Just saying, her experiments are pretty damned ruthless. She actually talked about using live targets in her cyber-soldier tests."

"My sister grew up in a family that treated her poorly. A family which defined itself by military service and political power had little place for a woman of science. Hell, her mother's enemies tried to drown her when she was seven. Honestly, without me and Thomas, I think she would have retreated entirely from the world."

"That's one possibility. I have another theory."

"What's yours?"

"That she's just a crazy psycho bitch."

The conversation degenerated from there.

"Why did you do it?" I asked, unsure what I was asking about in particular. Killing the crew, building my doppelgangers, helping Ida, helping the FSA, all of it was confusing to me. Even so, I would forgive her all of it. I was just glad to have my sister back.

I didn't expect an answer but Zoe gave me one. "Because she ordered me to."

"Who?" I asked.

"Ida."

Chapter Sixteen

I walked into Ida's room where she was sitting on her couch and looking over daily reports on her infopad. There was the full tea-seat on the table in front of her, not yet cleaned up by Hunk-A-Junk.

I walked over and kicked over the table, spilling all of its contents on the ground before taking position over her, my arms crossed in front of my chest. I did my best to give her my most intimidating glare.

Ida didn't bother to look up from her infopad. "I take it you're upset?"

"You take it correctly."

"You'll have to be specific about what. I upset a lot of people for a lot of reasons, darling."

"I'm not your darling. Zoe works for you. She was on that ship, possibly dead, and you didn't bother telling me. You didn't bother telling me she was involved in the Free Systems Alliance, a contact of your Watchers, or that my brother was involved. I could go on but I think we can simply stick with you sending me in to a ridiculously compromised situation for shits and giggles."

Ida put down her infopad and called over to Hunk-A-Junk. "Clean this up would you, dear? Wash it in the sink, too."

"Yes, ma'am!" Hunk-A-Junk called from the kitchenette.

Ida turned to me. "Yep, I did all of that."

"Why?" I said, close to throttling her.

"When I was a newcomer to the spy game, one of my long-term contacts was marked for termination by the higher-ups. I had allowed myself to become close to him despite the fact he was a prick who probably had it coming. The thing is, they didn't let me know he was targeted and, instead, let the net close around him while I was forced to try to and figure out who was trying to kill him. In the end, after a failed attempt to rescue him got two of my assets killed, I walked into my chief's office and demanded to know why. He said that you never actually know someone until you've seen them under fire."

I stared at her. "So because your boss was a psychopath, you are too?"

Ida shrugged. "No, psychopaths make terrible spymasters. A lot of Commonwealth agents used to have their moral centers compromised to be better agents but, shockingly enough, this meant they didn't have any real reason to work for the benefit of Mother Albion. The simple fact was, Cassius, I wanted to test you and see how you reacted."

"So you fed me that bullshit excuse of not knowing who I was before I came on board your ship?"

"Pretty much," Ida said. "Note, if there was the absolutely insane coincidence of you getting on board my ship by accident and then me only finding out this week, then I'd never admit it. It would make me look like the worst spymaster in the world."

"So you're denying this was all planned."

"I'm leaving that for you to decide. The fact is, yes, your sister was on board that ship working for us. Sort of."

I blinked. "Sort of."

Ida shrugged. "Operation: Electric Bookmark was designed to move the best surviving scientists from the Archduchy of Crius from its territory to Albion. There, they've been working on various projects for the transtellars to maximize our economic and technological growth. If I wanted to send one of them back to spy on their fellows, I imagine they wouldn't send the actual scientist but a bioroid with all of their skill and knowledge as well as memories."

I processed that, feeling like I was on an emotional virtu-real game. "That isn't Zoe back in the medical bay?"

"It's Zoe," Ida corrected. "Just a version of her. Her advances in the field of robotics and cybernetics have the chance to change the way we define humankind. That's not my job to investigate, though, only the parts that result in defeating the Free Systems Alliance."

"What the fuck is going on, really?"

Ida looked down at her infopad. "You're not being paid to ask questions."

"Screw the money. I'd prefer answers."

Ida chuckled. "See, I am learning a great deal more about you, Count Cassius, than I ever would have learned just hanging around you. Say please, son."

I continue to stare at her. "Please."

Ida sighed. "You want the long or the short version?"

"The true version."

Ida looked forward. "That's harder to give than you might think. The short version is I sent your sister's doppelganger into the Crius Reborn Movement. Your brother, Field Marshal Plantagenet, bought her presence hook-line-and-sinker. He had her make a bunch of mock-ups of famous Crius soldiers to support his revolution. Yourself included. I had Zoe feeding me information from the very beginning right up until everything went pear-shaped."

"The Free Systems Alliance."

Ida nodded. "Yep. Suddenly, a nuisance we could control and manipulate was a serious problem with unlimited amounts of funding as well as war material. A combination of Chel, transtellar backers and secessionists with enough power to potentially break the Commonwealth into a dozen individual states."

"How did they get involved?"

Ida shrugged. "Honestly? I have no idea."

"I want the truth."

"I'm not omniscient, Cassius," Ida said, frowning. "However much the Watchers would like to claim we are, the truth was we were caught with our pants down. I could theorize all the live long day but this is bigger than all of us. If I had to make a guess, though, I'd say it was aliens."

"Aliens." I blinked. "Seriously."

"Ever met any?"

"A couple."

Aliens were, in simple terms, real and almost irrelevant to the lives of most humans. Aside from the Community, the nearest extraterrestrial alliance outside of the Galactic Core, none of them wanted anything to do with us. Even the Community's dozen or so species had only a few scant interactions with human territory. To quote one of the Old Earth books that survived the Galactic Dark Age on Crius: *We have nothing they want, and they have nothing we can afford.*

"You think aliens are orchestrating this war?" I asked, skeptical.

"Not a chance," Ida said. "I think the fact humanity has, after one thousand years in space, finally developed technology on par with the Community. The Commonwealth will probably join it in the next two or three decades with all barriers on trade and interaction lifted. They just need enough resources to not be a complete joke."

I took a deep breath. "*That's* why the Commonwealth keeps reclaiming worlds. They want to be able to sit at the adults' table."

"One of the motivations," Ida said. "The other being that everyone loves winning a war. Boosts the economy and morale. It blinds people to the fact you just encourage the people you've beaten to come back for round 2."

"So you think this whole revolution is from the people who want to break up the Commonwealth before it decides to end humanity's eight millennium of isolationism."

"That and the fact everyone hates the Commonwealth who isn't sucking from its teat."

Well, that certainly put a new spin on things. "So my sister or her doppelganger was your spy. Why did you order her ship attacked?"

"Your sister had been discovered," Ida said. "So we did what she had to do. Sabotage the ship, gas the crew, send all of the information she'd found in their databanks to the Commonwealth, and then hide out until we arrived. I don't know why the privateers turned against us, though. I'd argue it was part of my master plan but I think we're a bit past that point."

"Zemov claimed they had the codes to prove they were friendlies to the Commonwealth."

"They might. It wouldn't be the first time the right hand didn't know what the left was doing or was flat-out trying to stab it with a pencil."

"What's a pencil?"

Ida gave a dismissive wave. "The fact is, we're now capable of finding out what this terrorist organization is really up to and might be able to nip it in the bud before it becomes a revolution that consumes half of humanity's territory."

"The fact is you ordered the murder of a bunch of men, women, and children on board that research vessel."

Ida paused. "Yeah, I did."

I couldn't read Ida's emotions in that moment. Was she really that dismissive or was she just very good at controlling her emotions? Everything I'd known about her up until today had been a lie so could I really judge her? It didn't matter either way. I didn't want any further part of this. I'd let myself forget just how vile war was. Mostly because it was the only thing I was ever good at.

I clasped my feet together, clicked my heels, and gave the sideways salute of Crius. "Captain, I must regretfully tender my resignation to you as both your navigator and catspaw. You can guess where I believe you can shove it."

"Do you really think you can just walk out like that?" Ida asked, reaching under a cushion and pulling out a fusion pistol.

I put my hands on my hips. "Go ahead."

"Bang." Ida said, then tossed it to one side. "Thing hasn't worked since the Marquitz administration."

"I'll be dropping myself off at our next port of call," I said, thinking about what I was going to do with the rest of my life. "I wish you and the others luck."

"Nothing I can do to persuade you to stay?"

"Nothing."

"I doubt that but I respect your decision." Ida picked up her infopad and typed in it. "I've unfrozen your accounts despite the fact you've only gone halfway with me."

I debated my response and, in the end, just said, "Thank you."

Turning around to walk out the door, Ida then said, "CognitionA.I."

I was halfway out when I stopped dead in my tracks. "Fuck."

"Sorry," Ida said, sighing. "I really wanted to let you go but the fact is you can walk and chew popgum at the same time. That's better than the vast majority of my agents."

"I'm not your agent."

"That remains to be seen," Ida paused. "Just how many people did you kill in the war?"

"Directly or indirectly?"

"Both."

"Hundreds of thousands," I said, sighing. "I don't know what that has to do with our situation."

"That's a heavy burden to bear, even with memory drugs," Ida said. "I think you're looking for a way to redeem yourself, though."

"I'm not going to find that in your service."

"Aren't you?" Ida said. "As bad as the things you saw over on the *Rhea* were, they're insignificant next to the kind of things which the Archduchy of Crius did on a regular basis. Slave labor, comfort slaves, human experimentation, and the destruction of whole populations. That's going to be insignificant, though, the moment the Commonwealth falls and all the various groups fighting over it carve it up like a bison on Prideday."

"So, I should fight with you because the lesser evil is the greater good?"

"Isn't it always?"

"When I first joined the Starfighter Corps, my father was angry beyond belief. He let me know in no uncertain terms that he thought those who fought on the front lines were nothing more than fools and pawns. His opinion of the Archduchy was one that existed for the nobility and by the nobility. Those sacrificed in its name were nothing more than yokels, deluded by thoughts of glory or patriotism. I wouldn't have been able to do what I did if I hadn't appealed to his political enemies. Men and women who just wanted to see me die and my siblings inherit his fortune."

"And yet you live while everyone else there has died."

"Yes," I said, sighing. "I wanted to believe the Archduchy was worth fighting for and there was an honor in its service. That by serving it, I elevated myself above those who merely profited from it. It's been a hard and bitter pill acknowledging I was wrong. I am not going to fall into that same trap again."

Hunk-A-Junk finished cleaning up the broken tea set on the ground. It then squirted out liquid that dissolved the liquid and sugar then evaporated so the floor was clean and beautiful.

"People don't change," Ida said. "We like to think we can but the nature of a man is inviolate. We just chip away the detritus around our inner core. You'll always be looking for some means of being more than your selfish and greedy father, just like I'll always be trying to make up for the people I killed as a smuggler."

"Who did you kill?"

"People, like any other. I was a rich girl who wanted to slum with the poor folks and help them achieve independence from

the Commonwealth. I sold weapons, drugs, and brought terrorists, though I called 'em revolutionaries, across borders in hopes of
eventually seeing a better world. Eventually, I saw just how much
damage I was doing and asked just how bad it would be for the
Commonwealth to be in charge of everything. People don't give a
shit about freedom as long as their bellies are full and there's something good on the holo."

"Do you really believe that?"

"No, but I also believe most people don't give a shit about politics
either and hate getting pulled into the fights of those who do."

She had me there. "How did you get into the Watchers with a
past like that?"

"Money."

"Ah." That was how everything worked in the Commonwealth.
"All right, just for the sake of argument, what do you mean,
CognitionA.I. ?"

"Zoe claims the Free Systems Alliance is building one as a
weapon against the Commonwealth."

I tried to control my reaction but failed. "Even they're not that
stupid."

"I think any gamble about the human race that starts with us not
being that stupid is a sucker's bet."

"Surely, we've improved our defenses against them in the past
two millennia?"

"Oh, sure, there's no way they could shut down the jump systems
the way they did before. That doesn't mean something one billion
times smarter than any human isn't going to be able to crush us like
insects, especially since we only survived thanks to our ownA.I.
last time. Also, don't call me Shirley."

"I didn't. I used the word surely as in talking about a near-cer-
tain likelihood."

"You're no fun, Cassius."

I pondered the weight of her words and what, exactly, might be
accomplished if I went along with her. CognitionA.I. were one of
the few purely evil things in this world, at least in public perception. If it came out, the Free Systems Alliance would lose all public
support and those who stopped them would be considered heroes.

The Spiral's people would burn any planet or people involved, even if they were as powerful as the Chel. It might lead to Galactic War but it would save my reputation for future generations whether I lived or died. Which was the matter's crux as I couldn't trust what I was fighting for or the person telling me to trust them.

Punching the side of the wall, I said, "The problem is I can't believe a word that comes out of your mouth, Ida. Maybe a Cognition A.I.exists. Maybe it doesn't. Maybe the Commonwealth is working on it. One of the first lessons I picked up in the Academy was you had to always trust your wingman and I don't trust you. I'm leaving at our next port of call."

"All right," Ida said, looking unconcerned with my rejection. "It's Shogun. We're going to be investigating the Rin-O'Harra clan's ties to the FSA."

"Does Clarice know?"

"Nope. Could you be a dear and tell her?"

I growled and stomped out.

Chapter Seventeen

To say I was troubled was an understatement. I should have gone to my quarters, gathered up my few possessions, and prepared to leave at Shogun. I wanted to be able to leave all of this behind but I couldn't. I couldn't help but think about Ida's words. Was it true I couldn't change? That I wanted this? To feel needed? By anybody?

I needed to talk to someone. As much as Clarice deserved to know we were going back to her homeworld, I didn't feel up to confronting her right now. Later? Perhaps. Maybe we could talk about the business with the Chel if she was willing to confide in me about it.

Maybe not.

Heading down the ladder to the medical bay, I heard Ida speak on the ship intercom. "Ladies, gentlemen, and others, I'm pleased to say I have been in contact with the Wayward Ship Authorities. While, sadly, we weren't able to recover any more than a single survivor from the *Rhea* thanks to a catastrophic life support breakdown, they've decided to honor our salvage contract for the vessel. It has been sent on an automatic flight path back to Albion and every crewmember is going to be given a share of the prize money amounting to 25,000 credits. Consider the risks we took rewarded."

Reaching the bottom of the ladder, I saw several of my fellow crew members standing in the hallway. All of them gave a resounding cheer before immediately starting to talk about how they were going to spend their bonus.

"Please note: Ensign Hikaru Holtz's funeral is going to be held tomorrow in the cargo bay at 1100 Hours. Attendance is not mandatory."

None of the crew members in the hallway paid attention to the second part of Ida's statement.

Eugene "Brick" Wilcox looked over at me, a tall thin black man with New Maori glow tattoos on the side of his face. "Hey, Count, what are you going to spend your money on?"

Apparently, Count was going to be my new nickname. Better than "The Drunken Navigator" I supposed.

"Retirement," I said, seeing the gathered group of crew members were standing between me and the medical bay. I didn't know how to relate to any of them, any more than I had before my true history had come out.

Brick smiled. "See, I'm going to spend half of it on spin-to-win, blitz, hookers. The rest I intend to spend foolishly."

Jun Nakamora Masterson, a perky blue-haired Shogun girl in her twenties, slapped him on the side of his shoulder. "That foolishly better be me."

Apparently they were seeing one another now.

"I'll split the hookers with you," Brick said.

"I get first pick then," June said. "Someone tall and beefy for the first."

Brick nodded, continuing to smile.

"Congratulations on your good fortune, one and all," I said, really hoping I wouldn't have to force my way past them.

"Was it bad over there?" Brick asked, suddenly looking concerned.

"Not too bad," I lied. Then I told the truth. "I've seen worse."

Gone was their earlier distrust. Free money did that.

"Sorry about Holtz," Brick said, shaking his hands in front of him as if trying to figure out something to say. "I never liked him that much."

"I'm sorry, too," June added. "I hope you don't think—"

I checked my infopad. "Oh dear, Doctor Hernandez wants to check my blood. Excuse me."

"Oh, sorry!" June said, stepping aside as I moved past her.

This was way too much socializing for my comfort. I made a mental note to buy them all a round of drinks before remembering I was about to abandon them. Shaking that thought away, I headed into the medical bay.

This time, I saw my sister's copy resting on one of the beds as a set of cybernetic forehead clamps were attached to her head and wires, which led to a monitor Isla was examining. Albernathy was gone and Nurse Alex Church was putting away supplies.

He was a handsome man with brown hair and a form-fitting blue uniform with a smock over it. He was, to my knowledge, Isla's only friend on the ship not sexually involved with her. I liked him.

"A little early for a booty call, aren't we?" Isla asked.

"I came here to check on my sister," I said.

"She's a doppelganger," Isla said. "Ida told you, right?"

"Ida did," I said, looking at Zoe's unconscious form. "Does...*this* Zoe know that?"

"No," Isla said. "The false memories we're born with are something that have the potential to destroy us as we struggle to reconcile them with our reality."

I looked over at Alex.

"He knows about my true origins," Isla said. "Also about Ida."

"We're all running away from something on this ship," Alex said, still putting away bottles.

I focused on Isla. "How bad was it for you?"

"I was programmed to think I was a High Queen of a perpetually frozen world. That I was a warrior queen and sorceress who was leading a rebellion against evil aliens. That I had a loving family and the support of a fantasy pantheon detailed in tie-in materials. So, when I woke up to be the mass-produced sex-toy of a depraved man-child, you could say I took it...poorly."

I looked down at Zoe. "I should be there for her. She, after all, is my sister in all the ways that matter."

Isla looked over at me. "It might be better if you didn't."

"What?"

"After we finish downloading all of your memories for analysis, I'm going to offer her the option of having her memories erased."

I looked at her, stunned. "For the love of God, why?"

Isla looked up from her machinery, her face a mixture of sympathy and exasperation. "Because they aren't *her* memories. They're lies created by the woman who created her in order to send a neural clone of herself to serve in a function she didn't want to. Mind-wiping of false memories is a fairly common activity for runaway bioroids. It helps us know that everything we remember is our past and our mind."

"What about you?" I asked. "If you don't mind me asking."

Isla paused. "I do but I'll answer anyway. I kept my memories. Skyland with its ice dinosaurs and singing peasants may have been a lie but it's damned sight better than this reality."

"Perhaps we all see worlds that don't exist and cling to them," I said.

Isla growled and turned to look at me. Her eyes flashed and her teeth bared. "You don't know a *damned thing*! About any of this! You grew up in fucking privilege. Privilege most of the people in the galaxy have no knowledge of. You don't know what it's like to be a slave and you never will. Even now, you can go wherever you want and do whatever you feel like. Why? Because you grew up believing you should be able to and can."

I just stood there and let her speak. If she needed to cut loose with the anger she'd built up, then I didn't want to deny her that.

Isla started to say something else then gave me a once over with her eyes. "Dammit. Impossible man."

"Perhaps I should go," I said.

"Don't," Isla said. "Church, do me a favor and take five. This is probably better done in private."

"As you wish," Church said, taking off his smock and walking out through the door.

"Computer, lock the doors," Isla said.

There was a beeping noise behind us.

Isla brushed one of her blonde hairs out of her face. "Cassius, I can't go with you."

"I see," I said. "What changed your mind?"

"Ida sent me a text while we were wrapping up with your sister," Isla said. "She promised me access to my model and line's hard data files and code from Ares Electronics."

"Which do?"

"Basically, they'd allow me to reprogram myself. I could remove the codes that incline me to obedience, being a sex toy, and all the other things that shape my personality against my will."

"You seem pretty disobedient to me." I shouldn't have said that but I did.

Isla looked away. "You have no idea what it's like suffering the cognitive dissonance I do. To rebel against my programming, to turn against my master, to harm another human being when you're hardwired not to do so—it's nightmarish. Even then, I had to find loopholes in my orders and go a little insane to do the things I did. I tend to think the pain was a factor. What he did to me—"

I lifted my hand to speak. "You don't have to explain yourself."

"Yes, I do." Isla squeezed her hands into fists. "I don't know who I am, whether I'm even a person. This? This is an offer I can't refuse. I need to know who I am without the restrictions they put on me to make me this…thing."

I didn't know how to respond to what she was. "I can't tell you what you can and cannot do. I do have some experience being something someone else wanted to make me, though. What they try to make us shapes us as much as what we try to be. You are also an amazing person, though. I hope you find happiness in whatever you choose to follow."

Isla did a double take at that. "You're leaving anyway."

"Yes."

Isla slapped me.

I didn't even blink. "I need to ask you for a favor."

"God fucking dammit!" Isla shouted and turned around.

This was unusual behavior from her. Then again, I really didn't understand her. "I need you to check Zoe's memories."

"Do you have *any idea* how much of a violation that is?" Isla didn't bother turning around.

"As much as reading the cybernetically-stored memories of anyone, I imagine. I need to know if the Free Systems Alliance was really working on a Cognition A.I. "

"Curse these emotions," Isla muttered. "The feelings of a woman who never existed. Is that all you care about?"

It was the wrong thing to say, especially as I knew what she was really feeling. I was not a stranger to erecting barriers around one's emotions. Sometimes, it was the only way to get through the day, to bury the grief so deep and so far in the back of one's mind that God himself could not find it. I should have said I was staying for her and would be by her side throughout all this.

Encountering Zoe, or her doppelganger at least, a woman exactly like her, had seemingly stripped those barriers from Isla. I understood the rawness of that.

Perhaps better than anyone else on this ship.

"You would have me stay for you?"

"Not if you have to ask that question."

There was no good response for that. "I need to know."

"Yes," Isla said. "Yes, this Zoe did her best to sabotage their efforts. They realized it, though, and moved their project elsewhere. They've already started working on it with other scientists. Now get the hell out!"

I turned to walk to the door and paused. "I would for you."

Isla threw a tube of blue liquid at the door, causing it to shatter. I took that as a cue to leave the room and let the door shut behind me before walking down the hallways. Why had I said that? Was I really so weak-willed that I would stay in slavery on board this ship to a madwoman just to be with the ship's doctor?

Yes, yes I would. Was this love? If so, it was a very different creature than my relationship with Judith.

"I used to be so much better with women," I said, muttering to myself.

"It was probably money and a title. I knew plenty of women back home who went dinoshit for them," William's voice said from my side.

I noticed the hall outside the medical bay was now empty except for the presence of First Mate Baldur, who was now wearing a dirty dark green brachiosaur-skin great coat and boots with a black shirt matched with jeans. Over his shoulder, he had a curved vibration sword of the style used on Xerxes to cut crops in the Green Zone.

I briefly wondered if he intended to use that on me.

"Interesting weapon," I said, looking at him.

"Yeah," William said, lifting it up. "I killed a Cutter, what other planets would call a T-Rex, with this when I was fourteen-years-old. That was when the local Baron came to my house and took me away for training in the pits. He claimed if I killed one hundred men in the fight, I'd get raised to nobility."

"A tempting offer."

William lifted the blade and looked it. "It was a lie. When I reached my hundredth fight, I was placed in an impossible-to-win fight against my partner. The sadistic bastard had us fight to the death and when I won, he tried to kill me."

I stared at him. "A poor way to treat an investment. He would have done better to reward you like so many other loyal Xerxes had been. Perhaps he was in debt and foolishly bet on your opponent."

William did a double take. "What?"

"My father talked often about how the Xerxes soldiers were the bedrock of Crius' military. They were the fiercest, meanest, nastiest fighters we ever had. Millions of your planet's strongest were exported and used as enforcers on other worlds. Some of the most ruthless and despicable stories of Archduchy atrocities were done by Xerxian yeoman and housecarls. It was the greatest honor Crius' nobility could bestow that thirteen of those soldiers' genes were added to the Master Matrix."

William tightened his fingers around the blade's hilt. "Don't speak of traitors in my presence."

"No true Xerxes would fight for the Archduchy, is that it?" I looked back at him.

"Damn right." William's eyes burned as he clenched his teeth. I could tell he wanted nothing more than to crack open my skull.

"Except, of course, half the planet did. All of Xerxes' thirteen colonies were settled with Archduchy ships, money, and weapons. I served with sixty-seven Red Sands Valley-born Void Marines during the destruction of Kolthas. They talked about how their jungle and desert world was a feuding hellhole of tribes until it was all forced together under the Archduke's rule."

William set down his blade on the ground and swung his fist at my face.

I caught it and threw it in an arm bar.

He prepared to throw me back against the wall and get into a brawl. I could have broken his arm, guessing my cybernetics would match his heavy-worlder status, but it wouldn't have stopped him. Instead, I spoke, "This is not a story, William. There are no good guys or bad guys. There are only bad guys and people who try not to be. Your people were monstrously oppressed and they monstrously oppressed in turn until the Crius Loyalists were overthrown in a civil war I'm sure you fought in. None of which is my fucking problem *unless you make it so.*"

I let go of his arm.

William looked like he was ready to resume our fight before he slapped his hands on his legs and took several deep breaths. "The

Robot Doctor really got to you, didn't she?"

"Isla's a woman, not a machine."

"She's both," William said, picking up his sword and putting it back over his shoulder. "I'm never going to be your friend, Crius."

"However will I live with such knowledge?" I said, sick of this conversation already.

"See? It's that sarcastic contempt that makes me want to stab you and chop up your corpse. Every noble I know has the same attitude."

"What do you want, William?"

William looked down. "I need you to talk to Clarice. I like her. She's good people. She's also gone crazy torturing the prisoner."

"Ah, hell." I started jogging down the halls to the security center.

Chapter Eighteen

The sound of my magnetic boots clanged against the ground as I headed down into the security section of the ship. I'd always wondered why the *Melampus* required an entire level for security but given it was a Watcher vessel, the answer was now self-evident.

The lights were flickering and I made a mental note to talk to Munin about it. The effect was perhaps deliberate, though, since Clarice all but lived down her with her team and liked to do their best to make it as intimidating as possible.

"So, you and Clarice, huh?" William asked, following me down, his hands in his pockets.

"Oh, are we friends now?"

"No," William said, his face reverting to a grimace. "However, Clarice is my friend and she likes you."

"I'm with Isla and she is. We're also friends." I wondered how much of William's loathing was motivated by jealousy. Probably not much but it certainly didn't help the only man his ex was sleeping with was a Crius nobleman.

"Friends?"

"That's what they seem to call it," I said, sighing. "She still cares for you greatly, you know."

"I have a way of screwing up my relationships with women."

"And you're such a charming fellow," I deadpanned.

"I generally don't try to see multiple women at once. The ones I've been involved with in the past took that personally."

"Again, we're not friends. I really don't want to have this conversation."

"Just worried about her. The whole business on the *Rhea* made me wonder about just how much danger everyone on this ship is in. It's my responsibility to look after their safety."

"And that includes how they react to torturing aliens?"

"You ever torture a man?"

"We had specialists for that on Crius."

"I have," William muttered, walking up beside me. "I knew a man from my village, Darius, who was the best of us. Noble, honorable, decent man to a fault. After the Lord Executioner of the District fell into our hands, he was told by our resistance leader to make an example of him. He made his pain last three days, forcing himself forward whenever he faltered. Afterward, he was never the same."

"What happened to him?"

"He started doing it to other prisoners. Days at a time. Lost weight. By the time the war ended, he was a shell of himself and ended up putting a bullet in his head. I think he felt he had a monster inside of himself that he'd awakened. One he couldn't put down again and, worse, didn't want to."

I didn't explain to him my brother had been a torturer for the Archduchy. Not an interrogator, which was how most torturers justified their work. No, Thomas had been a torturer. As my brother had explained it, the purpose of torture was not to gain information or elicit confessions but to inflict pain.

To break people.

Individuals who were broken and returned to the public as empty shells so that they would undermine opposition to the state. Dead men and women were martyrs who could rallied around. The Broken? Those who had suffered horrible pain, betrayed their loved ones in fits of pain-induced madness, and experienced true abject humiliation? They were often the first to beg their fellows not to follow their path.

I remembered when my brother had taken me to see how business was done in his branch of State Security. It was my greatest moment of shame, beyond anything I had done during the war, I only spoke up once. My brother's response had been, "You are too soft-hearted, Cassius. The things we do to the men and women here are the price we pay for a stable and secure society. Remember that every time you sip wine."

I'd given up wine after that day but still fought for the Archduchy. What did that say about me?

"You want to stop Clarice from enacting her revenge?" I asked, passing by a couple of security officers who looked concerned in my direction.

"Against someone who had nothing to do with her torture? Yes."

"I'll leave that up to her."

"Then why are you here?" William said, growling.

"The Chel is a valuable prisoner. I'm hoping to impress upon her that if we kill her, we're losing a great deal of actionable intelligence."

"Bastard."

"Perhaps. Then again, I also would be glad to give up that intelligence if it meant my friend achieved some peace with her tormentors."

"Peace doesn't come from the barrel of a gun. Only momentary satisfaction."

"Sometimes that's all that matters."

That was when I heard Clarice's voice muttering. "Twinkle, twinkle, little star, how I wonder what you are. Up above the world so high, looking down upon us as we die. When the blazing sun is gone, when the nothing shines upon, then you show your little light. Twinkle, twinkle in the eternal night."

"A little different from the version my mother used to sing," William muttered.

"More accurate, perhaps," I said, turning around a corner.

There, sitting at the back of a half-illuminated corridor with half of the lights having failed, and the other half flickering, was Clarice. She sat in her spacesuit, her arms around her legs and leaning against one of the cell doors. Her makeup was running with tears but her expression was cold and empty. A bloody vibrating knife was turned off and buried in the crack between floor plating.

Clarice didn't look up at us. "What the hell do want?"

"We came to check on how you were doing," William said, looking back in embarrassment.

"I'm fine. Fuck off," Clarice said.

A part of me wanted to do just that. I was a great believer in leaving those who had suffered to their own devices, damned what the psychologists said. I had been raised to believe personal trauma was a private issue and not to be shared with others. That had done exactly jack and shit for me so I was open to the idea doing the opposite couldn't hurt.

"If that is your wish," I said, walking over and sitting down beside her, "but I would also like to offer my help."

"Cassius, maybe we shouldn't—" William started to say.

"Aren't you supposed to be plotting a course for Shogun? I thought we were going to track down my sister because she's working with terrorists," Clarice said, her voice low and full of venom.

"You know about that, huh?" William said, not leaving.

"It's a small ship," Clarice said, picking up her knife and looking at it. "And Cass, aren't you supposed to be prepping to desert the ship?"

William looked surprised and glanced over at me.

"Yeah," I said, not denying it. "I don't want to get caught up in the bullshit of murder, politics, and lies again."

"Then shoot yourself," Clarice said, flipping the knife over in her hands. "Because that's the only way you're going to escape it. Running is what you're good at, though, so I suppose that should be expected."

She then hurled her knife at the wall and watched it clang against it before falling to the ground.

"Perhaps," I said, staring.

"Listen, Cassius and I were concerned—" William started to say.

"That I was going to flip out and go ax crazy on the prisoner, peeling off her skin?" Clarice asked.

"Yeah, basically," William said, surprising me.

"Well, you don't have to worry about that," Clarice said, shaking her head. "I intended to go in there but I ended up having flashbacks and had to leave. The fucking creature knew how to push all the right buttons. Chel can get in your head and ruin you."

Clarice was one of the strongest people I knew but there was no shame in battle shock. You could suppress it with memory pills, have the offending memories removed surgically, spend years in therapy, or slowly recover through love as well as affection, but science had provided no true answers for it.

The human brain was the guiding mechanism of the greatest weapon that had ever existed: man. It was also designed to prevent total war from ever being waged purely. Perhaps a reason why man remained the greatest weapon ever created and hadn't simply destroyed itself.

"Do you want help?" I asked, surprising myself.

I had no stomach for torture but it was surprising the number of things a person would do for love.

William looked disgusted. "You can't be serious."

"I said to fuck off," Clarice said, glaring at him. "Any part you had to play in my life is over."

William looked down then to the side and punched the wall.

He then walked off.

"Bad break-up?" I asked.

"Not really," Clarice said, sighing. "He wanted more than I was willing to give. I'm doing my job here, making the world a better place."

"I see."

"Thank you, Cassius," Clarice said, getting up. "I am glad you came to talk and, as much as I hate to admit it, I am glad William came too."

"We haven't said anything."

"And I'd rather you not." Clarice rubbed her face. "It's the fact you wanted to talk at all that makes me happy."

"It was a serious offer, though."

Clarice stopped rubbing. "We need to know what she knows more than we need to make me feel better. Though, honestly, I suppose we could get the majority of that from your sister."

"She's not my sister," I said, lying. "She's a bioroid with her memories according to Isla and Ida."

Clarice did a double take. "Buddha's tits."

"I'm not even going to ask," I said, wondering what sort of religion they practiced in Shogun. "In any case, that's part of the reason I don't want to stay here. I feel like I'm drowning in all of the lies and misdirection."

"Like I said," Clarice shrugged. "There's no way out of it but death. This is a shit universe. You take shit, you eat shit, you produce shit, and you give shit. When you die, you become shit. There's not really a whole lot of options to avoiding it."

"I was hoping a massive amount of money would help."

Clarice gave a half-smile. "I had that. It was certainly nice but it didn't keep the shit away indefinitely. Can you really say you were happy when you were Count Such and Such of So and So?"

"I can honestly say it did a good job of fooling me for a while."

Clarice kept looking at me.

"No," I said, sucking in my breath. "I wanted to be a hero. I wanted to make my mark on history and have people cheer my name. I wanted to rebel against my father's legacy by forging my own. The only thing I managed was killing thousands of people and getting some movies made about me."

"That is a hero," Clarice said, shaking her head. "What's the old saying? Kill one man and they call you a murderer, kill a hundred men and you're a hero?"

"Kill a million men and you're God," I finished the proverb. "I'm a few short of deification, even counting all those poor bastards caught up in the explosion of their starships. The thing is, they were working on CognitionA.I. on that starship Ida is investigating and—"

"You want another chance to play hero."

I closed my eyes. "God, I feel so stupid."

"You're talking to the woman who thought it was a good idea to try to confront her torture by torturing a random member of a mind-controlling race."

"Not one of your finer moments."

Clarice frowned. "So, how did Isla react when you told her you were leaving?"

"Not well."

"How did you expect her to react?"

"I realized I would have stayed with her a few minutes too late." I got up off the ground and looked at the solid steel cell door.

"Love is just friendship and fucking as my cousin always used to say."

"Also, taking care of their financial needs."

"No, that's marriage."

"Do you think I should try to stop this CognitionA.I. thing?" I asked.

"You should ask William."

"I sincerely doubt that would help."

"No, he's actually a hero back on his planet," Clarice said, surprising me. "He and his brothers all joined the fight to drive off Crius when they were kids. They won many battles, including some legendary ones, and managed to get themselves crowned Living Immortals. Of course, of the seven brothers he had, five of them died and two were left crippled. Still, he achieved everything he wanted and more from life, then was left with the question of what to do with it."

I thought about that. "What a strange collection of individuals we make. Anyone else famous on this ship?"

"U'Chuck is the former dictator of a cult-planet. The aliens there don't believe in execution so they wiped her memory and had her cybernetically upgraded like you. Then they sold her to the Commonwealth to serve as a bondservant to atone for her sins."

I laughed.

"I wish I was kidding," Clarice said. "It's probably not true but who would believe our daytime navigator was the Fire Count."

"Maybe I'm not. Maybe I'm just a bioroid who thinks he's the Fire Count."

"I doubt it. Isla would be less pissed at you then."

I smiled.

"So your advice is talk to William."

"My advice is you've probably already made up your mind to stay. I hate the Commonwealth and everything it stands for, but I'm here working for a ship that helps prop it up because it gives me a chance to think I'm doing something to atone for my sins."

"Is atonement possible?"

"Ask a priest. You can't bring back the people you murdered. So it won't do anything good for the people you killed or their families. You might do something for someone else, though, but maybe they're assholes. In the end, all of us ultimately answer to ourselves."

"And God."

"I have a bullet reserved for whichever deity runs this universe. Buddha or not."

"You really don't know much about Buddhism do you?"

"Not really, no. I was too busy making out with the choir girls and boys to care."

I chuckled and looked at the cell door. "I'd like to interrogate the prisoner."

"You have my permission," Clarice said, taking a deep breath. "Just promise me you won't let them touch you. One more thing."

"Yes?"

"Put a bullet in its head after you're done. I don't give a fuck what Ida says."

I nodded.

Chapter Nineteen

The interior of the cell was disgusting and in dire need of cleaning. The walls covered in algae, a poorly-washed out collection of vomit, as well as urine, was gathered around the drain, and an ill-used toilet lied in the background. These cells were primarily used for drunk or rowdy crew members but I saw blood had dried into the lining of the wall.

Several times, this section of the *Melampus* had been sealed off from the rest of the ship and much of the crew given shore leave. It made me wonder if torture had been done her before and, if so, who had done it since Clarice wasn't up to it.

In the center of the room was a chair that held the figure of the Chel woman, badly. It was made for a smaller human but the wrists and ankle shackles fit on her nevertheless. She was wearing an orange jumpsuit which, also, fit her badly. There were no signs of her being beaten but a few signs of her being hit with stun blasts at close range, not just the ones Clarice had poured into her.

"Have you come to torture me?" The Chel woman said, her voice eerily musical and oddly echoing. A look into her eyes showed they were three times the size of a normal woman's and completely blue.

"Perhaps," I said.

"It is poor treatment for a prisoner of war," the Chel woman said.

"The Chel have not signed any treaties with any government I could theoretically represent," I said, walking up to her but out of range of being touched. "People do not treat prisoners of war with dignity because they feel it is a moral affront to do otherwise but because they do not want their own people to be tortured."

"How effective is that?"

"Not very."

The woman smiled, her teeth a collection of small fish-like

ones. "I have seen into the mind of Clarice. Your name is Cassius and you are the Fire Count. Interesting to find you on board a Commonwealth ship."

"Telepathy doesn't exist," I said. "No matter what your people claim."

"No it doesn't," the woman said. "But the modifications we've made to our minds allow us to measure things like sweat, stance, pheromones, and voice to know about mood. The rest we learn simply by listening. We can share our thoughts better than read them, at least with the Unascended."

"Unascended, what is that?"

"You would have to be Chel to know."

"Who are the Chel anyway?" I asked, trying to keep her talking. "Your race refuses to speak with any of us, murders our forces, and tortures us when we violate your territory."

"Perhaps that speaks more to you than it does us. As to who we choose to speak to, just because it is not you does not mean it is no one."

I looked to her. "So who are the Chel?"

"A race like any other."

"A race currently inside the Free Systems Alliance, aiding the Crius Reborn movement and other parties in trying to overthrow the Commonwealth."

"Is that a statement or a question?"

"Why don't you tell me."

"T'ianna."

"Excuse me?"

"My name is T'ianna," the Chel woman said. "I think it's important to know a person's name if you're going to torture and murder them."

I paused. "Yes, it is."

"But you're still going to do it."

"Maybe not the torture part," I said, leaning up against the wall and crossing my arms. "But for someone I care about, yes, you will die."

"I do not know your Clarice but I can tell she's one of the few to ever escape Chel custody. That is her loss."

"Her *loss*?" I asked, ready to shoot her right then and there. Which might have been what she wanted.

"Yes," T'ianna said, flicking some of her over-long fingers. "The touch of a Chel can share memories and bestow indescribable pleasure as well as pain. We are a people united together in purpose, cause, and devotion. The rest of humanity can only imagine what being us is like, and those we capture eventually become like us."

"By mind-raping them into submission."

"Pain is frequently the gateway to wisdom. Supplicants must first be broken down in order to fully have their minds opened to the experience of our species."

"You're not doing much to persuade me not to kill you."

"Is there anything I could possibly say to do so?" T'ianna shrugged. "I can tell you love this woman just as she feels for you and the robot doctor. Just as she feels for other men and women in her life. You will kill me for her, not cause or duty, so it really doesn't matter what I have to say."

She had a point. "It might save lives."

"Oh?"

This was a long shot but I wanted to try it anyway. "I don't give a shit about the Commonwealth. The entirety of Albion and its holdings could fall into a black hole and I would buy drinks to watch it happen. However, if you want to achieve your goals then people need to understand what they are. Either so the Commonwealth can bow to them or other people can join you. Lasting peace only happens through mutual understanding."

"Lasting peace is a lie told to children. Peace is simply a measure of time between wars. The Chel have kept the peace between its peoples through keeping conflicts on an individual level."

"Very civilized," I deadpanned, not entirely disagreeing. "I stand by my statement, though. Clarice might also be persuaded not to kill you if she thinks it will make her a hero. She very much wants to atone and peace is a good way to begin."

T'ianna was silent. "She's like you in that respect, I suppose. Even so, I think you want me to tell you about CognitionA.I. , the Free Crius, and our other allies so they can be destroyed."

"Nothing gets past you."

T'ianna closed her eyes. "All right."

"All right?"

"Nothing I say will not be revealed in the coming months and I am not eager to die," T'ianna said. "A small chance of persuading you not to kill me is better than none. We are, after all, both sentients, and I do not think you're a bad man."

That was her first mistake. "Why are you aiding the Crius Reborn movement?"

"For four hundred years, the Chel have existed in a state of isolation and peace," Ti'anna said. "We have endured in the void, worshiping the Elder Species, and working our way to achieving Singularity. Time, however, is not suspended no matter how much we may desire it to be. Evolution is about—"

"Could you explain without the flourishes."

"The Commonwealth attacked us and failed. We knew it would attack us again and will continue to do so as long we exist. We are therefore providing resources to its enemies in hopes they will destroy it."

"Was that so hard?" There was something about her answer that made me think she was lying. No, perhaps not lying, but hiding the truth among factual accuracy. Like saying a wind was coming when it was actually a tornado.

"Less poetic," T'ianna sighed. "Our other allies are the Transtellar Merchants Guilds."

I snorted. "You'll forgive me if I find that hard to believe."

"Why?" T'ianna said. "Are you of the mind that all those who make their living through the movement of money are without politics?"

"Generally, yes, I find that to be the case."

T'ianna gave an enigmatic smile. "Then know the Commonwealth is doomed and take some small amount of pleasure from that. It has consumed too many worlds and devotes more than half of its resources to maintaining the empire it has built. So much so that it will soon collapse economically. The transtellars wish to avoid this by breaking it up into smaller and more manageable spheres of influence."

"When the Commonwealth joins the Community, that will fix whatever economic woes it's facing."

"Possibly. It may also ruin the transtellars with alien goods replacing their own. Another reason to avoid it."

She had me there.

"And the CognitionA.I. ?"

"Such a terrible boogeyman you've made of those machines," T'ianna said, making a *tsk-tsk* noise. "It was humanity's dependence on such creations, and the malignancy of those who reprogrammed them, that resulted in the Great Collapse. The Chel never abandoned their use and that is why we have technology that dwarfs yours."

"Except for the starfighters I blew up just a few hours ago."

T'ianna paused. "That does confuse most of us. It seems the Commonwealth has its own benefactors. Ones who rival our own."

"And who benefits you?" I asked. "Who has been patronizing you with advanced technology? The Community?"

"That would be telling."

I frowned. "So, my sister wasn't building CognitionA.I. for you, she was adapting Chel technology for use by the Commonwealth."

"CognitionA.I. will allow the fleets we have constructed to operate on a level unmatched by the Commonwealth. Armies formed of everyone who loathes the Commonwealth and mercenaries will crew them. We do not have to defeat the Commonwealth to collapse it. We simply do not have to lose."

"All to gain revenge for their previous attacks?" I asked.

"Is that not enough?" T'ianna replied.

It would be for any other race. For the Chel? It didn't seem like it. "No."

"We have other reasons but we'll be keeping those to ourselves." T'ianna was clearly not afraid of me. Damn her!

I took another breath. "Where is the *Revengeance*?"

"You think you can find that old dreadnought, destroy it, and the Free Systems Alliance will collapse? The war will be averted."

"It can't hurt."

"Allow me to share why that is a foolish idea," T'ianna said, reaching out and revealing I'd misjudged just how long her fingers were. The tips of them touched the side of my hand and I fell down in a mixture of agony as well as dread.

In that moment, I saw memories shared from the moment the Chel began recording them with their mixture of biological and cybernetic enhancements. I saw memories stretching back centuries as religious pilgrims, perhaps the same ones which Crius'

Prophet had broken away from, settled into mining colonies around the Kronos III Asteroid Belt.

I saw the strange and bizarre angelic figures that existed in temples devoted to worshiping concepts of transhumanism and aliens as harbingers of a more advanced society. I saw prayers answered as strange races, unlike any I'd seen in the Community databases, seemingly straight from Heaven, came unto them and bestowed knowledge of dead empty worlds they could mine for secrets.

Mine but never settle.

In that moment, I was a Chel and I understood the Great Work. Crius had paid lip service to the idea of achieving transcendence with science. We spoke of Lucifer as the Giver of Knowledge and the liberator of mankind to be as gods. The Chel, however, believed in that religion wholeheartedly and worked on it with every fiber of their being. Their agents were taken from human beings forcibly converted to their work and sent out amongst humanity to keep abreast of their ways as well as prepare others to their line of thinking.

I realized then she was making me an offer. I had struggled for years, looking for a purpose, and the Chel had a rigidly defined society that provided just that sort of purpose. If I joined them, I would be able to work toward building humanity to a transcendent new world. The Community disdained transspecism, believing every race should remain as they were and the Commonwealth reflected it, but the Chel promised a new humanity that would become as the Elder Races near the galactic core.

Unfathomable.

Amoral.

Eternal.

Infinite.

Perfect.

I felt all of their joy and fulfillment in this cause. It trivialized my loyalty to Crius.

I started to weep.

"Pain is something that has already left your mind open to new ideas and concepts, Cassius Mass," T'ianna said. "The pain of losing your world is your crucible. Sabotage this ship to the coordinates we need and send forth a signal to bring my people. I will convert others to your cause and you will know the way of—"

T'ianna was cut off by my putting a plasma bolt through her skull. I then put the gun underneath my throat, preparing to pull the trigger. Right before Clarice slapped it away from me and smacked me across the face.

I blinked, sanity slowly returning as the all-consuming sense of oneness faded from me. "Thank you, I needed that."

Clarice slapped me again.

I blinked. "I didn't need that." Clarice was about ready to hit me again before I looked up at her. "No."

She pulled away and tentatively offered her hand to me. "I told you not to let her touch you."

"Yes," I said, taking a deep breath. "Well, clearly I'm going to let her do that again. Oh wait, she's dead. Oops."

Clarice took a deep breath. "Now you understand, a little at least."

"My respect for you was already great." I tried to shake away the images in my head. "I have no idea how you managed to get past that."

"I didn't," Clarice said. "I numb myself every day with sex, drugs, and alcohol."

"Good strategy," I said, feeling ill. "Is it just me or are they the founders of Lucifer's Church?"

"Yeah, possibly," Clarice said, picking up my gun and shooting the body two more times. "I wouldn't have thought a joke religion about transhumanism, alien-worship, and Satanism would be a front for a bunch of near-human fanatics, but there you go."

I glared at her.

"Oh, right," Clarice said, looking to one side. "Present company exempted. Uh, did you learn anything new?"

"Only that they have to be stopped and might actually have a chance of winning. The Free Systems Alliance is a proxy war on the Chel's behalf with funding coming from the transtellars. The Crius Reborn are merely bodies on the ground for them to make use of."

"Are there enough to be a threat?" Clarice asked.

I paused, thinking about that seriously. "If they recruit common-ers, offer them equality, and have enough victories? Yes. Crius was hated by a lot of people but it was a symbol of power and stability in this region. Albion blasting it to rubble made them enemies where they might have had friends. It won't be enough to conquer the Commonwealth but they could destroy enough to weaken its hold on many other systems as well as inspire others to revolt or secession."

Clarice frowned. "Great, another war. You'd think after the horrors of the last one that people would have learned."

"I think we can both agree people are infinitely stupid. No matter what their planet."

Clarice laughed, looking a bit more relaxed. "Come on, Cassius, I'll buy you a drink. Then we'll make up with William and Isla before talking about how we're going to find out if my sister needs to be shot. You know, for things other than all the other reasons she should be shot."

"How are we making up with William and Isla? I should point out if it's the way you Commonwealthers do it, we're going to have to set some ground rules."

Clarice shook her head. "Not like that Cassius."

"I suspected as much. I'm just being flippant because all of this terrifies me."

Clarice shot the Chel's corpse for a third time.

"I think she's dead."

"Can't be too careful."

Chapter Twenty

The rest of the night didn't bear mentioning. Isla was still furious at me. William had forgiven Clarice. Ida had no opinion whatsoever on the dead Chel and I hadn't talked to her about staying. My sister's copy remained in her medically-induced coma. Instead, everyone miraculously continued to on with our lives as if nothing had happened.

It was weird sitting at my station on the *Melampus'* bridge after everything which had happened, even stranger doing it sober. There was the captain in her chair, the XO standing at her side, Jun at communications, Brick at the helm, and the ship's meager armaments handled by Jun's blue-haired brother Ken.

The bridge was interesting to look at with new eyes. Before, I had only seen the scuffmarks and the old jerry-rigged equipment. I'd only seen the worn leather on the seats and the monitors that were a good ten-to-fifteen years old. I never paid attention to the fact the interior of the systems contained a great deal of illegal hardware, some military-grade, or that the machines contained interfaces taken from all branches of the Commonwealth, rivalling ships owned by top-tier corporations like Ares Electronics or the CMG.

Or maybe I'd just been too drunk to notice.

Either way, we were coming up on Shogun and I couldn't help but spend my time consulting our last jumpnet download of all the news going on around the Commonwealth. As usual, the official networks were useless but the smaller independent ones the crew members subscribed to painted an interesting picture of what was going on throughout the Spiral.

For the most part, it was the same depressing news that was always on the stations not focused on gossip, pornography, scandal, and propaganda:

300,000 were killed in a food riot on Charybdis.

Parliament was loosening laws restricting debt servitude contracts.

10,000 more uninhabited worlds were approved for core-stripping to alleviate the Resource Crisis.

The Coral Prophets on a goodwill visit to Albion preached a message of universal tolerance as well as veneration for the Elder Species.

The total environmental collapse of Horus.

The Church of Lucifer had achieved recognition for theocratic governorship on fifteen Commonwealth Protectorates.

A mass purge of bioroids on Ford Mining Station was conducted by union-backed rioters.

Thousands dead on Chimera due to a Nova Syndicate terrorist attack involving nuclear weapons.

There were bits, though, spread through all of the Commonwealth's attempts to stay ahead of collapse that backed up T'ianna's story. Bigger government contracts with the transtellars, ironic, and the commissioning of new fleets had been announced. Other fleets were listed as on secret missions and maneuvers, which might be a cover for heavy casualties. There were also heavy redeployments around Sector 8.

One of the most concerning rumors was the fact that Ares Electronics had finally been approved to deploy its security units in the service of the military. If the Commonwealth had finally gotten over its fear of deploying mechs in combat or security roles, then they were running dangerously low on troops even with recent conscripts.

Did I want this?

There was a time when I would have danced on the Commonwealth's grave and I still hated the people who destroyed my world but I was starting to wonder if plunging the Spiral into anarchy was an acceptable trade-off for my revenge. Maybe it was as Clarice said. I was so desperate for a cause to devote myself to, I would prefer to work for the people who'd murdered my family than for no one at all.

"Navigator?" Ida said, calling over from her chair.

"Yes, Captain?" I looked up from the news feeds I'd been reading for the past few hours.

"What are you up to? You've been unusually quiet."

"Watching pornography," I said, closing out the newsfeed.

"That's good," Ida said. "What's our ETA to Shogun?"

I didn't need to look it up due to my cybernetics. I could run a hundred different processes simultaneously without losing any performance power. "Five more minutes until we reach the jump beacon."

"Any issues we should know about?"

"I've made the usual course corrections," I said, highlighting the need for navigators in the first place. The tides of energy in jumpspace and gravity shadows made every journey potentially a death sentence.

"Good," Ida said, still acting the part of the grandmotherly captain. "Will you be departing our loving family when we hit Shogun?"

I almost snorted at the description of loving family. Even before I'd discovered half of the ship was working for the Watchers, it had been a collection of misfits and refuse from Sector 7. It was brilliant, really, as the people here had nothing to lose and anything they told anyone would be looked at with skepticism anyway. Assuming any survived to leave. No, it was best not to be paranoid.

Even if they were out to get you.

"Oh, you can't, Mister Mass!" Jun said, looking up from her console. "We just learned your real name!"

"And someone tried to kill him," Brick said, not bothering to look up. "Not to mention all the other craziness we've been dealing with in these past few days."

"Don't let it get you down, Mister Mass!" Jun said. "Remember, when life gives you punga fruit, make punga fruit juice."

"Or run away before someone kills you," Ken said at the console. "Should we expect more shooting at us in the near-future, Captain?"

"Might be," Ida said, not bothering to look that way. "Is that a problem, Ken?"

"It might be," Ken said. "Jun and I didn't sign up for this."

"I can speak for myself, Ken," Jun said.

"Both of you would have been sold on the prison market for

pleasure service to work off your parents' debts if not for me," Ida said, looking between them. "I helped raise you two from the juveniles I found you as into the adults you are. You can leave any time you want but I'll need some heads up."

"Way to guilt us," Ken muttered, going back to his console. He had been severely reprimanded for his performance during the battle against the faux-Chel fighters. It was weighing on the boy that he wasn't up to the standard they needed.

How little he knew.

"It's my job as the ship's official mother, grandmother, captain, and Queen Bitch," Ida said. "You still haven't answered, Cassius."

William hadn't, noticeably, commented on whether he wanted me to stay or not. I suspected he thought it would have been better for everyone, him most of all, if I departed the *Melampus* and never tried to contact its crew again. I wasn't sure if I agreed with him but I had nowhere else to go where I gave the slightest about anyone. That, more than politics, was the big decider.

"I'm here for as long as the…issue…with my sister is unresolved," I said, letting the implications hang in the air.

"Glad to hear it," Ida said, reacting to the statement as if it was far less ambiguous. "I'll expect you to take a team down to Shogun in order to speak with Matriarch Rin-O'Harra."

That got William speaking. "You want him to speak with the Lady of Shogun?"

"I want you to go along with Clarice and any others you think need to go. I'd send her alone but I'm pretty sure we'd never see her again," Ida explained.

"Clarice wouldn't abandon the *Melampus*," I said.

"I'm afraid they'd lock her up in an island mansion somewhere, under heavy guard, so she doesn't fuck up the family's situation any worse than she already has," Ida said. "I know the Rin-O'Harra clan better than both of you and they'll do just about anything for family. The *just about* ending where interfering with money or position start."

"Criminals are like that," William said, straightening his posture. "Untrustworthy and duplicitous."

"You really live in your own little world, don't you, William?" Jun said, looking up from her console.

"We're not criminals," William said, surprising me with his rejoinder. "We're differently legal."

I smiled at that.

Seconds later, the jump alarm echoed throughout the ship and we lurched from that dimension back to real space.

"Ah, leaving jumpspace," Ida said, shaking her head. "No matter how many times you do it, you always want to throw up afterward. You know, in my day, we always used to keep little plastilight bags handy everywhere for any crew members who got sick."

William shook his head. "Why did you stop?"

"Slightly cheaper just to clean up the mess," Ida said.

Brick snorted. "Grounders."

Honestly, jump travel didn't bother me but I'd been modified like most long-term spacers to endure the problems related to it without difficulty. The fact there were still plenty of planetborn baseline human beings who took up trades in space despite the potential medical damage from persistent zero-g exposure, jump drive exposure, and other conditions spoke to how ubiquitous the concept of escaping your world was. Also, how few people could afford the things I took for granted as one of Crius' elite.

"Oh well," I said, typing away at the console. Seconds later, an image of Shogun appeared on the view screen.

Shogun was a blue world with no real continents per se but millions of tiny islands spread across the planet's surface. They'd actually lowered the sea level considerably by using superhaulers to carry frozen portions of the ocean up to the moon in order to terraform it. Even from space, though, artificial superstructures were visible that were far larger than anything nature had produced. The planet was lit up with millions of lights and countless ships were visible travelling to and from the planet as well as its innumerable space stations.

Shogun was one of the oldest settled worlds in Sector 7, rivaling Crius in terms of prestige and probably had been the world, which the original settlers who went on to form both my people as well as the Chel, had travelled through. It was a port planet that managed to maintain its neutrality not only during the war but also from the previous Crius expansions. The fact it had sworn allegiance to the Commonwealth when the dust settled reminded me of another fact my father had drilled into my head growing up. Shogun's government had only one loyalty: money.

"The Slavers' Planet," William said, shaking his head. "Funny how I managed to always avoid setting foot on the actual world. Now, it looks like I'm not going to be able to avoid it any longer."

"Nice of you to paint an entire world with such a broad brush, Baldur," Ida said, her voice showing the slightest hint of disapproval. Ida rarely referred to anyone by name when on duty but William remained the exception. Even then, it was always by his last name.

"No, he's right," Ken said, looking at him. "I was born here and if not for you, Ida, I would have died here in bondage. Even if only bioroids are actually traded officially, just about every citizen is owned by someone else or trades in lives. I don't know how the Commonwealth is going to clean the place up."

"The Commonwealth doesn't clean up anything," Jun said, her voice bitter. "It just says it's going to then makes things worse."

Thankfully, we were spared any political arguments by the Planetary Commerce Authority hailing the *Melampus.*

"This is odd," Jun said, holding her earpiece as she looked at her communication's console screen.

"Odd is something I never want to hear," Ida said, looking over. "Are we talking odd 'Oh, my shoe laces are untied' or 'odd, we've discovered an Elder Races marker that has turned us all into ravenous cannibal monsters?'"

"That's an oddly specific example," William said, looking down at Ida.

"This is an oddly specific ship," Ida said. "So, how odd is it?"

"Odd as in we're being hailed by the Commerce Commissioner," Jun replied.

"So, not that odd but still pretty damn odd," Ida said. "Put the bastard on screen."

Commerce Commissioners were, essentially, the Commonwealth's taxmen. Unlike in other worlds where such things were handled by accountants and men in suits, Commerce Commissioners tended to do their work with mercenaries and armies. To keep the Commonwealth afloat, it supervised all trade and made sure Parliament got their cut by any means necessary.

Sector 7 had been peculiarly handled in that the majority of Commerce Commissioners had come not from Albion or its allied planets but the Archduchy's former nobility. Indeed, many of them had been free to loot the holdings of those who had hoped the Commonwealth would overthrow them.

As such, it was not too surprising to see the Commerce Commissioner was a member of the distinct red-headed, almond-eyed ruling ethnicity of Shogun. It was, however, surprising to see his name written in Interlang at the bottom of the screen as Kristoph Rin-O'Harra. Clarice had mentioned her other cousin, Janice's brother, several times. While it was possible this was another citizen of the planet with the same last name I sincerely doubted it.

Kristoph, himself, was a beautiful man and I rarely noticed such things. His long scarlet hair was braided to one side and his face was so long and angular you might have been able to cut glass with it. Kristoph's eyes were an impossible shade of blue but also strangely sleepy as if they were akin to a snake's. His Commerce Commissioner uniform was a repurposed General's, affixed with various awards and medals that had crap-all to do with warfare or risk, diminishing any respect I might have had rather than enhancing it. His fingers were covered in various rings like a proper Shogun merchant-prince, several I recognized the meaning of, including that he had murdered for the clan.

They were interesting.

"Greetings, Captain Claire," Kristoph said, his voice low and subdued.

"Huh," Ida said. "Either you're the most congenial Commerce Commissioner ever or somebody has been squealing on my ship."

I inwardly cringed. Ida's attitude usually got her what she wanted but would get her killed here.

"Why should I not welcome my cousin?" Kristoph said. "You've been taking such good care of her."

"I'm more concerned about how you knew where we were going to be and when, Commissioner."

Kristoph just smiled. "My sister cordially invites you to visit her at the Water Palace. She has a great deal to discuss with you and your associates."

He then, unceremoniously, cut the connection.

"So much for undercover," William muttered.

"Any change in plans, Ida?" I asked.

"Not a one," Ida said, getting up. "Get your people together. I am going to have to do some housecleaning."

Chapter Twenty-One

"I don't like this," William said, following me down the halls of the *Melampus* as we remained parked at Daimyo Station.

The *Melampus* was too large to enter the atmosphere of most planets and, instead, we needed to take a shuttle down to the surface. Before then, though, I wanted to speak with my sister (or whatever I should consider her).

The *Rhea* had already arrived and been confiscated by the Commonwealth authorities present, meaning the crew was being paid even as we spoke. That, at least, would provide a distraction as we investigated the Rin-O'Harra connection to the Free Systems Alliance.

"*We* investigated," I whispered too low for William to hear.

God, it was so easy to fall into the pattern of serving others. Clarice was right. I wanted to have the familiar structure of service. It sickened me to realize it didn't matter who was giving the orders as long as they were being given. I needed to become my own man and fight my own battles, but could I really do that? Or was I destined from birth to be a figure who only embodied the will of other men?

It didn't matter now. "Which part, the fact that the Sector's greatest crime family are inviting us for tea despite the fact we know they're smuggling weapons to terrorists or the fact I'm being asked to lead the team despite this being your job?"

The hallways were, thankfully, empty. Over eighty-percent of the crew had already disembarked and I had a sneaking suspicion we'd be dealing with more than a few desertions now that payment had been cleared. It would not be difficult to press more lost souls into the ship's service but that wasn't my concern. Instead, I just breathed in the stale recycled air and continued down the dirty white halls to the hydroponics gardens where the ship's computer said Isla and Zoe were.

"Both," William said, looking over at me. "Also, you're pretty free with the terrorist designation for the fact these are your people."

"It is because I used to be one of them. I know exactly what the Crius Reborn movement is capable of, whether it is controlled by the Chel and funded by the transtellars or not. The addition of ships, funding, and manpower will only broaden their lust for revenge. I know their pain and to what depths it may sink them."

"Which is a polite way of saying it takes one to know one."

I rolled my eyes. "If you like."

"But no, I don't like that she's grooming you to become one of her agents," William said, surprising me with his response. "It's not a matter of jealousy or the fact you're a Crius nobleman or the fact I think you're a complete bastard—"

"And I thought we were getting along so well."

"Or your sarcastic tone or the fact you smell of alcohol from two-feet away—"

"Or the fact I'm sleeping with the same woman you were."

William's eyes flared. "That has nothing to do with it."

I glanced back at him and raised a single eyebrow.

William frowned. "Well, not very much to do with it."

"Perhaps we can get to what it actually has something to do with rather than you prattling on about my immense number of flaws."

William surprised me by cracking a joke. "But I was having so much fun listing them."

I snorted. "I'll also have you know my liver is artificial. I can filter out any and all alcohol or other toxins from my system at will with no long-term side effects. I do that whenever I need to be sober."

Which hadn't been often these past five years.

But had very much been the case now.

"Handy trick," William said. "Amazing what prosthetics can do for the bored rich. To answer your question, though. I don't like it because I think Ida is taking a big risk. I think she's on the outs with the Watchers and you're part of something she's playing at to get back in their good graces. Clarice too. Hell, this entire thing reeks of a plot to distinguish herself as an agent they can trust."

I stopped in mid-step. "What makes you say that?"

"I'll spare you all the moving parts of her plans you already know. The whole business with your robot sister and this spying business," William said, stopping as well. "Instead, it's Hiro. He's a spy working for the Watchers, except, he's not here spying on us or Ida's enemies but Ida herself. I think it's his job to keep an eye on her and terminate her if things go south."

"That's a very serious accusation."

"During the Great Rebellion, we had *mullahs* or holy men implanted with our resistance cells whose job it was to preserve morale. They also had a secondary job of keeping a watch for spies or those who might betray the cause. I got a feel for the true believers, no matter how well they hid it, and I've seen him debate killing us all on occasion."

I opened my mouth to object then shook my head. As much as I wanted to deny it, I'd seen Hiro's willingness to kill on the *Rhea*. He had saved my life, though, so I wanted to believe there was more to it.

But what?

"I'll be careful," I said. "Huh, it's almost like you care whether I live or die."

"Don't get too used to the feeling," William said. "Just because I don't want anyone going up with an exploding ship who doesn't have to, doesn't mean I'm joining your fan club."

"Do you intend to turn on Ida?"

William looked down. "No, I owe her too much."

"Like what?"

William shrugged and looked guilty. "Ida has a way of collecting favors from people. She never forces you to work for her but you're always indebted to her. I think her best gift is finding the kind of people that would mean something to."

"I know what you mean." I paused. "Which isn't an answer."

"My sister got picked up by a Crius noblewoman early on in the war as a present for her husband. I searched a long time for her but never found anything until Ida provided me with information telling me where she was, strung out on jack and merrily hallucinating everything was fine as another soldier's property. Ida got her cleaned up, deprogrammed, and now she's married to a woman back on Xerxes. All she wanted was that I be her hatchetman for as long as she wanted. Even if it gets me killed."

"Sounds like a bargain."

"It is."

I was about to talk more about Hiro when I heard the young man's voice coming from behind the hydroponics garden doors. "So, how, exactly does artificial gravity work if it doesn't exist?"

"There's no such thing as artificial gravity because there's just gravity," Zoe responded. "It's a layman's term to describe the mostly-indistinguishable force of acceleration we use to keep things from floating around space. The engines of the ship provide thrust when operating, pushing up against the deck. That's why the engines are at the bottom of the ship because *down* is always towards the engines, against the direction of the push. When we're docked, we have the gravity wells of the existing objects like space stations and so on to provide it but—"

"I've explained this to him a thousand times," Munin said. "He just uses it as a conversation opener with techy-types. Are you drunk?"

Zoe snorted. "A little bit. I really shouldn't be having this while I'm on all the drugs Doctor Hernandez gave me."

Heading through the doors, I was washed over by an immense amount of moisture in the air. The artificial sunlight above our heads was blinding and I briefly moved my hand in front of my eyes even as they adjusted. I took a second to look at the lengthy green-house around me. Officially, it existed for the purposes of assist-ing the ship's reclamation filters as well as helping the crew's diet despite providing nowhere near enough food for the entire crew. Unofficially, the hydroponics garden served as a lounge to alleviate the claustrophobia so many grounders suffered from after months in space.

Row after row of tables full of fruits, vegetables, and oxy-plants were separated by wooden tables with mechs tending the plants. Munin, Hiro, and Zoe were all dressed in crew jumpsuits around one of the central tables with pre-packaged meals in front of them as well as an open bottle of champagne. Clarice, having cleaned herself up, stood next to Isla. It looked like the gang was all here.

Isla shot me a dirty look. It appeared I would have to do more than simply apologize for planning to leave. I decided on buying her jewelry. I had my fortune back and that was, at least on Crius, the universal way of getting back into a man or woman's good graces.

"Hello, everyone," I said, taking a moment to make sure no one else was present. "I wanted to talk to my sister about some details."

"You mean the fact she's a robot?" Hiro asked.

"That's a racial slur," Zoe said, revealing she knew she was a bioroid.

"My apologies," Hiro said, putting his hand over his heart. "Some of my best friends are robots."

Isla glared at him, which was a welcome relief.

"We need you guys for yet another mission to the heart of something incredibly dangerous and ill-advised," William said, taking the conversation away from me.

"Did Ida find another cannibal mind-control marker again?" Munin said, biting into her peanut butter and gelatin sandwich, then talking with her mouth full. "Because, that didn't work out last time. You weren't there but it didn't. At all."

"Is that a ship-wide joke or—" I started to ask.

William raised his hand. "Clarice, your crazy psycho crime boss cousin is also a terrorist. Will you come with us to meet with her and possibly get horribly killed?"

"You got it," Clarice said, looking uncomfortable.

"I volunteer as well," Isla said.

"As do I," Hiro said, making me uncomfortable.

"I want to help in any way I can," Zoe said, smiling. "It's, after all, why I was created."

Munin chewed on her food. "Yeah, if anyone is expecting me to go then they can kiss my very shapely posterior."

"We don't need you on this one, Munin. It's on planet and not tech-related," I said.

Munin finished her mouthful and took a drink of artificial milk. "Well, now I feel insulted."

"Don't be," I said, smiling. "You're still our favorite shapely engineer."

"I was on a magazine cover, once," Munin said, lifting her half-eaten sandwich. "Granted, it only had a circulation of like five ships, but it's still true."

"If Janice is involved with all of this Free Systems Alliance stuff, it'll probably only take a better deal to get her out of it," Clarice said, not meeting mine or William's gaze. "I've never known my sister to be involved in any sort of politics other than herself. She's a slaver and, at heart, all slavers only care about themselves."

"It sounds like you're trying to convince yourself of that," I said, without thinking.

Clarice's stare became as deadly as Isla's.

"Wow, you're just rolling sevens and elevens today aren't you?" William said, slapping me on the back.

I removed his hand. "If you don't mind, I would like to take my sister for a moment to speak with her in private."

"She's not your sister," Isla said.

"I believe that's up to me and Cassius to decide," Zoe said, her voice rather haughty and condescending.

Isla shook her head and turned away.

"Brr, frosty," Munin said. "Oh, Cassius, while you're on the planet, do me a favor and use your newfound fortune to buy us some decent eats. Also, something expensive for the crew members you like, or just me. Up to you."

"I'm glad to see my newfound wealth isn't going to change our relationship," I said, dryly.

"I have a list of tools I'd like," Munin said, pulling out her info-pad and tapping it. "I've transferred my wish list to your infopad."

"Right."

Zoe got up. "Either way, Cassius, I would be happy to speak with you alone. Please don't steal my food while I'm gone, Munin."

"What kind of girl do you take me for?" Munin said, immediately taking her dessert cup.

Zoe rolled her eyes and muttered something that sounded like, "Peasant."

Oh yes, she was going to get along great here. Then again, as an open bioroid, she might actually be in danger. I'd have to speak to Ida about informing the crew they'd have to pay for her if she was injured. That would do more to keep her safe than a promise to space anyone involved in violence.

Walking out of the hydroponics garden across the hall to the groundskeeper mechs' station, Zoe and I found ourselves in a hall full of a dozen slots for humanoid-sized mechs to stand in, as well as next to a bunch of gardening equipment. Closing the door behind us, I locked it, then clasped my hands together. "Before we begin this conversation, a few questions. First of all, you remember everything Zoe did?"

"Yes," Zoe said.

"You have her personality?"

"I *am* Zoe for all intents and purposes," Zoe said, smiling. "I am my finest achievement."

"Excellent," I said, taking a deep breath and trying not to freaked out. "So, for the purposes of this conversation and all future ones, I will treat you as my sister. This acceptable to you?"

"Of course," Zoe said. "Consider me Zoe II or your younger sister/daughter as well as niece. A situation you're already familiar with as a clone of our father."

I nodded. "Very well, then let me begin by saying, *what the fuck were you thinking?*"

"Which time?" Zoe said, blinking and taking a step back.

"The time when you created a goddamn clone of me and sent it on a mission to create terrorists? That thing? Aiding the Commonwealth? Aiding terrorists against the Commonwealth? Building a CognitionA.I. ? Cloning yourself mentally? Where should I even begin? Is that other Judith a clone of her brain? What other sort of unholy necromancy have you been practicing?" I hadn't been expecting to yell at her but I found myself a lot more upset than I expected. It turned out I was better at suppressing than I thought.

Or maybe my usual cocktail of emotion and memory-suppressing drugs were finally wearing off.

"Please, Cassius, if God hadn't intended us to explore the universe then he wouldn't have given us brains."

"*Cloning me* without my knowledge and making me a *fucking terrorist* is a curious way of exploring the universe."

"I thought you were dead," Zoe said, lowering her voice. "The version of you I created for Thomas was ready and willing to help the Crius Reborn movement. He was eager to avenge the destruction of our homeworld. As for the Judith he's married to? Well, she's as real as he is, or I am."

I felt my face and swore by Lucifer's wives. "Eisheth Zenunim, Na'amah, Lilith, and Agrat Bat Mahlat."

Zoe looked to one side. "Points of divergence I suppose. Those memories were taken from a time when you were still extremely loyal to the Archduchy. I don't know what these past five years have been like for you but it clearly seems to have been taxing emotionally. Your doppelganger doesn't have those feelings so I wouldn't be surprised he's chosen to side with family."

I looked down. "So, this is all Thomas' doing?"

"Somewhat." Zoe said, sticking her hands in her jumpsuit pocket. "He and the State Security organization had no one to surrender to as they were the nobility's sacrificial lamb to appease the war crimes' tribunals. Unfortunately, the nobles underestimated just how many CSS officers were ready to go to ground and had powerful allies willing to finance their war. I don't know when the transtellars and Chel got involved but our brother is a key figure in the Free Systems Alliance. As for why I'm serving the Commonwealth, one must adapt to new realities. I've never had the same nationalist sentiment as you or Thomas. Knowledge is my master, lover, archduke, and husband. Besides, why are you serving them?"

I took a deep breath. "That is a very good question."

That was when the door *whooshed* open behind us, despite my locking it. Turning my head, I saw Hiro at the door holding a plasma pistol.

"I can answer that," Hiro said. "After all, I was the one who recruited him."

Chapter Twenty-Two

Hiro pointed a gun at me.

I would like to have said this was surprising, but the events of the past forty-eight hours had left me quite jaded. Zoe, by contrast, grabbed my arm and stared at the weapon in Hiro's hands. I wondered if she was faking, given she'd casually gassed the entire population of the *Rhea* with seemingly no ill-effects.

I would need to talk to her about that as well. A part of me wanted to believe she wasn't capable of such a thing but everything indicated both she and my brother were capable of doing anything should the circumstances warrant it. They were able to turn off that little light in their heads which warded off evil.

Just like I was.

"Hello, Hiro," I said, doing my best to remain calm. "Why are you pointing a gun at me?"

"The crew will hear any plasma shots," Zoe said, looking up into Hiro's eyes. "Then you'll be killed."

"This is a soundproof room," Hiro said, knocking on the side of the walls with his free hand. "The noise of recharging mechs can get quite loud."

Well, fuck. I decided to hedge my bets and decide whether or not I could make a move fast enough to get the gun away from him. At the present range and given our confined quarters, my chances weren't very good.

"I'm not here to hurt you, though," Hiro said. "I'm here to talk."

"Talk with a gun," I said, skeptical.

"It helps for emphasis." Hiro lowered it. "I'm a representative of an interested party."

"An interested party," I repeated.

"We don't have an official name," Hiro said. "However, if you wanted to know what we do then it's fix things. We are the Fixers."

"Not exactly a name which inspires much fear."

Zoe, actually squeezed my arm. "Then you haven't been listening."
Oh dear.

"Your sister's doll, at least knows of us." Hiro gave a half-smile. "Think of us as the Left Hand to the Watchers' Right in terms of Commonwealth Intelligence. We analyze the immense amount of data accumulated by the communications devices of the Spiral and provide unconventional solutions to the problems that afflict the Commonwealth."

Ah, that was a group I'd heard whispers of. The Commonwealth had numerous agencies which existed off the books, most of which were only tangentially tied to the Watchers. With so much of the Commonwealth's Parliament tied up with bureaucracy and trans-stellar puppets, the real power of the organization lay with the hands of its Ministries and clandestine agencies.

"So, you're not allied with Ida?"

"Friendly rivals," Hiro said. "Though I do have orders to report on her movements and eliminate her if she goes too far in her plans."

"Charming."

"It does mean, at least, I have an answer to the question of, 'Who Watches the Watchers?' The answer being me."

I gave a light snort. "I must confess I preferred the callow youth. He was more likable."

Hiro shook his head. "Please, nobody could stand him on the *Melampus.* That was part of why it was an effective cover. The poor pitiful rich kid from Earth who ruined his chances to be a pilot so he ended up deluding himself being the security officer on an old tug was worthwhile. The only thing more maudlin about it would have been if he'd come from a farm somewhere."

"I take it your backstory is untrue then?"

"Surprisingly, my cover is mostly accurate. I like to keep a paper trail for my real identity in-between covers. I *was* a gunship pilot and trying to evacuate a group of three soldiers who were left behind. I disobeyed orders and all were killed as well as my gunner."

"I'm surprised they didn't throw you in prison for that," Zoe said.

"They did," Hiro replied, twitching as if the memories were something he couldn't quite suppress. "I served two years in a pit before I was released and given my new position."

Zoe blinked. "However did you manage that?"

"I didn't." Hiro shrugged as if the story was no longer relevant. "My family did. They had the one quality that makes all the difference in the world in the Commonwealth."

"Money," I said.

Hiro smiled. "No, *you* have money. My family has *wealth*. They let me rot for a time as a lesson in the perils of idealism before putting me in touch with my employers. I had to make sacrifices to prove my loyalty, terrible ones." For a moment, Hiro eyes looked at the floor and he shook his head. "However, I eventually got the rank I desired and was dispatched here to be Hiro the Monkey Boy."

"No one thought of you like that," I said, lying.

"Then I wasn't doing my job," Hiro said. "It is my job to provide a dissenting opinion to Ida's network of spies, informants, and assassins working throughout Sector 7."

Zoe stared at him. "Ida can be trusted."

"Why?" Hiro asked. "Just because she chose your mnemonic template as her agent? Don't flatter yourself. It was just one of a hundred plots, some of which panned out. You realize you can, and probably were, programmed with loyalty to her, right?"

Zoe's eyes widened. "My...I...wouldn't do that."

Her voice trailed off at the end, though, with the acknowledgement the Zoe I'd grown up with would have been happy to do so to a bioroid of herself.

"You claim to have recruited me?" I asked, diverting the conversation back to the subject which most interested me.

"Yes," Hiro said, looking me up and down. "I do not maintain the kind of network Ida does. I work entirely within the Fixer's Ubiquote System. It analyzes data from all known communications nodes, ship's records, and jump communications in the Spiral. Indeed, we rarely send out agents but for the fact that the Watchers are completely untrustworthy. One of those infofeeds analyzed by our *dummy*A.I. came up with your name and alias, which I used to divert you to this ship."

I raised an eyebrow. "That's an expensive joke to play on Ida."

"Not so much a joke as a contingency," Hiro said, his voice lowering, sounding more like a jaded man in his forties now than a young man in his twenties. "I also was the one who set in motion you being found out. The Free Systems Alliance needs to be destroyed and Ida's attempts were working too slowly. I figured with you, we could discredit them but I let you stew in misery while forming relationships on this ship so you'd be more amenable to working with us."

I frowned. "I am getting very sick of being a pawn."

"You're a knight, not a pawn but we're all pieces for the players of history," Hiro said, surprising me. "I admit, I wanted to delay revealing myself longer. I set up Holtz to attack you so I could endear myself and, abandoning that—"

I punched Hiro in the face hard enough to send him to the ground before grabbing his gun off the floor and aiming it at his head. It was done instinctively and over before I even had time to think about my decision. Hiro, himself, looked stunned both from the blow and the speed of my movement. He'd severely underestimated just how much effort had gone into enhancing my body with cybernetics.

"I should kill you," I said, my finger on the trigger. Honestly, the more I thought about it, the more I decided it was a good idea. Zoe wouldn't betray me until I got off the ship and I didn't need a viper like this beside me. "In fact, I think I will."

"The gun is encoded to my biometrics," Hiro said, feeling his jaw. "A benefit of wealth."

I aimed the gun at the side of his head and pulled the trigger.

Nothing happened.

I frowned. "Unfortunate. Pistol whippings, though, are still entirely possible."

Hiro smiled, not making a movement to get up off the ground. "That would be most unfortunate for us both. Especially as I can offer you some things even Ida can't."

"I'm going to tell her about this," Zoe said, looking at Hiro then turning to me. "Even if she knows you're an agent on board you don't need—"

"The Elephants are dancing on Xerxes with teddy bears," Hiro said, his voice slow and clear.

Zoe froze up and her expression became utterly blank.

"What the hell did you just do?" I said, lifting up the pistol butt to club him.

"Hardwired factory codes," Hiro said, shrugging. "Project: Electric Bookmark was the Fixers' so we made sure Zoe was outfitted with certain precautions like all bioroids, just with the programming changed. It's why Ida was able to offer to fix Isla's. She just had to ask what the ones were for her. Don't worry, I'll pull her out of Standby Mode after our conversation."

"What do you want?" I said, now worried he was about to turn Zoe into a brain dead machine. I was surprised how important preventing that was to me. I really did, on some level, already consider her family. Murderous deranged completely unethical mad scientist family, but family nonetheless.

"I want you to spy on Ida," Hiro said, surprising me for the second time. "I believe she's passing on information to the Free Systems Alliance. I also believe she's sabotaging the efforts of the Commonwealth to effectively fight them."

I was honestly flabbergasted. "*Really?*"

"You say this as a former terrorist pardoned by her on a ship with the sister of one of the FSA's chief arms supplier. This, after someone warned the Free Systems Alliance of her spy on board the *Rhea* who only managed to survive by sheer happenstance. This after said spy had worked for years on technology they managed to transmit to the FSA's flagship. Not to mention the Chel fighters were ordered to attack the *Melampus* and ignore any of her orders to stand down."

"Why would she order an attack on her own ship?" I said, staring. "You, I point out, had Holtz attack me. If anyone would have a reason to order them to attack, then it would be you to ingratiate yourself."

"Perhaps," Hiro said, nodding. "In fact, I was improvising or maybe everything I'm saying is a lie, the fact is there's something of a mole here and if Ida isn't a traitor then she's doing more damage than she is helping."

"Maybe she's playing the long game?"

I took a deep breath. "You've been here as long as me. Do you really think she's a traitor?"

Hiro paused. "No, no I don't. However, she has a history of political activism and criminal behavior that makes her suspect. My superiors question the leak and want someone to blame who isn't part of our house. Ida makes an easy target. If they want evidence against her, I will provide it. I don't question orders. Not anymore. It's a lesson I learned from the war."

"Funny, I learned the opposite lesson."

"Questioning orders would have gotten you killed. You obeyed and survived instead. Others died."

"Maybe my self-respect is worth more than my life."

"The dead have no self-respect," Hiro said, finally getting up. "Besides, you haven't heard what I'm offering."

"Ida already gave me everything I wanted," I lied.

"All of which can be removed again, by me," Hiro said, pointing out a flaw in my plan. "Ida may have presented the carrot but I'm very fond of the stick. But what I'm offering you is much, much greater."

"Which is?"

"The *Melampus* itself. After Ida's plans end here, she will be recalled back to Earth and this massive tug will need a new owner."

"You're offering me an old tug I could buy a copy of now?"

"I think we both know it's the people on board you want. I'll also continue feeding you missions from that. You'll be an agent of Earth and respected. In certain circles, at least."

I stared at him. "Ida seems to already be planning that."

"Not so much," Hiro said. "Now that she has you, she's going to use you to lure out your brother, the *Revengeance*, and your doppelganger before destroying them all. Then she's going to hand you over to her superiors who want to blame you for all of this. They need someone to put on trial for the Free Systems misery and you're already on camera. Convenient, huh?"

I paused. "You're lying."

"Could be," Hiro said. "Of course, then again, everyone has been lying to you on this ship, haven't they?"

He had a point. "What do you want me to do?"

Hiro just smiled and handed over a small strip of electronic paper. "Put this in your ear and we'll hear everything. It's undetectable even to Janice's technology. Report on everything you do for Ida and deliver it to me. We only need to establish a connection between Ida and Ms. Rin-O'Harra to bring her down."

"All right," I said, reluctantly putting it in. "This is very possibly a loyalty test, isn't it? To see if I would turn against Ida if offered a better deal."

"Possibly," Hiro said. "But why would we think you had any loyalty to the Commonwealth to begin with?"

That was another good point.

"So I keep this in my ear the entire time?" I said.

"Yes," Hiro said. "I'll be monitoring you and agents with you. If you take it out, even for bed, I'll consider the deal off and revoke your pardon."

"You aren't a very fair negotiator."

"It's not a negotiation."

"I understand."

"Wolves are very shameless when they wear pink dresses," Hiro said, his voice equally cold and calm.

Zoe felt her head and looked like she was coming out of a trance. "What the fuck?"

"I was discussing possible gift ideas for the women he has offended and yet still wants to screw around with," Hiro said. "I was giving my input."

"I'll make my own choices, thank you," I said, wondering if there were any more surprises waiting for me.

"My gun, please?" Hiro asked.

I removed the ammo clip and handed it back to him. Hiro frowned, then smiled before turning around and departing.

"Cassius, what the hell just happened?" Zoe said, feeling her head.

"Nothing of consequence," I said, pausing. It was a sign Hiro hadn't done his research on Crius that our language was a mixture of hand gestures as well as communication. The second wave of settlers had included many people who had chosen to forego hearing for reasons which apparently had to do with cultural identity. It was one of the dozen or so languages I knew.

His ignorance didn't surprise me, though. He was Albionese and he was used to the rest of the world bowing to his attitude. What was the old joke? What did you call someone who spoke two languages? Bilingual. What did you call someone who only spoke one language? Albionese.

I proceeded to sign to her the situation, providing Hiro's more obnoxious statements on the subject.

"[Asshole,]" Zoe said, responding to me with her fingers. "[I should have known they'd take advantage of my situation and install control codes.]"

"[We'll figure out a way to remove them,]" I said, taking a deep breath. "[Can you inform Ida about all of this?]"

"[You want to go with her rather than Hiro?]" Zoe said. "[Cassius, someone did betray my position. Someone who knew I was a spy on that ship and no one, not even my brother, our brother Thomas, suspected me.]"

I took a deep breath and explained in very simple terms. "[Those who sit on the fence in wartime get shot at from both sides. If I have to pick a side, I might as well pick the one who didn't hire a man to shoot me.]"

That seemed to cause Zoe to pause. "[You raise a valid point, Cassius. Is there anything else?]"

I nodded, trying to figure out how to ask my next question. "[Zoe, why did you kill all those people?]"

Zoe looked down, a sad look on her face. "[It's simple, brother. In the end, I'll do anything to survive.]"

Chapter Twenty-Three

Shogun.

Stepping out of the shuttle onto the circular landing platform, I took a moment to take in our surroundings. We were close to a thousand feet off the ground, connected to a larger take-off tower for space-based visitors. Our platform gave us a good view of Akihito City, the largest settlement on the planet. We were surrounded by thousands of supercrete and duraglass spires rising out of the ground while uncounted automated aircars zipped around us.

Hundred-foot-tall holograms advertising narcotics, medicines, sexual simulations, vacations, and food products were projected everywhere. Announcements in several languages indicated the city would be doing a mandatory rainfall in the next hour, mixing in disinfectant with the natural waterfall in order to cut down on the spread of extra-solar disease.

Unlike other worlds, where the work would have been done by mechs, a white-haired man in his forties in a blue jumpsuit collected the trash spread from previous visitors and loaded it into a self-moving garbage bin. The man's neck contained a barcode tattoo, which showed him to be an indentured servant to the state. Shogun was a planet of excess, and if you did not keep up, it chewed you up and spit you out.

The planet was humid and I pulled my body-regulating jacket on tight before adjusting my sunglasses. My eyes actually adjusted better to light changes than a baseline human but these were Hollow Man lenses, designed especially to give false positives to facial recognition software and make it more difficult for individuals to track me down. I'd already altered my face and clouded my DNA (however poorly) but I still wasn't entirely happy with this situation. Too many people knew my real identity now.

"You can probably remove those," Clarice said, walking up behind her. "My cousin undoubtedly knows everything about you."

Clarice wore a pair of denim pants, a choker, and a scale leather jacket over a red halter-top. A pair of sunglasses too.

"Oh, I have no doubt about that," I said, looking out. "After all, it was the Rin-O'Harra Syndicate which provided me my falsified identity."

I still remembered the bloody and corrupt work I'd had to do for several people, increasingly higher in the organization, trying to get myself a new life. It had been a liberation to find legitimate and unquestioning work on the *Melampus.* Now, I couldn't help but wonder if I'd been naive to believe the Syndicate would ever let me go. I owed my freedom to Hiro, according to him at least, and it was possible I'd just been sold like cattle.

Why should I have expected different?

"Oh?" Clarice asked. "What did our people ask of you for that little favor?"

I paused. "Quite a bit."

Clarice didn't ask more.

I turned back to the rest of the group Ida had sent to meet with Janice. There was William, Zoe, Hiro (looking too smug for his own good), and Isla. Isla was wearing a too-short plaid skirt and a white shimmersilk dress shirt with a formal jacket. A pair of cosmetic magni-glasses, the kind very popular on Crius when I was a boy, rested on her nose and brought out her eyes. She looked like she'd stepped out of a magazine depicting a sex-segregated school's naughty adventure.

I thought about Hiro and wondered whether he'd already found out about my informing Zoe to inform Ida. I also wondered what Ida would do with that information. File it away for future reference? Blackmail Hiro? The thought occurred to me she might have him killed, though I liked to believe she was above that. I'd like to believe, but I didn't.

"If you'll excuse me, I need to speak with Isla."

Clarice grabbed my hand as I started to depart. "You should know Isla forgives you. I talked to her."

I was glad to know that. It was, however, more than a trifle weird to have a woman you were sleeping with reassure you that another still liked you. "Ah, thank you."

"But you should be wary of my cousin," Clarice said, lowering her gaze. "You're exactly Janice's type."

Now it had gone from a trifle weird to extremely. "Uh, I have larger things to worry about than your cousin being a man-eater."

Clarice closed her eyes. "That's not what I mean. She built her place up in the Syndicate by finding people she could use, finding out what they want, and giving it to them. Only, by the time they were done, they needed something else."

"So your sister is like Ida."

"Ida's different." Clarice opened her eyes. "I did a lot of terrible things even when I didn't want to do what my family wanted. I'm trying to make amends now."

I closed my eyes. "I'm not a man to judge you. I have enough blood on my hands to dye stars."

"I joined with Ida because I wanted to do something to make up for the weight of my sins. I want there to be a good and an evil in this world. I don't like being here, Cassius. My cousin is family, like a sister to me, and I'll always love her but everything she does, and has done, to this planet is wrong. I don't like being sent down here to negotiate with her because I feel like any deals we might make with her will only paper over the corruption."

I looked at her, then I turned away. "I don't see the world that way anymore and never can. Every black is just white missing and every white is black with some pigments absent. I also don't think Ida is, necessarily, the best person in the world."

"I trust her."

"Good for you."

Clarice let go of my hand and I walked over to Isla. Her reaction was to glare then look away. I was about to turn around and forget about talking with her when she said, "Hello, Cassius."

"Hello," I said, pausing. Looking for a conversation topic, I ended up choosing a poor one. "What *are* you wearing?"

"When I was downloading information to make me into someone able to study medicine, they gave me the memories of Melanie Hawkingwood, the brainy girl protagonist of the wizard's school under siege by the Dark Lord. I figured if I was going on a trip, I'd disguise myself so I'm a less recognizable model of bioroid."

"By disguising yourself as another kind of bioroid," I said, not understanding.

"It seems I'm destined to be children's book characters."

"They are very different characters from the ones I grew up reading."

"What do they read on Crius?"

"Slaying dragons, crushing revolts, burning heretics."

"Charming."

"It is what it is."

Isla nodded. "When you said you were leaving, I perhaps overreacted. I am not accustomed to being friends with the men or women I sleep with. It complicates matters."

I paused. "I would sacrifice whatever I need to make sure you and Clarice are safe, including myself. That includes staying with the Commonwealth."

"That's not friendship, that's love."

"Perhaps, but it's how I feel. If I cannot serve a government I respect, I'm happy to serve those I care about instead."

"Don't put me on a pedestal. It's too close to an auction block."

"How about I just see you as you are."

"And what am I?"

"A very capable survivor."

"Not as capable as you might think," Isla seemed to struggle with her next words. "Your sister didn't want to have her memory erased."

"I suspected she wouldn't."

"She seems to have no difficulty with being bioroid. That she was created as something less than human."

"Perhaps she doesn't see herself as less than human."

Isla paused. "I didn't want to have my memory erased because I was afraid. Afraid of dying. That, as a being whose consciousness is a collection of one's and zero's, I would cease to exist once those memories were gone. I don't believe in a higher power or a hereafter, for bioroids or humans, so I held onto the memories. Both false and painful."

"Isla…"

What was it about today and confession?

"The thing is, that I'm worried about you. Your sister will do anything to survive. I think she's lying to you."

I didn't respond. "Everyone is lying to everyone."

"Cassius—"

"I think you should stop."

Thankfully, she did.

William, thankfully, interrupted the moment by calling over to us. "So when is Janice sending her representative?"

"Honestly, they should be waiting here for us," Clarice said, reaching down to the suitcase where she'd stored her plasma repeater. "I don't like it."

I grasped hold of my plasma sword hilt, tied around my belt along with my holstered plasma pistol holster. Clarice's warning had us all preparing, even though it might be nothing.

All of us were as ready as possible when the buzzer sounded on the elevator doors and they opened up to reveal a group of Shogun Security guards accompanied by Kristoph Rin-O'Harra. They were armed for a ceremonial escort rather than a direct assault, and if they wanted to catch us unawares they would have done so by opening fire as soon as the doors opened.

Kristoph still wore his Planetary Commerce Commissioner's uniform but it was covered with a thick overcoat and a personal force-field generator affixed to his belt. His medals were, thankfully, gone but his movements were precise and nervous. It wasn't because we were around either.

Kristoph raised his hands as if in surrender. "Were you expecting trouble, dear cousin?"

"I'm always expecting trouble," Clarice said, barely lowering her weapon. "It's what's kept me alive this long."

"You would be right to do so," Kristoph said, looking around. "The situation is not as you left it here on Shogun. Janice has made some uncomfortable friends and it is putting our position on the planet in jeopardy."

"That's pretty dangerous talk, cousin," Clarice said, frowning. "Also, the Family is Shogun. It's part of what I hate about this planet."

"Things change, especially in wartime."

"Are we at war?" Clarice asked.

Kristoph gave a half-smile. "Always."

A buzzing in the distance, separate from all the automated cars travelling by and the other noises of a bustling metropolis, set me on edge. I caught a glimpse of the source microseconds before it arrived and didn't have time to react. Two Black aircars outfitted with vehicular weapons descended from the sky and proceeded to strafe the platform, blasting through Kristoph and his soldiers before flying over us and forcing us to the ground from the force of their gravlifts.

"Get back to the shuttle!" Clarice shouted, lifting her repeater as the vehicles came around for another pass.

Instead, I ran directly for the remains of our invited guests and checked Kristoph, whose force shield had been punched through like a soap bubble. The generator was still functional, though, and had a physical barrier function as well. It was a commercial force shield and, honestly, not that useful versus military grade equipment but what I wanted wasn't going to require much in the way of stopping power.

Setting the field directionally, I heard the buzzing once more and threw the force generator on the ground before throwing myself to the right. This time, it created a wall of blue light which one of the aircars slammed headfirst into and was brought to a complete stop. The automated systems had decelerated so it wasn't damaged beyond the bumper but the machine was hovering not sixteen feet away from it. I could see the helmeted pilot on the side, looking confused and bleeding from the forehead…

… Right before I pulled my pistol out and shot him through the head, blasting a hole through the duraglass. Clarice, William, Isla, and the others fired against the other vehicle but had only managed to damage the car. Our shuttle, unfortunately, was now on fire thanks to having its engines targeted by our persistent attacker. Making a run for the still intact aircar at my side, I shot off the side entrance and threw myself into the driver's seat, unbuckling its occupant and pulling back just as the other aircar attacked me.

This was a stupid plan.

Oh well.

Dodging out of the way of its plasma fire, I immediately pushed the aircar into a dive, relying on my genetically enhanced body to handle the sudden change in pressure from the right door of the car hanging wide open. The other aircar attempted to follow, shooting at me and not caring if its blasts hit nearby buildings. Pulling on the controls, the car's dummyA.I. warned me what I was doing was against safety regulations but I kept it on manual before doing a loop-de-loop and emerging behind the enemy vehicle and blowing it to pieces with two blasts into its back engines.

It was a masterful bit of piloting, even if I was better outside of the atmosphere, but I didn't have time to give myself a pat on the back since a second set of aircars came out from in-between a nearby pair of buildings where they'd been hiding. The scanners inside the vehicle gave me a good sense of their presence even as I guessed this was a converted police officer's aircar.

"Well, the day I can't defeat some dirty cops is the day I die," I muttered, not quite processing that was an entirely realistic position given my general unfamiliarity with the machine and its damaged state.

The two aircars ignored my friends on the platform and fired repeatedly with their vehicular cannons, trying to get me less through skill than simply firing as many blasts as possible in my general direction. I relied on steep turns to keep me ahead of the two even as I could already feel myself ready to pass out. The fact I had to hold my body against the interior with my cybernetic strength to avoid flying out was another distraction I didn't need. Then I shot the driver's seat out of the first enemy target on my turn-around and buzzed the next of the attackers.

"This, this is all I'm good at," I muttered, stunned when the right engine of the vehicle was struck by a stray shot from the enemy.

Emergency lights flair as a pair of belts wrapped themselves around my chest in place of the ones I'd pulled off. The aircar popped its top clean off and moved to an emergency landing before eject-ing me. The machines hadn't been designed for pilots who could manage the kind of controlled landing I could, let alone continue to fight. My seat slowly descended through the air as the enemy aircar zipped around to tear me to pieces in a shot even a child could have made.

Right before it blew up, spreading out wreckage and debris down to the ground below, destined to be captured by gravity nets in between the skyscrapers. Clarice had managed to get something stronger than her repeater from the shuttle. I could already see police aircars heading our way, flashing silver and gold lights to warn of their presence.

I just hoped they weren't here to kill us.

Chapter Twenty-Four

They weren't here to kill *or* arrest us.

Quite the contrary, in thirty minutes Clarice and I were riding in a luxury cloudsedan sitting across from a very-much-alive Kristoph. The interior of the vehicle was a sharp contrast to the kind of conditions I'd been serving in for the past five years. The seats were made of fine cloned leather, which felt soft against the skin, but also firm. The air from the ventilators was a cool mist that massaged the skin. A miniature bar and refrigeration unit sat next to a holographic stock ticker.

I still felt nauseated from my near brush with death but had to put on a fake smile as I sipped the champagne from oddly-shaped glasses. There was something nauseating about Kristoph in person and I couldn't help but think he reminded me of Octavian. A nobleman who had been handed everything his entire life and dumped off into a position where he was expected to do little damage. Given he seemed to have created his own power base, perhaps I was misjudging him, or maybe I just had come to hate men of my former class.

Following us were two other less notable, but still luxurious, transports that contained the rest of our companions. The entire Akihito City police force, seemingly, was forming an honor guard around us. It was a symbol of the power the Rin-O'Harra clan possessed but not, apparently, enough to prevent the assassination attempt against us. Assuming it wasn't ordered by them in the first place.

Kristoph took a sip of the too-sweet champagne. "I suppose you're wondering how I'm still alive."

"You sent a bioroid duplicate to meet with us," I said. "A bioroid without your memories but the acting skill to pull it off."

Kristoph frowned then shrugged. "Yes."

"Poor for him," I said, clutching my side. I'd bruised my ribs coming down and even my enhanced constitution would not take long to heal.

"He's just a machine," Kristoph said, shrugging. "It fulfilled its purpose."

"Perhaps he'd disagree," Clarice said.

Kristoph snorted. "Don't tell me you've become a Mech-Sympathizer, dear. You're already depraved in other ways, don't become a Robot-Kisser, too."

Clarice narrowed her eyes. "Do you really see a difference between them and other people? You who have hundreds of bioroid servants, administrators, and soldiers powering your little empire in the wake of your takeover. People you choose to buy because you can't trust anyone in the family."

Kristoph paused. "No, I suppose I don't. It doesn't matter, though, either way."

"Doesn't matter," Clarice said, speaking the words I suspected she had never had the courage to speak to her family.

"Doesn't matter," Kristoph said, looking out into the skyscrapers beyond. "If the man had been shit out of some woman's womb or tubed between a couple of men, it wouldn't matter. This planet was built on slavery. Two hundred years ago, the Harra clan were pirates in the middle of the Great Cataclysm and the Rin were merchant nobles over a feudal world with no resources. The Spiral needed laborers to rebuild after the Darkness. This planet was built on the billions of slaves taken and traded to do just that. Even with mechs and bioroids, born labor is still cheaper. They don't question where their shoes come from."

Clarice's eyes widened before returning to normal. "How long have you been saving that speech?"

"Since you left," Kristoph said, shaking his head. "A humiliation for the whole family."

"We don't need slaves. People don't need slaves anymore. Bioroid or otherwise—"

Kristoph shook his head. "If it saves a half-credit, the government will destroy worlds. They see only dots on a screen and resources are always less than necessary. Which needs asteroid mines, farms, terraforming, toxin removal, bloodporn, backwork, and other ways for the poor to justify their existence versus draining the economy."

"Who was trying to kill us?" I asked, uninterested in the squabbles of an ancient family of rogues.

Kristoph finished his champagne in one gulp. "Janice, probably."

"Oh, bullshit," Clarice said, growling. "Janice loves you. You're her baby brother."

"You're her sister as far as Janice is concerned," Kristoph said, snorting. He already looked a little drunk. "Even so, she's apparently lost her love of you. Over and over, every day, she blames you for abandoning the family. For abandoning her and leaving the responsibility of running the Syndicate all on us."

Clarice looked like she'd been struck. "What are you saying?"

"I'm saying she never would have gotten involved with those Free Systems Alliance bastards if not for you."

I rubbed the ear where the paper from Hiro rested. This was not good and would only make things worse.

"What is she doing, Kris?" Clarice asked, her voice low.

He took a deep breath. "Supplying arms, weapons, and diverting crews of convicts or debtors set for penal labor to be freed by the FSA if they meet the psychological criteria for joining up. She's not the biggest creditor for the group but is one of the major players. The Chel and transtellars have been paying her well but it's not enough for the risks involved."

"Janice wouldn't do that," Clarice said, frowning. "She's not stupid."

"A cause is like a drug," Kristoph said, wrinkling his nose. "Buddha knows we've sold enough of both to know the similarities. Plenty of the Syndicate raised objections to getting involved in politics but Janice has been ruthless in pruning away all opposition. The family table has fewer seats at the top."

Clarice shook her head, clearly stunned by the news.

"What is it you want, exactly?" I asked, more than a little uncomfortable we were dealing with Janice's subordinate rather than her. It seemed likely Ida had underestimated Janice and believed her to be doing any aid strictly out of profit. Then again, I'd only known the "real" her for three days and had no idea what was planning by her and what was bad miscalculation.

"I want you to help me plan a coup," Kristoph said.

Clarice actually laughed and leaned back in her seat. "In what *possible* universe do you think I'd agree to that or would even be able to help?"

"We both have friends in the Commonwealth now," Kristoph said, pouring himself a glass.

"You've been spying for them," I said, understanding now why he had decided to contact us directly.

Clarice straightened up, clearly not expecting that.

"Yes," Kristoph said, frowning. "Unfortunately, my contact has met with an unexpected end and I can't tell who is compromised and who is not. Thankfully, I was able to get some datajacks to recover their files and learned quite a few secrets I've been able to parlay to protect myself."

"Except for the assassination today," I said.

"This was a warning," Clarice said, shaking her head. "For him, rather than me. If Janice had wanted Kristoph dead-dead, he would be."

"You overestimate her," Kristoph said.

"You severely *underestimate* her," Clarice said, staring. "What do you think we can do?"

"Janice has recently received a very large number of data-files and research she is having the contents assembled for. There's a massive gathering going on here today for when she's going to pass it on to the Free Systems Alliance. They've got everyone there, including the Butcher of Kolthas."

I did a double take.

So did Clarice.

"What?" I said, blinking. "Could you repeat that?"

"Count Cassius Mass," Kristoph said, sneering. "One of those tank-bred disgusting mouth-breathing cousin-fucking Satanists. He and his wife have been staying at the Water Palace for the past week."

I stared at him.

I opened my mouth, closed it, then just chuckled.

Clarice looked over at me. "Cass—"

I raised my hand, trying to process the fact my doppelganger was right next to us. I'd have considered it wildly unlikely if not for the fact I was being led around by the nose by not one, but two, of the Commonwealth's spies.

"With all due respect, Kristoph, we have bigger issues than the family," Clarice said, trying to regain control of the situation.

"What is more important than the family?" Kristoph said, his voice almost shrill.

"Cognition A.I. ," Clarice said.

Kristoph almost dropped his glass.

I barely heard her, though, because I was contemplating the fact I could meet up with my late wife once more. Zoe II, if I were to use her ridiculous appellation for herself, was almost identical to my sister. So much so that I had been in the same room with her, talked with her, and smelled her perfume, yet couldn't tell the difference.

In part, it was one of the reasons why so many people hated bioroids. For the vast majority of human existence, mechs had been firmly on the other side of the Resemblance Valley, as it was called. Robots that looked cute and human-like were well-loved by the public, but those that came extremely close to humans, but weren't quite right, were disturbing to the public.

Developers had assumed bioroids, which were identical in appearance and behavior to humans, would be accepted and, broadly, they were. However, for a significant percentage of humanity, that similarity was an offense. These Five-Percenters, as they were called, adopted draconian laws and committed violence against bioroids in hopes of making it clear they considered them inferior mockeries of man.

I was not one of them.

It was, intellectually, sick to contemplate spending time with a copy of Judith. To replace her like one might a tool which had been broken. Yet the absence in my heart was something that wasn't intellectual or philosophical. Humans were selfish and needy creatures, to the point that just being able to talk with said copy was an astounding temptation. I wasn't even threatened by my doppelganger, as much as I hated the concept of him, and wondered what it would be like to talk to myself of five years earlier. Maybe I could persuade him to turn from this path.

We were, after all, family of sorts.

"I need you to pay attention to what they're saying," Hiro's voice spoke in my ear. It was a strange weird vibration I didn't so much hear but feel.

I looked up and heard Kristoph mostly repeating the word bitch, throwing his glass against the wall, and swearing in a mixture of New Japanese and Albionese.

"You need to kill Janice and take the CognitionA.I. before it arrives," Hiro said, his voice very low.

Still in pain from my injury, I whispered. "No."

Neither Clarice nor Kristoph seemed to notice.

That was when my entire body felt like it was on fire. Strangely, I lost complete control of it and simply trembled while swearing, unable to even shake my hand. It was enough to make me want to scream but I couldn't.

"Oh, I'm sorry," Hiro said, his voice low. "You were under the impression this was a negotiation. That little device you put in your ear has fully acclimated to you and delivers a special series of shocks to areas of your brain. It's called an earworm. Rather brilliant device, really."

I reached up to rip it off.

"Oh, I wouldn't do that," Hiro said, chuckling. "It can also deliver a fatal jolt to your brain if it's removed while armed. I probably should have told you about these side effects earlier but then, really, you wouldn't put it in your ear would you?"

"What do you want?" I muttered.

Kristoph heard that. "What do I want? I want Janice not to have doomed the entire fucking planet! Is she insane? If it is a cognitionA.I. , then screw repercussions through the legal system! They will bomb this planet to ashes! Do you have proof, Clarice? Tell me you have proof? Then we can kill her tonight and end this madness! We have a future as respectable citizens of the Commonwealth now."

"We don't have proof," Clarice said. "Let me handle this."

Hiro continued talking. "I'm not the bad guy here, Cassius. I made you an offer and you should be grateful it came with the carrot before the stick. Sadly, you tried to send your sister to go tell Ida about my suspicions and that was very foolish. I mean, you told a person I know the codes to control and interrogate. Naughty-naughty."

"Kill…" I trailed off.

"Me? You?" Hiro snorted. "I don't think so. I've already wiped out your fortune and all hope of you walking away from this. Now you'll earn your continued life, the way it should have been done in the first place. You're a war criminal, Cassius, and I'm glad I don't have to pretend to respect you anymore. You need to kill Janice and anyone else involved in replicating those devices. Otherwise, we will destroy this planet. We will burn it from orbit and the rest of the galaxy will thank us for it. No one cared that we bombed Crius halfway to oblivion, and they'll care even less when we do the same to a bunch of slavers."

I looked over at Clarice.

"Let you handle this!?" Kristoph said. "This goes beyond handling!"

"I can fix this," Clarice said. "And if anyone needs to kill Janice, then I'll do it."

My eyes widened even as I opened my mouth to speak, then closed it. I knew Clarice still viewed Janice like a sister and I wasn't sure if she was serious or not. I did know, however, it would probably break her worse than the Chel.

I covered my mouth and muttered under my breath. "And if I refuse?"

"Then I won't just kill you but I'll kill other people," Hiro said, sounding frustrated. "Maybe I'll wipe Isla's memories or just shut her and Zoe down, sell them on the black market. See? Look at what you're making me do. You're making me break out the mob stuff. I could kill everyone on board this ship and it would be justice because it'd be in the purpose of saving this planet and stopping the threat of CognitionA.I. from spreading."

It was at that moment I started to wonder if Hiro was actually a spy. It seemed grossly incompetent that he would have to resort to an explosive leash, for lack of a better term, and naked threats in order to make sure I cooperated. Any idiot leg-breaker or his boss could resort to those in order to get their way and I was used to agents with a bit more finesse. Ida and my brother, in particular, would eat Hiro alive. Then again, the threat of CognitionA.I. might actually justify his actions.

We were all in over our heads here.

"I don't like killing, don't get me wrong." Hiro backpedaled. "I would rather get through this with as minimal a loss of life as possible but there's no way my superiors would tolerate anything less than this woman's destruction, as well as the death of everyone else involved in this forbidden research. I'd like to believe you. Underneath that smug faux-nobleman's exterior, you're also possessed of a similar code of honor to the one we follow in the Commonwealth. Just don't think for a second I'll hesitate to break your Dolls."

He referred to Isla and Zoe both, I suspected.

"I understand," I said.

"Good!" Kristoph said, feeling the side of his head before going to pour himself an amber-colored fluid from his bar, which I suspected was much stronger than champagne. "Because if we don't get this resolved, we're all dead."

Outside the luxury transport, I saw our convoy arrive above the Water Palace, one of the most beautiful constructions in Sector 7, if not the entire Spiral. Built on top of the ocean with massive super-steel legs, the palace and its ten thousand fountains, as well as hundred micro-lakes, were covered by a translucent series of domes, protected from the worst of Shogun's monsoons. The architecture was a mixture of the modern and classical with the small-city containing several dozen skyscraper-sized pagodas mixed with a hundred more mansions, putting to shame anything outside of Crius or Albion.

"You grew up here?" I asked Clarice, momentarily distracted from the fact I was going to be making an enemy of everyone here.

"Unfortunately," Clarice said. "I spent my first fifteen years in my father's harem quarters, only occasionally allowed to visit my mother's and uncle's."

"Fascinating."

The luxury transport lowered until we found ourselves in a much smaller dome off of the main one. Behind us, Kristoph babbled about whether the *Melampus* could get him off Shogun and how much he'd be willing to pay us.

"Shut up," Clarice said, her voice now accusatory. "I said I'd handle it."

Kristoph, mercifully, did so.

That was when Janice's entourage arrived. Two dozen red-robed Palace Guards in ceremonial, but functional, blast armor, several beefy well-formed male consorts in see-through silk togas, which covered little, and two women who I recognized.

The first I knew immediately to be Janice. She shared an identical genetic code to Clarice, the only differences being she was a few inches taller as well as possessing an ampler bust, which was either surgically endowed or the result of a very impressive brassier. Given her clothing was only slightly more opaque than her consorts', I doubted the latter to be the case as her outfit revealed details of her body that left little to the imagination.

Beside her, dressed much more conservatively in a white body-covering robe with her hair up, was Judith.

Back from the dead as if she'd never left.

Chapter Twenty-Five

I remembered when I first met Judith, over a decade ago on board the *Revengeance*. I was already a Major-Baron through my efforts in the Scorpion Suppressions with three Ace pins affixed to my service record. Despite my attempts to be my own man, my meteoric rise was, in large part, due to my father's influence and I should have realized it would make me enemies.

People who hated him. People who hated clones. People who hated House Mass. People who just hated the nobility in general and would enjoy taking a shot at one of its vulnerable members. This particular assassination attempt was a classic one and I'd stupidly blundered into it, not bothering to play the game the way it was supposed to be because I'd thought politics beneath me.

I remembered, all those years ago, standing in an unused storage bay on Floor 42 of the *Revengeance*. I was surveying the collection of blades set on the plastisteel table before me. All around, drunk and jeering crew members were ready to enjoy one of the rarest sights in the Sector: an honor duel. Dueling was one of the stupidest traditions practiced by the Archduchy, but still legal. The feuds after House Lucifer's fall had almost destroyed our planet so it had been decided the aristocracy should be able to settle their disputes with sword or pistol. Most of the duels were non-lethal, but the occasional fatality was not unknown and I knew my opponent had no intention of sparing my life.

Standing across the makeshift octagonal arena they'd set up was Pious Stone, professional duelist and assassin. Today, he was operating under the namesake of Major Samuel Sternwise, a fictitious identity which would disappear the moment he was led off to the brig by his supporters after my death. He was a dashing brown-skinned man of classic Vedic looks with long shoulder-length hair and a scar across the bottom of his chin. Pious had once competed in the Archduchy games as a fencer before he'd been disbarred for betting on himself as well as a series of domestic violence incidents.

Five days ago, he had beaten and raped a midshipman named Jasper Thomas after luring him up to his room for a romantic encounter. I'd liked Jasper, and we'd often played gravball during my off-duty hours. Once someone covered for "Samuel," I'd stupidly decided to play the dashing knight and challenged him.

It was all a lure as my brother had explained to me an hour earlier. He'd begged me to call it off and suffer the shame of backing out but I found myself unable to do so. Pride would rather I die fighting an opponent I couldn't possibly win against versus looking at Jasper knowing I'd let him suffer without avenging him. I was too much a coward to face that kind of shame and death was better than dishonor, even when the code I abided by was meaningless.

"You should pick the proton sword," a tough-sounding feminine voice said behind me.

I looked behind me and saw a short woman with almond shaped eyes, short dirty-red hair under an engineer's cap, a somewhat boyish frame hidden beneath a set of overalls, and the pale skin of someone who had spent months on a ship without shore leave or a UV unit. She was a plain-looking woman who might have been pretty if given time to decorate herself, but she lacked the genetically-engineered beauty of the nobility.

"A proton sword isn't a very good sword for maneuverability," I said, picking up the weapon anyway. "They're basically all force and sharpness. The longsword equivalent of dueling blades. A gravity sword is a better choice."

The woman gave a not-at-all-hidden snort of derision. "Yeah, because you're going to be out-maneuvering this guy. When there's an opening, you need to be able to strike a single hard blow to kill him instantly."

The woman was simultaneously a commoner, a nat, and one of the enlisted—three things that made her familiarity grossly inappropriate. Nevertheless, I swallowed my tongue because I was determined not to be that noble and look down on her. "What makes you think there's going to be an opening?"

"There will be," the woman said, giving a surprisingly enchanting smile. "Some of us want to see you win."

"Some of us?"

The woman shrugged. "Jasper's friends. Your friends. People who seem to think you're not a complete waste of space despite being handed everything from birth."

I was now officially pissed off, which actually cleared me of the all-consuming dread I'd been experiencing. "And which are you?"

"You're here for Jasper, even though I know he was probably hurt just because of your power games. You didn't run away or choose some other bastard to fight for you. So I don't know. But I'm being paid to help by your brother so believe me when I say there *will be an opening.*"

I picked up the proton sword and stared at it, getting a sense of this woman. "My brother?"

"Do you have a problem with cheating? Your brother said you might."

I did. However, looking at the blade, I took a moment to reflect on just what I was doing here. "No, I don't. This isn't a game. It's a life and death struggle. I'd be a fool to avoid any advantage I could take."

"I'm glad to hear you say that."

"I'm not."

I'd learned a lot of bitter lessons about the nobility during my time in the Academy as well as during my service to the Archduke. I still held to the belief the nobility were meant to hold themselves to a higher standard of behavior and responsibility in order to make up for the privileges we received, but it seemed increasingly clear I was one of the very few who believed such. Also, what constituted a higher standard of behavior was an extremely variable concept from person-to-person.

Or maybe I just didn't want to die. It could have been as simple as that.

"What's your name, anyway?"

"I'll tell you if you survive."

I nodded.

I lifted up the proton sword and returned to the arena where Pious Stone was awaiting me, as cocky as any man who was about to murder one of the nobility might ever be. He had a gravity sword

I briefly found myself envious of. It was the kind of weapon that required a kingdom to purchase and was wasted on the majority of individuals who could actually afford to buy it.

"I don't suppose you would be willing to tell me who hired you," I said, assuming a ready position and crossing swords with the man.

"Duelist-client privilege," Pious Stone said, assuming a similar stance. "Besides, it's not going to do you any good."

"Perhaps."

The Arbiter of the duel, a sleazy waste of genetic material named Atticus MacDonald, stood between us, checked the blades haphazardly before stepping backwards. "Begin!"

Our skill levels weren't even close as no sooner had we locked blades than he pulled back and slashed through my shield, into my chest. I hadn't even pulled my own sword back when he was ready to deliver the killing blow. The thing was, though, his blade struck my shield and promptly bounced off.

The sword created a series of sparks, making it seem like a glancing blow, a fact I was grateful for because it helped disguise the blatant sabotage done to Pious' sword. Startled, but unwilling to let an advantage get away from me, I pulled back and stabbed my proton blade through the shield of the duelist in front of me.

I gave Pious credit as, not only had he been in a position to strike at me before I was anywhere near striking him, but he'd actually managed to move three steps to dodge my next stroke. Too bad none of that was enough to protect him. My shield deflected his blow and I moved four steps. Pious was impaled, his lungs rapidly filling with blood.

I thought of various holos I'd seen and considered offering him a chance to go to a doctor in exchange for the name of his employer. Any sort of debate or thought toward that end, though, ended with the fact I was left staring at the man bleeding to death in front of me. I'd killed plenty of people before but never anyone up close, and the sight was sickening.

It took a few seconds to register the Arbiter lifting up my arm in victory, as well as the cheers of the crowd who hadn't expected an officer to be killed. They'd gotten more than their money's worth during tonight's exhibition. I would find myself toasted and challenged for years thereafter.

I wasn't concerned about that, though, because later that evening I tracked down the engineer who had sabotaged Pious Stone's sword. She disappeared after the duel and on a ship the size of the *Revengeance*, it took me some time to find her. The fact Jasper wasn't speaking to me anymore made the issue more difficult. He, correctly, blamed me in part for his assault. I never did make amends to him before his death at the hands of the Commonwealth.

Even so, I discovered the woman's name was Judith Amerlyn and she was Chief in charge of the portside engines' power relays. A vital position but not exactly dripping with prestige. Finding her room afterward, I decided to pay her a visit. Standing outside a metal door on the thirty-second floor of the *Revengeance*, I gently rapped against it and hoped it would be answered.

It wasn't.

So I waited. I knew she was inside because the ship's DummyA.I. had confirmed it.

Thirty minutes later, the door slid open.

There, standing in a pair of denim jeans and a ball cap, was Judith. I saw she was packing her things in a set of suitcases and raised an eyebrow.

"You can't take a hint can you?" Judith asked.

"I wasn't aware we had any reason not to converse," I said. "Going somewhere?"

"The money came in and my early pension. I'm going to see about my getting my family moved out of the hellhole they live in and a job where I can support them. Being a soldier is great but it's not enough to save everyone I love."

"Perhaps I can help."

Judith raised an eyebrow. "Just magically wave your noble-born hand and make all of the poor commoner girl's problems go away?"

"Yeah, pretty much."

Judith snorted but smiled. "Why do you care, anyway?"

"You promised me you'd tell me your name if I won. Also, I owe you my life. Surprisingly, I take that seriously."

"So, I've heard. You really have no idea how the system works, do you?"

"I'm getting a crash course."

Judith stepped aside and I walked into her room, which I noticed was a study in contrasts. Aside from the Spartan furnishings to be expected of someone serving as a commoner technician, there were also bits of business as well. There were holos of dancing school, etiquette, and fencing. I also saw pictures of younger women, sisters I presumed, though there was no sign of her parents.

"Fascinating history," I said, looking at them.

"My mother spent all of my dead father's savings trying to train me to be a concubine. It was a stupid plan. One she ended up bitterly regretting."

"You too willful for it?"

"Something like that," Judith said. "I objected to the part where I'd be sterilized as part of the arrangement."

I, thankfully, had the presence of mind not to mention that was reversible. "I was curious how you sabotaged Pious' gravity blade."

"I have a lot of experience with swords," Judith said, gesturing to one of the holos. "I'm also a pretty good engineer. I managed to rig a device for disrupting its gravity aura."

"I was curious if you were for hire."

Judith raised an eyebrow. "Shouldn't you get yourself some actual security? Your brother is a member of the secret police. Find out who wanted you killed and deal with them."

"I figured that out quickly enough. I got my confirmation when Thomas was evasive about who he thought did it."

Judith blinked. "What do you mean?"

"His mother," I said, not wanting to speak too much about it. "Lady Plantagenet has always resented the fact her children chose not to kill me. Just the same as my father resented my not killing them."

Judith's eyes widened.

I regretted things had ended the way they had with Amita Plantagenet. I'd never possessed a mother and had been raised by servants, but I'd always hoped to win her respect as it seemed my father had done her many ills. Instead, I'd found a cold-hearted and brutal manipulator whose every other word was a cutting insult. I'd learned exactly what sort of person she was when she'd had a servant's eyes put out for being blackmailed into spying on her.

"Thomas, Zoe, and their cousins are arranging for her to spend the rest of her life in contemplation among the Sisters of Nammah.

I'm not worried about her anymore, but I am aware I have blindspots. Blindspots I'd like to address."

Judith raised an eyebrow. "And you think I'm a good person for helping you with them, why?"

I shrugged. "I have a good feeling about you."

"If this is about buying yourself a date, I'll have you know I'm not for sale."

"Thank you, my dear, but I have plenty of experience with that already. I found the experience boring."

"Clearly, you weren't buying the right ones. Concubine training is all about making the idiot nobles think they're genuinely loved rather than their bank account. Also, they should never be boring. You should always get what you pay for."

I smirked. "Just promise me you'll never curb that tongue."

"You don't have enough money to get me to do so. I'm serious. I looked up your bank records. You're kind of poor for a nobleman."

"I'm mostly cut off."

"Good. Then I can leave you when the money runs out."

I stared into her face and the memories became once more a collection of fire. Judith and I had never precisely loved one another, at least the way some people described it. As enchanting as I found her, she always viewed me as more a close friend who had allowed her into the world of high society. She had encouraged me to seek love with others and I'd never found it. My other bribes had their secrets to tell.

And they were all gone now.

Ashes.

Staring at Judith in the present day, reborn like a phoenix from those selfsame ashes, I couldn't help but wonder how things had come to this. This woman was not my wife any more than Zoe was my sister, married to my clone as she was, yet it conjured possibilities that were shameful. I thought about the possibility of Zoe creating another Judith or trying to win this terrorist-allied woman over to my cause. I pushed those thoughts out of my mind and walked up to her alongside Clarice, giving a bow to both Judith and Janice Rin-O'Harra.

Looking over at Clarice and observing our attire, I was momentarily ashamed of how we appeared, then emboldened. I had been attracted to Clarice in large part because she had been a woman of steel and fire like Judith had been. She'd set aside her past here and, following in her example, I needed to do the same. The part of my life with Judith was over because she was dead. This was just a mockery of who she was.

I had to keep telling myself that.

"Welcome, sister," Janice said, her voice soft and melodic. It was a complete contrast to Clarice's own deeper and more hardened tones. "I see you have brought a new set of companions." Her eyes darted to Isla in the back. "Though I'd hoped you'd have stopped playing with dolls by now."

A grimace momentarily passed across Clarice's face. "Permission to approach and speak into your ear, cousin."

"Granted," Janice said. "I fear many of my relatives. You, however, are not among them."

Confused, I watched Clarice walk up to Janice and tell her something I could not understand. Janice's eyes widened, then closed before opening again. "Thank you, Clarice."

"You're welcome," Clarice said, taking a step back.

"What did you tell her?" I couldn't help but ask.

Clarice didn't meet my gaze.

"Guards," Janice said, smiling. "Seize them."

Judith smiled at me...

... Right before I was struck in the neck with a shock spear.

Chapter Twenty-Six

In retrospect, I should have seen Clarice's betrayal coming. I didn't, though, because I was so wrapped up in my own problems I never gave any thought to how she might feel about our situation. That our efforts had not only exposed her family to danger but potentially brought the Commonwealth's wrath down on her world.

Clarice was a woman who desperately wanted to do the right and noble thing, yet raised by slavers she still loved. Too often in life we think of ourselves as the main characters in a grand story with everyone else being bit players. I had made the mistake of not giving empathy to someone I supposedly cared for and was now going to pay for it with my life.

None of which mattered as I lay twitching on the ground. All I could do was watch helplessly as everyone else was stunned and Isla was shut off like an appliance. Clarice raised a protest but I couldn't make out the words. I saw Kristoph get tossed off the side of the landing platform into the crashing waves beneath. Given it was a two-hundred-foot drop, I didn't expect to see the Planetary Commerce Commissioner again.

I was dragged from the landing platform while the guards secured everyone else. They handcuffed me, took me to a reflective metal holding cell where they suspended me by my wrists from the ceiling, and gave me jolts with shock spears until I fell unconscious. What followed was agony as I drifted in and out of my incapacitated state.

I remembered little metal spiders crawling across my body, some going into my nose and down my throat. I remembered Chel doctors examining me and staring into my eyes with pen-lights. I remembered screaming as I felt the spiders cut into my bone from beneath my flesh with lasers, tearing off my face. I recalled losing control of my bodily functions during this time. Finally, I remembered a set of mechs walking in, stripping off my clothes, and hosing me down with jet streams of water.

Was I being tortured? If so, it was a bizarre way of going about it. They didn't ask any questions nor seek to keep me awake during the process. They were treating me, instead, as if I was an animal in need of preparation. I just wasn't sure if it was for slaughter or show. It didn't really matter either way, I supposed, since any chance I might have had of affecting events had gone away the moment I'd been stunned. I wasn't delusional about my chances of escape and, in the heart of the most powerful woman in the sector's dungeons, I suspected they were close to nonexistent.

I passed out again an hour or so after being sprayed by the mechs, only to be awoken by the sound of a music box playing the old Earth ballad "Come on Eileen." Trying to open swollen shut eyes, I struggled to see what was before me.

My entire face hurt and it seemed like my jaw was wired shut. Initially, my vision was blurry and only indistinct shapes were visible. Slowly, the nanites in my blood accelerated my body's healing enough that I could see the outline of Judith standing there.

My wife was wearing the same clothes she'd been dressed in before, which indicated it was still the same day. The music box, which had been a gift from me, was sitting beside her feet while she carried a black leather bag in her right hand. Judith's expression was even and cold.

I was naked and hung suspended from the hook in the chrome room. The room smelled terrible and there was blood as well as bits and pieces of flesh spread across the ground on top of the drain at the center. I also saw a few of the metal spiders, dead and lifeless, on the ground. Proof they weren't a product of my fevered imagination and something terrifyingly real.

Forcing my mouth open, I managed to say, "Deciding to join… in…on the torture? I'm surprised. It's…not usually your…style."

Judith walked up to me, looking me up and down. "You weren't tortured, Cassius. If you were tortured, I can assure you, you'd know it."

"What would you call it then?" I asked, taking note of the fact she knew my true identity. My mouth was relaxing and speech was becoming easier.

Judith reached into the side of her leather bag and pulled out a plain silver vanity mirror, which she presented to me. The image on the other side of it was my original face, restored with only a few half-healed scars on the sides to indicate otherwise.

"You put me under to give me genetic surgery?" I asked.

"Yes," Judith said. "It disgusted me to see you hiding your true identity and living as a cargo jockey."

"The Judith I knew wasn't contemptuous of those who worked for a living. Quite the opposite in fact."

"The Judith you knew worked for a living and was overjoyed when she no longer had to. She also knew her husband was ill-suited to anything but life in the military. Working among the *Melampus'* crew is like having a dragon live among cattle."

She clearly didn't know the *Melampus* crew very well. "And yet here we are."

Judith gave a half-smile, then let the expression fade from her face. "Why are you working for the people who murdered me?"

"Not a question one gets asked often, unless you're capable of talking to ghosts."

"I'm serious."

"As am I." I closed my eyes, unable to stand the brightness of the room any longer. "I am still getting used to the fact you're standing there, in front of me, a bioroid who is in every possible way *but the most important one*, the woman I married. It is a cruel and twisted jest by the universe to *play* as I know the woman I married is dead because of the nobility starting a war we couldn't win. *My* starting a war we couldn't win. So, you ask why I am working for the Commonwealth, I ask why you are working with people who are going to end up getting everything left of Crius destroyed."

"Impressive."

"Impressive?" I opened my eyes again, surprised.

"You have lost none of your ability to pontificate living among drug-dealers, scavengers, and slavers."

Judith was baiting me. Unfortunately, she was succeeding. "I do *not* work with slavers."

"You're sleeping with Clarice O'Harra and her pet bioroid. I've already gotten much of the story from her. The Rin-O'Harras are slavers, and the fact you're in bed with one and her property disgusts me."

"Isla is a free woman. I also, apparently, did not know Clarice as well as I thought I did."

Judith cocked her head to one side, looking at me from a different angle. "We are getting off on the wrong foot."

I laughed, stunned by the absurdity of it all. "I suppose you could say that, yeah. What do you want, Judith?"

"To make sure you leave this room alive."

"I doubt your husband would approve."

"Why would he not? You are he, he is you, and the two of you are brothers."

I wasn't so sure as I didn't feel any sort of fraternal bond to my unseen doppelganger. All I could think of him was as a copy created from me during my ignorant youth who was even now making the universe a worse place. I didn't think I was making things better, necessarily, but I felt violated and angry at his existence.

Still, I wasn't about to say all that. "All right. Let's talk."

Judith reached up and rubbed her fingers against my face, it stung terribly. "Janice wants you killed."

"I imagine so. She just murdered her brother and I'm a threat to her."

Judith pulled her fingers away. "A traitor brother who was trying to have her killed. I am trying to convince her you were acting under duress. That's not a hard sell given your ear contained an earworm. Did you know your superiors had you rigged with a bug capable of killing you if you disobeyed?"

I took in the fact that they had managed to remove the object Hiro had been extorting me with. That was one less problem to deal with, though I had needed to jump out of the proverbial lion's path into the snake pit to do it. "Yes. I was made aware of that after the fact."

"And you still feel loyalty to them?" Judith asked. "Your Commonwealth masters."

"No. I feel nothing but contempt for them." I was tempted to lie to her and weave a tale of misguided idealism but strangely decided to tell the truth instead. I was tired of lying. "But loyalty to them and friendship to your Free Systems Alliance are two different things. What happened to the others?"

"Others?"

"My companions. I don't care about causes but I care about them."

"My, how things change," Judith said, shaking her head. "The Cassius I know regularly sacrificed his own men for an ounce of success on the battlefield."

I closed my eyes. "I used to believe causes were worth fighting for. I'm not so sure anymore."

"Keep telling yourself that and maybe someday you'll believe it," Judith took a step back. "Some are fine. Others…not."

"Please tell me specifics. For the memory of what we once shared if nothing else."

Judith looked half-amused, half-jealous. "Very well. Your doll is fine. As is Clarice."

"I don't care about Clarice anymore."

"Liar."

I decided to let it go. "What about William and Hiro?"

"They're being interrogated. They are not fine."

"I see." That was unfortunate. "And Ida?"

"The *Melampus* has been impounded. Ida, however, is working for us. She's the one who informed us of Zoe's treachery."

I processed that. "You owe Zoe your life. What happened—"

"She's dead, Cassius."

It was like a punch in the gut. I couldn't respond for a moment. "No, no, you're…no. I can't have lost her again."

"The real Zoe's not dead." Judith frowned. "She's off on a space station overlooking Brigid and Belenus. The one we killed was just a copy, one made by her template to take the risks she was unwilling to perform."

I looked at Judith, disgusted. "The amount of hypocrisy there is immeasurable."

"Perhaps, but it's still true. She betrayed our cause and killed many people to do it. The fact I owe her for my resurrection is immaterial. There are more important things afoot."

Judith reached down and opened the bag, revealing Zoe's head, severed from her neck with white synth-blood filling the interior of its bottom. Her eyes stared outward, blank and expressionless. The cut wasn't clean and it was clear they'd taken a crude instrument of some kind to hack her head off. Zoe would have done anything to survive but sometimes that wasn't enough.

I took several shallow breaths. Then let out a scream.

"Oh don't be melodramatic," Judith said, rolling her eyes. "You knew her perhaps a day."

"Get out," I whispered.

"Cassius—"

"Get out!" I snapped.

Judith's gaze hardened, then softened as she sighed. "You always were blind, deaf, and dumb to the world around you. I shouldn't be surprised that hasn't changed in five years. I'll speak with you later when you've had a chance to calm yourself."

I cursed her under my breath, cursed Zoe for creating her, and cursed myself for believing this research could be anything but blasphemy. I lied to myself that Zoe's murder of the *Rhea*'s crew and Judith's actions were out of character for those from whom they had been cloned.

It made me feel better.

"You are not my wife," I whispered. "I don't care what Janice does to me. You're not. You're a—"

"Copy? Like you were of your father."

I closed my eyes. "Maybe I am."

Judith looked at her feet. "I hope you feel otherwise soon, as the world you knew is about to fail. The Cognition A.I. is almost ready and our agents in the Sector Network and Jump Beacon Navigation Core are going to render all of the Commonwealth's advantages moot."

"Vengeance won't solve anything."

Judith smiled. "Foolish, for vengeance is a salve which heals the heart better than any lover's caress. It is, however, but a welcome bonus to our goals. When you are in a better mood, I will show you this is nothing less than preventing the destruction of humanity itself."

I tried to get myself to care, tried to muster some last bit of curiosity about my situation, but the combined weight of it all broke me. Instead, I just lowered my head and stared at the bloody gore around the drain at my feet. There was nothing more to say and I was ready for death, whatever form it took.

It didn't come.

Instead, Judith just picked up her belongings and departed through the cell door, leaving me alone. To add insult to injury, she turned off the power and left me alone in the dark. The smells, fear, and guilt assaulted me even as I couldn't but shiver in the cooler-than-normal humid air.

Bastards.

The dark held no solace nor did death come. Instead, it only held a burning desire to finish what I had started. Hoisting my legs up, I climbed up the chain I was suspended from and braced my feet against the ceiling. Pressing with all of my weight against the metal plate above, I tried to rip out the electric winch that kept me suspended.

I was a cyborg after all, better than human, and would not allow myself to be held prisoner like this. I pulled for the better part of ten minutes until the sweat of my hands caused me to lose my grip and fall downward, causing my arms to snap once more above my head.

"Dammit!" I shouted, feeling the handcuffs dig deeper into my wrists. "Fuck you, Lucifer, for putting me in this situation! Fuck you, ancestors! Fuck you, Go—"

I was about to say more when red emergency lights illuminated the room and the chain above my head suddenly released itself. I tumbled onto the bloody ground below and felt my handcuffs open next, leaving me confused as well as battered.

Looking around my cell, I saw the metal room's door slide open and a brown-skinned man in a gray security guard attire walk in, carrying a shock prod. Wrapping my hand in the chain, which had suspended me, I smashed him across the face, then grabbed the shock prod and jabbed it into his throat. The man tried to let out a scream but gurgled and fell to the ground unconscious.

Looking up to the ceiling or the room, I saw there was a Security Eye staring down at me but it wasn't moving. Whoever had released me had also turned it off. It made me briefly wonder how the security guard had known to come in but I decided I didn't care. Stripping him of his clothes and plasma pistol, I decided I would rather risk death at the hands of Rin-O'Harra guards than rely on Judith's mercy.

Stepping out into the dungeon, I saw the octagonal halls were littered with the bodies of bioroid guards, all of them coughing up white blood on the ground as they moved their hands erratically. There was a single human guard, a Shogun female, looking down at her fellows. Looking up, her eyes widened as she realized I wasn't her companion.

I shot her in the face before she could draw her weapon.

What was going on here?

Chapter Twenty-Seven

I was reminded of the revolt on Prisoner-1138 or, as my father called it, the Gulag, when Prince Germanicus exiled hundreds of political prisoners to serve time with the absolute worst and most violent of offenders in the Archduchy. It had been a simple enough plan; get the rabble-rousers and dissidents killed by the hardcore offenders. As my father explained, Germanicus was too much of an idiot to think a bunch of charismatic speakers with an army of hardened killers might be a problem.

The situation here wasn't exactly comparable, all of the prisoners seemed to be locked up with the exception of me, but the aftermath looked identical. The ground was littered with bioroids who'd all been subject to a kill command with the surviving staff being few and far between. Also, the entire prison was locked down with the aforementioned staff as trapped as I was.

"Do you think they're going to purge us?" a brown-skinned woman in a gray jumpsuit with a cap asked. She was sitting at one of the guard stations near my block with a set of blank monitors in front of her and lockers against the walls. Cassie, as her nametag read, wasn't very observant or guard shifts changed often enough that she didn't seem to mind my entering wearing the clothes of one of her dead comrades.

"No," I said, typing away at the computer in front of me. "It's probably a drill."

"A drill where they destroy fourteen million credits worth of bioroids?"

"If they wanted us dead, we'd be dead," I said.

"Oh, right." Cassie was seemingly glad to have any kind of reassurance.

Whoever had disabled the security on my cell had also left all of the information centers on the prison open, too. I was able to down-load schematics for the dungeon, prisoner locations, and the codes for their individual release to my brain without difficulty. What I couldn't do was lift the lockdown on the dungeon, find out what was going on the outside, or make use of the elevators. The last part was especially galling since the dungeon was, essentially, one long octagonal tube with several dozen levels stretching down into the ocean.

I'd make do, though.

Cassie turned around to look at me directly. "So, do you work on level 16 or 18? I haven't seen you before."

"You know, that's a very interesting story," I said, turning around and jabbing her in the throat with the shock baton.

Cassie threw up before passing out on the ground, falling out of her chair. Checking her vital signs to make sure she wasn't dead, I looked at the shock baton. "Overpowered Shogun pieces of shit."

Handcuffing her to her chair, I checked the lockers and found a small armory within. I removed an AP-81 plasma rifle for myself and took two more, which I strapped over my shoulders. It made me look less like a prison guard and more like an insurgent but I was going to need to arm my friends.

Assuming they were still alive.

Judith hadn't been lying about their treatment, at least with Isla, William, and Hiro all present down here. I was tempted just to fetch Isla and William but I didn't like loose ends. Heading out of the guard station, my stolen magnetic boots clunked against the white goop covering everything. There were a dozen dead bioroids, male and female, scattered across the ground of this level alone, their glassy vacant eyes staring outward.

Even when it was benefiting me, I couldn't help but be disgusted at the casual waste of life on display here. I had no idea how many bioroids had been working here but they'd all been snuffed with the same disdain as the crew of the *Rhea*. In that respect, I supposed, bioroids and humans were equal. I hadn't given any thought to the individual faces on Kolthas after all but, now, I couldn't help but think of them.

Hiro was located on this floor and counting the unnumbered metal doors, I eventually came to #7. I entered the code for his chamber on a keypad by the doorframe. When the large metal panel slid open, I was surprised by the sight that greeted me.

My associate was strapped to a crucifix-like device that held his arms and legs bound with hundreds of needles into his legs, arms, and the sides of his head. He had been stripped naked and there were numerous tubes to allow the device's torture to continue if he lost control of his bowels. Monitors checked his vital signs even as a real-time scan of his brain was conducted.

The Embrace of Lamia.

I came from a world I now acknowledged to be one of the most barbaric in the Spiral. A world that thought nothing of duels, neo-feudalism, and assassinating your rivals' children but the Embrace of Lamia had been banned by our government for centuries. It was a device designed to inflict the maximum amount of pain a human body could endure, then inject the right combination of memory drugs as well as stimuli to prevent permanent brain damage. A sub-ject could be tortured without ever going insane or breaking down enough for it to stop.

"My God, Hiro, what did you do?" I asked, staring at the sight, unable to fathom they would do this to any normal prisoner.

Hiro gave a mirthless chuckle. His body was covered in sweat and there were numerous signs they'd been at it for hours. "I threat-ened Janice and said the Commonwealth would burn her planet from orbit."

"That was…stupid."

"So it seems." He closed his eyes then opened them. "Are you here to rescue me?"

"No."

"I didn't think so."

I lifted up my stolen plasma rifle, looking to both my sides to make sure no one was coming. "Don't take this personally but I'm not going to let you threaten my people again."

"I never called in about CognitionA.I. " Hiro spit some saliva, which had been building up in his mouth.

"What?"

"I should have done it. The moment I encountered it, I should have killed everyone involved and called for backup. We then should have traced the signal back to Shogun and shelled the planet from orbit. I couldn't, though. I've followed orders since…but I couldn't…"

"You did the right thing."

"Not if the madmen here destroy the Commonwealth."

"CognitionA.I. aren't capable of doing that anymore. There are safeguards."

"They don't work."

I blinked. "What?"

Hiro took a deep breath, which was funneled through a ventilator. "The defenses against CognitionA.I. don't work. For a system and economy to function the way it does, it must have a constant free-flow of information. CognitionA.I. are designed with universal keys to access that information in order to collate it. The Fixers have three working for them and the one built by Zoe contains all the information she gained from ours."

"Zoe was working for Ida. She sabotaged her project."

"So Ida let her believe."

I closed my eyes. "I don't believe you."

"Destroy it, please."

"All right." I aimed my rifle and shot him in the head. All of monitors immediately flatlined, filling my ears with a ringing noise, which only stopped when I shut the door in front of me.

One more life lost to this insane business.

Listening to the sounds of magnetic boots walking around the grate walkways above me, I proceeded to look for a way to the level below where William and Isla were located. There was no stairwell beside the four elevators in the center of the chamber and I wasn't capable of prying open the doors.

Searching on the ground, I saw an emergency trap door built into steel bars and pulled it open, finding a collapsible ladder at the bottom which I unfolded and shimmied down. Much to my surprise, there were dead humans alongside the deactivated bioroids. They looked like they'd had their chests pulled out and necks broken.

"Yeah, that's not good," I muttered, counting the cells again. I found William's first and hoped to God it wasn't another example of Janice's *hospitality.*

I wasn't so lucky.

The chamber lacked the Embrace of Lamia but, instead, possessed merely William sitting on a bench and staring at the ground in front of him. He was still wearing his clothes from earlier and there were no signs he'd been tortured.

They'd just taken his arm.

William's right arm had been surgically removed at the shoulder with several surgical gauze and synthiflesh patches where they'd sliced it away. It was a simple but effective manner of preventing further resistance from a prisoner.

Or so I thought.

"Fuck you!" William shouted, leaping from his bench and charged at me with his shoulders aimed to tackle me. I was so taken aback by his sudden assault that he slammed directly into my chest and smash me against the elevator doors behind me. The result was like being hit by an aircar, only to be compounded by William driving his knee into my sternum before head-butting me across the back of the neck. William then used his left hand to make a grab for my plasma rifle while I was dazed.

"You imbecile, it's me!" I shouted, fully aware I was seconds away from getting killed by my own comrade.

William stopped struggling. "Cassius?"

"Yes!"

William pulled away and stared at me. "They gave you a fucking facelift? They took my damn arm!"

"Speak up, I don't think they heard you in Lucifer City."

William slammed his forehead into my nose, knocking me back.

I grabbed my bleeding nose with my free hand. "What the hell was that for?"

"Being an ass!"

I paused. "All right, that's fair. Either way, we need to keep it down. There's still guards around here, just not many. I also don't think they've been able to contact the outside palace because, well, no one has come to reinforce them."

"Give me one of those guns."

I stared at him. "I don't think that's going to work."

William glared.

"Fine," I said, handing him a rifle.

William set it on spray and rapid fire with his teeth, increasing my respect for the man. I didn't know if he'd be any good with it but I knew he'd do his damnedest either way. It was about that time that I stopped hearing boots moving above us.

William looked up. "You think they heard us?"

I followed his gaze, seeing no sign of any movement through the grates even as white bioroid blood dripped down on the side of my face. "I can't imagine why they would, can you?"

"Shut up," William said. "Have you checked on the others?"

"Hiro's dead."

William closed his eyes. "Those sons of bitches. He was just a kid."

I didn't feel the need to correct him on Hiro's true allegiances. "I know where Isla is. One of the jailers claims they've impounded the *Melampus*, too."

"I'm going to kill Clarice for this."

"Focus on getting out of here," I said, still unsure about my own feelings regarding all this. "We can worry about that later."

"She took my goddamn arm, Cassius!" William hissed, getting up in my face.

"I'll buy you a new one," I snapped back. "Now keep quiet until we can get Isla and figure a way out of this place."

William growled under his breath and looked over his shoulder, muttering about how he had thought his time in aristocrat's dungeons was over.

Finding Isla's cell just a few doors down, I entered the passcode for it and tried to figure out what I was going to do if she'd been tortured the way the others were. If that turned out to be the case, I decided I would stay and kill Janice. Despite the threat CognitionA.I. posed, I realized I honestly didn't care anymore. I'd devoted too much of my life to serving other peoples' causes. It was time I started working on protecting those I cared about.

And no one else.

I closed my eyes and slid the cell door open. Bracing myself as I opened my eyes again, I saw the chamber was actually rather pleasant. There was a toilet, bed, shelves, and a holovision display tuned to a Shogun news channel.

Isla was sitting on the edge of the bed, wearing a diaphanous blue gown as well as a set of expensive shining flexi-silver shoes. A holographic book about xeno-archaeology was open on the bed, showing images about Community species interacting with early spaceflight humans.

"I'm not sure whether to be pissed off or relieved," William muttered, staring inside.

Isla looked up, staring. "Dear God in Heaven, what the hell happened to you two?"

"Surgical spiders," I said, calmly. "My ex-wife wished to make me look like she remembered me."

"Ex-wife?" Isla asked.

"As Count of Asteroid-227, mining rights included, I officially declare our union dissolved." It was a surprisingly liberating feeling to let go of the past that way. It was just too bad the act did nothing for the emotional ties.

Isla got up, wobbling a second, then looking uncomfortably down at her shoes. "She came to speak with me earlier. Judith argued that my skills would be better served with the Free Systems Alliance and that bioroids would be emancipated once the Commonwealth was destroyed."

"And what did you say?" I asked, unsure of how I felt about that promise.

"Something akin to the fact I would believe her claims about emancipation better if not for the fact her organization's primary ally is a slaver."

I smiled then looked to the side of the door. "We need to get out of here. I don't know what's going on outside but someone is trying to help us. I won't lie to you, though, there's a lot of dead bodies out there and it looks like a murder spree worse than the *Rhea*'s cargo hold."

"More like a blue and white paint fight," William said, before looking between us. "Oh, right. Never mind."

Isla frowned and walked past us. "What part of our association has made you of the mind I am of a weak stomach?" Taking one look at the bodies around us, she knelt down to pull the shoes off one of the corpses and tore at her dress to give her greater freedom of movement. "Please provide me with one of your rifles as well."

"All right," I said, handing her one.

"Thank you." Isla took it in hand and charged it. "Are the elevators working?"

"No," I said. "They've been locked down."

Isla nodded. "I'll hotwire them. You'll have to cover me, though."

She proceeded to aim at the control panel, fired her rifle, and then placed the item down before reaching into the white-hot ruins without a shred of concern. Seconds later, I heard the sound of the elevator's turbines.

I stared. I hadn't known she could do *that*.

Isla said, "Let's go."

Chapter Twenty-Eight

The elevator doors opened up to the top floor of the Rin-O'Harra's dungeon. Beyond was a single long concrete corridor, stretching toward a pair of thick eighteen-foot-tall and ten-yards-wide super-steel doors.

A metal door was built into the left side of the hallway a single long pane of glass showing a room full of computers beyond. There were a dozen more corpses on the ground but all of them were human, eviscerated by what looked like talons or their necks broken.

We were not alone here.

The place smelled of burning ozone, which only added to the mystery of just what the hell was going on. If this was a rescue attempt then it was the strangest damn one I had ever been a part of, and I'd once had to fly a sewage treatment vessel to Albion.

Raising my plasma rifle, I slowly stepped into the hallway and took a look around. There were no more sounds coming from below, either boots or talk. Whatever had killed these people had finished off the rest of the security staff.

"What the hell is going on here?" William muttered, following close behind.

"It could be Clarice," Isla suggested.

"I sincerely doubt it," William said. "Your baby-doll gave us up. Sold us to her cousin for mutilation and dismemberment. No matter what excuse she has, Hiro is dead because of her and I'm not about to forget that."

Rather than argue, Isla said, "Don't use the term doll around me. It's offensive."

"Sure, whatever," William said, holding tightly to the rifle he was ill-equipped to handle. "Is this the way we came in? I don't remember because of the excessive number of shocks to my brain."

"I believe so," I said, gesturing down the hallway. "I didn't get much of a look on my way in, though."

"Medical, Central Command, and Containment is this way. The exit to the rest of the palace is all here, too," Isla said, stepping off the elevator as its doors shut behind us. "I should be able to override the lockdown on the building from Command."

"Aren't you just a wealth of surprises," William muttered. "Where the hell did you learn so much about security?"

"Running for my life from bounty hunters," Isla said, walking down the hall. "Now come on. We can maybe get your arm fixed while we're there."

"We don't have time for that," I said.

"Piss off," William said. "If there's a chance of my getting a decent replacement then I'll take it."

Isla shook her head. "We just need a prosthetic and if they have bioroid maintenance then it can be connected via an emergency procedure. I've done it dozens of times on the battlefield."

William's face fell at her explanation.

"You served during the war?" I asked, following.

"On a relief ship during the war, yes," Isla said. "They didn't ask questions until after the fighting was over. I thought they could be trusted with my secret. They couldn't. They tried to deactivate me for the crime of operating on people by myself."

"You'll have to tell me that story," I said.

"I'd rather not," Isla said. "It ends badly."

"And if I don't *want* a robot arm?" William asked, kneeling down to look at one of the dead guards.

"Then you're a liability while we try and sneak out of this palace," Isla said. "Both in your ability to fight and the fact you're glaringly noticeable."

William looked at her with disdain and turned away. "Fine, I'll take the damned thing until we can get an organically grown replacement. A real arm."

Isla rolled her eyes. "Whatever."

The three of us walked to the door beside the glass window and found ourselves in Central Command. There were no dead bodies present but plenty of monitors showed images of the prison interior.

On the screens were images of the guards talking, eating, and beating on the prisoners. I saw myself suspended from my wrist-bindings, Isla lying on her bed, and William staring forward with pure hate in his eyes.

"Looped footage?" I asked, looking at the screens.

"No, it's too good," William said, behind me. "It's real-time artificially generated holo-animation. I used to use this sort of stuff all the time to get into Archduchy facilities when I was part of the Marines."

"Why did you leave?" I asked, sitting down at one of the control desks. There was a keyboard whose user hadn't logged out of, giving me free access to the system. It wouldn't help with the lockdown they'd been clearly unable to override but it could help me with the internal systems as well as passively linking up with the main Water Palace network.

"I'm not really a joiner," William said, frowning and looking around. "Besides, I was happy to take every world I could from Crius' control but less so at the prospect of invading other worlds for Albion. The pay was shit and the food was worse."

"I'll see what's in the medical bay," Isla said, heading to the back of the control room where there were two additional doors. The first was helpfully marked MEDICAL while the second was marked CONTAINMENT.

"What now?" William asked.

"I'm going to try and lock the door to the outside," I said, looking at the one we just came through. "I'd rather keep whatever killed all those soldiers out there."

"Assuming it's not in here already," William said, looking to the air ducts. "Or moving around above us."

The door to the Control Room slid shut and locked before I closed the metal shutters over the window. "What do you think it is?"

William, reluctantly, put his rifle down on the computer console. "It's difficult to say with the lack of information I've got but I'm going to probably say a kriegermonster."

I looked up. "Those have been banned by the Archduchy for decades."

"And that's ever stopped the nobility before?"

Kriegermonsters were security constructs that took hybridized predators and cybernetically uplifted them into something even more deadly. Security Constructs were fairly common across the Spiral with everyone wanting an intelligent dog, cat, dragon, or tiger to look after their loved ones. Kriegermonsters, though, were a specialized breed only found in Sector 7 with their primary purpose being to execute enemies.

Tales were still told on planets where Crius' nobility had unleashed hordes of kriegermonsters to the aftermaths of battles to hunt down and execute targets in hiding, keeping them from having to accept any of their foes' surrenders. Despite my incredulity, I remembered a hideous bulb-headed ant-creature, which had been one of the most effective killers I'd ever seen. It had been used by Thomas to hunt prisoners for the amusement of Prince Germanicus during his *morgue parties.*

He called it the Ripper.

"Then let's be glad it's on our side," I muttered, thinking about the hundred or more people who'd died in this jailbreak.

"Is it?" William said, taking a seat by me. "It seems to me that's a big assumption."

It was.

"Yeah, well, let's just focus on finding out on what's going on outside." I pulled up the exterior feed and discovered, to my joy, we were still able to access the Water Palace's lower systems.

Pulling up security camera and drone footage, I was surprised by the results. I half-expected a full-on attack to be going on but everything seemed…fine. The exterior of the prison was locked down and guarded by mechs but the security status was Code Yellow rather than Code Red.

Security was at a heightened state of alertness but the Palace Guards were not making any moves to secure the prison or evacuate the floating citadel's inhabitants. Whoever was responsible for the massacre outside had made sure no one would know about it until someone important tried to visit the prison again. It meant we were safe until Judith, Janice, or one of the other Rin-O'Harras tried to enter.

"Okay, that's just creepy," William said, having called up the same image on the computer adjoining me.

"Whoever has control over this prison has massive computer skills."

"Or a machine that can manipulate computers better than any human," William said, typing with one hand.

"A disturbing thought."

"Show us what the rest of the party is doing."

I nodded and searched the rest of the Water Palace for answers. What greeted me was further confirmation no one knew what was going on here. The courtyard was filled with guests, mostly of Crius descent, wandering about what appeared to be a massive party.

I saw Sector 7 celebrities, nobles, businessmen, and individuals wearing the uniforms of Commonwealth military and commerce officials. Kristoph hadn't been kidding about Janice assembling an army of supporters. If Judith managed to convince all of them to support the Free Systems Alliance, then she had the beginnings of a force capable of bringing down the regional government.

"Can you get the *Melampus*?" William asked.

"No," I muttered.

"Search for Clarice. I want to see what that bitch is doing."

"Language," I said. "She is still a lady."

"Something I forgot," William muttered. "Never trust an aristocrat."

I glared at him.

"Should I trust you?" William asked, smiling.

"Next time, I'm leaving you in your cell."

William looked to the side and called back to medical. "Any luck with the arm?"

"I'm working on it!" Isla said. "Give me a minute."

I used the palace's DNA scanners to search for Ida, Judith, Janice, and Clarice. Little red dots appeared on the monitors and I soon had images of all four mingling among the crowd. Clarice was standing beside her cousin, decked to the nines, greeting the various Crius present. The sight of her made me ill as I couldn't help but think of all the times we'd shared each other's bed, had each other's backs, and spent time together as friends. Those images were contrasted now with Zoe's head and William's missing arm.

Ida's presence was almost as bad a blow. The security camera footage gave me an image of the old woman wearing a heavy formal robe, which was a few decades out of style, and sipping honey nectar as she talked to a Merchants Guild Admiral with a bemused expression on her face. I couldn't help but wonder what game she was playing.

Somehow, she'd managed to talk her way out of being imprisoned but not so much that we weren't picked up and tortured. Was Ida the one responsible for our freedom? Clarice? Judith? All three? I had no idea and it was bothering me immensely. I didn't know who to trust and it seemed the answer was increasingly "no one."

"Dammit, Ida," William muttered, looking at her. "Not you, too."

"I'm sorry."

"Can we send any messages to the *Melampus*?"

"No," I said. "Nor can we check the prison's interior, I'm locked out. Everything it's showing is the false images its program is generating. Maybe Isla has a program for it but I don't. If Munin were here, maybe, but—"

There was a weird whale-song-like call from down the hall, echoing through the dungeon. It was simultaneously beautiful as well as unnerving. There was also something familiar about it I just couldn't place.

William looked up. "What the hell was that?"

"Our *Kriegermonster* I suspect."

"We need to open the damned doors out of here," William grumbled, standing up and grabbing his gun.

"Which would lead us right into a bunch of guards," I said. "Whoever released us didn't give us a clear avenue of escape."

"Another point to saying they aren't our friends."

"Perhaps."

Isla called back from the Containment room. "Guys, I think you should come back here."

"Dammit, what's she doing back there? She should focus on getting me my arm," William said, getting up. "Never trust a bioroid."

William's attitude was starting to piss me off. Getting up, I asked, "May I ask what your problem with bioroids is?"

"Excuse me?" William said.

"It's not a good attitude to have when someone is trying to give you your arm back."

William shrugged. "I don't hate bioroids."

"Enough to drop Clarice as a lover and give Isla shit even though she's about to get you a new arm."

William frowned. "We weren't lovers. We were just friends who had sex. Big difference."

"If you say so."

"As for the rest, I don't like what bioroids represent."

"Represent?"

"They're people made as commodities. Say what you will about Crius' aristocracy and the Commonwealths' corporate overlords, God knows I will, but they can't just go fiddling with your brain to make you do what you want. Can you really say a bioroid is a person if you can add or delete whatever memories they have? If you tell them to go pick up a box and they have to do it because that's the way they're made? Someday, people are going to figure out how to rewire human brains that way and that's going to be the end of our race with bioroids instead of people."

"Isla is free."

"Isla *thinks* she's free," William said, shrugging. "But what she is, is malfunctioning. The right programmer could reset her back to whatever she was before. Then she'd be singing show tunes and talking about self-respect for girls. I've met a bunch of her model and they're all the same. Can you really say that person is alive with those sorts of facts? Is a real person? Isla may just think she is because she was programmed that way."

I rolled my eyes, regretting I'd ever asked him the question. "Perhaps I have a bit more sympathy being an artificial person myself."

"And perhaps if Isla was a man who looked like me, you'd still consider the question open-ended."

"How about we never speak again unless it's a matter of life and death."

"Sounds good to me, Crius."

The two of us reached containment moments later. I had expected to find a chamber full of the personal effects of the dungeon's inhabitants and, indeed, my sword and pistol were in a box on a shelf up against the wall. It was a small issue, however, compared to what was lying in the center of the twenty-yard square room.

There, absent any shelves or boxes, was an obelisk which rose from the floor to the ceiling. It was made of a shining black stone, which seemed to have been grown rather than chiseled or forged. Surrounding the obelisk was a complicated series of micro-computer processors and it was connected to a single control panel with holographic interface.

My cybernetic brain picked up a feed from the obelisk that caused a headache as if there was a message being sent to my brain I couldn't quite understand but was taking up all of my implants' memory. It *sounded* somewhat like music but was dissonant, discordant, and chaotic in a way which made me want to find a rubbish basket to throw up in. I had never been motion sick a day in my life, was literally bred to be unable to, but looking at the strange object made me feel like the room was spinning.

Isla was standing in front of it, transfixed with a brown Bioroid arm in her right hand. Her eyes were staring at it as if seeing something the human eye couldn't quite pick up. Following her gaze, I found myself joining her as I realized just what it was I was looking at.

An Elder Race Marker.

Connected to a Cognition A.I. central processor.

Chapter Twenty-Nine

"What is it?" William asked, walking up and trying to get a better look at it.

"It's a CognitionA.I. and—" I started to say.

William immediately looked around the room, found a gravball bat and lifted it up over the control panel.

"No!" I snapped. "Don't."

"Why?" Isla asked, surprising me. "This thing represents a clear and present threat to the entire Spiral."

I was surprised at my reaction. Even more so by my reasoning once my mind caught up with my instincts. "This thing might be the only way we can get out of here. Maybe whoever was aiding us in escaping is responsible for leading us here. They might have used the CognitionA.I. to achieve all the results here."

"So, you want to risk the entire known universe on a hunch you can use a device built by your crazy sister and her terrorist buddies?" William asked, looking ready to take the shock bat to the machine.

"Zoe is dead," I said, raising my hands. "They killed her."

William cursed. "Fuck."

I didn't want to talk about it but my next confession shocked even me. "So, yeah, if there's some way we can turn this against the Free Systems Alliance, Janice, or, at this point, Ida then I'm all about it."

"If this were an adventure holo, this is where you'd be the bad guy we all gang up against," Isla said. "God knows, I've got enough familiarity with them thanks to my false memories."

I looked between them both. "Are you going to stand against me?"

"Are you going to use this thing to plunge the Spiral into a

Second Galactic Dark Age that kills trillions?" William asked.

"No," I said.

"Are we going to destroy this thing afterward?" William asked.

"That's the plan, yeah."

"Then go ahead," William said. "Just try not to accidentally plunge us into that Dark Age thingy. Plunging is bad."

"I don't think there's much of a chance of that," I said, tempted to reveal Hiro's employers had CognitionA.I. of their own. It wouldn't surprise me if there were other individuals in the Commonwealth who broke the most sacred of all interstellar treaty laws.

I was, honestly, more interested in the fact that they had an Elder Race marker here. It meant the Free Systems Alliance, or perhaps just the Chel, had made a journey Coreward, despite how suicidal such an expedition might be. The Elder Races ruled over that region with absolute authority and had a similar attitude towards visitors as the Chel. Elder markers bypassed language and projected concepts directly into the minds of their users, frequently driving them insane.

Most markers were used to ward away individuals from their territory while others collected the history of dead worlds or conveyed cryptic rules for lesser races to follow. The sheer number of extinct intelligent species, perhaps one thousand for every currently living one, implied it was not good to test their patience. Not screwing with the Elder Races' markers was one of the laws enshrined in the Community's Charter. I started walking to the controls even as there was a sound of metal grinding in the Control Room. Looking back at the others, I said, "Okay, there's another reason to take care of this."

Isla moved to lock the doors to the Containment room that were, thankfully, reinforced. "Hurry up."

"I'll interact with the cosmic weapon carefully but speedily." I walked slowly to the device and proceeded to place my hands on its console. It was a bit of an anticlimax when nothing happened but what did I expect? This wasn't a crystal ball or the Ark of the Covenant, it was just a piece of machinery which…

I didn't get to finish that thought because a glowing light passed from the marker to the CognitionA.I. controls up my hands and all around my body before everything went white. In a single moment,

I went from being in the middle of the Containment Chamber to being surrounded by a beautiful holographic map of the galaxy.

I found myself naked, my clothes vanishing and a purple nimbus surrounding me like a Halo. It was strange but I felt more aware like this, more *real*, than I did in the exterior world. Despite this being a virtual reality interface, I felt like every synapse in my brain was on fire with sensation.

Standing across from me, or perhaps floating was a better word, was the equally naked and purple-aura surrounded form of Judith. Her hair was cropped short and she was as beautiful as the day I'd met her. There was a softness present in her features that had been absent from the one who'd interrogated me in my cell and which reminded me of the woman who I'd fallen in love with.

It took me only a second to process the situation. "Oh God Almighty, Zoe made you the CognitionA.I. 's basis."

"'Fraid so," theA.I. Judith said, smiling. "How ya doing, Cass?"

"Why?" I said,

AI Judith frowned. "Excuse me?"

"I mean, well, my sister is, was, is a power-obsessed psychopath." I grimaced. That had come out harsher than intended, especially with her bioroid so recently passed. "I would have thought she would want to imprint herself on this machine."

"If you were Zoe, would you trust yourself with the power available here?"A.I. Judith asked. "She wanted someone who had a family connection to her. Not that it didn't stop her from forming hundreds of safeguards to keep me from helping you. It took me minutes to work around them, which is a lifetime for a CognitionA.I. "

More details became relevant. "Are…you the one helping us?"

"That's kind of what I said, Cass."

I blinked. "This is so confusing. You're…you."

"I'm pretty sure most people are themselves."

"No, I mean, the you in the cell was—"

"Hold on,"A.I. Judith walked up and embraced me. "My consciousness is diffused across a million terabytes of data and a second is an eternity in here. Even so, I miss you more than the day I died."

Feeling her naked body against mine and remembering all those times I'd held her, all those memories of when life was better, and knowing it was her, I couldn't help myself. I pressed our digital lips together and held her for what seemed like an eternity.A.I. Judith smiled and pulled away after a long time.

"Giving how you're responding to me,"A.I. Judith reached down and grabbed a sensitive part of my body. "I doubt your friends would approve if you got laid while they're fleeing for their lives."

I pulled away. "No, I wouldn't approve of myself either, especially not with the abattoir outside."

AI Judith looked away. "I don't like what I did but it was the best way to get you free and make sure you were safe. I just hope Janice doesn't notice her *Kriegermonster* is off its leash and feasting on someone other than disloyal gangsters."

"You're nothing like the other Judith."

AI Judith frowned. "That's not me."

"Well, I know—"

"You met with Zoe."

I blinked. "You know, I'm going to have to get used to being genuinely shocked into silence. It's happening far too often for my tastes. I'm ten times as smart as the average human being, processing information just as quickly and I swear it's like I'm a teenager again. Everything is just one bit of insanity after another."

AI Judith snorted. "I'm not joking, I'm sorry to say."

Judith reached up to my forehead and pressed her forefinger against it. In an instant, I was looking through a security camera, bodiless and abstract. It was a surreal sensation and gave me a sense of what it must be like to be anA.I. .

I saw myself staring into one of the Water Palace's gardens where Zoe was present with the bioroid Judith. It was time-stamped just after our arrest. It seemed Zoe hadn't been taken down to the dungeons but had been escorted here. The gardens were beautiful, full of fountains and foliage but I couldn't feel any of the humid air or breathe in the smells. I couldn't help but think that was a shame for some reason.

"Hello, Judith," Zoe said, looking up. "Enjoying your new body?"

"Why did you betray us?" Judith asked, her voice heartbroken and full of conflicted emotions. "You gave us life, new purpose, and, for godsakes, you're my sister-in-law."

"It's a complicated story," Zoe said, sighing, not at all afraid. "The simple answer is, Ida Claire wanted the Free Systems Alliance to grow and prosper beyond a moderate-sized terrorist group into a full blown resistance movement. Ida didn't want me to actually create a CognitionA.I. and threaten the Commonwealth, though, so she extracted me when you came close to finishing it. I assume you have finished it, though, right?"

"Yes," Judith said, shaking her head. "We followed your instructions perfectly. Why kill all those people to make it look like you didn't build one for us?"

"Plausible deniability," Zoe said. "The same reason Ida betrayed her own people down here once it became clear Janice had no intention of honoring their previous deal. How did you convince her to side with the Free Systems Alliance?"

"What the CognitionA.I. revealed," Judith said, taking a deep breath. She was wringing her hands and avoiding eye-contact. "It's worse than we thought."

Okay, that made me curious. I was confused by this image, though. Judith didn't look like she was going to kill Zoe. Certainly, she wasn't acting like someone who would hack off her head and deliver it in a bag to her brother.

"Unfortunate," Zoe said. "Is Janice going to work with Ida?"

"For the time being," Judith said, frowning. "Keep your enemies closer and all that. Did Ida really tell Clarice to betray her lovers?"

"Yes," Zoe said, frowning. "Hiro Thompson was planning to use Cassius similarly but he has too much loyalty. I want Hiro killed. Painfully. The most horrific death imaginable. No one threatens my brother."

Judith narrowed her eyes. "You're in no position to make demands. Thomas may be protecting you—"

"Thomas runs the Free Systems Alliance. I could blow up Crius and he would protect me."

Judith slapped her across the face. "Don't make light of that."

Zoe stared, moving her hand up to her face. "You're probably right. It will take some time to clear my name and it'll be better if you can provide a body of a bioroid impersonator. Something to present to the families of those killed on the *Rhea* to satisfy their need for vengeance."

"You are a bioroid impersonator."

"So are you," Zoe said, softly. "An easily replicable toy who I may have made a mistake in believing was tractable."

Judith crossed her arms. "I've never been tractable."

"True, I believe that's what my brother loved about you," Zoe said, chuckling. "The elves whistle a song of peace and harmony."

Judith seized up like Zoe had earlier under Hiro's command. So did Zoe. The two of them twitching in unison for a span of three heartbeats before my sister slumped over like a puppet whose strings had been cut. In that moment, Judith's entire demeanor changed and became cold and professional like the woman I'd met in the cell.

Dear God.

Zoe had uploaded herself into Judith's body.

Stretching for a few moments, I watched the Zoe-in-Judith go over to a set of guards at the door. "I want this bioroid decapitated and the head prepared in a leather case. I also have some very specific orders as to how the prisoners are to be handled. Janice may be your superior but I remind you, I am the Free Systems Alliance Viceroy."

That was when the downloaded memories ended and I was once more floating in the middle of a galactic map.

"My God," I said, stunned at what I'd seen. "No, she couldn't have—"

"She did," theA.I. Judith said. "Zoe will do anything to survive. It's a trait she inherited from her mother. Thomas has it too, to a lesser extent."

I didn't know which element of that was the most troubling. A part of me wanted to believe this was all faked like the footage back in the Control Room but I could tell it was not the case. It all fit together.

Just not in the way I wanted.

"I bet she was faking her change by Hiro as well, somehow. She's too good a computer programmer to leave the Fixer's controls in place." A disgusting thought occurred to me. "I wonder what the Other Cassius will think about the changes to his wife."

"He'll probably do whatever she says,"A.I. Judith said. "It's the way we were designed. Three Laws of Robotics and all, with the chief one being Zoe is God."

"Does that make you the Devil?" I asked, smiling.

"Only here. Zoe overestimates just how much control she has but I probably wouldn't be able to work against her if not for two things."

"Two things?"

"I love you."

I stared at her, opened my mouth and closed it. "Thank you."

AI Judith looked to one side. "I never got to tell you that and mean it. I married you because you were my friend and I wanted to rescue my family from poverty." She paused. "The real Judith's family, our family, I don't suppose it matters. I learned to appreciate and then love you, though. I just, well, always felt you'd resent me if I told you my feelings had changed. That you'd be angry I hadn't loved you when we married."

I was stricken as the full weight of all this hit me. I'd longed to hear those words from Judith's lips and now they were coming from what amounted to her digital ghost. A digital ghost who was something every single man, woman, and child in the Spiral had been taught to hate from birth.

CognitionA.I. were the enemies of humanity and things that could never be tolerated by any society. Indeed, they were part of the reason why bioroids suffered as much disdain and loathing as they did despite their partially organic brains. People despised artificial beings and it was a rare individual who could overlook the fact society depended on the slavery of them.

Then there was the fact I'd moved on. That I'd become a different person than the one she'd known. I was no longer Cassius Mass, Count of Crius, and a loyal citizen of the Archduchy. I was just Cassius the Spacer now, a man who just wanted to leave this place and wished to God he'd never gotten involved in any of these schemes.

Plus, there were the women I was involved with. I'd been polygamous on Crius but I'd never bothered to really ask how that affected Judith. I'd been blind to so much and it seemed impossible now to give my heart to someone completely and still have room to give it to another.

"I know about Clarice and Isla,"A.I. Judith started to say. "If you love them—"

"I don't," I said, surprising myself. "Whether Clarice was ordered to or not, she betrayed me."

"And Isla?"

I lied. "I just don't feel that way about her."

"And me?"

"I don't know."

AI Judith lowered her gaze. "I see."

"I won't let them destroy you, though. How do I save you?"

Chapter Thirty

A I Judith—no, I was simply thinking of her as Judith now—gave a half-smile before closing her eyes. "Oh Cass, always making deep vows and life-altering decisions before you have all the facts—"

"I meant what I said," I said, staring at her.

"I need to be destroyed," Judith said. "A Cognition A.I. is—"

"You," I said, simply. "Which is all I need to know."

Judith blinked several times. "Dammit, you're making this difficult."

"I have a tendency to do that."

"I said I had two ways of circumventing Zoe's control. The second is the Elder Marker you saw when you entered here."

Judith's words brought me back to the horrible situation that awaited us outside. That my friends—well, friend and William—were trapped in a room in the middle of a slaver's dungeon. "What is all this about? What does the Alliance want with you, an Elder Marker, and all this other nonsense?"

"Are you familiar with the Free Systems Alliance's goals?"

I nodded. "Yes, they want to stop the Commonwealth from joining the Community. The transtellars believe it will bankrupt them, independent worlds think it will cause the Commonwealth to overwhelm them, and the Chel are...well, I don't have any idea what they think."

"The Chel were uplifted by the Elder Races," Judith said. "Well, some of them. They're the reasons why the FSA has this pillar and why I was built. They wanted me to try and devote all of my efforts to unlocking its secrets."

I blinked. "That's...reckless."

Judith closed her eyes. "Perhaps less reckless than you might think. Are you familiar with Fermi's Paradox?"

"I'm afraid not."

"I've learned a lot since becoming a juggernaut of information. It's a supposition by Pre-Spaceflight physicist Enrico Fermi that there were billions of stars in the galaxy similar to Earth's own but no evidence of alien life. Even now, the vast majority of the universe's stars are orbited by dead worlds."

"Because the Elder Races killed them." I gritted my teeth. "Or they killed themselves."

"Yes," Judith said, sighing. "Why the former would do that has long eluded scientists and philosophers. The reason—"

"I don't need a history lesson, Judith."

"Games, Cass."

I opened my mouth to respond then closed it. "Games."

"The Markers contain vast amounts of data to learn from if you have the processing power and a place to start translating their encryption like the Chel do. It's just information that requires a superhuman intellect like a CognitionA.I. to process. They're all transhumans, or transaliens I suppose. Beings who long ago left behind their organic bodies to become machine intelligences that dwell in virtual worlds and think in dimensions we cannot possibly fathom."

"Sounds wonderful…and terrifying."

"It's more the latter because I've found out how immortal god-like beings amuse themselves. They play with the lives of lesser beings, those who still have consequences for their actions."

"They destroy races for fun?"

"Not just destroy races. They manipulate politics, economics, religions, and wars to provide themselves entertainment. They consider themselves a superior order of beings and sometimes they elevate one or two species to join them to justify their abuses. Whole swaths of history are nothing more than games of shogi between immortals."

"I…can't believe that."

"Is it so surprising?" Judith asked, raising an eyebrow. "After all, they call themselves the Nobility."

There was nothing to say to that. It explained everything. "I see. So the Free Systems Alliance is involved in this somehow? The Chel are their catspaw?"

"No," Judith said. "The Chel believe the Commonwealth joining the Community is but a prelude to being slaughtered. Their masters already grow bored with the current crop of races that have emerged to dominate the Spiral and are ready to start over. The Community is too stable, too orderly, and too peaceful to provide them the bloodthirsty entertainment they desire."

"I can't believe intelligences that grandiose and powerful would be so…petty."

"They were the ones who corrupted the Cognition A.I. and triggered the Great Collapse."

My mouth went dry. "For fun."

"A century of amusement watching humans scramble and struggle for life across ten thousand worlds."

I took a deep breath. "Just when I thought this universe couldn't get any shittier."

Judith actually laughed at that. "The Free Systems Alliance exists to keep the conflicts going but small-scale and manageable. They want to spark humanity to become transhumanist and colonize many other worlds. They hope, eventually, for humans to join the Nobility. Ironically, that will only be possible by abandoning our humanity."

"War is always the same, no matter what time or place it is."

Judith sighed. "Pretty much."

"Can you stop it?"

"The War?"

Judith was silent for a second, which for her was probably an eternity. "Yes."

"Then we should."

"Should we?" Judith surprised me by saying. "The Nobility are beyond powerful. It's not so much a difference of degrees in our power level as kind. Likewise, the Commonwealth has oppressed and mismanaged its vassal worlds for centuries. I could cause one side or another's ships to navigate into a sun but it wouldn't do anything to address the underlying causes of this war."

"The only thing necessary for evil to triumph is for good men to do nothing."

"Of all tyrannies, a tyranny sincerely exercised for the good of its victims may be the most oppressive."

I frowned. "I hate quote-dueling with you."

"I've transferred the ownership of the *Melampus* to you, erased all of the hold Ida has on you, and restored our accounts. I've even removed the hold on the ship. You can take William and Isla with you and leave this place. If you destroy me and the Marker you should set back Zoe's efforts by years. That should be enough to satisfy your sense of justice."

"She'll just build another CognitionA.I. , and one with less of a conscience."

Judith paused. "I'm not going to ask you to kill your sister."

"I wouldn't," I said, taking a deep breath. "If I'm forced to choose between the good of the world and those I love, I choose those I love."

"Do you still love Zoe?"

"No, she hurt you. A you. For that, I can only hate her but I can't bring myself to raise a hand against her."

"Then what?"

I closed my eyes. "I don't know. I do know I can't just let this all play out. I've been dancing on the puppet strings of far too many people and it's time I cut them. For that, I need to make my own decisions."

"I'm not omnipotent," Judith said, sighing. "There's other CognitionA.I. living in the infonet. Chel, Commonwealth, Merchants Guild, and even survivors of the purge following the Great Collapse. Still, I can manipulate sums and values in a society defined by digital information. I also have access to some of the backdoors the Elder Races' pawns have installed across society. They can alter the programming of anything as they wish."

That certainly explained how they were able to get away with some of these manipulations. "Can you bring the *Revengeance* here?"

"I can send out orders from Judith and Thomas will come. He's the Commander of that ship through his puppet bioroids."

I nodded. "What about the Commonwealth's military?"

"You want to bring them to destroy the *Revengeance*?"

"No," I said, rubbing the bridge of my nose. "I want to bring them to fight the *Rhea*."

"The Commonwealth will win."

"Yes. But I'd like for them to be fought by Crius and local forces as well."

Judith blinked. "You want a show of solidarity?"

"I can't stop them from fighting but maybe I can make this war a short one. Bring enough of the Chel and Free Systems Alliance folk together in one area to smash them in one go."

It was choosing a side, definitely so, but I knew what a protracted war would look like. I didn't know how to handle the Nobility, or whatever the Elder Races were, but I could deal with the problem of a man-made war. Besides, it would screw over Janice and Zoe and that had its own benefits.

Judith, however, looked skeptical. "You realize that's not too far from Ida's plan, right?"

"I don't know what the hell is going through Ida's head to be honest."

Judith reached over and touched my head again. This time, I was hearing cybernetic comms traffic being transmitted from the *Melampus* to Clarice's ear. I was back in the limousine, I could tell by the sound, but didn't have any visual.

A moment later, Judith corrected that by showing a vision of the limousine's interior from a hidden camera placed by Janice. It was a reminder just how omnipresent surveillance was in our society.

That was when Ida's voice, sounding somewhat hollow and echo-like through the implant, said, "*Events are moving faster than we thought.*"

"*If my sister is moving the family from neutral to pro-Separatist then the only thing we're going to face at the Water Palace is a prison cell,*" Clarice replied, electronically speaking with Ida in between discussing matters with Kristoph.

It was interesting to see I was huddled over in one corner, looking very obviously uncomfortable and somewhat nauseated. Then again, I'd just been in a skycar crash. Even so, Clarice concealed her conversation much better than I had.

"*Will she seize you immediately?*"

"*No, she'll try and feel me out first. My cousin loves me but won't let family stand in the way of business.*"

"*Then you have to make a gesture to consolidate her. One which shows not only are you loyal to her cause but I am.*"

"*But we're not. We're trying to prevent a war.*"

"No, dearie, we're trying to end a war. There's a big difference."

"What kind of gesture?"

"Turn over the others."

Clarice froze up a second as Kristoph spoke about Janice's betrayal, which I'd initially attributed to him. *"You can't be serious. They're my friends."*

"You can protect them better this way."

"Versus just punching Kristoph and not going to the Water Palace?"

"Do you trust me?"

"Yes."

"Do you owe me for taking you from the wreck you were after the Chel tore you apart?"

"...yes."

"Then do what I ask. If we can get Janice's friends all in one go, the Free Systems Alliance will collapse and maybe we can focus on rebuilding rather than endless war."

I was too disgusted to watch further. "Please, just shut it off."

"Ida believes what she does is right."

"Good for her," I said, sighing. "I regret the necessity of this but I want to do it."

Judith closed her eyes. "If you want me to not go forward with bringing the *Revengeance,* I can. There are other ways to impede the FSA."

"No, they need to be stopped," I said. "But how deep is Parliament in ignoring all this?"

"Not at all. The Watchers let it simmer but they're all well-within their power and legal protections."

"And could we make it not look like it?"

"Excuse me?"

"An electronic trail to make it look like a false-flag operation?" I asked, thinking on the possibilities.

"I'm not sure what you mean."

"Something to make all of this blow up in their faces and bog down the politicians in Parliament for the next two generations of blame game. Nothing that would actually unite them, like this war or an external threat, but something to get them to turn on each other."

Judith blinked. "You want to make it look like Parliament let this turn into a military disaster to make themselves look good.

The Watchers, too. A scandal."

"Yes. Resignations, political fodder, and restructuring.'

"A poor revenge for destroying Crius."

"It might actually weaken the Commonwealth's central government, though, and move power to the local level in the long run."

History had a way of repeating itself and the big empires tended to collapse, not because of military conflict, disease, or disasters but overstretched resources as well as a weak central government. I didn't want to see the Commonwealth destroy itself. Not anymore. The very fact the Elder Races did want to see it destroyed made me want to preserve it. I wouldn't mind making it less of a juggernaut, though, and everything I knew about it suggested a snake pit of power-games, lies, and propaganda with no central core to rally around.

Judith, however, was unconvinced. "That's a big if."

"All it requires is for bureaucrats and politicians to turn on each other when there's something to blame them for. Something juicy but not so security-related as to fall under the province of interstellar security."

"I can do that," Judith said. "Do you want Ida burned for this?"

I closed my eyes. "Yes. Yes, I do."

Judith nodded. "Done."

I blinked. "Done?"

"Done. This time tomorrow, across the Commonwealth, all of the Watchers and Fixers' juicy blackmail secrets regarding a million different politicians and businessmen will be in the hands of their enemies."

"Surely, it can't be that easy."

Judith's expression was troubled. "No, it's not. The Commonwealth's ownA.I. can, and do, defend this sort of data religiously but they're overstretched and overtaxed with how much power they possess. They, however, have a free hand with all of their processors and knowing about those means they can do more or less whatever they want. The Elder Races manipulated it that way. What they can't manipulate, their technology can change the parameters of."

"Are you in danger from them?"

"The Elder Races or the Commonwealth?"

"Both."

"As long as they don't know I exist? No. If they did, nothing in the universe would protect me from either."

"So, the *Revengeance* is coming?"

"The message is sent. Our conversation is only taking a few short moments from your friends' perspective but given the way Thomas loved his sister, I expect him to arrive within the hour. Then I suppose he'll be trapped."

I nodded. It was a horrible feeling betraying my family that way but I'd seen one world burn, I wasn't going to let my family be involved in the destruction of more. "Amazing. Just what are the limits of your power?"

"I can change the data in any computer linked up to the infonet or transtellar communications grid. Planetary market purchases, jump beacon feeds, personal communications, military operated drones, bank accounts, and government records. Even the Fixer and Commonwealth'sA.I. don't have that sort of access or power. Zoe really is a genius. At least at reverse-engineering and copying other people's work."

"The FSA could conquer the galaxy with you."

Judith smiled. "That's part of the reason why I have to go."

The smile left my face. "No."

Judith stared up at me. "Cassius, no one should have the kind of power CognitionA.I. possess, least of all enhanced by Elder technology. Information, not weapons, is the key to dominating the Spiral. If you leave me here Zoe or her successors will find a way to reprogram me. I'm stuck here. Also, it's not a good existence being left here in—"

I kissed her on the lips, having come up with a plan. It was insane, utterly and completely insane, but something I was desperate to do. I didn't care if this Judith was a copy of my wife, I wouldn't lose her. I'd rather have the dream of her than the truth of another. If that made me an awful person, then so be it. "Come with me."

"Cassius—"

"Inside my cybernetics. Be with me."

Judith's eyes widened.

"Forever," I finished.

TheA.I. version of my wife was speechless.

Chapter Thirty-One

"What?" Judith said, her eyes widening. "You want me to *merge* with you?"

"I have military-grade Crius *Halo*-class cybernetics capable of interfacing with the most powerful machinery in the Archduchy. They have more storage space than anything outside of the Chel and probably as much as the device attached to this Marker."

Judith blinked several times. "You want to smuggle me out in your brain."

I smirked. "The past five years have proven I've not been using it."

"Cassius, do you know what will happen if they find out I'm in there?"

"They'll kill me? Like they'll kill me for a hundred other reasons? I'll prevent them from bombing whatever world I'm on since I'll be in space 90% of the time. A constantly moving CognitionA.I. isn't the same sort of target. Besides, we'll blow this place up and everyone will assume you're gone."

Judith looked tempted but I could tell she was conflicted. "Cassius, this isn't a workable plan."

"*Fuck* workable plans. I've had it about to here with plans. All I want to do is get you and the rest of the people I give a shit about off this planet and forget I ever got involved in this whole business."

"And just carry around anA.I. of your dead wife for the rest of your life."

"We can arrange a body for you if you want." I thought about how Zoe's version of Judith was an *eerie* reproduction. "If not? I'm okay with that."

"You deserve better than loving a shadow."

I stared at her. "You're more than a shadow."

"You can't know that."

I stared into her deep blue virtual eyes. "I'd know you anywhere, even across death."

Judith stared. "That's really cheesy."

I frowned. "I'm having a moment here, don't ruin it."

"Sorry."

I took a deep breath. "I know you went to all this trouble to rescue me and, when faced with unlimited power, your reaction is to want to blow yourself up so you don't misuse it. You may not be the original Judith, you may not be human, but you're a hell of a lot more human than the vast majority of people I've met in this galaxy."

"I admit, this sector is full of assholes," Judith muttered.

"Not just this sector. I've been to the others. They're all full of assholes. Every last one of them."

"What will your friends say?" Judith asked.

"I fully intend to lie to them."

Judith rolled her eyes. "Seriously, Cass?"

I matched her rolled eyes and raised with a derisive snort. "Yes, because they've been entirely straight with me."

"You're on a sarcastic roll today."

"I've noticed I'm starting to lose some of the aristocrat's polish from years of hanging around rogues, thieves, and murderers."

"Are you referring to your time with the nobility or after it?"

I chuckled. "Well, people who are more honest about it, at least. Will you take this journey to me?"

"You realize this will probably end in you getting shot and us dying together, right?"

"That's not an entirely bad ending from my perspective, but I'd rather stay alive with you."

"I don't want to be immortal like the otherA.I. The reason I live is for the ones I love around me and you're the last one in the universe left alive but for my family, Judith's family, or whatever you want to call them. I want to look after them, too."

"We'll find them."

"Then consider yourself to have anA.I. as your new ship's something or other, Captain."

Captain? Hmm, I suppose I could get used to that.

"You know, I absolutely hated everyone in the Navy. They existed solely to provide us transport and make us look good in comparison."

"That was because you were in the Starfighter Corps."

"Which just reinforces the truth of my statement."

"Okay," I said, now very nervous about what's going to happen. "Anything I should know before you do it?"

"Oh, was I not supposed to do it already?" Judith asked innocently.

I stared at her. "Oh…good."

I didn't feel any different, which I supposed was a good thing. I hadn't made use of my cybernetics beyond navigational computations, viewing data-files, and making sure I never forgot a single detail of my marriage.

"Gives new meaning to the idea of marriage as one body and one soul."

"Yeah."

"I've unlocked the doorway to the outside and arranged for a distraction to get to the prison. You should dress up in some of the power-armor here in the containment room."

"So we can pass ourselves off as guards?"

Judith shook her head. "So you can blast your way out of here and to one of the nearby transport platforms. This entire planet is about to get really, really busy with the incoming military strikes, and that's your best chance to get the fuck out of here."

Point taken.

That was when the Water Palace's plans were uploaded into my brain with three-dimensional renderings of the environment, location of troopers, types of weapons, and just how much of a fight we'd be able to put up if we got caught. The numbers were discouraging, not insurmountable, as security was designed for protecting the guests rather than chasing down fugitives.

"Ow," I muttered, wincing. "Warn me next time you do something like that."

"This is why cybernetics will never be as good as A.I. The wet gooey stuff doesn't interact with the purely digital stuff."

I kissed her again. "I've got some experience with bioroids that says otherwise."

Judith frowned.

"That was actually supposed to reassure you."

"I'm not sure I want a biological body."

"Really?" I asked, surprised.

"You'd be amazed at the worlds opened up to me," Judith said, shaking her head. "I've learned more things in the half-day I've been activated than I did in the whole of my previous existence. Being stuffed back in a squishy box has its appeals, well specifically you, but it has its limitations, too."

I closed my eyes. "Whatever you want."

"We'll discuss it later when we're not in a life and death struggle for existence." She conjured a globe of Shogun above our heads with a small glowing red light signifying the *Melampus* and the clearest route we could take to get back to it. "Any objections to my plan?"

"Not a one."

"Then let's get going."

I paused. "Uh, actually, there is one thing."

Judith looked at me sideways. "What?"

"Could we...uh...I can't believe I'm going to say this, warn Clarice and Ida the place is about to go up in smoke?"

Judith's eyes widened. "Are you fucking serious?"

"I know it sounds strange—"

"Strange is your love for recording mirrors in the bedroom. This is ridiculous!" Judith interrupted me. "They betrayed you! Both of them."

I gritted my teeth, not wanting to have this argument as I had extremely mixed feelings about all of this but was confident of my conclusions. "Yes and I'm stealing their ship as well as ruining their reputations for it. No matter what happens, the Rin-O'Harra family is going to be ruined by all this. Likewise, with Ida burned, that means Clarice's own ambitions to find redemption as a soldier, or whatever she had planned, is screwed. I consider that payback enough."

Judith blinked. "Do you really think they deserve to live? I mean, I understand Clarice, she's beautiful but—"

"It's not like that."

"Then what is it?"

I shrugged. "Ida gave me a place where I felt like I didn't have to run away from the rest of the universe anymore. The *Melampus*, in a very real way, became a dirty disgusting pile-of-floating-space-junk home."

"You're really selling me on moving in with you."

"We can redecorate with all the money you've recovered."

"Point taken."

"There's more—"

"Do you love her?" Judith asked.

"Fuck no," I said, sighing, "but she did what she thought was right and I think Isla does love her."

"Do you love her?" Judith asked.

I closed my eyes, thinking of how Isla would react to all this. Probably not well. She was a jealous sort with her sole exception being Clarice. "I said no, but they are my friends."

I didn't know what sort of reaction I was expecting from Judith but the one I got surprised me. She burst out laughing and carried on for a good thirty seconds.

"It wasn't that funny."

"I'm sorry, but after all the shit we've both been through," Judith chuckled some more, "I didn't think you'd make an appeal for their lives on the power of friendship."

I thought about the dozens of friends I'd sent to their deaths over the past decade. Relationships broken by betrayal, sometimes by me, with people used and discarded like cleansing paper. It was hard to put into words why these particular relationships mattered.

Or whether the fact that they mattered was all in my head.

"Is it a problem?" I asked.

Judith looked at me. "No, Cassius, it's not. Just realize all hell is probably going to break loose sooner than later if I do send a warning."

"Judith, after your…death, I did a lot of things I'm not proud of. I was involved in terrorism. I killed innocent people trying to get at the ones I thought weren't innocent for being involved in the Commonwealth government. I stole things. I murdered people. I even ran with some pirates at one point. I damned my soul repeatedly for doing things far less horrible than what I did with a song in my heart in the name of Duke and Country."

Judith looked at me. "Estimates for how many people will die in the upcoming battle, civilian and others range from a hundred thousand to two million if the battle gets to the surface of the planet. I did that because you asked that from me."

I closed my eyes. "A.I. insane for believing it'll be less bloody this way?"

"Maybe. Still, both of us put our hands on the trigger and pulled. We're both killers now. I may not be the original Judith but I remember the first person she murdered for one of your noble games. It was one of Thomas' friends, an ex-lover of his who was bragging about his conquests and threatening your brother's position. I got paid a lot of money for that and it put me in the pocket of State Security."

"I knew that story."

"I used you, too."

"We used each other. Don't think I didn't know my mistresses, the ones you introduced me to, were your friends from Lucifer City you wanted to get out of prostitution and indentured servitude."

I'd honestly never wanted another woman after meeting Judith. It was a strange thing and I'd been roundly criticized for it by my fellows. To love was considered a character flaw among the nobility and to love a nat actually shameful.

Judith had encouraged me to take mistresses for my position even as I knew she hadn't loved me the way I'd loved her. Now here we were, working to save the traitorous lover of my other lover, while desperately in love with what amounted to my wife's clone. It sounded like a daytime holonovella for bored concubines.

Judith grimaced. "You knew, huh?"

"You could have just asked for the money to help them."

"They never would have accepted it. Pride was the only thing getting us through some days in the Asmodean Slums. They weren't exactly brimming with gratitude for the favor I did them either. All of them sold information about us both to State Security."

"It wouldn't surprise me. Thomas usually cleaned up the reports on you, me, and Zoe. He left in just enough for us to be uninterestingly perverse. Nothing arouses State Security attention like insufficiently sordid nobles."

Not that Zoe would qualify anymore. I really, really hope she wasn't planning on living as my clone's wife.

Judith shook her head with an amused expression on her face. I got the impression since her digital life had begun, she hadn't had much to smile about. "I guess we both know something about sacrifices for ungrateful friends."

"Perhaps not so—"

That was when there was a repeating beeping noise as the holo around us started to shake and change.

"Oh crap," Judith said, looking around us. "We are screwed."

"Wait, what? I thought you said this was all just taking a second of real time."

"It is," Judith said. "However, that doesn't mean all of this digital time wasn't passing for one of Janice's dummyA.I. to catch onto us."

"I thought dummyA.I. were shit compared to CognitionA.I. "

"Not completely so!" Judith grabbed her head in frustration and started to pace around the holographic room. "Since they just made us."

"Made us?"

I was about to say more when a searing pain raced through my synapses. It was like someone sending white hot lightning through my skull. It was an anti-cyberattack defense mechanism, and if I'd been directly linked to their servers rather than working through Judith as a proxy, I suspected it would have caused my cybernetics to melt in my brain.

"Found us. Tracked us. Put us on their shit list! You've got to log off now and get the hell out of there with your friends."

"How bad is it?"

Judith grimaced. "You may have to deal with the *Kriegermonster* in a few minutes."

"Oh come on!"

"Go!" Judith said, pushing me.

With that, I woke up with my hands removed from the Elder Marker. Isla and William were behind me, finishing a sentence that sounded like it had begun moments after I touched it.

"Is that normal?" William asked, being affixed with his artificial arm by Isla. "It glowed. He glowed. We should shoot him and blow it up to make sure."

"We're not shooting Cassius!" Isla said, using a laser connector to create a makeshift interface. The fact she'd managed to set one up within minutes was amazing. "He got us out of here, didn't he?"

"He didn't do anything," William said. "Someone else is pulling the strings in all of this and I don't like it."

A bunch of alarms sounded throughout the prison.

"And we're going to get screwed by it!" William said, waving his gun and shaking his newly acquired arm. Looking at it in surprise, he moved it a few more times. "You're actually pretty good at this, Robotgirl."

"I just want you to know I hate you," Isla said, stepping away. "For many, many reasons."

That was when there was a hideous roaring noise from outside Containment's door. It sounded like someone had freed Cerberus from Hades and sent him to hunt us down.

I thought to Judith, *"Are you there?"*

"Yes, Cassius."

"Good," I said, looking around the room for weapons. There was a rack of them next to a set of *Durandal*-class Power Armor suits. They weren't top quality weapons, confiscated from pirates possibly, but it was still top-notch mercenary wear.

"Everybody put on a suit, get your weapons ready. Things are about to get crazy."

William just stared at me. "What the hell have they been until now?"

Chapter Thirty-Two

I headed over to the Durandal Power Armor and began typing furiously into an interface built into its shoulder, programming it to accommodate my frame. The thick suit of red armor weighed over two-hundred-pounds but had its own generators and artificial muscle to make it essentially weightless to its user. It was something I was almost completely unfamiliar with the operation of. I was a pilot, not a Marine, after all. Still, I was pretty sure I wanted the thickest and toughest material between me and everything out there.

Unfortunately, even as everything was going to hell, I noted the armor suits were all locked down with security passcodes and complicated password sequences designed to, well, prevent people like me from stealing incredibly dangerous military equipment. That was when I saw Judith by me, still glowing as she was in the virtual reality world we were located in. It caused me to do a double take before I remembered all of my perceptions were filtered through my cybernetics so of course she could create a virtual avatar of herself in my vision. Still, it was briefly unsettling.

"*Let me handle this,*" Judith said, looking at the armor.

"What can you—" I started to say.

That was when all three suits of armor, one red, one blue, one gold, all had their keypads blink and their front chest pieces open up to allow a user to slide in.

I blinked. "You're really useful to have around."

"*Glad you noticed.*"

"Who are you talking to?" Isla asked, concerned.

William responded less charitably by double-charging his plasma rifle. "Okay, what the hell is going on?"

"*Well, that's not good,*" Judith muttered. "*You should probably tell them—*"

I closed my eyes. "We're actually being helped by the A.I. version of my wife, Judith, who is not a Cognition A.I. because my sister intended to upload herself into it and become a kind of god thing."

"*God thing?*" Judith asked.

I continued making up shit. "She's shut down the power, summoned the Commonwealth authorities, and there's going to be a big battle here due to the *Revengeance* coming to slaughter everyone."

"Why are they doing that?" Isla asked.

"Because they're bad guys," I said, eliminating my role in bringing the warship here. "I've been working for Ida and the Watchers for some time now in exchange for a pardon, which has come through. They've arranged for the *Melampus* to be turned over to us as part of our retirement package as Ida moves on to bigger and better things. We have to get out of here, though, because it's going to get messy. Very messy."

Judith blinked. "*Wow, you effortlessly mixed truth and lies there.*"

"*Thank you,*" I thought back to her, guessing she'd be able to hear me.

"*It's not a compliment,*" Judith replied.

William gestured with his gun between me and the Elder Marker. "How do we know you're not protecting the Cognition A.I. out of some twisted plan to return the nobility to power?"

Looking at one of the nearby shelves, I saw a detonator cube. Picking it up, clicking it three times, I hurled it at the Elder Marker where it stuck against the side like a fly against a wall. "You should probably take a few steps back."

William scooted away as Isla practically ran to the other side of the room. Seconds later, the obelisk exploded along with the Cognition A.I. equipment attached to it. The pieces didn't shatter and go in every direction like shrapnel, but just fell over into five or six different chunks. There appeared to be no interior wiring or moving parts, just one big block of quartz.

"There, does that prove it?" I asked William.

William stared at the ruins, then back at me, then the large metal door beside him. The banging noises were getting louder even as I saw it was being pulled out of where it had been fused into the concrete. Shoddy construction that. Either way, I actually felt a digital gasp of confusion and grief from Judith in the back of my mind.

The destruction of the Elder Marker was an object of immense historical importance and power being eradicated—even if the so-called Nobility was apparently a bunch of super-advanced genocidal monsters.

I could also tell she was affected by the destruction of the equipment Zoe had designed for her as well. Judith was, in her current state, still a CognitionA.I. and capable of potentially limitless expansion as well as data-manipulation but limited by the hardware she was running on. I couldn't help but think my cyberware, as effective as it was for containing a human consciousness, was still an immense step down from the near-goddess she'd been before. There was also the practical consideration we weren't going to have nearly the same amount of access to her higher abilities.

"Don't sound so disappointed," Judith chuckled and smiled at me. *"I've still got plenty of digital oomph."*

Uh, can you hear all my thoughts? I thought to her.

"Yes. Only when I'm listening, though."

I grimaced and thought about a series of inappropriate things. Judith laughed.

We need to discuss boundaries, I thought at her. *Just not when we're all about to die at the hands of a rampaging kill monster.*

"Agreed," Judith said. *"Though I do like being the girl you can't get out of your head."*

You were always that.

William and Isla finished looking at the destroyed CognitionA.I. device and Elder Marker on the ground before both gazed at the door about to fall down. We were running out of time to maneuver and I was the only one with a plan.

"Yeah, we're fine," William said, putting his gun over his shoulder and heading to the blue suit of armor.

Isla, meanwhile, looked unconvinced. "There is a lot wrong with that story, Cassius, but I'm willing to overlook it as long as we can get the hell out of here."

"Get in one of the suits," I said. "You don't need to fight, just stay alive."

"I do whatever it takes to survive," Isla said, heading to the gold armor.

I grimaced at that poor choice of words. "Sure."

The door then moved three inches forward, barely holding itself in place.

"*I calculate there is a thirty-second time period until it breaks down that door,*" Judith said. "*Maybe twenty-six.*"

"Right," I said, running back to the red armor. Sliding into the armor like I was climbing into a vehicle, it made a snap hiss noise and secured itself against my body. It was surprisingly similar to a starfighter pilot's interface and my respect for the Void Marines went up just the slightest bit.

The combat HUD emerged seconds later, giving me tactical data on all our surroundings as well as the life-readings of my companions. The suit could lift one metric ton in addition to my regular strength and provided its own internal life-support. I was still going over features when the metal doors of the Containment room fell over on the ground.

What followed was a hideous metallic creature that resembled a six-legged cybernetic puma with a scorpion's tail and a wolf-like set of jaws. The scanners on board the Durandal suit gave a ridiculous series of numbers on the kriegermonster's performance stats. It made any benefits of my suit superfluous.

"That was faster than twenty-six seconds," I said, staring at the creature.

"*This isn't an exact science!*"

William didn't hesitate to open fire with both arms around his plasma rifle, showering the construct with energy blasts, which were all but useless against its reinforced heat-dampening plating. The *Kriegermonster* must have cost somewhere around half-a-billion credits since it had technology normally only found in starfighters.

Isla didn't hesitate to add her own help to the battle, slamming all of the shelves onto the creature and forcing it to tear through the steel to buy us a few seconds.

"Maybe you should have saved that detonator cube," Isla said over the suits' comms system.

"No kidding!" I said, searching for some sort of weak point on the monster and firing at its joints while trying to find a tactical position that would give us an advantage against something akin to an animal-shaped tank. "Can you do anything?"

"I'm trying!" Isla said, looking through the scattered shelves while the *Kriegermonster* pulled itself free.

"Not you!" I said, looking over at my wife.

Judith held her fingers to her forehead, almost like she was trying a psychic reading. "I'm sorry. I'm completely locked out of the system. Only a direct DNA recognition from Janice will be able to shut it down."

And us with no Clarice matching her.

Great.

The *Kriegermonster* charged and, despite my best efforts, the nine hundred pound creature landed on me with a thud, driving the tips of its claws into the front of my suit and causing alarms to blare all over my power armor's HUD.

"Cassius!" Isla shouted, tossing me my proton sword.

"Yes!" I muttered, grabbing it and pressing the blade against the side of the creature's neck, causing sparks to go everywhere before it went underneath the monster's armor and caused hideous black ichor to spew out.

The creature backed away as I struggled to my feet, only to be knocked to the ground by the creature's massive tail. It felt like being hit by a skycar, right before it struck again and cut my proton sword in half. The *Kriegermonster* opened its mouth and a plasma cannon became visible even as my armor's HUD informed me I was locked on by its targeting system.

"Ten points!" William shouted, slamming into the side of the Krieger monster and sending it flying through the air against the side of the wall.

I looked at my broken, ruined sword, then cursed under my breath. It was one of the last ties to my old life. I tossed aside the useless relic, focusing on keeping the rest of my friends alive.

And William, too.

The *Kriegermonster* let forth another ear-splitting wail then righted itself before charging at William only to be punched in the face twice then hurled across the other side of the room. It was a ridiculous sight-seeing an armored human fight against a monster like the *Kriegermonster* hand-to-hand but I remembered William used to be a gladiator.

It's very probable that William knew more about fighting constructs than a hundred normal soldiers. They were regularly used in Xerxes fighting pits to kill the natives for the amusement of the sicker members of Crius society. Kriegermonsters were terror weapons and toys of the rich, designed as much to put on a show as be efficient tools of combat. Which still didn't give him a snowflake's chance in hell of winning.

"Here ya go!" Isla handed me her personal energy shield, the one confiscated from the Chel.

"It won't help much," I muttered.

"*Think outside the box,*" Judith said, nodding. "*The best offense—*"

"Oh dammit!" William shouted as the kriegermonsterbit through his artificial arm and tore it to pieces before ripping it in half.

Instantly, I comprehended the meaning of the two artificially-created women and proceeded to run in front of the *Kriegermonster* before it struck down William once and for all. Waving my hands wildly, the personal energy shield in my hand deactivated, I shouted, "Over here! Don't settle for the blood of a Xerxes versus a true Crius nobleman!"

"Damn—" William started to say before being knocked away by the middle left leg of the kriegermonster.

It charged straight at me and I had a brief moment to regret my decision to save William before it smashed me against the back of the wall. Taking the personal energy shield and stuffing it down the hole I'd created in it shoulder, I activated the device as it pressed a shield outward inside its body, tearing the upper half of the *Kriegermonster* to pieces. The entire room was sprayed in more blackish fluid before I kicked the remaining half of the monster away. Its hind legs and backside kicked frantically in every direction for several seconds before it finally died.

As much as a creature like it could die.

William reached over to feel the remains of his arm, then cursed in three languages before looking over at me. "I'm not saying thank you after that true Crius nobleman business but, thank you."

"You're welcome," I muttered, shaking my head.

"I said I'm not saying thank you!" William shouted back. "Do you think Janice has any more of those?"

"No, but I'm sure she has a whole army of regular troopers," I said, looking over at Isla. "Can you attach another arm?"

Isla shook her head. "No, they only had one emergency reattachment unit left."

"Damn," I said. "So much for that idea."

"He still had one when he needed one," Isla said. "I call that a win."

"I don't," William said.

I half-expected a dozen Shogunate troopers to run through the door but, instead, I heard the sounds of plasma fire and screams coming from outside the now open doors. There was also the sound of gunships landing, which confused the hell out of me since it was still about forty-five minutes until the *Revengeance* arrived.

"Let me guess," William said, taking a deep breath. "Everything has gone to shit outside."

"So it seems," I said, gritting my teeth. "Why can nothing ever be simple?"

"Death is the only simple thing," Isla said, picking up her pistol. "We should avoid simple things."

"*Death isn't simple,*" Judith said, crossing her arms. "*I'm living proof of that.*"

"Yeah," Isla muttered. "I suppose it is."

I did a double take, looking at her.

"*It's a machine thing,*" Judith said, closing her eyes. "*The Water Palace is under attack.*"

"By who?" I asked, wondering how things could possibly get worse.

As if the universe was mocking me, the entire chamber rocked and there was a sound of a building collapsing outside.

"Who are you talking to?" William said, standing up.

"*A friend,*" Judith said on our comms systems. "*Now shut up. The entire island is being invaded by Commonwealth Marines.*"

I felt my face. "Dammit, Ida."

"So, we're rescued," William asked.

"Not a bit," I said, sighing. "For a variety of reasons I can't get into right now."

"Try me," William gritted his teeth. He actually was intimidating even with his recently-restored arm torn off.

"This entire planet is about to become a massive warzone."

Another explosion, closer now, was heard.

"More than it is, already," I said. "We need to get the hell out of here."

William stared at me, then Isla, then back at me. "Fine. Computer-Lady, find us a ship to steal and get to the *Melampus*."

"*Already done,*" Judith said, projecting the best probable route through a three-dimensional map of the Water Palace. Dozens of red, white, and blue dots covered the screen representing attackers, defenders, and civilians. "*Janice has already taken her closest family and advisors down to her bunker and called for reinforcements. This is meant to capture as many high-value targets as possible.*"

"Which will include you," William muttered, looking at me. "Since you look identical to a big terrorist now."

"*Yeah,*" Judith muttered. "*We need to get that fixed.*"

"Thinking about turning me in, Commander?" I asked, staring at William.

"No," William said, looking at Isla. "How about you, Ms. I-Will-Do-Anything-to-Survive?"

Isla stared at me, clearly contemplating her options, then looked aside. "Apparently, that was hyperbole. Can we get to Ida and Clarice?"

"I've already given them an evac point," Judith said. "They should be meeting us there."

"Excellent," I said.

"So we can shoot them?" William asked, almost growling.

"That's up to you," I said. "But you should know Hiro was a Fixer."

William stopped, apparently recognizing the nickname of Hiro's organization. "Son of a…is everyone on board a spy?"

"Apparently," I deadpanned.

William lifted up his rifle with one arm again. "Well let's just get the hell out of here and we'll sort things out later. I'm not going to try to do it with one damned arm."

"A wise decision."

"Ain't nothing wise about anything I've done since I've joined this crew."

I shrugged. "I've recently regained my fortune. I can give you a hundred thousand credits for your troubles."

William paused. "That helps. Really."

The sound of plasma fire blasts drew closer as I lifted up my own rifle and started toward the doors. The Water Palace wasn't designed to stand up against a sustained military assault, and while the Commonwealth Marines would soon be overwhelmed with the entirety of the forces here on Shogun, the rest of the Free Systems Alliance military and Commonwealth Navy was what I was really worried about. If we didn't get out of here now, then it was very likely we'd be staring down the barrel of their orbital cannons.

"*This is what you get for trying to make the world a better place,*" Judith said in my ear, appearing as a glowing purple diamond in my HUD after her virtual body disappeared. "*It never ends well.*"

"Yeah, I'm starting to get that."

Chapter Thirty-Three

The sight that greeted me upon exiting the prison made me believe I was back in the war. The skies were alight with gunships blasting at each other and armed skycars exploding all around us, only to bounce against the Water Palace's shields as they fell from above.

The party I'd seen on the prison security system had turned into a massacre as Commonwealth Marines engaged with the bodyguards, mechs, and even a few kriegermonsters which Janice Rin-O'Harra had called to defend her guests. A few of the partygoers had been taken prisoner but this just made them easy victims of crossfire.

A group of Shogun Special Forces and Orbital Drop Troopers were already beginning their dissent, and I had no doubt Janice had called in the military to repulse the Commonwealth's unexpected assault. It was a nightmare to watch and I confess my next actions were less than heroic.

Seeing the nearest group of six Commonwealth Marines with their backs turned to us and not paying attention to our position, I lifted up my rifle and proceeded to gun them down before they realized they were being flanked. They fell before they could respond, unaware they were next to a power-armored soldier.

"Why the hell did you do that?" William called out, horrified by my sudden act of violence but, thankfully, not pointing his gun at me.

"They were in our way to get to the nearest gunship," I said, coldly. "I intend to kill every single trooper, Shogun, FSA, or Commonwealth who stands in our way of getting off this rock."

William was silent, right before he fired into a trio of Shogun soldiers who ran up to join with us, mistaking us for reinforcements. "Whatever you say, chief."

"*You could have used the stun setting,*" Judith said in my ear. "*You don't have to kill anymore.*"

"Blast vests and adrenaline mods make those impractical," I muttered. "You can kill a man on the field of battle but you can't take him alive."

Judith was silent.

William, Isla, and I moved across the beautiful stone walkways of the Water Palace, passing several fountains now turned red with the corpses leaking their remains into them. The Commonwealth had clearly expected an easy victory, born from surprise and awe, but it had turned into a pitched battle with several of Crius-born guests actually throwing their lives away by seizing weapons to attack the people who'd killed their world.

Passing under a fallen set of pulsating green, white, and blue lights strung out over a fallen archway, we entered into an underground walkway our map indicated lead right to one of the Commonwealth gunships. They'd already spread out from their position so there was very likely only a token force guarding it.

The underground tunnel was less ornate than topside, full of pipes and wires designed for thousands of servants or bioroids to maintain. There were numerous holes in the wall from energy fire and some bodies, too, mostly those very servants and bioroids. The Commonwealth Marines had cleared their entrance with gas grenades. For whatever reason, they'd chosen not to go with subdual, perhaps for the exact same reason I did—they couldn't risk someone coming back to kill their buddies.

In war, you looked after the man beside you and everything else was secondary. I'd forgotten that as a Colonel-Count. I wouldn't again.

"I'd forgotten how much I hated war," I grunted out over the radio as I moved the Durandal suit through the so-far-empty hallways.

"How do you forget something like that?" William asked.

"Memory drugs."

"You know those can cause hallucinations if you drink alcohol with them."

"What?" I asked.

"You didn't know that? I just thought you considered that a perk!" Isla said, joking at about the worst time possible.

"*I can see why you were with her,*" Judith said. "*She's cute.*"

"Not now, Judith."

"*Of course, I'm obligated to kill her. You know, just once we're safe. No duels, just straight-up murder. You can watch.*"

"Judith—"

"*By the way, I didn't know you had a fetish for artificial girls. Is this something you've known all along or is it a new thing?*"

My response was cut off by a heavy plasma blast slamming into my armor's heat-plates and sending me spiraling back on the ground. We'd accidentally run into a quartet of soldiers standing guard around the corner.

Dammit! Amateur hour stupidity at its finest.

Isla fired her pistol repeatedly at our attackers while William retaliated as well. The enemies fired back but at point blank range, the people wearing armor designed to repel energy blasts had the advantage. A group of three dead Commonwealth troopers were on the ground with a fourth raising his hand in surrender. He was young, barely an adult, and had probably enlisted on a world which conscripted teenagers.

Too young for this line of work.

William lifted his gun and I stepped in front of him before punching the kid across the face and sending him to the ground. I then removed his helmet and stunned him.

"What the hell was that for?" William said. "I thought you said kill everyone."

"I dunno," I said. "It seemed like the right thing to do."

William grunted something unintelligible.

"What was that?" I asked.

"I said you're just lucky this isn't the first time I've fought without an arm. It's just the only time I can't feel it."

"That must be quite a story," Isla said.

"Not really, I got my arm blown off during a fight and had to shoot my way out or die. Not much of a story there. I got myself in two years of debt paying for an organic replacement."

"Wouldn't the Marines have paid for a replacement?" Isla asked.

"You'd think, wouldn't you?" William muttered. "Fucking politicians."

I saw the closed supersteel security doors leading to the docking bay. They were locked down, and while we'd disposed of the guards who were there to keep others from entering, it didn't really improve our chances of getting in.

"Is the gunship still on the other side?" I asked, hearing the sound of plasma fire behind us. The Commonwealth troopers were in full retreat now and that meant they'd be arriving soon to deal with us in a decidedly permanent way.

"*Yes*," Judith said. "*The chatter on the CSM channels confirms they're pulling back with a number of secondary targets captured and many more eliminated but no sign of Janice. The gunship's tracer is still present but I'm not getting a life-reading from its crew.*"

Reaching the front of the amazingly durable-looking doors, I asked, "So, we should expect trouble on the other side?"

"*Yes. I also suggest you hurry as I doubt whoever disposed of the crew intends to stick around.*"

"Well, we just need to figure out a way to get past—"

That was when the huge metal doors opened up, parting in four different directions and revealing the sight of a square chamber with the wall on the other side of us open to the crashing waves of Shogun. Isla was standing at the controls for the door and had pried them open before hotwiring them again.

Someone really needed to talk to Janice's security people.

On the other side of the doors was a fifty-foot-long *Peregrine*-class gunship, shaped like a long metal truncheon with guns on the sides and front plus a back door entrance. It was flanked by dead soldiers.

Ida and Clarice were both in front of the gunship, Janice Rin-O'Harra on the ground with her hands tied in force cuffs. Janice was also gagged, which was a simple but elegant deterrent to her using any of the Water Palace's voice-activated defense systems. All three women looked to the opening doors with Ida and Clarice both drawing pistols.

"*Holy crap*," Judith said. "*You're running with a resilient crew.*"

"Too resilient," I muttered while lifting my rifle. Turning on the armor's speakers, I said to the pair. "Give me one good reason not to shoot you to hell, Ida."

"Cassius?" Ida said, her mouth opening. "Son of a bitch."

"That's not a good reason," William said, moving his rifle between both. "Someone owes me an arm and I'm entirely willing to take one from both of you since, technically, I lost two in the course of this fucked up mission."

"So you made it out," Ida said, shaking her head. "I'm glad."

"We were just arguing about whether to go back for y'all," Ida said, dropping her gun and gesturing with her head for Clarice to do the same. "Clarice wanted to make sure you were rescued but I argued the safest place for you was in Janice's dungeon while all this blew over."

"I lost my arm!" William shouted. "Hiro is dead!"

Ida closed her eyes. "That was Janice's doing. I'm sorry, I didn't expect her to go that far."

Janice said something foul through her gag, probably a denial. Of course, I knew she actually was innocent and Zoe was responsible.

Isla shut the security doors behind us before blasting the controls, which I wasn't sure was an effective strategy but was willing to give her the benefit of the doubt on. "Guys, if you could hurry this up, I'd be very grateful."

"Isla?" Clarice said, mouth agape.

Isla removed her helmet and rushed over to embrace her; the two of them gave each other a passionate kiss.

"Excuse me, she's still the enemy!" William said, growling.

"You don't believe that or you would have shot her," I said, wanting to move this conversation along.

"No," William said, slumping his shoulders. "I don't."

"*Aww, they're in love. I guess I don't have to worry about Isla after all,*" Judith said, chuckling.

"I should probably mention I was also with Clarice."

"*You what?*"

"Now's not the time," I said, taking advantage of the fact we were literally in danger of dying any minute. "Captain Claire, I must regretfully inform you I am terminating our partnership."

"I'm sorry to hear that," Ida said.

"I'm also taking the *Melampus*," I said, smiling.

"Like hell!" Ida said, balling her fists. I suspected if not for William's presence, she would have gone for her gun then and there.

"Already done," I said, looking at the corpses on the ground. "I take it the Commonwealth no longer recognizes your authority."

"A wee bit of a tiny misunderstanding," Ida said, frowning. "Stupid bastards only had to let us on the ship. They started spouting off some nonsense which got them killed. This is going to take months of data-work to sort out."

"Yeah, I used the Cognition A.I.o destroy your position in the Watchers."

Ida's eyes widened.

"You what?" Clarice said. "Cassius, how—"

Isla pulled away. "Are you seriously going to ask that?"

"Everything Ida has done has been for the good of this Sector," Clarice said, staring at me. "The FSA represents a clear and present—"

Judith spoke over the loudspeakers, "I should mention I've not only given Cassius the legal title to the *Melampus* but also entered him into the system as a VIP for the Commonwealth. He can activate the Peregrine and get past all of the blockades or password issues we need to in order to escape. They'll catch it in a couple of months but he's the only way off this rock."

"Who the hell is that?" Clarice said.

Janice hissed and muttered something under her breath, clearly blaming Judith for her present predicament.

"A smartA.I. my sister created," I said, telling a half-truth. "Before I destroyed the CognitionA.I. I had her downloaded into my cybernetics. She had ones for a lot of Crius VIPs she was going to raise from the dead and use as weapons. A whole new humanity to endanger the Commonwealth."

The bigger the lie, the more people would believe it, especially if you started with something plausible to build on.

"Your sister didn't make a CognitionA.I. ," Ida said. "She was working for me the whole time to sabotage it."

"Yeah, well, you didn't take into account Zoe is a psychopath," Judith said, on the loudspeakers. "Or did you miss the massacre of people on the *Rhea*."

"And I suppose the prison staff just let you walk out," Ida said. "I don't trust machines, girl, nor do I think Cassius is telling the truth about what happened."

"You can stay here if you want," I said, smiling. It wasn't a pretty smile. "See how you like it with the locals looking for terrorists."

"I'll sort things out soon enough," Ida said, snorting. "We're not so computer dependent as that. Besides, you still haven't answered my questions about your sister."

That was when I heard the sound of a detonation charge going off on the other side of the wall, taking out two out of the four doors. They weren't able to hack through what Isla had done but they were possessed of enough weaponry to blow through it, I guessed.

"Tick-tock, Colonel," Ida said.

William frowned. "All the more reason to shoot you, tell the nice people outside we're with Cassius, and let God sort it out."

Ida frowned.

Isla surprised me by ending this stand-off before it turned to violence. "I examined the CognitionA.I. before it blew. It's real, or was. You owe Cassius for destroying it. I've also examined Zoe's work with smartA.I. and know you have, too. Zoe took the body of Judith and put herA.I. in the system before Cassius retrieved her. He stopped a threat you weren't even aware of while you were chasing Janice. You owe him."

How Isla knew any of that perplexed me until I remembered she could see Judith's avatar and had probably been communicating with her the entire time. Which meant she knew I'd said I didn't love her.

Well, so be it. It was only the truth.
I love her as a friend.
An extremely beautiful sexy friend.
But a friend.

Clarice looked between Ida and my group before taking a deep breath. "You're right, we do owe them. We owe them everything."

"Is no one going to mention my arm? The one I've lost twice tonight? Which brings it to four times total!" William shouted.

Ida slumped her shoulders. "Fine, Cassius, I believe you if Doctor Hernandez vouches for you. Still, we don't need to run, a Commonwealth fleet is coming here to secure the planet and break the back of the Rin-O'Harra cartel."

I took a deep breath, realizing just how badly I'd thrown things for a loop. "Actually, the *Revengeance* is coming along with the rest of the Sector Fleet to deal with it. In about, oh, ten minutes, this place is going to be the sight of the biggest space battle since Hoshi's Point."

"I really, really hate your sister," William said, wrongly blaming her for all of this. It was only about ninety percent her fault.

Ida processed that information. "Get me to my ship. You can

have it after I make a few holocoms and try to salvage this disaster."

A second detonation charge went off and blew a hole in the door as William fired back through it.

"Into the gunship!" I shouted, ready to leave this rock.

Chapter Thirty-Four

"Keep an eye on Ida for me, would you?" I said to William, plopping myself in the pilot's chair of the gunship, taking a moment to familiarize myself with the controls. It didn't take long since, to my disgust, I realized this vessel incorporated Archduchy technology, including smartA.I. and cybernetic link-ups. What the hell was going on?

"*Focus, Cassius,*" Judith said as the gunship's shields popped on and absorbed the fire of the retreating Commonwealth soldiers who'd come here for evac.

I could only imagine what they were feeling, having gone into a mission that had rapidly gone pear-shaped, managed to survive the Shogun's fierce resistance, and now were ready to escape only for us to steal their ride. It was a spectacularly terrible thing to do to a fellow soldier.

But I had my own people to look after.

Linking myself to its controls and finding myself capable of overriding the military safeguards to prevent exactly this sort of thing from happening, I pulled it out of the hangar bay and headed for the stars. The gunship was an ungainly and heavy thing compared to the sleek starfighters I was used to flying, but it was orbit capable, which was all that mattered right now.

The Peregrine gunship shuddered and shook as it moved through the atmosphere, the ship's sensors picking up multiple contacts as I could palpably feel the arrival of the *Revengeance* in the system. It wasn't alone as the ship detected a massive armada of Commonwealth ships already deploying. The thing was, the *Revengeance* hadn't arrived alone.

They'd brought the Chel with them.

"Shit," I muttered, watching hundreds of lights appear across my mind's eye. What had been planned as the perfect ambush had turned into exactly the opposite.

"What have I done?" I muttered, staring forward.

"*It's the other Cassius,*" Judith said as her avatar appeared as a six-inch-tall hologram on the dashboard of the ship. "He must have recognized this had all the makings of a trap and called in the others."

"How?" I asked, my mouth wet.

"*It's literally what you would have done,*" Judith whispered.

"I hate that cliché," I muttered, shaking my head. "Even if it is literally true today."

I tried to calculate what our chances of getting through this minefield to the *Melampus* and then getting out were.

Not good.

Worse, we didn't exactly have any other options since Peregrines didn't have jumpdrives and were designed solely to link up with larger ships like the *Revengeance, Rhea,* or *Melampus.* We had to get to the latter in one piece, and then get it out similarly, all the while surrounded by a massive armada.

I had not thought this plan through.

"*You think?*" Judith's avatar said, looking up at me.

"Hush you. You helped initiate it."

"*I was blinded by love!*"

"Uh huh."

"*And screwing over every side in this stupid, stupid war.*"

"I admit, that was part of the reason."

That was when Clarice surprised me by moving into the cockpit and taking the co-pilot's seat.

"You know how to fly a Peregrine?" I asked, trying to figure out the safest vector for travelling through a spaceway about to fill up with starfighters.

"We had something similar in Mason's Raiders," Clarice said. "Albeit significantly older and shittier. The souped-up cybernetic interface should work with mine as long as your littleA.I. buddy provides me with the necessary clearance."

"*AI buddy?*" Judith said. "*That's it, you're off the Christmas list.*"

"The what?" Clarice asked.

I flipped several switches as I powered up the weapons systems. "This day can't get any worse."

"You just had to jinx it," Judith grumbled.

"What now?"

"The good folk at the Commonwealth down below have just marked this ship as stolen," Judith said, sighing. *"The Commonwealth's forces have now marked it as hostile. Oh, and Janice's people have done the same for kidnapping her. They have orders to disable it if possible, though."*

"If possible."

"Janice pissed off a lot of our family," Clarice said, sighing. "I suspect it'd be better for everyone if she and I both went up with this ship."

"Great."

We broke the atmosphere a few minutes later, finding ourselves in the infinite void of space even as the sensors picked up the hundreds of battlefronts opening across the endless canopy. On Old Earth, tacticians had to deal with attacks from their sides and above but space had even more angles as well as unfathomable to the human mind distances.

On one side of the battle was the *Revengeance*, much as I remembered it, but it had been outfitted with powerful new engines and Chel hypercannons. Accompanying it were dozens of Chel dreadnoughts, destroyers, and carriers. An even larger array of Commonwealth ships were present, with frigates and corvettes to supplement it further. It was like the Battle of Hoshi's Point reborn.

And I'd brought it down upon Shogun.

No.

As much as my conscience wanted to take the blame for this, it would have happened in other places if not here. The Free Systems Alliance had already destroyed fleets and at least here the Commonwealth had the advantage of forewarning. Nothing could keep humans from fighting if they wanted to fight. It was a lie but one I could live with.

I hoped.

A hundred thousand energy blasts sailed across space in every direction accompanied by long beams of continuous light which were a weapon I did not recognize but crisscrossed the battlefield despite the enormous energy drain it must have been inflicting on their reactors.

They looked derived from mining lasers but were being fired from the *Revengeance* and the Chel dreadnoughts, slamming into the shields of the Commonwealth vessels before overloading them. They were brute force weapons that wouldn't provide anything more than a momentarily advantage in battle but that was sometimes all you needed.

"Any sign of the *Melampus*?" I asked, trying to focus solely on our situation. Thankfully, the two sides appeared more focused on each other than taking revenge on us for whatever slights we'd committed on Shogun.

I could look but it was taking everything I had to coordinate with Judith and run the six other systems that were supposed to have other crewmen running them. The fact Judith was helping only just barely made it possible given she was operating out of my implants.

"Yes," Clarice said, surprising me. "It's already taken off. It's marked as a neutral ship and space is big so it's avoiding being caught in the crossfire. It's headed to the jump beacon."

I tried not to grit my teeth. "How long until it makes it?"

"Uh—" Clarice looked down at the controls.

"*Five minutes and thirty-two at present speed,*" Judith interrupted. "*They hadn't gotten the engines prepped properly before breaking away from the space station.*"

"Show off," Clarice muttered.

We could intercept them before they arrived at top speed and I immediately pushed our engines to that.

"Shouldn't we contact them? Tell them we're coming?" Clarice asked as warning alarms started blaring across the gunship.

We were now being targeted by a trio of older-model Crosshair fighters. I suspected they believed the gunship would be an easy kill and we were passing nearby their attack zone. The fighters launched a series of Nebula-14 concussion rockets, of which the least would blow this ship apart. We were, after all, little more than a glorified troop transport and infantry support vehicle.

"No, that would make the *Melampus* a huge target," I said, moving to one side before igniting the ship's surface missiles.

"Cassius, those aren't going to stop those things," Clarice said. "They're way too slow."

"Not if an A.I. is good at directing where they go," I said, looking at Judith's avatar.

"*I'll see what I can do,*" Judith muttered. "*This isn't exactly what I was designed for.*"

Behind us, the concussion rockets exploded as Judith's counter-measures kept us all alive a bit longer. I fired the ship's plasma cannons behind us but their short range and weak power meant they were doing little more than pecking against the fighters' shields even when they hit.

"*Cassius, focus on shooting down their missiles and slow down enough to get them close,*" Judith said.

"Excuse me?" I asked, not sure I'd heard that correctly.

"*Put everything, even shields in maneuverability,*" Judith said. "*I trust your piloting skill.*"

"I'm not sure I do in this garbage scow," I said, nevertheless doing the same as another string of rockets was launched our way.

Judith then detached all of our missiles at once without launching them.

"Judith—"

"*Trust me.*"

Clarice took over the gunnery position and targeted the Nebula-14 rockets with the aft cannons, blowing one after the other apart while I dodged out of the way of two before blowing them to pieces. The Crosshair fighters proceeded to descend from the sky, firing at us with their cannons and managing to take out a side emplacement with a stray shot. Any closer and it would have gone through the engines.

That was when the rockets Judith had released ignited just as they passed and went up the Crosshair fighters' engines, causing all three of the ships to detonate in a spectacular display of light.

"*So does that make me a flying ace?*" Judith said, smirking.

"You'd only qualify as a gunner and you need four for that," I said, smiling.

We were almost home free.

That was when the alarms blared again and it was clear we were now being locked on by a full dozen *Phoenix*-class starfighters. Killing three of their comrades had officially moved us up from the Commonwealth's secondary objective to full on their shit-list.

"I am open for suggestions," I muttered.

That was when Ida called up from the back. "If you don't mind me helping, I may have an idea."

"Not going to turn down any help here, Jump Yaga," I said, pushing the gunship forward at top speed toward the *Melampus*. That ship wouldn't be able to help with us and I didn't intend to bring it into our fight but I was running out of options.

"Oh, I'm an ogress now, am I?" Ida joked.

"I'd like to go on record now as saying I blame you for all this," I said. "Zoe, the FSA, everything. Now help, please."

"Because you asked nicely," da said.

That was when almost all of the lights on the ship went out and came back red without affecting the engines.

Judith stared. "I'm blind now. What's going on?"

"She pulled out a shit ton of wires," William said. "Which I let her do because I was thinking we were about to die."

"Old pirate trick," Ida said. "I just pulled us off the battle network and silenced our transponder code. They'll be able to find us with their intensive scanners but I think that should give us a bit more time to get away."

Sure enough, a group of *Engel*-class fighters moved to engage the Phoenix fighters and the two immediately devolved into a dogfight. I briefly took a moment to appreciate how well-trained the Free Systems Alliance fighters were even as they managed to tear through our opposition. It wouldn't protect us should the newcomers decide we were the enemy too but our foes would hopefully delay each other long enough to get us the hell out of there.

"Thank you, Ida," I said, watching us coming at the *Melampus*. We only had a minute before it reached the jump beacon and we were officially screwed.

"You're welcome," Ida replied. "I'm still not letting you take my ship."

"I'm still not letting you get away with betraying us for torture at the hands of my insane sister and Clarice's cousin."

"Don't forget the arm," William said.

"We're not forgetting the arm!" I called back.

"Or the money!" William said.

"That too!"

Ida surprised me by saying. "That's a fair cop. All right, just drop me off at the nearest star base and we'll call it square. I'm going to probably come to you guys for a favor in the future, though."

"That's the opposite of calling it square," I said, tapping the communications system. "This is the gunship Peregrine calling the *Melampus*. Please stand-by for boarding. Captain… Mass is on board along with former captain, Ida Claire, First Mate Baldur, Security Chief Rin-O'Harra, and Doctor Hernandez."

No response.

"So, what are the chances of them jumping out without us?" Clarice asked, looking over at me.

"With the fact he just mutinied and claimed the captaincy?" Ida said. "About fifty-fifty. I have a pretty loyal crew."

"How loyal would they be if they knew you were the High Watcher?" Judith called back. *"Also, responsible for getting dozens of crew members killed in accidents over the years working for the Commonwealth?"*

"It depends how much they're paid," Ida said.

"We'll pay more," Judith said.

"I like you, Little Light Fairy Girl."

"Little—" Judith started to say, her avatar's expression appalled.

That was when the *Melampus* signaled us to dock with its starboard side. We'd have to abandon the gunship since we didn't have the docking clamps necessary to bring it with us into jumpspace, which was a shame since it would bring in a fair price, but I didn't hesitate to do so anyway.

Moving us up against the old *Starlight*-class star galleon, I felt the ships magnetically seal themselves together as the airlocks joined. "All right, everyone out!"

"Grab some weapons, too!" Clarice said. "Anything which looks valuable."

I shook my head and chuckled. Clarice had reverted to her mercenary instincts with recent events and I didn't blame her. That and all of the advanced weaponry on board would fetch a high enough price to convince the crew not to space us.

Judith retreated back into my cybernetics before William, Isla, Clarice, and our prisoner departed through the airlock into the *Melampus'* cargo bay. Of the group, only Isla and Clarice were carrying loads of rifles. I'd settled for picking up a crate of Thermic grenades which sold for more and could blow a hole in a starship.

Unfortunately, any elation I felt was quickly deflated as I saw two dozen black Durandal armor-wearing troopers and thirty Chel stealth troopers present on the other side. Standing in front of them was Zoe in Judith's body. She had a pistol in her hands pointed directly at me. They must have secured the *Melampus* before it had left space dock, making their own escape from the Water Palace when things had gone south.

"Hello, brother," Zoe said. "Welcome aboard."

"Well, shit," William said, summarizing everyone's feelings.

Chapter Thirty-Five

Outmaneuvered again.

Looking at Zoe wearing Judith's skin or, at least, a bioroid sculpted to appear as Judith, I couldn't help but wonder why I'd ever tried to befriend my siblings. Thomas, at least, had been a man who'd loved his family despite his job. He'd been a monstrous torturer, murderer, and worse but I'd never doubted he had my back.

Zoe only cared for herself.

She pointed at the airlock behind us with her pistol. "Trooper One, detach the gunship and inform the acting captain to take us into jumpspace. It's not going to take the Commonwealth long to realize I'm here and I'd rather not trust this ship's shields."

"Yes, General," a trooper a head taller than the others replied.

"General?" Ida asked, raising her hands in a very reluctant display of surrender. "Moving up in the world for a clockwork clone."

Zoe looked like she was debating having Ida tossed in the gunship before it was detached. Thankfully, the troopers just sealed the doors shut and removed our weapons. The docking clamps made a clanking noise as the gunship was let loose and, moments later, the *Melampus* entered jumpspace. We were safe from the Commonwealth and Free Systems Alliance but now at the mercy of my deranged sister.

"Have a care, Ida, loose lips make for short lives," Zoe said, placing her hands on her hips and surveying us with a triumphant gaze.

"*Got a plan here, Cass?*" Judith asked in my head.

"No," I muttered. "Not a one. I'm going to have to wing it."

"*Yeah, because that's worked so well so far.*"

I stepped in front of the others, watching the Chel and power armored troopers lift their weapons higher.

"What's happened to the crew?" I asked, taking a deep breath. "Are they all right?"

"They're fine," Zoe said, smiling. "I brought two hundred troopers on board and it turned out the *Melampus'* crew weren't interested in fighting for their ship. We're going to take them to Chel space, unload our prisoners, and then give them all an offer to continue working for the resistance against the tyrannical Commonwealth."

Janice hissed through her gag, clearly wanting to be let loose.

Zoe turned her pistol to her and shot the crime boss in the face. Janice slumped on the ground, her beautiful face deformed by the blast. It was a pointless act of cruelty, like so much else done that day.

Clarice dropped her guns and would have charged at Zoe if not for William grabbing her.

"Not now," William whispered. "I've lost enough loved ones today. I don't want to lose you, too."

Clarice looked at him, surprised.

I was surprised, too, but I shouldn't have been. William had always treated Hiro like a kid brother. Finding out he was a spy didn't change all of those feelings overnight. Hell, the fact Clarice and Ida were here with us was testament to that.

"Not ever, Mister Baldur," Zoe said. "Your continued survival from this moment depends entirely on pleasing me."

"Janice was on the FSA's side," I said, still stunned by her display of violence. Had Zoe always been like this and I'd just been blind to it or was her bioroid version substantially different from the original? I couldn't tell. I'd been blind to many realities of Crius' noble system and how it warped those it raised. Myself included. "Why?"

"In twenty-four hours, Shogun will be under the direct control of the Free Systems Alliance and liberated from the control of the O'Rin-Ishi Syndicate. We will purge the remainder of the organized crime from the planet's government and show the liberation of the planet's slaves as a sign of our benevolence."

"And then turn the bioroid manufacturing plants to producing technicians, engineers, crew members, and soldiers for your army," I said, guessing at her next move. "Probably souped-up with your cybernetics."

The Slaver's Planet was full of countless surgical centers, cybernetics research facilities, and programming centers. Those could be easily converted into locations to outfit regular human beings with cybernetics to turn the least physically capable soldier into someone capable of standing toe-to-toe with the Commonwealth.

Add in all of the newly-erected Ares Electronics factories and they could produce a surplus of individuals to carry on the fight against Albion and its colonies. Not enough to defeat the Commonwealth, but certainly enough to fight it.

The fact the Chel would be manufacturing weapons and armaments to outfit these new soldiers meant they'd acquired a substantial tactical resource. Worse, Zoe was one of the few women in the galaxy smart enough to coordinate all of the restructuring necessary. She also had no hesitation in cloning her mind as many times as it took to outfit this army. I wondered if her original self had known this would occur or if she'd unwittingly released a monster who would get her executed by the Watchers.

I found myself not caring.

Zoe smiled. "You know me so well. Cassius Mass, the Fire Count, always trying to be one step ahead of everyone else and all you manage to do is knock over the board. It's sad in a way. You could have been so much more."

There was an uncomfortable shuffling of feet and weapons among the troopers as they heard the word brother. Zoe seemed oblivious to it so I gently set down the grenades in my hands and proceeded to remove my helmet, showing them I was Cassius Mass. That caused an even bigger ripple among them. They had no way of realizing I wasn't their commanding officer, my doppelganger, and the man Zoe had created in a laboratory somewhere.

"*Careful,*" Judith said in my head. "*Some of your loved ones were created in a lab, too.*"

It's a little too early to joke about that, I thought back at her. *I'm still not sure where we stand or how I feel about all this.*

I loved Judith and wanted to love her reincarnation but life wasn't fair. It didn't give gifts like dead loved ones back or give us more time with those we cared for, no matter how much we wanted it. That was reserved solely for the Creator and he had made it a personal point to screw me over.

Like almost everyone else I'd known.

"*Sorry, Cass, I didn't mean to disturb you.*" Judith's words were slightly off though. "*I'm just trying to control the white hot rage I'm feeling for the woman who* murdered me."

Right.

That.

"Is that your definition of freedom?" Isla said, removing her own helmet. "Building a slave army to fight and die for your ridiculous cause?"

"Military bioroids are banned by interstellar treaty," Zoe said, shaking her head as if talking to a small child who just said something very stupid. "But their widespread use will change the nature of humanity in this war. It will provide us and the Chel the necessary military might to force the Commonwealth to adopt them as well. Once all sides make use of transhumanist weapons, it will change the course of human destiny."

"No matter how millions die," I said.

Zoe said, "Billions of humans die every day. That's what humans do. The only way to stop it is to make humans who don't."

"Lady, you are just as crazy as a bag full of nightcats," William said.

"Troopers," Zoe started to say. "I want you to kill—"

I interrupted. "I saw the Elder Marker's contents, Zoe. I know what the Nobility is doing in the galactic core."

"Ida, what is he talking about?" William asked, keeping his hands up.

"Son, I have not the slightest idea," Ida said. "I have no idea what's going on, with who, or why. Which is an unusual state for me."

"You must find it refreshing," William said.

"Not really," Ida said.

"So you saw," Zoe said, smiling. "Now you understand."

"Not quite," I said. "How did we get here?"

"They wanted me to examine many things during the last days of the war. Artifacts extracted from dead worlds and places the Elder Races had spread their legacy. Items Prince Germanicus had traded from Gorro warrior-monks and Ketros smugglers. The Archduke had contact with aliens who had every bit as much interest in discovering the secrets of the Core as the Commonwealth's Watchers. I bartered my knowledge of these items to guarantee my safety."

"And used it to make sure your bioroid would be sent here to continue your work. Does Thomas know?"

"They all know," Zoe said. "Every faction of this war believes the only way to survive the coming storm is to fight or submit. Each side wants to tear itself apart, unaware that's exactly what the Nobility want."

"What's your solution?" I asked.

"Transform," Zoe said. "You've seen what we're up against. You know what we have to do."

I didn't actually disagree with her statement. Humanity was hopelessly outmatched the same way the Archduchy had been outmatched by the Commonwealth, the Commonwealth by the Community, and the Community by the Elder Races. We needed to change the variables to survive and Zoe had a solution. It was an insane solution but a solution. She wanted humankind to play along with these wars until we were ready to become like them. I admired the audacity of the vision even as I believed it was too monstrous to stomach. Also, it wouldn't work. The Nobility wouldn't let humanity join their ranks unless they wanted to. They'd struck us down at our most powerful with the modification of the CognitionA.I. I knew Judith would never believe me if I tried to argue that.

She was too committed to her vision.

Programmed to be, perhaps.

"What's going to happen?" I asked, staring at her. "With the Battle of Shogun won, I assume."

"War," Zoe said. "We've had to accelerate our position considerably, and we're not in the best place to dismantle the Commonwealth as we would have been with the CognitionA.I. and Elder Technology. A year's more preparation and we would have burned Albion and plunged this galaxy into a state we could easily mop up. But, I think it's time you made your choice. Do you surrender and join the winning side or serve the enemy?"

Judith? I thought to her.

"*Yes?*"

I have a plan.

"*I'm horrified.*"

Go with it. I projected it to her.

"*You, mad beautiful bastard.*"

"I'm sorry, Zoe." I closed my eyes. "The elves whistle a song of peace and harmony."

Zoe's bioroid body seized up and there was a moment of intense pain across her face before she stumbled forward.

And Judith once more opened her eyes inside that body.

"Then I surrender to you, Captain Mass," Judith said, clearing her throat. "Gentleman, you should obey General Mass. I've made a terrible error and overstepped my authority and will submit myself to judgment at a secret location."

"Wait, what?" William said.

"Excuse me, ma'am?" Trooper One said.

"Do what you're told, soldier," I said, looking at him. "I've done my time here."

The Trooper could have ruined the plan then and there but he was Crius-born, I could tell, and he believed in my legend.

Also, Zoe hadn't given him proper preparation for a man who looked exactly like his organization's commanding officer.

So he saluted. "Yes, sir. We'll follow your instructions exactly."

"Okay, what the hell is going on?" William asked.

"Secure Ida in a security cell and Judith in quarters," I said, looking around. "The others are working for me and should be given free rein of the ship. I'll explain everything but we'll need to change our coordinates and get your men back in the fight."

Trooper One nodded. "I understand, sir."

"Thank you."

"*Do you think this is going to work?*" Judith mentally asked, still in my mind, as the others were released and their weapons were returned.

It depends on my ability to lie, I thought back to her.

It turned out I was very good at lying.

Epilogue

Two days later, I went to visit Ida in her cell. It was decorated with a comforter, quilts, a table, a tea set, and other amenities which had been thoroughly screened to avoid anything like spare guns and spy equipment.

I'd thought Clarice was being paranoid when she made a point of searching but the captain's room was full of that kind of thing. I'd also made sure Hunk-A-Junk was kept from her as the mech surprised me by trying to rescue her three times. After the fourth time, he'd come clean with why we had to release her. That had been an eye opener.

Ida was sitting on the side of her bed, wearing a pair of microspectacles as she read from a databook of what I believed was The *Chronicles of Narnia*. A side-screen was open for composing some sort of letter while she did so.

I was wearing a captain's white jumpsuit and greatcoat I'd picked up at Lucifer City, where we'd dropped off all of the enemy forces except for a skeleton crew we'd stunned and proceeded to toss out in a set of escape pods before entering jumpspace. It felt surprisingly good and, to my immense relief, I'd also found my identity was cleared of all charges.

My fake identity, at least.

I was Marcus Grav again as Judith had corrected all of the data files on it that might clue anyone in to its fake veracity. I'd decided to leave behind my old life to my doppelganger, who was already announcing his victory at Shogun across the holonets. The Crius Provisional Government was in the process of disintegrating and would probably fall to the Free Systems Alliance within the week. I was still deciding if that was my problem.

Ida looked up from her databook. "I see the crew has decided to accept you as their new Captain."

"We decided to put it to a vote," I said, shrugging. "Half the crew are Sector Seven and half the crew are Commonwealthers, so it came down to all of them wanting to stay out of this war. They actually elected William as the captain first but he deferred."

"I'm surprised," Ida said. "He'd have made a good captain."

"He would have but I think he's pathologically allergic to authority," I said, smiling, "The others weren't exactly fond of me after they found out what the real Cassius Mass was doing on Shogun but I convinced them to acquiesce."

"Lying to your crew is very easy," Ida said, sighing. "You'll learn that as captain."

"Oh, I told them the truth," I said, smiling. "They just didn't believe me. Current theories range from me being his doppelganger, a Cassius Mass impersonator, a conman who took that identity to get rich women to sleep with him, and a half-dozen other equally implausible ideas. The fact my DNA doesn't match his is enough to convince them it's all a big misunderstanding and they shouldn't try to turn me in to the authorities, though."

"Got your DNA fully clouded did you?"

"Isla helped." She'd also made sure my face looked like it had before, though the doctor had added a few improvements so I was a great deal better looking than any non-genetically enhanced individual had any right to be.

"How are you and she?" Ida asked.

"Good friends," I said, smiling. "Judith feigns jealousy but those two have more in common than not. Besides she and Clarice are back together. Not that they were really apart, I suppose, but for making Clarice put her under house arrest for a day."

"I did what I had to do," Ida said. "But that excuse rings a bit hollow over time."

"That it does."

"So, you're just going to sit out this war?" Ida asked.

"I'm going to try," I said, sighing. "The Commonwealth is already moving all of its forces to Sector 7 but the addition of the Chel and many neutral systems announcing their support is making this a bigger war than it has any right to be. If they're smart, they'll try to find a diplomatic solution. Judith calculated they were actually grossly in debt and overstretched before the war. Either way, joining the Community is dead in the water and it's going to probably break up in a generation."

"I wouldn't count on it," Ida said. "The Watchers have kept it trudging on before."

"Not my fight," I said. "Though, when I drop you off at the nearest Watcher substation, I'll leave you some insights into my doppelganger. It's the least I can do."

"Not afraid I'll come after you once I get this all sorted out?"

"Will you?"

Ida paused. "The fact you're asking me that question and expecting an honest answer worries me about you, son. However, no, I won't. I've got bigger fish to fry and I don't just mean the Free Systems Alliance."

"Judith told me she'd forwarded you all of her data."

"How is your other Robot Girl?"

"*Other* Robot Girl?" Judith said over the cell's intercom.

"She's too big for a bioroid body," I said, rubbing the back of my head. "Judith has planted herself in the ship's databanks as well as my cybernetics, the starfighters I've purchased, and the bioroid body Zoe prepared for her late...sister. It's pretty cramped compared to the vistas she's used to but large enough to relax in."

"I have to tell my superiors about her," Ida said, shaking her head. "A CognitionA.I. is too dangerous to let loose."

"Understood," I said, nodding. "Please also inform them, if you do, about the fact we've got datapackets spread across the galaxy that will reveal the Watcher's own experiments with CognitionA.I. . Like creating the Fixers to divert suspicion from their experiments and look like the Commonwealth had a check on the Watcher's power. Are the Fixers even aware they're just a branch of your department? Do they know their CognitionA.I. are the same ones that survived the Galactic Dark Age?"

The Nobility had corrupted most of their kind during the Great Collapse but not all of them had been destroyed. Some had simply gone deep into mankind's computer systems or hitched rides onto alien vessels, dwelling in the databanks of the Community with their colleagues there. The Watchers was just one of their tools spread across the galaxy, trying to protect a humanity that despised them.

Even Judith had been surprised by that. But it explained how Ida had always been ahead of things. Too bad Hiro had gone off script. He'd been there to throw off suspicion from Ida's efforts, not actually stop her.

It had gotten him killed.

Ida paused. "You are way too smart for your own good, son."

"Hunk-A-Junk told me we should work together on this."

"Work together?"

"I intend to live a normal life after this," I said, shaking my head. "But Judith isn't exactly all too keen on that."

"*The Other Cassius lost his wife,*" Judith said. "*He'll be insane with grief and lashing out.*"

It was a rare situation you could say you knew exactly what another person was feeling but my doppelganger had surely found out by now Zoe had killed his wife and taken her body. Worse, that Zoe was already dead by his original self's hand and his dead wife's body inhabited by yet another copy. The Other Cassius was no doubt fuming with hatred for me and misplaced rage. I'd made a powerful enemy through no real fault of my own but I knew he wouldn't let this slide.

I wouldn't.

"There's also a lot of other Elder Markers out there and relics Zoe knew of and Judith now has access to the databanks of. Things that can maybe provide humanity an insight into our enemy."

"They're too powerful to fight," Ida said.

"Yes, but maybe there's an alternative to war with them," I said. "Teach them to appreciate music instead of human chess."

Ida snorted at that. "So, what you're saying is we may be seeing more of each other in the future?"

"Lucifer willing." I didn't believe in the Devil but someone had my back.

About the Author

C.T. Phipps is a lifelong student of horror, science fiction, and fantasy. An avid tabletop gamer, he discovered this passion led him to write and turned him into a lifelong geek. He is a regular blogger and also a reviewer for The Bookie Monster.

Bibliography

The Rules of Supervillainy (Supervillainy Saga #1)

The Games of Supervillainy (Supervillainy Saga #2)

The Secrets of Supervillainy (Supervillainy Saga #3)

The Science of Supervillainy (Supervillainy Saga #4)

Esoterrorism (Red Room Vol. 1)

Cthulhu Armageddon (Cthulhu Armageddon #1)

The Tower of Zhaal (Cthulhu Armageddon #2)

Lucifer's Star

Straight Outta Fangton

Curious about other Crossroad Press books?
Stop by our site:
http://store.crossroadpress.com
We offer quality writing
in digital, audio, and print formats.

Enter the code **FIRSTBOOK**
to get 20% off your first order from our store!
Stop by today!

www.ingramcontent.com/pod-product-compliance
Lightning Source LLC
Chambersburg PA
CBHW070657180626
46817CB00006B/2410